IRENE D. CROUT

Tate Publishing, LLC

"Zephyr" by Irene Crout
Copyright © 2006 by Irene Crout. All rights reserved.

Published in the United States of America
by Tate Publishing, LLC
127 East Trade Center Terrace
Mustang, OK 73064
(888) 361-9473

Book design copyright © 2006 by Tate Publishing, LLC. All rights reserved.

No part of this publication may be reproduced, stored in a retrieval system or transmitted in any way by any means, electronic, mechanical, photocopy, recording or otherwise without the prior permission of the author except as provided by USA copyright law.

This novel is a work of fiction. Names, descriptions, entities and incidents included in the story are products of the author's imagination. Any resemblance to actual persons, events and entities is entirely coincidental.

ISBN 1-5988623-2-4

DEDICATION

This novel is dedicated to my loving sister, Betty Lou, and my dear friends Rose Abbie and Sylvia Detleft, all of who never gave up faith in me. My thanks to Marilyn B. for her help.

Best wishes
Irene D. Crout

Chapter 1

A shot rang out, scattering the birds from their lofty perch in the Florida pines.

The sound of gunshot was not alien to this part of the woods, with the cabin less than a mile away. However, this time of night usually brought stillness to the woods, more suitable for beast than man.

As the birds settled back on their branches, the rustling of their wings covered the last ricocheting sound that remained from the single shot fired moments earlier.

The warm, humid breeze had started the boy's blood to coagulate before it could seep into the moist sand. He lay there, numb from the pain. He knew he was dying. The gun had been well aimed. It took every ounce of strength he could muster to make an attempt to let someone know. With his fingernail he gouged in the sand, just as the nausea overtook him. His muscles relaxed one by one. Finally, there was just the occasional twitch of a nerve as it gave its final jerk. The brain could no longer reply to its demand. He was dead.

Chapter 2

I've been searching for more than an hour, Hank thought, as he cast the light on his watch.

He felt panic grip him. But as he had managed to do so many times in the past, he held it in check. There had to be a good reason for Jack's not going back to the cabin before dark.

Even the local hunters didn't brave nights in these woods. Florida was still in part wilderness, and unexplored.

The stillness of the night was broken by the screech of a bobcat, making Hank feel uneasy. His main reason for coming here was to relax. To get himself together. Hunting with a few of the men had been thrown in for a little extra fun. Since he had been elected sheriff he had experienced quite a bit of discord among his men. Things had happened so fast in his life. Sometimes he felt he had no control over situations. He kept step behind the glow from his flashlight, feeling that even controlled his footing.

His wife of eight years and he had been having problems. So far they had been kept pretty quiet, thanks to his friend and second in command at the department, Colonel Don Watson. He and Captain Ray Yarbrough were the only two people he considered friends, though he had many acquaintances. They always came at the last minute and pulled his fat out of the fire.

Basically Hank Myers was a figurehead over the department, and didn't do much at headquarters. The captain and the colonel took care of just about everything. The first four years, they had formed his character and determined his destiny. It was at their prodding that Hank sought reelection. They made it easy for him.

Hank wished the colonel were present now; he always felt more secure with the colonel.

By this time, Hank had walked almost a mile from the cabin. When he turned towards it, he could no longer see the light shining from the window, though he could smell the smoke coming from the fireplace. He had built a fire and just gotten it nicely started, when he noticed that Jack was overdue in coming back to the cabin. Paul Travers, the third hunting companion in the group, didn't seem as alarmed or concerned as Hank had been. Reluctantly, he went with Hank to look for Jack. He walked a little to the east of Hank through the woods. Hank had heard no signal of his locating Jack, either.

All this time Hank had kept the light directed towards the ground, except when he paused to listen for any human noises coming from the area. Then, he'd searched the surroundings with the ray of light, and proceeded on the road. Suddenly, the light reflected off something. Hank moved the light a little, to help his eyes focus on the object. His pace quickened until he was almost running. When he reached the object, he couldn't believe his eyes. He closed them, hoping when he opened them again the object on the ground would no longer be there.

Reality rushed over him, weakening him. His legs like rubber no longer were able to support his weight. He fell to the ground on his knees, placing his hands over his face. He felt as if every ounce of his blood had rushed to his feet, making them feel like lead. He broke out in a cold sweat.

"*OH MY GOD,*" he whimpered, then he started to cry. His whole body was racked by soul-wrenching sobs. He let out a blood-curdling scream that once more drove the resting birds from their perch.

Travers had just started back to the cabin, feeling that by now the sheriff was back there having a drink to take the chill out of his bones. He hadn't wanted to come out and look for Jack anyway.

Travers heard the scream pierce the darkness to his left. Even before he had directed his light in front of his footsteps, he started to run, causing him to fall over a decaying tree. Chills went up his spine when his hands touched the slimy wood. This added to his anxiety and his already pounding heartbeat.

When he reached the place from where he had heard the scream it seemed like he had run for hours, though actually it had been only a couple of minutes. The sight was illuminated by the sheriff's dropped flashlight. Travers' eyes were glued to the blood on Jack's chest. He walked over to the sheriff and placed his right hand firmly on Hank's arm, bringing him to his feet.

Feeling the hand, Hank began to cry uncontrollably.

Travers slapped him across the face, feeling a great satisfaction in having to do so. "What the hell is the matter with you, Hank?" He asked. "You'd better pull yourself together. We have to figure out what to do."

Hank looked at Travers through swollen eyes, and shook his head from side to side.

"Come on, Sheriff," Travers urged. "We'll go back to the cabin and think this thing out." Travers' manner was more subdued now than it had been a few minutes before. He knew this would take a calculating mind. Somehow he had to get to a public phone and call the colonel. The colonel always had the answers, but even he would have to work hard to pull this one out.

"Listen to me, Sheriff! You stay here in the cabin. I'm going out to the highway and call the colonel."

Just the mention of the name seemed to calm Hank.

"Tell him to bring Jim Deets with him, and to stay off the radio... we've got to have time. I don't want this on the radio. The wrong people might hear it."

Travers had to agree with him there.

By the time Travers reached the main road, the overcast conditions had dissipated, allowing the full moon to shine through. Often when he had passed this phone booth he had wondered why the phone company had placed one out in this God-forsaken location. Tonight, he was glad it was there, whatever the reason.

Colonel Watson leaned back in the swivel chair, placed his hands behind his head and propped his feet up on the desk. He glanced at his pointed western boots. *They've seen better days,* he thought. He removed one foot from the desk, held it over the wastebasket, and casually dusted the sand from it. Placing his foot back on the desk, and his hands behind his head, his cold, piercing eyes stared off into space, and then focused on a plaque hung on the opposite wall. *What a joke that was,* he thought. Words of praise, preserved for posterity by being deeply engraved into the gold-plated metal on the wood. Everything that anyone could ever want, it said. That was the trouble with engraving; it was there to stay. It seemed strange, he thought. Since it had been presented, ten years had gone by, and a lot had transpired. Gold watches are usually given for service, but they gave him a plaque only for looks. *Not much to show for ten years of your life, but what the hell can you expect,* he asked himself. He was sure to take the blunt of the repercussions that went out after everything blew sky high. He being the low man on the totem pole.

Oregon was a long way off; here he had the situation well in hand. He'd vowed when he had pulled out of Penbrook, never again to be placed in such a position. He had just happened on the right place at the right time for this job. When he'd stopped at the Red Tiger Bar, his only thoughts had been to get out of the hot Florida sun, and have a beer. He had sat at the bar, staring into the beer with his thoughts elsewhere. He hadn't noticed the man who occupied the stool next to his. The white turtleneck sweater was in sharp contrast to the shoulder-length, black, wavy hair. He was a handsome man, but slight in stature. From their conversation that first night in Fort Manson grew a relationship which led to the position he now held. The colonel didn't hold the same feelings for Hank that he knew Hank held for him.

He felt his being dubbed second in command by the local paper was a feather in his cap. He knew in reality he was first in command, pulling the strings for Hank to perform like the puppet he was. Never again would he place himself where others had command over his life. Yes, he had worked himself into the position he now held, with one thing uppermost in his mind: to take everything in the world he could grasp, no matter who, or what, got in his way. Actually, he never felt in jeopardy. There were others who stood to lose much more than he, so he was confident they would always cover him just to save their own tail feathers. They were high-ranking, influential people, with the authority to wheel and deal and with no questions asked. *Someone is always going to skim off the top, so why not let it be me?* he thought. Just the power he wielded, being able to make or break a man, brought a half smile of triumph to the corners of his mouth. He had done just that. Many men were serving time now because they had stepped out of line.

He never really trusted anyone. He would lay the groundwork as soon as he started to feel he was being undermined. The rest would be taken care of by the state attorney's office. They worked together, hand and glove. There had been a few hairy times, but when you play on the fear in men you can control them.

Fear was a constant undercurrent at the department. The colonel saw to that. He carefully chose those allowed in his tidy little clique. A man who was hard pressed with his back to the wall was a prime candidate for his organization. His lack of scruples, hardness, and cold calculating mind fortified him for his position. Colonel Donald Watson of the Fort Manson Sheriff's Department, Leeward County, Florida, had things just the way he wanted them.

The light on the button lit up, signaling that a call was coming in on his private line. He pressed the left button and picked up the receiver. Placing it to his ear, he said, "Yes." He listened, while slowing taking his feet off the desk.

His facial expression never changed. "Where in the hell is Hank now?" he asked.

"Hell, I never thought he would freak out. You'll have to calm him down before I get there if you have to give him something." Watson clinched his teeth, and the muscles tightened in his cheeks. He listened to Travers' conversation, then said, "I'll pick up Deets and we'll be on our way in a matter of minutes."

Being very precise and deliberate, Watson put the phone back on the hook. His computerized mind clicked.

Pushing the swivel out, he rose to his feet and sprang into action. Then he reached for the leather jacket hanging on the clothes rack. Watson's gait was rapid as he walked down the hallway.

"Hey, Colonel," Watson heard a familiar voice call. He stopped and waited for Detective Bob Pool to catch up to him.

"What is it? I don't have any time for something lengthy."

"I think we are going to have some trouble with Becky," Pool said in a subdued voice. "All of a sudden, she's showing up with conscience pangs."

"Damn that redhead. I knew it was bad business bringing her into the action," the colonel said, while running his hand through his hair. "I don't like women being involved, I never have. They're too emotional."

"Well Colonel, it's better they get screwed over than us. At least they're built for it, and you aren't."

Starting out the door, he turned and said, "Look, Bob, I have to go now. Try to keep her cool, until I can get to her and put her straight." He turned around, looked at Pool and asked, "Jim Deets is on patrol in the Pondella area tonight, isn't he?"

"I think so. Why?"

"Never mind. I don't have time to explain. Get on the radio and tell him to meet me at Waverly Corners. Then tell Brown, the dispatcher, that Deets has been put on special detail for the rest of his shift. He's to tell someone else to take his zone." Without another word, he turned and stepped through the doorway. The door closed behind him with a muted bump.

The dispatchers' room was always busy and noisy, with crackling calls coming in over the radio. The recent remodeling job had made things more convenient. The computers were readily accessible, where before someone had to keep running into another room to gather the data asked for by the men out on patrol. The computers cut down on manpower time, and made the whole department more proficient.

There were two calls coming in at once.

"Car 57, stand by. Go-ahead 72," Brown said.

"Give me a 10–29, locally on spelling it out M-A-N-U-E-L R-U-E-Z," the voice over the air said.

"10–23," replied Brown, he turned, punched out the name on the computer's keyboard, and the screen printed out *no known wants*. Brown called, "Headquarters to 72."

"72," said the voice.

"That's a 10–54, 10–29, 10–26," Brown said in an even-toned voice.

"10–4," the deputy acknowledged.

"Go ahead, car 57," Brown commanded.

"57, get a hold of DOT, and tell them the light at Ortize and Colonial is malfunctioning."

"10–26," Brown replied, and made a notation on a tablet nearby.

For a few seconds the radio silenced. Brown reached for a cigarette and lit it, as he noticed Pool approaching him from across the room.

Pool had just hung the duty roster back on the wall. He had found the name he was looking for.

"Get hold of 505 and tell him to 10–25 the colonel at Waverly Corners," Pool told Brown.

The dispatcher faced the microphone and delivered the message. Then he waited and looked back at Pool, knowing there would be further instructions to fill the gap that left open in the area.

"Deets will be on special detail the rest of his shift tonight, so place another cruiser in his zone."

Without further discussion, Pool turned and left the dispatchers' room.

The radio once more gave out numbers by faceless voices, and Sgt. Brown answered.

Pool walked down the hall to his office, pondering the urgency that had taken the colonel out this time of night, especially after he had told him about Becky and the flack she was throwing up. It seemed to Pool there couldn't be anything more important than getting her back in line.

Pool had allowed himself to be placed in this situation that now was slowly tightening. He was a bright man. He had a streak of laziness, tinged with a little greed. Pool had a good education, though the degree made him no wiser. He had been approached in confidence about teaming up with the colonel and his men. Seeing a chance to make it quick and get the hell out, Pool thought, *Why not?* He was smart enough to know that a good thing doesn't last forever. In fact, he was surprised the sheriff had been elected for a second term. His predecessor, Thomas, had thrown a strong opponent in his way. Anything can be rigged to look good. With the colonel running things, how could he lose? Pool figured, why not take one more chance?

But he was wise enough to never express his views out loud. He knew he had to stay on top of things. He was aware of the skullduggery going on in the department. A certain degree of trust existed among the choice few, but the colonel was very careful not to tell everyone everything. Whatever they knew, they knew better than to repeat, even to each other. They all received a skim off the top, but each received different amounts.

The colonel had an incredible memory, but he possessed a book he carried with him everywhere. Pool recalled a time when a badly decomposed body was found out east in Highland Hills. After the initial investigation, a mere formality, the body was tentatively identified as a resident of Roseland Center, an institution for the mentally retarded. No one pursued any form of information that turned up. They just said it was a poor soul who had wandered away, got lost, and died of exposure. The wedding band on the corpse's finger and the presence of fishing pole, bait, and tackle close by was never made public.

The colonel got out his book, and with his pen made a mark on one of the pages. That was how easy it was to be checked off his list. Woe to the one at the top. Pool often wondered how hard it would be when it came time to get out. There was a lot of undeveloped land in Highland Hills, and likewise in Cape Corrine. A body could be out there for months, or never be found. If it were, the buzzards would have feasted on it, while the sun rotted it beyond recognition. Though Pool didn't like to admit it, the colonel owned him, just like everyone else in the clique. If he didn't own them, he maneuvered them so they feared for their life or their job. His name was probably on the colonel's list too. He hoped at the bottom.

Chapter 3

The traffic was light on the way to Waverly Corners.

The colonel arrived ahead of Deets, so he pulled off the road and waited. The reflection from the traffic light illuminated his car: Red.... Green....Yellow corresponded with his character. Watson lacked emotions, and because of that everything in his life was geared, like the cold changing lights. He was sitting on the yellow now.

It flashed to green as Deets pulled up. He looked at the colonel, waiting for a command.

That's how Watson liked it, his men performing without questions. This gave him an ego boost that started his adrenalin pumping. He had already thought of how he was going to handle this situation and the adrenalin was a stimulant. He never required an upper like some others in the department.

"Pull your car off the road and park it over there behind the gas station," he barked, pointing to the secluded area.

The automatic door lock released with a click, allowing Deets to step into the colonel's world. He got into the car and sat down on the plush seats. *This is living,* he thought.

Then they were off, north, towards the Carroll County line on Route 41. The colonel spared no rubber.

Finally, Deets broke the silence. "Where we headed, Colonel?" he ventured to ask. It was not wise to ask questions of Watson, but he chanced it. He couldn't imagine where they were going, or whom they were going to meet.

When the call came over the radio for him to meet with the colonel, he didn't think it strange. They had gone many times on the spur of the moment to pick up a stash, make a payment, or dole out a warning to someone who might have stepped out of line. Now Deets just sat there. He knew to leave well enough alone. When the colonel didn't respond to his question, he knew the answer would come in due time, so he played the waiting game. But Deets did take into consideration the direction in which they were traveling. It had to be something really important to take the colonel anywhere near the Carroll County line, he decided.

In general, people believed that all law enforcement agencies stuck together and cooperated with one another. Not so in this county. Leeward County was like a thorn between two roses. Neither Carroll County to the north nor Baron County to the south condoned the way Leeward conducted its sheriff's department force. The counties had very little to do with each other and when it became necessary to work together, animosity could be felt. It made Deets wonder, under the circumstances, how long it would be before one of the two counties blew the lid off the colonel's regime.

Finally the car slowed and veered to the right, off 41.

The colonel spoke, "We're faced with a nasty situation tonight, Deets. Everything we do has to be done quickly, but carefully. You remember the Manning kid? His father runs the wrecker service in the East End."

"Sure." Deets replied.

"Well, he's dead at the sheriff's cabin."

"How?"

"I don't know yet," Watson said.

"Was he alone?" asked Deets.

"No. He was with the sheriff and Paul Travers."

"Who found him, Colonel?"

"Hank, of all people, and from what Paul told me he's in pretty bad shape."

"How are you going to handle this, being so close to the county line?" asked Deets.

"We sure as hell aren't going to bring Carroll County into this. They would have a field day with this one," the colonel replied. "I've already put part of the story into motion, when I had you meet me at Waverly Corners. We couldn't call out on the radio about the incident, not with his father monitoring the police calls into his wrecker service, now could we?"

Deets thought he detected a hint of sarcasm in the colonel's voice.

The colonel slowed down, pulled the car to the side of the dirt road, and stopped. Off in the distance a pair of headlights was bobbing up and down, fast approaching them. It was Travers that was coming out to meet them with the four-wheel-drive jeep. He stopped, as the trail of dust that had been chasing him overtook the men. This annoyed Watson as the dust settled on the car. Showing his disdain, he exhaled a blast of hot air.

"I'm sure glad to see you," Travers said as he approached.

"Well let's get this thing started and over with as soon as possible," the colonel said, hopping into the jeep.

The other two men scurried in right behind so as not to aggravate further. Travers took off with a lunge, and they went bounding down the road. Once again the dust chased them, lapping at their wheels.

The cabin was situated deep in the woods. Few knew of its exact location. Five minutes later, without conversation, they pulled around a bend in the road, took a hard right, and drove up an incline leading to their destination. Before the motor had been shut off, the colonel was at the cabin door. He was like a fire horse when the bell rang. He thrived on excitement and the challenge that situations like this brought. When he opened the door, Hank looked up from the hole in the floor he had been staring at.

Hank felt a rush of relief flood over him when he saw the colonel standing in the door. He rose.

The colonel closed the door, before the other two men had a chance to enter.

"Don't worry, Hank, I'll take care of everything. It's obvious you aren't in any condition to handle it."

Just the sound of the colonel's voice started Hank crying like a baby.

The colonel placed his arm around Hank's shoulder and guided him over to a day bed in a corner of the room, saying, "Come on over here and sit down. Now, tell me exactly what happened. Was Travers with you when you found Jack?"

Hank shook his head. "No, he wasn't. He arrived a few minutes later," he said through gasping sobs.

"OK now, settle down. We have limited time to work this out, get hold of yourself," he spoke sternly. "You're going to have to contact the boy's parents. We'll put out a news release later. We'll wait as long as we can. Did Paul give you something to settle you down?" he asked, changing the subject.

With the colonel rendering his support, Hank began to collect himself.

"Yes, he gave me something." The sheriff proceeded with his story, giving the colonel all the details he could remember.

When he was through Watson instructed, "Put on a pot of coffee and rustle us up something to eat. Travers and I are going out but we'll be back in a little while, Hank. I'll leave Deets to stay with you." The colonel stood up and was out the door before the sheriff could reply.

Travers and the colonel drove the sheriff's jeep to where the body lay, taking only a few minutes. The full moon shone brightly, lighting up the whole area. The colonel's flashlight gave just the light needed for the detail work in their investigation.

Travers looked at the boy lying on the ground. He paused, muttering something under his breath. The colonel approached Jack's body. He reached down, grabbed Jack by his pecs, picked the torso up off the ground, dragged it, and propped it against a nearby tree.

Jack's lifeless hand left furrows in the sand as his body was dragged. The colonel observed the markings and deliberately walked through them with his pointed boots, wiping them out.

Travers approached the colonel. "Will we notify Carroll County?"

The colonel glared at him. "There's no need for that. He wasn't in Carroll County when he died," the colonel said as he bent down and picked up a spent 30–30 cartridge. Then he reached in his pocket and brought out a hand filled with several empty cartridges. He let them fall to the ground, slowly...one by one, like dirty snowflakes.

"Now for the record," he said, "it's obvious this was an accident."

Travers watched in silence, daring not to question.

The colonel looked at him and said, "I'll drop you at the public phone on the highway. Call Captain Yarbrough; tell him to come out here. You stay out there and ride in with him. We will meet you both back at the cabin." Colonel Watson pressed the button on his watch. He glanced at it under the moon's light. The digital flashed 9:36. "He should be here by a little after 10." He started toward the truck and motioned for Travers to follow.

They rode to the highway in silence. A moment or so later the colonel pulled the jeep to a halt, and Travers got out. He walked across the highway toward the lonely phone booth.

Captain Ray Yarbrough had put in a long day, working on a case they were trying to clear up. He filed his report, then got ready to go home and catch a few hours of sleep. He was tired, but he didn't like the thought of going home to an empty house. He would rather have had a bed companion.

Rose would be out of town until Thursday. Maybe he wouldn't go home, he thought. He still knew a couple of available beds he could crawl into. Since he and Rose had gotten married, he had kept in touch with some of his lady friends, but didn't get the action he once did with them. He had always had trouble with women, one way or another. He was good looking enough, with his tall, husky build and dark hair.

That's what drew women to him, but it didn't take long for his charm to wear thin and his rotten disposition to show through. He had a short fuse. He made his own laws and felt everyone else was out of step. He not only deceived himself, but others too. The captain had a methodical mind, able to remember details. He liked women, all women, but his preference ran towards women who were neat in appearance and could be an asset to him.

The position Yarbrough held in the department placed him in the public eye, and he thrived on that. He enjoyed being the center of attention.

His home was plush, with all the modern conveniences. He and Rose entertained a lot. He had two sets of friends: those who enjoyed the better side of life and were straight, and those who were under his influence, considered to be on the unusual side. Both groups lived by their wits, for he found little interest in anyone who could not carry on an intelligent conversation.

At one time Yarbrough could have leaned towards a more religious life, for he possessed a sixth sense. But he finally chose the direction that supplied him with the finer things in life, without his having to put out much effort. He used gut instinct to survive. Thus far, it had worked well. But now that instinct was signaling trouble. Trouble from a female narc who worked under him in the Civil Investigation Division.

For awhile they had a thing going between them. He seized the opportunity for a little fun, but he was never quite sure how she felt.

Their relationship diminished after he met Rose. The affair with her topped off a working relationship they had while working at the city police department. When Hank had been elected sheriff, they had both changed their employment to the county. He had made captain at the age of 33, and was the youngest to ever attain that high a rank. He was placed in a supervisory capacity over C.I.D., and the lady narc was schooled and placed under his command. He knew her moods, and she had changed recently. In fact, lately she had occupied a lot of his thoughts. He knew something had to be done before she stepped too far out of line.

Yarbrough closed the file, and was just removing the key from its lock, when the phone buzzed. He hoped it wasn't something that would tie him up; he needed some sack time. Seeing it was his private line, he sensed the long hours that were ahead of him. Only a few people knew his private number. In fact, periodically, he had it changed. He felt that kept him one step ahead of the game, by always being unpredictable. He opened the top drawer of his desk with his left hand and picked the phone up with his right.

"Hello," he said, sitting down in the chair with a plop, letting his weight drop without restraint. "What in hell is he going to do with the body?" he barked. For a moment he listened silently, then said, "I think he's asking for trouble if he doesn't bring Carroll County in on it." He paused again. "But it is their county!"

Travers never thought he would have such a hard time getting this phone call through. He knew the captain played hunches, and that his reluctance was due to that feeling kicking up.

"I'll have to go home and change cars and clothes first," he told Travers.

"The colonel wants you to be here by a little after ten. He says we're working against time." There was a pause on the other end of the line, then Travers asked, "are you there, sir?"

"Yes, I'm here. I was just thinking. Tell the colonel I'll be there as soon as I get the jeep." He hung up the phone, leaving Travers with a dead line.

Yarbrough was in deep thought as he drove over the bridge to North Fort Manson. Just what he needed, another problem before he got his lady narc put straight. Any investigation of the cabin incident would naturally fall under his jurisdiction.

The clock on the dash read 9:48 when he pulled in his driveway.

"Hell," he said out loud, "I hate to wear these clothes out in those woods." But he didn't dare take time to change. He knew how far to push his luck with the colonel.

He had no emergency lights or siren on the four-wheeler, yet he knew if he pushed the speed limit he wouldn't be bothered. The law recognized his jeep, and he was the law in this area, so he pushed the pedal to the floor. He had worked on the jeep, making it heavier for just this purpose. Normally they were not built to travel the speed he was driving.

Yarbrough pulled up to the cut-off road in a little over ten minutes. Travers stood waiting by the side of the road. He pulled off the macadam onto the dirt road, and stopped.

"Man, I sure am glad to see you," Travers said. He felt more relaxed in the captain's presence.

"Now tell me what happened, and I want all the details," Yarbrough demanded. He listened while Travers told him what had taken place since the Manning boy hadn't shown up back at the cabin, and how the sheriff had found the body. He told him everything with the exception of the planted spent cartridges.

"Why would the kid do a thing like that?" Yarbrough said, more to himself than to the man riding with him. "I just talked with him yesterday. He was helping his dad on a towing job out on Route 82. I was coming back from Clinton and saw the wreck, so I pulled off the road and talked with them for a couple of minutes. Jack told me he was supposed to go back to base tomorrow. He said he was real happy in the Army, and was considering staying in and taking engineer training." Yarbrough paused for a moment, then said, "His dad could have used his help. Since that car fell on his legs awhile back, he's had to take it easy. But the old man wanted the kid to live his own life, do what he wanted, and not feel obligated to him. The boy enlisted last year after he graduated from high school." The captain was carrying on the conversation by himself, to sound it out.

When they arrived at the cabin, the colonel opened the door. Yarbrough entered, looked first to Colonel Watson and then to Deets, acknowledging both with a nod. Hank sat at the table drinking a cup of coffee. To him he spoke. "Sheriff."

Hank rose from the table without a word. He placed his cup in the sink, turned around facing the men, and said, "Well, let's get on with it."

The colonel took over. "Deets, you stay here with the sheriff and help him close up the cabin. Travers, you go out to the road and call the ambulance. Give us enough time to get to the scene. All of you go out to the main road and wait for us to bring out the body. The captain and I will go to the scene of the accident, do our investigation, and take care of everything there."

The sheriff shook his head in agreement. "We'll meet you at the entrance to the dirt road," he told both as they made their exit.

The colonel drove along the winding, rutted, dirt road through the woods. The moonlight showered everything with a soft subdued light, bringing objects into focus for yards.

Yarbrough was set aback when he first saw the boy propped up against the tree. It appeared to him as if the kid had gotten tired and sat down to rest—that is, until he saw the hole in his chest. *This rest was permanent,* he thought.

The colonel maneuvered the truck up to within carrying distance and stopped. Both men got out of the truck at the same time.

Yarbrough walked all around the tree, surveying the surroundings, being very observant. Knowing the victim made the investigation harder, he thought to himself. He bent down, picked up a couple of the empty cartridges and smelled them. "I wonder if it took this many shots for him to get his nerve up to fire that one fatal shot?"

"What the hell do you mean? This was an accident" the colonel said from where he stood, removing burlap bags from the back of the truck. He was quite aware of everything Yarbrough was doing.

Yarbrough eyed the gun lying beside the body. The barrel was in a peculiar position in relation to the body. He considered the angle it would have fallen to, after it had fired the fatal shot. Yes, he reasoned, it was possible. Yeah, sure it was. It might have fallen in that direction after his grip loosened. *His death's grip wouldn't have to be pried from this gun,* he thought.

As the colonel approached him with the bags, Yarbrough spoke. "There's something here that's not kosher; something just doesn't feel right."

"There you go with your feelings again," the colonel said, more in disgust than in jest.

"I can't help it, Colonel. I'm just having a hard time believing this kid shot himself accidentally. Did anyone find a note?"

"No," he snapped. "Come on and help me wrap him up in these bags, so we can get back into town. We've already lost too much time. We can do our investigation at the station."

The body, in the sitting position, was difficult to lift. When they picked Jack up his bladder discharged, splashing urine on the ground.

Yarbrough swore under his breath. Usually he didn't get involved in the actual dirt work in his job. He was involved more with the interrogation of suspects. He'd never had to dirty his hands literally before. Yet he had always known that some day he would experience such a situation.

They placed the body on the bed of the truck, rolling it to the back to keep it from falling out. Picking it up once was sufficient, Yarbrough thought as he walked back to the tree, stooped, picked up the gun, and retrieved the empty shells. He paused and looked at the scene, implanting it in his memory for future reference.

The colonel barked, "Are you ready to get out of here?"

Yarbrough flashed the light around one more time, then walked to the truck.

Watson drove slowly, as if he were carrying a load of eggs. The cabin was dark and closed up when they passed.

"They must be out on the road already," the colonel said. "I wonder if the ambulance is there."

Yarbrough didn't hear him; he was deep in thought.

The revolving light from the ambulance cast a rosy glow over the area, blending with the moonlight. Watson backed the vehicle up to the ambulance, its doors wide open, waiting for its passenger. The attendants exchanged a few words, loaded the corpse, and closed the doors. They headed toward Fort Manson with lights flashing.

The five men, the colonel and sheriff riding together, transported the four vehicles back to the city.

Paul Travers drove the sheriff's jeep. Deets drove Jack's truck. Ray Yarbrough in his jeep brought up the rear of the procession arriving in the city in a little over twenty minutes.

As he passed Hudson Bridge Parkway, and the road that would take him home, Yarbrough wished he were headed there now. He knew there would be hours of paper work, reports, news releases, and the toughest job of all, telling the kid's parents. Looking at his watch he saw that not quite three hours had elapsed since he'd received the phone call that summoned him to the cabin. He probably wouldn't see bed before tomorrow night now. He was glad he'd popped a pill before he left the office.

Everything seemed quiet when they reached the station. The colonel decided before going in they would discuss the incident with no one until Jack's parents could be notified. The sheriff led the single file line into the building. Everyone went straight to his office and Deets, being the last one in, closed the door.

The men discussed what had to be done and who would do it.

The duties divided among five men didn't take as long as Yarbrough had expected. He was able to head for home at two o'clock. By the time he left, the sheriff and the colonel had already headed for East Fort Manson and Jack's parents.

Travers and Deets loaded into one car as Yarbrough arrived at his. The men waved at each other and parted ways.

The traffic was at an ebb. Bed wasn't far off, Yarbrough thought. He was dead tired. Still something kept gnawing at him, but he couldn't identify it. He gave it up. The few hours that were left were for sleep. He was still in his clothes, removing only his shoes before he collapsed. Tomorrow was another day and he'd be able to think with a clear head. He fell into a deep sleep.

Chapter 4

The station was quiet, except for a few calls coming in: the normal domestic fights, a few barroom brawls, and nuisance complaints of kids racing up and down the streets on their motorcycles. Corporal Eva Eaton had just turned to speak to her shift companion when the phone rang again. She answered.

It was Steve Doty, of the Fort Manson *News Leader,* inquiring about the shooting at the sheriff's camp.

She spoke in haste, "What shooting?"

Doty repeated his words. "I have been informed that there was a shooting at the sheriff's camp and I would like to confirm the details."

"Sir, I don't know of any shooting taking place tonight or any other night out at the sheriff's camp. I don't know where you acquired your information, but you've been misinformed."

He replied, "If I can't find someone there to tell me anything, I'll have to go ahead and print what my source gave me." He then placed the receiver back on the cradle. *There was no use trying to intimidate her,* he thought, *it might make her hostile for future news releases.*

Doty reached for the sheet in his typewriter and gave it a quick jerk upward.

The typewriter relinquished it with a growl. The paper brought a frown to his face, as his eyes scanned it. Then, as by some unseen force, he was propelled upward to the pressroom. He'd be in time to make the last morning edition. He'd have to be satisfied with that now. *At least,* he thought, *it would make the city edition.* The papers for the outlying areas came off the presses first; therefore, they sometimes lacked the later developing news.

Prior information from his source had always been reliable, so why worry now, he thought. Of course, the sheriff's department would have a rebuttal to print. After first getting their story straight, they would come to the paper to make their point. They had all been through this before, so he expected it as soon as the first paper hit the street. That could be as early as 3 A.M., for that was about the time the delivery people started picking them up. With the magnitude this story had, it was sure to cause a furor.

Peggy Tyler watched as Eva slowly hung the phone back on the hook. Her face had a puzzled look. "What's the matter, Eva?" she questioned.

Eva looked at Peggy, as if startled from a daydream. "That was a queer call, Peggy. Do you suppose I should call the captain?"

Peggy answered her with another question. "What did I hear you say about a shooting?"

Eva sat down and reached for a cigarette. She lit it, drew in the smoke, and let it out slowly. While she gazed into the spiraling smoke from her Salem, she regressed her thoughts. One more doubt crept into her mind. It seemed as though she'd had many doubts lately. Living alone now, she had a lot of time to think. At first, after Ron had been killed, her mind could think of nothing but him. He was so young, and had so much to live for. It seemed like a nightmare the night the sheriff came to the house to tell her that Ron had been shot in the line of duty. He and a fellow officer were trying to commandeer an escaped convict. Once over the shock, she had set out to find a job to support herself. When Sheriff Myers offered her a job, she jumped at it. It saved her from having to go through a lot of interviews. She remembered nights, when she and Ron had lain in the dark, smoking cigarettes and talking before their final good night kiss. Ron had voiced his concern about certain departmental proceedings. She hadn't given it much thought then, for she had wifely duties to occupy her time. Ron was a born worrier, so she had thought at times he placed things way out of proportion. Lately, however, doubts had begun to creep into her mind too. Maybe Ron hadn't been overreacting. There were times that he would start telling her about some crisis that had happened at work, then, seeing her face questioning his veracity, he would cut off in mid sentence and change the subject. How I wish Ron were here now, Eva thought. The way that last phone call was handled would tell her plenty.

Peggy was still waiting for an answer. Finally, she broke the silence by clicking her fingers in front of Eva's face. "Eva, come back!"

Eva blinked out of her trance-like state, snapping her thoughts back to the phone call. "Huh? That was Doty, of the *News Leader*. He wanted to know about a shooting at the sheriff's camp."

"What shooting?" Peggy queried.

Eva answered with a shrug of her shoulders, then said, "I told him I hadn't heard about any shooting, but he wouldn't take no for an answer. He's going to go ahead and print the story his 'source' gave him."

"What in the hell makes him so damned confident? Why is he pursuing this? Why not wait until he can get the story from the sheriff in the morning?" Peggy asked, perplexed.

"Well, I don't know what makes him tick. He reminds me of someone who has an ax to grind. As long as I've been here, he's personally delivered a paper to the department every morning. Lays it right here," Eva said, patting the top of the desk with her hand. "I remember one morning the presses broke down, and the papers didn't hit the street until eight o'clock. When he came in his eyes were all red and bloodshot. It must have been hours past his normal bedtime. Something else could have kept him up, but I don't think so. I think he just waited to personally bring the paper to the department. There is something about his manner. Once he enters those doors." She made a gesture towards the double glass doors with her hand. Then her mind raced back to the phone call. She could take a chance and wait until morning. She paused. Then again, she thought, it might be important, and if it was, the captain would need to be notified now. He would need time to take proper action.

"You'd better call and tell the captain," Peggy urged. "Let him make the decision on how to handle it. When the sheriff and the colonel left, the sheriff said the captain would take care of any emergencies that might come up, and that he wasn't to be disturbed."

Eva picked up the phone and dialed. It rang six times. She was ready to hang up when a sleepy voice answered slowly.

"Hello."

"Captain. We just had a strange call come in from the newspaper, wanting confirmation on a shooting at the sheriff's camp."

That abruptly brought Yarbrough to an upright position. "Oh, hell! What did you say? Nothing, I hope." He spat this out, before giving her a chance to answer. "Never mind. I'll get dressed and be back down in a few minutes. In the meantime, keep your mouth shut."

He had never talked to her like that before. Startled, she took the dead phone away from her head and replaced it with fresh doubts.

"He'll be right down, and he said not to say anything to anyone," she told Peggy.

The phone rang. She was glad. It took away the necessity to answer the questions she knew Peggy was ready to ask.

"Leeward County Sheriff's Department, Corporal Eaton speaking. Can I help you?"

The drive to the east end of town usually took twenty minutes when the traffic was normal. This time of night, though, most of the drunks had gone home to sleep it off. All the bars closed at two except for private clubs. So the traffic was light, yet they drove without haste. Neither of them was in a hurry to reach Jack's house.

Residents on the Mannings' street were mainly middle-class, hard-working people. The Mannings had managed to make a good living. They had a little more than the average family on the block. They had lived there for many years, and made many friends.

Watson pulled up to the curb and stopped.

"Well, we might as well get it over with," Hank said. Knowing Jack was an only child made this an even harder task for him.

The house was dark, in sharp contrast to the well-lit street. The entranceway was shaded with shrubs.

Hank reached out, put his hand up to the door, hesitated, then knocked. He waited for a minute, and knocked a little louder.

A light came on in the back area of the house, then another in the living room. Finally the porch light came on. The curtains parted. Mary Manning peered out the window, and, seeing who it was, quickly opened the door. "Hello, Hank. What's the matter?" she asked, realizing his being there at this time of night indicated something was wrong.

"May we come in, Mary?" He asked.

She opened the door wider and motioned for them to enter. By now she was beginning to feel apprehensive. Her heart started to pound like it would burst through her chest.

Her husband came down the stairs, quickly tying his robe belt.

Hank was the first to speak. "Mary, Bill, we have some bad news for you. Sit down so we can talk with you."

Grasping hands, they led each other to the couch and sat on its edge, their eyes searching the sheriff's face for a clue.

Hank took a deep breath to fortify himself against his task. "You know that Jack was up at the camp with us today hunting. Well, I'm afraid he's not coming home."

Trying to control herself, Mary started to sob. She'd built so much of her life around Jack. Now it was as if her life itself was being snuffed out.

"What happened, Hank? Was it a hunting accident?" Bill asked.

"We don't know for sure, but they've," Hank couldn't put a sentence together.

"What the hell are you trying to tell me? That my son killed himself? He didn't have any reason to do that. He was due to go back to base tomorrow."

"I know that, Bill, but I found this note at the cabin," Hank said, as he reached in his jacket and pulled out a piece of paper. "I assume it's for you. It had no name on it, but who else would he write to?"

Bill reached for the note, unfolded it, and read it aloud. "I can't stand this pressure any longer. I tried to tell you, but didn't know how. I didn't have anyone else to turn to, so I figured the only way was to try to put it down on paper. Not being able to see your face somehow may make it easier to say."

Bill ended his reading abruptly. Mary looked at him, pleading with her eyes for him to continue.

"There is no more, Mary," Bill said, answering her unasked question.

"There has to be," she sobbed, grabbing the note from his trembling hands. Her eyes hungrily searched the paper for an answer to the questions running rampant in her mind. She started to weep uncontrollably.

Bill put his arm around her, and they cried together.

The colonel had stood in the background while the sheriff took care of the unpleasant task. Now he stepped forward and said, "We'll take care of the arrangements for you Bill, if you want us to. We've already had the body taken to Carpenter's Funeral Parlor, unless you would rather it go someplace else."

"Thank you both, but mama and I want to do this one last thing for our boy."

Hank lowered his eyes to the floor. "Bill, if there is anything we can do, please don't hesitate to ask." Hank felt his heart tearing too, but he didn't dare show it.

"There is one thing. See if you can keep it out of the papers."

Hank looked up at Bill and said, "It's as good as done."

Bill rose from the couch and started toward the door. Hank rose too, and he and the colonel followed. It was obvious the Mannings wanted to be alone in their sorrow.

As the door closed behind them, Hank breathed a sigh of relief. They left in the car, with the colonel driving. They rode in silence for several minutes.

Finally, Watson could tolerate it no longer. "Why didn't you mention that note to me, Hank?"

"I think, with all the confusion and excitement of the night, it slipped my mind." In reality, he would like to have kept the note for himself. When he saw the condition the boy's parents were in, he relinquished it grudgingly.

Well, where did you find it?" Watson asked, trying not to place too much emphasis on it.

"We were closing up the cabin and I noticed a piece of paper on the floor. It must have blown off the table when the door opened. I didn't see it until I leaned down to turn off the gas valve."

"It doesn't tell a hell of a lot though, does it?" the colonel said.

"Well, maybe Jack felt they would know what he was referring to, when he wrote about pressure," Hank offered.

Or maybe you would, Watson thought, wondering whom the note was really meant for.

This was one time Hank wished the colonel would be still. He didn't care to listen to his talk. It would require giving his attention to the conversation.

By now the colonel had pulled up to the red light at Palm Beach and Flower. He often would slip through a light late at night, but this night he sat and waited for it to turn green. He needed the time to think.

"Don," Hank said. "I'm not going back into headquarters. I'm too tired. There isn't anything so urgent that it can't wait till morning." He hopped out of the car, got into his jeep, and was gone in a matter of moments.

Solitude at last! The colonel sat there staring through the windshield. He watched the lights shine from the department windows, glowing through the darkness. They taunted him to enter, but he, too, was feeling weary. He put the car into drive and headed for home. The morning would be a busy one and he'd need a clear head to cope with the new crisis. He always did take care of the hard core things. *In the morning,* he thought, *I'll have my act together and be able to handle whatever arises.* Watson hadn't seen Yarbrough's car parked in back of the jail. If he had, he would have let the sleep wait, and gone in to see why Ray was still at the station.

The colonel made his trip home in record time. The stress of the night was catching up with him as he crawled into bed. Even with fatigue overcoming him, he thought how nice it would be to have the warmth of a woman's body next to him. He fell into a deep, dreamless sleep.

Chapter 5

Boy, what a mess this is, Yarbrough thought, as he settled down in his chair. *How in the hell did someone find out about this before the official release? The men know better than to discuss departmental procedures. No one knew about the incident except the ones who were there, and they surely wouldn't say anything. They have as much to lose as anyon*e. Yarbrough sat holding his head in his big brawny hands, engrossed in thought, when a light knock came on the door. It didn't interrupt his deep thinking. The door being ajar, Eva could see what appeared to be a man in torment or just exhausted, leastwise the latter. Of all the men she worked in close contact with, she liked Yarbrough most. It wasn't a romantic involvement, just a platonic thing. Sure, he had taken her out a couple of times; but each date was a guise, as they kept their eyes on a suspect.

She knocked a second time, more loudly, to attract his attention.

He looked up in response. "What is it, Eva?" he asked.

She still didn't know what the news story was all about and she didn't intend to ask. She was patient. She'd learned from previous experience that he would eventually tell her. He almost had to tell her in this particular case, for it was she that had talked to Doty.

"Captain, have you been in contact with the paper yet?"

He ground his teeth together, pursed his mouth, and then shook his head. "No. Come in and tell me exactly what that bastard had to say. Him and his sources!" He motioned for her to take a seat.

She entered the room, turned, and shut the door behind her. Then she leisurely walked over to the chair in front of his desk and sat down. The slowness gave her time to think about exactly what had been said.

He was visibly shaken at her casual approach. As she placed herself in the chair, she saw that she had added to his misery and was sorry she had lingered.

She repeated the telephone conversation as nearly as she was able to remember it. He didn't say anything for a few minutes. It seemed like hours to her, as she waited to be either dismissed or given a command to carry out.

Finally, he spoke. He sat on the edge of his chair, resting his elbows on the desk, with his forehead cupped in his hands.

At first she had to strain to hear him. He was talking with his head down, and the sound directed toward the desk. She knew she dared not miss a word; if she did, she would not be able to ask again what he'd said. She was glad when he rose, for it made it easier to hear him.

He walked around behind her chair, as if he didn't want to see her face as he spoke to her. He would need her help to carry this off, without bringing too much disgrace on the department. Lately, it seemed that things had not been going as smoothly as they used to. Things were coming to light or surfacing and greater effort was needed to cover tracks. He realized there was no way they could rule the roost forever and not expect to be dethroned. Although the previous sheriff had been king of the mountain for twenty years, it was only when young blood came on the scene that he lost the race, his last bid. Now with Hank Myers in his second term, they were sure they were on the way to a long reign. The payoffs and the people who paid under the table were the same, but narcotics had added a new element to this regime. The stakes were a lot bigger now and so were the dangers. If somebody screwed up, it wouldn't be him! As the captain related the events of the evening, Eva sat silent. Walking within arm's reach of her, he placed his left hand on her shoulder.

The touch of his hand felt like a hot poker. She did all she could to not show her disdain and she didn't understand why. A feeling she never knew existed awakened inside her. There had to be more to the tale then he told her. She'd find out in due time.

"Eva," he said, "call the paper and get that bastard Doty on the line."

"I think it's too late to stop the story he was going to print," she said.

"Maybe not. We'll try anyhow. Let's hope the damned presses broke down. It wouldn't be the first time with that slip-shod outfit."

She started for the door.

"No, call from here," he said.

She approached the desk, pressed his private line, picked up the phone, and dialed.

The switchboard was off, so the call went directly into the newsroom. The phone rang, mingling with the sounds of the teletype.

"City desk," Doty drawled into the mouthpiece, never taking his eyes off the copy he was reading. He had acted from reflex. He was able to read copy and carry on a conversation at the same time, without missing a word of either. The voice alerted him. He knew it well, without the caller having to identify himself. "What can I do for you, Captain?" he said, a smirk crossing his lips.

From prior experience Yarbrough knew better than to throw his weight around Doty. He couldn't be intimidated. "Corporal Eaton tells me you've picked up on a hot tip, Doty. What gives, or are you keeping it a secret?"

"Well, Captain," Doty began, with a patronizing tone in his voice. "I called over there to gather the facts on a lead I had, but no one wanted to give me any information. My sources are reliable, so, without your verification, I decided to go ahead and print it. You can read about it in the morning paper, at least in the city edition."

The captain was livid. He knew with Doty it was a battle of wits, and he was fighting to keep control. "How damaging is it? Can you tell me that?"

Doty was jubilant. He wet his right index finger on his tongue, and made an imaginary mark in mid air, chalking one up for his side. "Well, Captain, I heard about this apparent suicide. If I had my way, I would have printed that word with quotes and underlined it; but you see, I also have a boss. So the story said he shot himself at Sheriff Myers' hunting camp in Carroll County."

"Who said it was in Carroll County?" the captain interrupted.

Doty ignored his intrusion. "You know the ambulance trip telephone calls instead of radio the condition of the body people present at the scene. The general run of details." Doty had had his fun; now it was up to Yarbrough to get off the hook.

"Who gave you the details?" the captain over emphasized the last word.

"Sorry," Doty said smugly, "I can't divulge my sources. You know the privilege of the press."

"Listen, Doty, I know the sheriff and the colonel will want to talk to you tomorrow."

"I'm sure they will," Doty agreed.

"They've both gone home, so they won't know about this until late morning. For your sake, I hope the story doesn't put us in a bad light." He was immediately sorry he'd said that, for he knew Doty would pick up on it.

"Why, Captain, is that a threat?"

"Doty, at least think of the boy's family. They don't need to be brought into any vendetta you might have with the department."

"Captain, I am thinking of the family, even though you might not think I am. It's just that I go about it in a different way than you do."

Yarbrough had had enough.

The phone went dead in Doty's hand. He placed it back on the cradle and returned his eyes to the copy in front of him. He could smell it. He could feel it. He was hot on the trail of a story. He had always been alert to the situation at the sheriff's department. They covered their trail well, but one day he knew he would be at the right place at the right time.

Doty's cool control would have made him a good cop. He had considered law enforcement once, but decided on journalism instead. It was a hell of a lot safer too, at least until he took on the Leeward County Sheriff's Department. He knew there were good cops. He couldn't believe they were all corrupt. But until he was able to separate the wheat from the chaff, he didn't trust any of them. The thought of those cocky bastards in their pert green uniforms galled him. But he had to give Myers' department credit. His was one of the best-looking and neatest outfits, judging from the ones he had come in contact with in other counties.

Doty thought of how well protected the city was. There was an abundance of law enforcement agencies in this city. The sheriff's department as well as the city police, and the Florida Highway Patrol south of the city. For some unexplained reason, the sheriff's department always seemed to have the upper hand. They managed to make all matters their business, whether they were or not. Doty's goal was to one day dethrone Myers and his raiders. He wanted to see them behind bars. Tonight's incident made it evident it had to be soon. When the corruption was exposed, it would go all the way up to the state attorney's office, he was sure. The whole damned structure would shake right to its foundation.

Betty had gone to bed by the time Hank arrived home. She hadn't expected him back until Thursday. That was another thing he'd have to face come morning. Tonight he was too tired to give it any more thought. She was easy to handle, and always had been. But he was exhausted; once he fell into bed, he never moved all night.

Betty got up to shut off the alarm. No matter how late Hank would get in the alarm was always set for six o'clock. Before leaving for work he had time to shave, shower, and drink his coffee while he scanned the paper.

Betty looked at the bed and noticed him lying there. She was curious as to why he'd cut short the hunting trip. With him home, she'd have to prepare breakfast. She left the room as he rolled over in bed. He watched her exit through the doorway. Betty placed his coffee on the table. She smoothed out the creases the rubber band had made in the morning paper with her hand. She knew he didn't like to fight with the pages.

He entered the room as she laid it on the table. He sat down without saying a word to her. She quietly busied herself around the kitchen. Soon she'd have to get the children up for school.

Hank unfolded the paper with his left hand, while he sipped coffee with his right. Suddenly his eyes hit the story. He dropped the cup, splashing the hot coffee in his lap. The only heat he felt was from the flush on his face. A picture of Jack Manning smiled up from the page at him. Next to that was another suicide article, about a young man who had jumped off the roof of the county courthouse. The same banner headline was used for both deaths. Hastely, Hank read the article.

Hank did all he could do to finish reading the article. He was ready to fly by the time he read the last detail. "Who in hell gave the information to the press?" he shouted aloud. Betty grabbed a towel and began cleaning up the spilled coffee.

"What information?" she asked.

"Did anyone call here last night?" shrieked Hank.

"No. Why?" she asked, puzzled at the question. She'd always told him about calls that came in while he was out. "What's the matter, Hank? You look terrible." As she finished wiping up the spill, her eyes fell upon the newspaper, and the picture of Jack. She raised her hand to her mouth to stifle a gasp. "Why didn't you tell me what happened?" she asked.

"You were in bed when I came home. I just hadn't gotten around to it this morning," he said softly. He stood up and pulled his shirttail out of his wet trousers. "I'll have to change clothes and leave for headquarters. I have to find out who gave out that information before I okayed it."

Hank pushed the chair back and it gripped the floor instead of sliding, tipping over with a bang. "Damn," he muttered. Making no effort to pick it up, he hurried out of the room.

Betty stooped down to upright the chair. She sat down on it and read the article about Jack's death, slowly moving her head back and forth. She couldn't believe it. Not Jack, that wonderful young boy who had been so enthusiastic about life. She heard the front door close. She hoped he'd be gone all day.

The dust from the school bus hadn't yet settled when Betty's mind turned to the morning's events. She walked slowly up the sidewalk with her hands in the pockets of her housedress. With eyes lowered she watched each step she took. She stepped inside the door, closed it, and immediately leaned back on it. She and Hank knew the Mannings well. She ought to call them, she thought, and give them her condolence. If she didn't they would think it odd. Maybe she should ask Hank first. Why had he kept the information from her, she wondered. She turned and flipped the deadbolt switch. That had become a mandatory action since Hank had taken office.

Marriage had been a lot different from what she had anticipated. Their courtship had been short, and the whirlwind marriage had given her little time to think things through. She had overlooked the faults of the man she loved, until they started to build up and fester into a sore spot. She soon learned that Hank possessed a very quick temper. Her thoughts flashed back to her stay in the hospital after Hank had beaten her. Only through the grace of God, and the colonel arriving on the scene, was he kept from doing her worse harm. He had gone wild over such a trivial little thing. Now she couldn't even remember what it was all about.

The colonel had her taken to the Baron County Community Hospital, and registered under an assumed name. Then he took Hank to Sarasota to a private clinic. That had been the only other time she had seen the look in Hank's eyes that she saw this morning. It frightened her. She had convinced herself that things were working out for them. He had started to go to church with her and the children. He'd even become an active member in the church activities. Their problems had been kept quiet due to the colonel's influence; yet she had misgivings about him. He made her uneasy and she didn't know why. It was always the colonel that came to Hank's rescue. Hank leaned on him, mentally as well as emotionally. She believed the colonel actually enjoyed Hank's dependency and the trust he put in him. She wondered if it might be a slight case of jealousy on her part. After all, she thought, a man should lean on his mate. She had been told that the first ten years of marriage were the roughest. After eight, she wondered if she could make it through another two years, either mentally or physically.

She didn't have close friends; Hank never had time to socialize. She kept herself occupied with the house and the kids. The two children had come close together. At first she wondered whether it was wise to start a family so soon. It hadn't given her and Hank time enough to get to know each other. Hank had had time to sow his wild oats. She was without family. Her parents had died when she was young. When she turned eighteen, the aunt who had raised her died, leaving her alone again. She had been terribly lonely. When she met Hank she felt her life was about to acquire some order. Boy, how wrong she had been. She had to make the best of what marriage had to offer her. Just being a cop's wife was hard enough, but now the marital problems seemed to be multiplying. The toughest thing of all was she didn't know why. She only knew that she felt more at ease when Hank was gone. Having him close made her uncomfortable. She still loved him, she was sure of that. But he had changed somehow. Lately he had been like a stranger to her. She hated to admit it to herself she was a little frightened of him.

Yarbrough was stewing by the time the sheriff arrived at the department. To make matters worse, he knew Hank had seen the morning paper by the look on his face.

The hallways were full of activity, with the shifts about to change. Hank worked his way through the confusion, ignoring several greetings from his men as he passed by. Arriving at Yarbrough's side, Hank glared hard into his eyes. The coldness sent a chill up the captain's spine.

"Come into my office, Ray. I want to talk to you," Hank said as he walked away.

Yarbrough followed him into the office and closed the door.

The sheriff reached his desk just as the door closed. He wheeled around and spoke in a cold, deliberate tone. "Someone in this department is undermining me." Then he shouted angrily, "Who in hell gave out that information on the Manning suicide?"

"I don't know, sir. The paper called here last night and asked about the shooting. Eaton called me. She didn't know what Doty was talking about."

"Is she still on duty? I want to talk to her," Hank growled.

Ray didn't hesitate walking to the door. He opened it, stepped through and was out of sight for a few seconds. Then he returned with Eva Eaton closely behind him. He motioned for her to enter the room, and he closed the door after her.

"Sit down here, Corporal," Hank said, pointing to a chair. "I want to talk to you. Start from the beginning and tell me just what happened last night with that phone call from the newspaper."

Eva drew a breath and began, "There isn't much to tell, sir. That reporter Doty called and asked me about a shooting up at your camp.

I told him I didn't know anything about it. He said if no one wanted to give him a statement, he would use the information he'd received from his source. I called the captain at home, because you said you wouldn't be available, and he was to take care of anything that came up." She sat silently, waiting either to catch hell or be dismissed. She had read the story, and it didn't put the department in a good light, whatever the motive.

The sheriff was silent, but his facial expression said what his mind was thinking. "You can go, Eaton. Pass the word. If any more calls come in regarding the Manning boy, direct them to the colonel or me."

Having his name omitted from the directive gnawed at Yarbrough. It was obvious that the sheriff didn't think that he was capable of handling the situation. He hoped Eva hadn't picked up on it.

Eaton acknowledged the sheriff's command. "Yes, sir." She opened the door quickly and was startled to see the colonel standing there. She was suddenly overwhelmed by the size of the man looming over her; she quickly stepped sideways and relinquished part of her area as they passed. "That guy gives me the creeps," she said to herself. As she closed the door, she heard the colonel speak.

"We have an appointment at the News Leader in thirty minutes."

"My God," Hank proclaimed. "I promised Bill Manning I'd see that there wouldn't be a press release on the death. Now there'll be twice as much publicity."

The colonel sat down and calmly lit a cigarette. "I really think it's to our advantage to give the details, and our version, instead of just letting the informant's story stand as public record. It will look better to make some kind of rebuttal in this instance."

"Of all things, they put another suicide article right next to Jack's," Hank said, as he lowered himself into his chair. "What the hell are they trying to prove anyway?" His hands grasped the edge of the desk. He went weak just thinking about it.

Yarbrough leaned over to pick the newspaper up off the desk. He studied the front page. He narrowed his eyes, cocked his head, and thought for a moment.

"Kenneth Carson," he said. "Say, isn't that the kid we were talking to the other night, while we were cruising the bar lots?"

"Yeah," the colonel replied.

"I never realized he worked right over here in the courthouse. He sure didn't strike me as being the kind that would take a leap," Yarbrough proclaimed.

"Must have gotten hold of some bad stuff," the colonel replied nonchalantly.

Hank's phone buzzed. He picked it up. "Sheriff Myers." His face paled as he listened to the voice at the other end of the line. "But, sir, I had nothing to do with the story. Just as soon as I can get over there, I'll have this mess straightened out. No, I don't know how they got the picture." When he replaced the phone, it was obvious by the look on his face that the person on the other end of the line had hung up on him. Not many people hung up on the sheriff.

Hank sprang into action, as if propelled by a bell going off in his head. He opened his desk drawer, removed a map, unfolded it, and laid it out on his desk. "Now, let's get this straight," he said as he pointed to the section of the map where his camp was located.

The other two men moved in closer to the desk to view the map.

"Right here is the cabin, and here is where we found the body," he said, pointing with his finger.

The colonel was the first to make a comment. "But Hank, that's inside Carroll County. We don't dare tell them we moved the body without calling in a neutral agency, especially when it was in their jurisdiction."

"I don't intend to tell them it was anywhere but in Leeward County. Because his father at the garage was monitoring the police calls, we communicated by telephone. If it weren't for Doty jumping on the story, we could have filed it as an accident, and we wouldn't be going through all this bull."

Yarbrough took the paper from under his arm where he'd tucked it as he bent to peer at the map. "I wonder who this city policeman is who gave his views on how the investigation should be carried out?"

As the colonel headed for the door, he turned around and looked at the two men standing by the desk. "They've got nothing but a bunch of a** holes over there. Those that aren't just old men biding their time to retire, are only good for writing tickets and directing traffic. And then someone has to tie a string around their finger so they can tell their right hand from their left." He reached for the doorknob.

"One other thing," Hank said, his eyes narrowing down to slits, as he looked first at Yarbrough and then the colonel. "Find out who leaked the story to Doty. I want you to make him disappear, dead, do you understand me?" Not waiting for a reply, the colonel was out the door. The only sound was the whoosh of the door closing against the padded jam.

Chapter 6

Steve Doty checked his watch as he pushed the glass door open and headed for his desk. He would have welcomed two or three more hours sleep, but this was better than sleep or food or even...by god... sex. This was confront-the-lions-in-their-den day. No, he mentally corrected himself. Not lions, no. There was something noble and brave about lions. These were more like jackals, pouncing on anything or anyone that ventured by. He mentally began running the gamut of animals that reminded him of the sheriff and his major-domo, the colonel. "And for vultures," he said aloud, as he poured himself a cup of coffee. "Weasels," he smiled, as he walked toward the desk.

His butt barely hit his chair when Corcoran's husky voice yelled out to him.

"Doty! In here!"

He sank into the comfortable armchair, set his coffee down on Corcoran's desk and waited for the lecture he knew was coming.

"You got my message about the meet with the sheriff's department?"

Doty nodded.

Corcoran was nervous, and trying, as usual, to hide it with bluster. "I hope to hell you haven't put my head on a chopping block. When I okayed that story last night I didn't know the sky would fall in this morning. Give me everything you've got on it. Don't spare anything. Wait, do you think we need to get our attorney in on this?"

Doty swallowed a chuckle. "I don't think so, Corky. They're coming on a fishing expedition. They'll spurt and blow like they usually do, throw out a few threats and try like hell to intimidate us. But what can they do? Our story was fact."

"Maybe so, but it makes me damned uncomfortable having those goons looking over my shoulder. I've got advertisers to worry about. Regardless of what you think, you self-serving bastard, this paper does not revolve around the sheriff's department"

Doty sipped his coffee and half listened to Corcoran sputter on and on. He'd known Corky for twenty years, and loved and admired him. He had that special quality that went into a good newspaperman. He liked to think he had it too. They both wanted the same thing: to report the news and keep the public informed. And, along the way, destroy the jackals, and the vultures and the weasels.

Maybe he had gone out on a limb with this one. He'd played a long shot, but it was paying off. Otherwise there wouldn't be such flack.

Corcoran paused for breath, and Doty jumped in fast.

"Now wait a minute, Corky. Remember that murder last year, the young boy killed by that known sex offender, the mental patient? Remember how you bellowed when the sheriff released him on insufficient evidence? And then the guy's parents got him out of the state, where he killed another kid? Remember how you said that you knew the loved ones would be hurt by spreading the gory details all over the paper, that they would have to relive the horror all over again? But that it was necessary to expose the negligence and ineptitude of both the state's attorney's office and the sheriff's department."

It was true, Corcoran thought. Hell, that's why he'd got into the racket, to use the printed word to change the things that needed changing. With it he had the power to bring about glory or destruction. He knew that power had a staggering effect on the public. He didn't consider himself a god or a judge, just a little man trying to sort out the good guys from the bad guys.

"Besides," Doty said gesturing toward a plaque hanging on the wall behind Corcoran's desk. "You got an award for that story. This Manning suicide is just the tip of the iceberg. Trust me on this, Corky. You know my hunches are good. This whole mess is going to blow wide open. Just give me a little time."

He paused, waiting for Corky to say something.

Instead, he stood up from his desk, fumbled at straightening his tie and muttered, "They're here."

Doty turned and looked toward the door. Sure enough, it was the boys in green. He'd like to see both of them in hell. Or maybe just high water, wearing cement shoes.

Corcoran moved toward the door, extending his hand to the sheriff. Myers ignored, it walking past him into the office. He glowered at Doty still sitting in his chair. He walked to the far end of the desk and stood waiting for Corcoran to cross behind him.

The colonel closed the door and stood in front of it.

"Won't you sit down?" Corcoran said, gesturing toward a chair in the corner behind the sheriff. "How about some coffee?"

Myers ignored the offer and started on his attack. Doty listened as the diatribe droned on and on. His eyes shifted from the sheriff to the colonel standing stiff against the door. *He really is a tall drink of water,* Doty thought, noting that Watson's hat was nearly level with the top of the doorframe. *Damn those sunglasses,* he thought to himself, *I'd like to see his eyes, just once. I'll bet he wears those damned reflective glasses to bed,* he laughed to himself. He studied the big aquiline nose, the square jaw, and the hard mouth. *He's got a neck like a bull,* thought Doty.

Suddenly he noticed the sheriff pull a map out of this pocket and spread it out on the desk. He leaned forward to see what Myers was pointing at.

"This is where the Manning boy was found, and, as you can see, it's in Leeward County. With your lousy judgment and poor taste you've not only hurt the kid's loved ones, you've deliberately lied about the location. The Mannings are experiencing enough heartbreak without you spreading malicious lies. We would have shielded them all together by not releasing the information about the acci...suicide." He hoped no one had caught his goof.

Corcoran stood and listened, taking the insults thrown out by the sheriff. After all, he had always been a fair man, he thought, he would listen and try to be impartial. He had always bent over backward to help the underdog. He'd squelched many a story to protect an innocent party. There were people in the trade who wondered how he had kept his job after allowing good stories to go un-printed. He didn't shy away from controversial stories, but he wasn't an editor who published gory details just to sell papers. He had a heart, he thought to himself, except when it came to the sheriff's department.

He glanced over at Doty and then back to the map. He and Steve often butted heads, but on this one subject they were in complete agreement. They both wanted to see the control and power taken away from these two tyrants who manipulated people to satisfy their own means.

Corcoran knew if he didn't conform, they would eventually destroy him. Even so, it was a game he couldn't stop. Couldn't and wouldn't. Damn it, a man had to stand for something. And besides, he rationalized, they hadn't succeeded in touching him or his staff. Not yet, anyway!

"Sheriff Myers, I printed the story as it was reported to us," Corcoran interjected. "If there is-"

The sheriff cut him off in mid sentence. "That's another thing. Which fed you the information? I want the name of the person who gave you the story."

"You know we don't give out names, Sheriff. The story was phoned in. We checked the facts, and we printed it. We did try to get an okay from your department, but your people refused to give us any information."

The sheriff was having trouble keeping his temper. "I want a detailed follow-up story using our quotes, none of that unidentified source crap."

"I'll get a steno and you can give us the story. We'll print it word for word."

"No," the sheriff said defensively. Then immediately his words were hard as nails again. "I have work to do. I can't stand around here all day. I'll issue the statement on my letterhead. You'll have a copy by noon."

Doty couldn't help but jump in. "Will that statement go to the TV station and the other news media as well?" He could see the panic in the sheriff's eyes. The boobs hadn't even thought about the television coverage. What a bunch of jerk offs.

Myers leaned over to pick up the map. "Just print the story the way we give it to you, and that's all." He carefully folded the map and placed it in his pocket. "And the next time you print something connected with my department, I want to see it first!"

The colonel already had the door open and stood waiting for the sheriff to pass through. In thirty seconds they were down the hall and gone.

Doty spotted the worried look on Corcoran's face and laughed aloud, "Well, they certainly know how to make an exit, don't they."

They stared at each other for a minute and Corcoran smiled, shaking his head.

"I sure hope the people are as smart as I give them credit for being," Doty said. He was hoping that the sheriff's story would put some doubts in the minds of the public. The paper had a good rapport with the city and state boys, but the sheriff's department was a hard nut to crack.

Corcoran sank back in his chair and loosened his tie. "What a piece of work that bastard is. And the colonel. Did you notice how he stood there the whole time? He never moved a muscle; he was like a statue. My God, that guy scares me. The sheriff is just a well-rehearsed demagogue, but that colonel is really evil."

Doty nodded in agreement. "I just hope they've overplayed their hands this time." He picked up his coffee cup and headed for his desk.

Ordinarily, by this time of the morning Doty would be off somewhere following up a lead or working on a story. Not today. He intended to wait patiently for the sheriff's statement. He glanced at his watch, then turned on his computer terminal and started typing.

He was still at it when he heard a voice behind him. He whirled his chair around to see a tall, thin-faced young man in a green deputy's uniform smiling at him.

"Mr. Doty, I'm Jimmy Dale from the Leeward County Sheriff's Department." The young man extended his hand.

Doty was baffled. It had been years since anybody from the sheriff's department had wanted to shake his hand. And he couldn't remember when anybody from there had a smile on their face.

Okay, I'll play your silly game, he thought to himself, as he reached out and shook hands. He was impressed by the strong grip. "What can I do for you, Deputy?"

"Well, I'm here to deliver this to the editor, Mr. Corcoran," he said, raising a large manila envelope in his left hand.

Doty glanced over to Corky's glass-enclosed office. "Looks like he's gone to lunch. But, I'll be happy to see that he gets it." Doty reached out to accept the envelope, excited by what he knew it contained.

"All right." Dale said, putting the envelope in Doty's hand. "I just want to say that I'm a real fan of yours, Mr. Doty."

A fan? Steve thought. He was really puzzled now.

"Yes, sir. I've read your articles for years. As a matter of fact your byline is the first thing I look for when I open the paper."

"Pull up a chair," Doty said, gesturing toward the straight back next to his desk. Dale moved the chair closer and sat down.

"Now, tell me something about yourself, Dale. Are you new at the department?"

"Yes sir, fresh out of the academy." Dale smiled again. "I'm this month's general flunky. You know, delivery boy, messenger, pick up, gopher. First, I had a tour on the roads with a patrolman. Then phone detail. They move me around all the time. I'll be happy when they give me a permanent assignment, doing something worthwhile."

This kid was too good to be true, Doty said to himself, as he continued the questions. "How did you happen to pick the sheriff's department?"

"Well, I wanted the city, but you know they have that budget problem and they've frozen all hiring for six months. I didn't want to wait that long and chance not getting on. The sheriff had an opening so I jumped in."

Jumped in is right, Doty said to himself, *I hope you can swim, kid.* "So, how did you happen to get into law enforcement, Jimmy?" He was beginning to warm to the boy.

"It just seemed right to me. I don't ever remember wanting to do anything else, even when I was small."

"That's great" said Doty, trying to see behind the young man's eyes. This boy was like a breath of fresh air. Either he was the best damned con artist he'd ever seen or the kid was really sincere. Either way, he was in for a hell of a ride with the sheriff's department.

"I want to wish the best of luck with your new job," Doty said. "I hope it's as rewarding and fulfilling as you expect it to be."

"I'm sure it will be," Dale said, as he rose from the chair, moving it back to its original position. "I intend to make it my life's work."

Let's hope that life is a nice, long one, thought Doty. He rose to shake Dale's hand once more. "If there's anything I can do for you, or, well, you know. Don't hesitate." It wasn't often that Doty offered his help to anyone. He was a little surprised to hear himself say the words.

"Thanks, Mr. Doty, I appreciate that."

"Call me Steve."

Dale smiled again, as he turned to walk away.

Doty watched him as he crossed the pressroom and passed through the glass door. He couldn't help feeling a little sad. *A really nice kid,* he said to himself, *those sharks will chew him up.*

"Back to business," he said aloud, as he ripped open the manila envelope and pulled out the official-looking document with the sheriff's fancy letterhead on it.

Chapter 7

"Let me handle it." The colonel said, leaning back in his overstuffed chair. "You keep your mouth shut."

Yarbrough nodded. They had agreed that Becky needed to be placed in line.

Watson started to press the button on his phone when it buzzed. A call was coming in on his private line. "Hello," he said, picking it up. He listened and then motioned with his hand to Yarbrough, pointing to the phone. He silently moved his lips, forming the word Carter.

Yarbrough leaned forward, listening. This call had been a long time coming.

"Well, Billy," the colonel said, "I think tonight would be better. I have a little business to take care of here first, how about seven?" He was silent again while Billy talked. "Alright, seven-thirty. Tell Lemmon, he knows where."

Watson pressed the button to disconnect Carter, then buzzed for the duty secretary. "Tell Detective Gibbons to step into my office at her earliest convenience, providing that it's in the next five minutes."

Yarbrough rose and moved to a chair by the wall. He crossed his legs and lit a cigarette.

When Becky entered the room she wouldn't be able to see him, unless she turned directly in his direction. That was how he wanted it.

A soft rap at the door broke the silence.

"Come in," the colonel commanded.

The door opened and a petite female with flaming red hair entered the room. She shut the door and moved her 110-pound frame toward the colonel's desk.

He motioned for her to sit down in the chair in front of his desk. As she lowered herself, he started to talk.

"Becky, I've had some things brought to my attention, and I'd like to get your views on them." He didn't like dissension in his organization, and he intended to make that crystal clear.

When she was called to the office, Becky thought she was in for a lecture. She had often been called in with other officers for high level meetings to map strategy in the sheriff's war on drugs. But this was the first time she'd been singled out, and she was worried. The way the colonel phrased his sentence placed her a little more at ease. Then suddenly reality hit her. She spotted Yarbrough out of the corner of her eye.

She had discovered him sooner than he wanted her to. He had taught her well. She was always quick to pick up on her surroundings. Her life literally depended on it when she was out on the street, mingling with drug people.

The colonel saw things weren't going as he had intended, but he charged ahead anyway. "It's been brought to my attention that you are not happy with certain departmental procedures."

Her green eyes opened wide, and sparks flashed as she glanced toward Yarbrough. She directed her words to the colonel. "Sir, I feel some things aren't being handled, as they should be. I spoke to Captain Yarbrough about it and he told me to go about my business and forget it. Some things are hard to overlook, sir."

The colonel sat silently while Becky cited times and instances. When it appeared she had finished, he rose from his chair, walked around the desk, and leaned against the front of it facing her. "Becky, I have a job for you. That is, if you think you're cut out for it."

The change in his attitude startled her. She had thought this was going to be the end of her job in the narcotics division. She was really confused now.

He looked into her face, waiting for her reaction.

She always looked at a job as an opportunity, and he knew it. She had made several successful arrests, and the men felt she was a credit to their team. Maybe Yarbrough was right. Maybe she was just getting too big for her bikini. Better safe than sorry.

"What is it you want me to do, sir?" she asked.

"I hope you will understand the importance of this particular assignment," Watson said, still searching for a reaction.

"What is it, sir?" she asked a second time, eager now for the information that would put her back into circulation. Since she had spoken out against procedures, she had been reassigned to the stolen vehicle division. She knew that it was a ploy to punish her, and she knew, also, that Yarbrough was behind it. She wanted to get back to narcotics; that was her niche, and she loved it. Besides, she knew a lot of time and money had gone into educating her as an undercover agent. The course on bugging devices alone had taken six weeks. Whatever the colonel wanted, she was game.

"Well, it's like this," the colonel said, stepping away from the desk and winking in Yarbrough's direction. "We need to know what the public defender's office is up to. In simple terms, we need a plant, somebody to make contact on the inside." He paused, then walked behind her chair. "You're a beautiful young woman, Becky. With your face, your charm, your body, and your know how, I think you're just the one to get us the information we need." He paused again, waiting for her to speak.

"Do I understand you right, sir? You want me to have an affair with the public defender, and milk him for information?" She had said in one sentence what he had beaten around the bush for five minutes to say.

"No, not the public defender himself, Becky. He's too smart for that. We would aim you at one of the junior assistants. They aren't too well educated in dirty politics yet." He slowly started to pace the floor in the area behind her chair, while she still faced his desk. "How you do it is up to you, Becky." It was obvious from the tone of his voice what he meant. "We chose you for this assignment because of your good record with the department. We felt that you could use a new challenge in your work. That, plus the fact that you aren't married, made you our first choice." He couldn't tell if she was swallowing the hook or not. "And, let's face it, everybody can use a change of luck in their love life." He smiled broadly as he walked around the desk and sat down facing Becky again.

The comment went over her head, or she just ignored it. She could taste the intrigue in the colonel's offer. This would put her back in the undercover work she loved. "Yes, sir, I'll do it," she said, shaking her head affirmatively.

"Splendid," said the colonel. "Do you know anybody at the public defender's office? Anyone who might be a likely candidate?"

"I know most of the guys when I see them. Wait, there is one. His name is Mark Sims, and he tried to hit on me at the Pelican Lounge a few weeks ago."

The colonel smiled again. "That's our boy. Start laying the groundwork, find out his habits, his hangouts, his weaknesses, his likes and dislikes. I don't have to tell you how to do your job, Becky. You're a pro." Watson had gambled and won. She had taken the bait and was running with it. He knew she was obsessed with the work and wanted to get back into it after cooling her heels for a few weeks. Besides, he needed her. No other female in the squad would go so far as to literally put herself on the line. Up to this point, he hadn't been able to get her involved deeply enough in any situation. She was completely under his control now. Her a** was not only on the line, it was his!

"Okay, Becky. You go back on duty and I'll get back with you," the colonel said, dismissing her.

She got up out of the chair and turned toward the door. She glanced towards Yarbrough. Their eyes met. The smirk on his face irritated her. She gave him a dirty look as she made her exit.

After the door closed, both men looked at each other and broke into laughter.

"That stupid redhead doesn't know if she is bored or punched," Yarbrough said.

"I'll bet it's been bored many times; and from what I hear, it's not too bad either. What about it, Ray?"

Yarbrough smiled, and they both let go with a low-grade laugh.

The colonel looked at his watch. "I've got a few things to wrap up. Meet me back here a little past seven."

Yarbrough rose and started for the door. "Okay," he said. He was being dismissed, just like Becky. He was smart enough to know when he wasn't wanted. The colonel didn't have to draw him any pictures.

Watson turned to the papers on his desk and picked up a pencil. A sudden rap at the door brought a frown to his face. Before he could respond, the door swung open and the sheriff crossed the room to his desk.

"Listen, Don, I've got to get out of here." There was a slight tremor in his voice, and Watson could see he was agitated.

"What is it, Hank? What's wrong?" the colonel asked, trying to hide his surprise.

The sheriff sank into the desk chair and placed his hands on the arms, as if to steady himself. "I just need to get away for a few days, that's all."

"Okay," the colonel said. "Where are you going?"

"I don't know. Just away. If anybody asks I had to go to Tallahassee on business."

"Alright," the colonel nodded his head in agreement. "Will you be back for the funeral on Wednesday?"

"Lord, no!" Myers gasped. "I can't face, no!"

The colonel's mind was racing. "No problem. I'll phone the Mannings, and make an excuse. I'll take care of the flowers and make sure the department is well represented at the service."

The look of panic seemed to ease momentarily in the sheriff's eyes.

What the hell? thought Watson. *What set him off?* The sheriff was falling apart before his eyes. "Get a hold of yourself, Hank," he said firmly. He had seen this weakness in the sheriff before, and he reveled in it. It made his hold over Hank even stronger. He played the dependable friend and compatriot role well. Oh, yes, Hank could count on the colonel to save his hide. "Why don't you go out to the camp for a couple of days?"

"No," Myers yelled as he shot up from the chair.

The mention of the camp brought a queasy sensation to the pit of his stomach. He swallowed hard, making an obvious attempt to steady himself. "I'll just head north for a couple of days."

Watson didn't want the sheriff running around in public making a spectacle of himself, but he sensed there was no way to stop him. *Besides*, he thought, *If he is going to come unglued I'd rather it not be around the department.* He reached into a desk drawer and pulled out a pint of scotch and a shot glass. "How about a nip to steady you, Hank," he said as he poured.

"No, I can't. My stomach," he didn't finish the sentence. Instead, he took a deep breath and turned toward the door.

"I want to know where you are, Hank. Call me on my private line, or the car phone. If you don't get me, leave a message with the switchboard and I'll call you right back."

The sheriff nodded and closed the door behind him.

"Damn," the colonel said as he reached down, picked up the jigger of scotch and downed it in one gulp. He turned and walked to the window. Separating the mini-blinds with his fingers, he watched Hank get into his jeep, turn left out of the parking lot, and head north toward the bridge. He sat down and leaned back in his chair. He stared off into space for a few minutes, then reached for the phone and buzzed the main desk. "Is Paul Travers on duty today?" he asked curtly. "He is. Tell him I want to see him right away!"

The colonel poured himself another scotch, then screwed the lid back on the bottle and replaced it in the drawer. He emptied the glass and turned it around and around in his hands. He was still playing with the shot glass when Travers knocked on the door.

"Come in," he said, and motioned Travers to the chair in front of the desk.

"What can I do for you, Colonel?" Travers asked in his usual servile manner. He knew that Watson was the real boss of the department, and he had made up his mind long ago that pleasing the colonel would guarantee his job.

"I'm putting a cap on the Manning kid's suicide, and I need a few more pieces to complete the puzzle." As he spoke he pulled open the desk drawer and dropped in the shot glass.

"Okay," said Travers, waiting for the questions to begin.

"Fill me in on what happened that day."

"Nothing much. The whole weekend was pretty dull," Travers said, describing how he and the sheriff had driven to the camp together and how Jack Manning was waiting for them in his truck.

"How did you happen to be invited?" the colonel questioned.

"I don't know. The sheriff said he wanted me there. I tried to beg off, but he kept insisting. I figure I was there just to cook and clean up."

"So what did Jack and the sheriff do the day of the shooting?"

"They went out about eight that morning and stayed 'till almost noon. I don't think they shot anything, at least they didn't bring anything back to cook. They had some lunch, sat around talking for awhile and went back out about two."

"What were they doing out there?" Watson asked.

"Beats me. Target shooting I guess. I heard gunshots off and on all afternoon. I cleaned up the dishes and took a nap. The sheriff woke me up when he came in the door. That was about dusk."

"Then what?"

"He asked if there was some coffee, and I said I'd fix some. Then he went over, sat down at the table and started cleaning his rifles."

"Did he seem upset, or anxious about anything?"

"No," Travers shook his head, trying to remember exactly what the sheriff had said to him. "He seemed to be someplace else, real quiet. But then, you know the sheriff never talks a lot anyway."

"So, did he say why Jack hadn't come back with him?"

"No, he didn't mention him. Not until it began to get dark. He went out on the porch three or four times and called to him. Finally, he told me he was going out to look for him. He said if he wasn't back in twenty minutes I should come looking too. I waited fifteen then I started out. You know the rest. When I got there the kid was lying on the ground and the sheriff was bending over him crying."

"What was your opinion of the Manning boy?" the colonel asked.

"I liked him. He seemed like a nice enough kid. I used to see him at his dad's wrecker service. I know he really had a thing for the sheriff."

"What do you mean, thing?"

"Well, you know, it was obvious he admired him, looked up to the sheriff. I guess you'd call it hero worship." Travers was careful never to call Myers anything but "the sheriff." He might refer to him as Hank with other people, but never to his face or in front of the colonel. Travers liked his job and wanted to keep it.

"How often did you see the Manning boy at the camp?" Watson asked.

"Lots. The first time he was in high school. He used to be up there almost every weekend. The sheriff seemed to enjoy having him around. They'd hunt a little and fish, cut some brush, shoot some birds, things like that."

"One more question, Paul. What do you think happened to the kid? Do you think he killed himself?"

"Maybe. But it doesn't add up to me. I think it was more like an accident. The kid didn't seem like the type to kill himself."

"Okay, Paul. Thanks for filling me in."

Travers got out of the chair and turned toward the door.

"Incidentally," the colonel said. "Who do you think tipped off the newspaper?"

"I figure one of the mobile medic guys, don't you?"

"Could be," Watson said as Travers closed the door behind him.

The colonel sat staring into space, mentally rerunning everything he knew about Jack Manning. "That boy deserved everything he got," he said under his breath.

The rap at the door startled him. Before he could speak, Yarbrough poked his head in and said, "It's late. We need to get on the road."

The colonel checked his watch, gave his desk the once over, and locked the top drawer.

On the way past the front desk, Yarbrough told Eva Eaton they were going out on the road.

She nodded, and checked their names off on her duty pad.

Both men routinely adjusted the bulge under their arm as they went through the door of the department into the parking lot.

"Have you noticed how some of the men are carrying two weapons?" Yarbrough asked as he slid behind the wheel of the unmarked vehicle. "They can only fire one at a time."

The colonel laughed, as he opened the car door, bent his head low and sat down. "Yes, but they can be using their second gun, while you're reloading yours."

"Well, if I haven't hit what I'm aiming at by the time I go through one round, then I might as well hand in my badge," Yarbrough said jokingly.

"Thank your lucky stars you don't have to worry about the time element involved, unless you have a contract out on you. So, you'll be able to keep your badge."

Before he started the engine, Yarbrough picked up the radio mike and spoke. "555 to headquarters."

"Headquarters to 555," came the acknowledgment.

"10–8," the captain replied.

"10–8 19:10 hours," the dispatcher said, putting them into service, aware they were on the road.

"Where we supposed to meet him?" Yarbrough asked, as he swung the Ford into traffic.

"He's going to be down at Maple Manor with Corporal Lemmon. He's meeting one of his suppliers in the area. We'll wait for them in that dark secluded area off the end of Maple Street."

They rode in silence, until the colonel spoke. "Incidentally, the Manning kid is getting himself buried on Wednesday. I want you there representing the sheriff and the department. Take Deets with you and Travers, and anybody else that's not on duty. Oh, and order a nice spray of flowers for the wake. Charge them to the sheriff's account."

"Isn't Hank going?" Yarbrough asked.

"No, he's in Tallahassee on business."

"What business?" the captain questioned.

"Just business." Watson answered.

Yarbrough was smart enough to let it go. He turned right off the highway and entered a housing development of ten square miles of middle-class homes, mostly duplexes. At one time they had been owner occupied, but now were mostly income rentals.

"We'd better call in and put ourselves out of commission. It would be embarrassing to be called into service during our meet," Yarbrough laughed, picking up the mike. "555 to headquarters."

"Headquarters to 555," came the reply.

"10–6, 10–7, 10–48."

"10–4 19:32 hours," replied the dispatcher.

"We wouldn't want to give anyone the idea there was a bust going down, would we?" Yarbrough laughed as he clicked on the bright lights. "You did say the end of Maple Street, right?"

"Yeah, right down there," the colonel said, motioning towards the roadway that left the blacktopped street.

The captain pulled up at the end of the street and stopped, shutting off the motor. They sat in the darkness, listening to the sounds of the night.

"This area has really gone sour," Yarbrough exclaimed. "Even the adults call this place drug heaven. There are a lot of potheads living in here, but I know a lot of hard-working, legitimate families here too. They work their asses off and payday barely gives them enough to go around. Yet the bastards keep butting their heads against the wall."

"Yeah, not everybody can work for the sheriff's department," the colonel said sarcastically. "Here comes a set of headlights."

A car pulled off onto the dirt roadway and stopped. Two men got out and approached the Ford.

The captain released the door locks with a click that broke the stillness of the night. He then started the car, ran up the automatic windows and turned on the air conditioner.

Larry Lemmon opened the back door and slid all the way across the seat. Carter followed, then closed the door. "What do you know, men?" he said, breaking the silence.

Neither Yarbrough nor the colonel liked Carter or trusted him. They needed him, pure and simple, and they tolerated him because of it. They had little information about him, and he volunteered even less. They knew he was dangerous, and wouldn't hesitate to kill if the opportunity presented itself. Every time the colonel saw him it reinforced his desire to eliminate Carter from the operation as soon as possible.

"What's the word on the shipment?" Yarbrough asked gruffly.

"Day after tomorrow, Wednesday night. That is unless there's a delay."

"What kind of delay?" the colonel asked.

"Hell, I don't know. Just a delay. Anything could happen. An engine, a breakdown, coast guard. Who knows? As of now the freighter should be in place about midnight Wednesday."

Lemmon tried to smooth the wrinkles. "If there's any problem we'll know in plenty of time. The contact will have all the information."

"Who is the contact?" asked the colonel.

"None of your damn business," Billy spat back.

The colonel bristled. Before he could speak, Lemmon jumped in again. "We don't know yet, some skirt from Texas. She's due in tomorrow. She checks into a local motel and phones us with the information. As soon as we hear, I'll be on the phone to you, Captain. We can work out the cover operation then."

Yarbrough nodded in agreement.

Carter could feel the tense atmosphere in the car, but he didn't really care. He only wanted what they could offer him, protection. Along with a way to unload the merchandise coming in. He knew he was the main man in the operation and that no matter how the colonel felt about him, he couldn't eliminate him without queering the whole setup. He enjoyed upsetting the colonel, and made a point of it every time they got together. He wasn't sure how far he could push, but as far as Billy was concerned the sky was the limit.

At 32, Billy Carter was cagey, and usually kept one step ahead of trouble. He made sure before settling in an area, that there were men in authority who could be bought. One fact he was sure of was that he would never run out of places. There was always someone on the take. He could speak with authority. He had been from one coast to the other. He'd really hit pay dirt here. Fort Manson had exceeded his expectations by far. He never figured things could run so smoothly. He was provided all the protection and cover-up he could hope for. Transactions were carried on in the open, as he'd never experienced before in all his years in drugs. Like tonight, he thought, watching the colonel's jaw tighten. Who would ever believe he could be setting up a shipment with one of the highest-ranking officers in the county? At first, he had found it hard to convince his supplier that they were on the take, and not just setting them up for a bust. Fact was he had hit the mother load in Fort Manson.

"Okay Carter, we don't have all night, you know," Yarbrough growled. "Give us everything you have up to now."

"Well, the freighter Calico left Columbia on the 28th of last month. It's loaded with first class, high-grade Columbian red and gold. The code name is Zephyr. You line up the boats to meet it out at the fifteen-mile marker. Bring it back in, and I'll take it from there." Carter reveled in giving the big guys orders. It gave him a high just thinking about all the authority he had. "That gives you a little over two days to get your ducks in a row, Colonel."

Watson didn't like anyone telling him what to do, particularly this low life. He wanted to reach around and grab him by the throat. Instead, he swallowed hard and said sarcastically, "You don't have to worry about me having things ready. While you're here though, I want you to know that I'm not crazy about the people you've been bringing into your organization."

Before Carter had a chance to comment, Watson asked, "Are you sure they can be trusted?"

"Hey, man, you never kill the goose that lays the golden egg, do you?" Carter answered, as he opened the door and got out, not giving the colonel a chance to respond. Billy was sure he owned them, and he proved it to them every chance he got.

As Lemmon slid across the seat, the captain put his arm over the seat back to block his exit. "Make damned sure there are no screw-ups on your end. You get your brother down here fast, so he can make the scene. I don't want any attention drawn to him or you while waiting to transport and distribute the merchandise. And keep close to that sick lunatic. I want to know everything he does, chapter and verse." He removed his arm and Lemmon got out of the car without a word, only a nod.

Yarbrough waited for Carter and Lemmon to leave before he pulled back on the street and turned on his lights.

The colonel was still smarting from Billy's words. "I want that damn slime ball out before the next shipment. Do you hear me, Ray? I want him washed out to sea. I want the bastard dead."

"Okay, I know, Colonel. That's why we've got Lemmon in there covering things."

"So what the hell has he found out?"

Yarbrough wondered himself, but didn't dare let on that Billy was too smart for them. "Up to now, not a lot," he said, then quickly added, "but this shipment should change things. Lemmon knows his creditability is on the line. He'll handle it."

"He'd better," the colonel mumbled.

"Where to?" Asked Yarbrough.

"Let's cruise up Route 41 and see what's going on at the clubs north of the bridge."

Yarbrough reached down and turned on the radio. He thought of the colonel's little black book. Three guesses whose name was at the top of the list.

Chapter 8

Doty checked his watch against the clock on the wall. 8:20 P.M. He would leave at 9 sharp. That would give him thirty minutes to make the meet. He reviewed the whole thing in his mind for the tenth time.

The call had come in at 4:32. The whole thing was suspicious. It sounded too damned smooth. The voice had promised him information about the drug dealing in Fort Manson. He tried to remember the exact words, trying to evaluate the tone in the voice, the manner. *Oh, hell,* he thought to himself, *the whole thing is fishy. It's a setup for sure. I'll be damned if I'm going to walk into a trap and get my head blown off.* He shuffled through the papers on his desk and checked his watch again. *I'll leave a note in my desk for Corky,* he said to himself. He took out a yellow lined tablet and picked up a pen. "Dear Corky," he began. He stared at the words trying to think what to say next. What was there to say? I think someone's going to blow my head off, so I'm going out to meet him and give him an easy target? Oh, yes, and I think it's the sheriff and his bunch of bums so if I turn up dead be sure and report my suspicions to the sheriff and his bunch of bums that will investigate my murder. He laughed at how stupid the whole thing was. No, there wasn't any use in writing to Corcoran telling him if he turned up dead that it was murder. Hell, Corky was smart enough to know that, even if he couldn't do anything about it. Anyway, he decided, it wouldn't hurt anything to make a note of where he was going, just in case. "Had a phone call this afternoon from a man wanting to meet me at the old Mermaid restaurant on south 41 at 9:30 P.M. Says he has information on drug smuggling in Leeward County."

Doty shoved the tablet in his center desk drawer. *Hell, I can always tear it up later, he said to himself.* He checked his watch again, then turned on his computer terminal and punched up the article he'd been working on for the last three years. He skipped through to the last page and picked up the sentence he had left unfinished.

    A certain breed of person, he began typing, is necessary for dealing in narcotics. It's only the crafty ones with devious minds who are capable of staying alive in that jungle of competition. They are the type who like the smell of death lapping at their heels. They perform at their best when their adrenalin is pumping full force. They are a dangerous type, and would never fail to eradicate someone to save their own skin, or to place a million-dollar deal on the street. They owe their allegiance to no one.

    Fort Manson is a prime location for drug smuggling and dealing. Located on the southern banks of the Caloosahatchee River, it is just fourteen miles from the Gulf of Mexico. The large river is part of the inter-coastal waterway, which is a shallow draft passage across Florida, flowing through rivers and connecting canals. Many endless secluded lagoons and coves exist along the waterway. The seventy-five mile trip across state winds through some of the wildest territory in South Florida. The accessible route benefits drug traffickers. Small boats can be hidden, undiscovered, for months in the miles of mangrove-covered shorelines. When the need for them arises, as during a drug shipment, smugglers use them for their exit to Miami and the East Coast.

    Freighters frequently travel these waters. They load phosphate at the tip of Gasperilla Island, to transport to ports around the world. Gasperilla is one of many hundred islands along southwest Florida's coast. Beyond them stretch the boundless waters of the Gulf. Freighters used in smuggling are used for legitimate hauls between trips. A freighter on a marijuana run could make the round trip, including the time spent loading it, in about two weeks. The freighters are owned by the drug organization and are capable of carrying as much as two million pounds of marijuana. They run an average of four trips a year, stopping at various points within the main freighter lane. They lay anchor and wait for boats in the fifty-foot class to come to it and unload part of its cargo. As many as fifteen boats weigh anchor and unload at one time. The fifty-footers distribute the cargo to smaller boats ranging in size from eighteen to thirty-six feet. The smaller boats move unnoticed up the waterways, inlets, and coves, where the cargo is eventually transferred to campers and trucks with trailers. A year's haul for a freighter can amount to a hundred million dollars worth of marijuana and eight million dollars in cocaine.

A freighter enters the area in an almost casual manner. It's totally impractical to think all the coastline, with its many inlets and coves, can be patrolled. The main risk is an accidental discovery by the Florida Marine Patrol.

The islands are a perfect set-up for smuggling, and the dealers know it. Wealthy people own most of the island property. The majority of the owners just winter there. Some rent their houses out during the summer; others close them up. The islanders believe that their activities shouldn't generate curiosity. Therefore, they maintain their privacy. They have done little to spoil nature and natural habitat. The islands have been left as nature made them, wild and peacefully quiet.

Drug smuggling requires a very well-organized machine. The higher echelon-

Doty stopped suddenly and looked at his watch. "Damn," he said to himself. The watch read 9:05. He punched the save button on the computer and clicked the off key. He opened a desk drawer and took out a pocket tape recorder. He shoved it and an extra tape into his pocket and headed for the door.

He made all the lights on 41 and arrived at the deserted restaurant at 9:25. He pulled around the back and shut off the motor. He reached over to the glove compartment, unlocked it, and pulled out the Colt .25 automatic, wrapped neatly in a bandana. He knew it was loaded; he always kept it loaded. If he ever needed it, this would be the time, he thought. He could feel the sweat running down the sides of his face. He was getting too old for this. He shoved the gun under the seat. The realization that he could never get it out in time to stop someone bent on killing him made him laugh out loud. He was a sitting duck! *Not only am I getting old,* he said to himself, *I'm getting paranoid.* He peered out into the darkness trying to see something, anything. He took the tape recorder out and set it on the seat beside him. He pressed the *on* button and then immediately the *pause.* He was ready. Where was the informant? Maybe he changed his mind. Maybe somebody stopped him from coming. He'd wait until 10 o'clock and that was it.

No doubt about it, he was petrified. He could feel his heart pounding through his shirt. He'd only been this scared once before the patrol in Korea in 1954. He was sure then that he was going to die. He was feeling that same way now.

"Doty?" A voice called to him from out of the darkness.

"Yeah, I'm Doty." He was caught off guard and suddenly forgot how scared he was.

The shadowy figure approached the rider's side of the car, hesitated while he looked around the parking lot, then opened the door and got in. He glanced at Doty, looked out the back window and said, "Drive."

Doty started the car. "Drive where?" He asked.

"Just drive. Take a left and head south on 41."

Well, if this kid is an assassin, the sheriff is pretty hard up for hit men, he thought. He tried to get a look at his passenger's face. Doty began to feel embarrassed that he had been so scared.

The boy lit a cigarette and turned to Doty. "Do you have it?"

Doty's mind was working a mile a minute, and he didn't understand what the question meant. "What do you mean it?"

"The money, do you have the money?"

"Oh, yeah. I could only get you three hundred."

"I told you five!" The boy was annoyed.

"I know, but it's the best I could do on such short notice. I can get you the other two tomorrow."

"I won't be here."

"Well, I'll send it to you. Just tell me where."

"You've got to be kidding" The boy said sarcastically.

"So, what's your name?" Doty asked.

"No names," the young man said with determination.

"Okay," Doty agreed. "How did you happen to call me?"

"Easy. You're out to get the drug guys. Everybody knows about your war on drugs. Every pusher in Leeward County knows you're out to put him away."

"Suppose you tell me what I'm buying for my hard-earned money."

"Information. A lot of information. And let's have the dough."

Doty reached up behind the sun visor, pulled out a long white envelope and handed it to the young man, who opened it and counted out the bills.

"Listen, I need to call you something. Just give me a name, anything." Doty reached down and slid the *pause* button on the recorder.

"Alright, call me Ed."

"Okay, Ed. Now, what have you got?"

"What do you want to know?"

"Everything. Start with how you figure in the thing. Are you a pusher? A runner? What?"

"Dope, just a dope, sucked in by dope."

"Okay, you're a dope. Are you from here in Leeward County?"

"No, I came down here six weeks ago from New Jersey with a girl I know and her brother. They went on to Miami and I stayed behind to look for a job. The girls at the beach were a real turn on and I thought I could find a construction job. Instead I got caught up in the drug scene."

"And now you want to get out?" Doty asked.

"Yeah. I'm heading for Miami tonight. I'll work my way up the East Coast and probably go back to Jersey."

"Why are you so anxious to get out?"

"I'm scared, man. I've never been so damn scared."

"Scared of whom?"

"The whole damn group. But mostly the main man."

Now we're getting someplace, thought Doty. "Okay, who's the main man?"

"A dude named Billy. Billy Carter. That's not his real name, I know that much, but that's the name he uses. He used to be a cop, someplace in the east, New York, I think."

"Where does he live?"

"Hell, I don't know. He hangs out at a house down at the beach."

"Where, what area, what's the name of the street?"

"I don't know the names of the streets, I just know it's close to the beach."

"Okay, how did you get involved with him and the group?"

"I met him at a bar north of the bridge, the Beachcomber. He came over and bought me a beer. He told me he could help me get a job and offered me a ride back to the beach. He was with a guy named Greg who rents the house I told you about. Anyway, we got to the house and they had some grass, good stuff, plenty of it. I passed out and woke up on the floor the next morning. I hung around and they told me they could use me."

"Use you how?"

"Well, mostly I pimped for them. I'd spend the days on the beach lining up kids for them."

"To pass drugs?" Doty asked.

"No. Mostly just to party with. These guys are heavy into enjoying themselves. I'd furnish the kids for their games."

"How did you get the kids to party?"

"Easy, offer them a joint and some free booze and they can't wait to join in."

Doty was a little skeptical. "Are we talking sex parties?"

"Sure, what do you think? They partied four or five nights a week. Usually small groups, maybe once a week there'd be twenty or more. Some couples, mostly singles."

"Young girls?"

"Girls, guys, whatever. These boys swing both ways."

"So, you played the pimp, rounding up young kids for sex parties."

"Mostly. Occasionally I'd go out on deliveries. Mostly to the black section. Sometimes with Greg, twice with a guy named Jake and once with this Billy Carter. They'd pull up like to a bar and I'd go in with the goods."

"They'd keep the drugs at the house?"

"No. I looked all around. They always had plenty, but they'd bring it in in paper grocery bags. I don't know where they kept the main supply but it wasn't at the beach house."

"Were you around for any of the shipments?"

"No. The last one arrived the week before I got here. But I picked up a lot just listening."

"Let's hear about it," Doty urged.

"They use freighters, big ones, out of Columbia. Mostly marijuana, some cocaine, but they don't pass that out at the parties. They put anchor a mile or so out and bring the stuff to shore on smaller boats. From there it goes inland and is picked up by vans, trucks, pick-ups, and all kinds of vehicles. It's a hell of an operation."

"No worries about the law?"

"Not really. They seem to have plenty protection, at least at the local level. They don't play around at sea, so I figure they don't want to tangle with the feds or the coast guard. But when they hit land nobody sweats."

"You think the police department is in on it?" Doty asked.

"I think it's the county Mounties. I notice they stay out of the city as much as they can, but they seem to run wild in the county. And another thing, there's a guy I see with Carter sometimes named Larry. I know I saw him one night at the Beachcomber, and he was in a sheriff's deputy uniform."

"Did you ever hear his last name?"

"No, just Larry. Nobody uses their last name, man. Only first names. In this kind of racket knowing too much can get you killed."

"Is that why you're getting out? You think somebody might kill you?"

"It could happen, man. I heard them talking yesterday about wasting some dude that owed them for some grass. I enjoy a good time like everybody else. But these guys play for keeps."

"I wish you could give me some more names. Did anybody ever mention who the big guys are?"

"Naw. The only name I ever heard that wasn't a first one was Carter. Except for somebody they call the captain. This captain must be a contact up the line. I figured it was a captain like in the military. Or maybe the captain of a ship."

"Did you ever hear anybody mention a colonel?"

"No. Just the captain."

"Do you know when the next shipment is coming in?" asked Doty.

"Soon, man. They're getting ready for it, I figure this week, or maybe next. Which is another reason I want out of here."

"Tell me some more about this Billy Carter."

"He's about 150 pounds, maybe 5'9"-5'10", mean bastard, small dark eyes that see right through you. Scary eyes; it's like when you look at them you don't see anything. I mean, there's nothing there. No emotion. Like they're dead. I mean, he makes my skin crawl," Ed paused, then took a deep breath and continued. "Anyway, he enjoys hurting people; he likes to slap people around, particularly female types. It's like he gets some perverted satisfaction in giving people pain."

"Did he ever hurt you?"

"No. But then I stayed away from him. At least until last night."

"What happened last night?" Doty asked.

"Well, he had been making it with this young blond boy in the bedroom and I guess the kid passed out from the booze. Anyway, he cornered me in the kitchen and decided I was going to be his pansy for the rest of the night. I told him I wasn't in to boys, just girls. He wouldn't take no for an answer. He grabbed me, I wrestled away from him, then he picked up a knife from the sink and I think he would have cut me if Greg hadn't come in. I got the hell out the back door and spent the night on the beach. I decided this morning that if I wanted to keep my balls I'd better get them the hell out of here. Everything I own is at the beach house but none of it is worth going back for. I stayed under a pier until sundown, then I phoned you."

Doty began to feel sorry for the kid.

"There's a Waffle House a mile or so down the road why don't we stop and get some coffee and a bite to eat."

"Are we out of Leeward County yet?"

"Oh, yeah. This is Baron County. We left Leeward three miles back."

"Okay," the boy said. "I could use some coffee."

The colonel sat quietly as Yarbrough wove the car in and out of the traffic north of the city. The night was unusually busy; the calls were coming in fast and furious. A signal 10 announcement awakened the cop in the colonel. He picked up the mike not bothering to formally identify himself by number. Everyone knew his voice.

"You'd better put a BOLO out on that signal 10," he commanded.

The dispatcher replied, "I've already notified the F.M.P.D., sir."

The airways went silent until once more the dispatcher's voice came on and began an all-points bulletin on a stolen car. "1995 White, Cadillac El Dorado, white interior. License number: 11 *PLAIN* 77659. The keys were left in the vehicle while it was parked at the Nottingham Apartments, 4406 North Broad. Sergeant Brown, Leeward County Sheriff's Department, Florida," the voice stated his status with authority.

Silence again, then the radio started crackling once more with calls coming in and going out.

"555 headquarters, 10–8, north of the city." The colonel placed them back into action.

"10–8, 555. 22:25 hours," the dispatcher answered.

They cruised the streets, looking for signs of someone who might need help, or just looking for trouble.

"Headquarters, 555," came over the air. The colonel picked up the mike. "555," he replied.

"There is a signal 24 in progress at the South Trail Seven-Eleven. Code three."

The captain immediately took the blue light off the seat, placed it on the dashboard, and turned the siren on. He headed toward the convenience store at top speed, traveling down the center of the highway.

They were the first officers on the scene. As they pulled up they saw a black man running up the street to the left of the store. Yarbrough sprang out of the car, drew his gun and pointed it in the direction of the fleeing man.

"Stop! Sheriff's department!"

The man kept running and Yarbrough squeezed the trigger. The man fell to the ground. Yarbrough kept his weapon trained on the prone figure as he and Watson slowly approached.

"The nigger. That's one less for the welfare lines this week," the colonel said, as he used his foot to nudge the black man's hands, first one then the other. By this time people had started to gather.

"There's nothing to see here, break it up and go back home or go on with whatever you were doing," the colonel said to the bystanders.

Other department cars were on the scene by this time. As the men placed their guns back in their holsters, Watson turned to a deputy standing nearby and said, "I'll call the coroner and the meat wagon. You disperse this crowd. You stay and get statements from the clerk and anyone else that was in the store." He turned to another deputy. "Find something to cover him up."

With the preliminaries taken care of, the colonel and the captain got back in their car. The crowd started to thin out as they drove away.

Off to the left of the lifeless body was a clump of bushes. A young man of seventeen or eighteen crouched in the darkness, not daring to make a move or a sound for fear he would be detected. He sat there long after the ambulance had gone and the last thrill seeker had left. He trembled, more in fear of what he had witnessed than what he had done an hour earlier. This had been the first time he had ever seen a man shot in cold blood...or even shot at all. He began to dig a hole in the dirt under one of the larger bushes. When he finished, he brought out a shiny gun from under his shirt. He wiped it off with his shirttail, shoved it in the hole, and covered it with dirt. He packed the earth down with his hand, then his foot, and stood up. He tucked his shirttail in and casually strolled out onto the highway, crossed it, and stuck out his thumb to the traffic heading south. He wanted to be out of this nightmare as soon as possible.

"Did you notice that nigger didn't have a gun?" the colonel asked Yarbrough.

"Yes, after I got down to him, lying on the ground," he replied in an unemotional voice.

"Make sure you get the report from the deputy I sent in to talk to the store clerk, before you make out your report for the sheriff," the colonel told him.

"Okay," Yarbrough said.

"Hey, isn't that the Cady car?" he asked, pointing toward a light-colored 1988 Mercury sedan moving in front of them.

Picking up the mike, the colonel pressed the button to talk. "555 to headquarters."

"Headquarters, 555."

"Give me a 10–28 on 18 plain 89187," the colonel demanded.

The dispatcher came back, "10–23." In less than a minute he had the requested information.

"Headquarters, 555. It's registered to a Michael Erwin Cady and Eileen Cady."

"10–26" the colonel replied.

"That's the cocky little bastard that's been hanging down at Carter's place," the captain told the colonel. "I pulled him over one night after he came out of the Bock Lounge. He defied me to hit him. I would sure love to lay him out one time. He's always out drinking, and as far as I know he doesn't have a job."

"No wonder Carter knows him," the colonel added sarcastically. "I'd like to eliminate his type. They're too full of wise ideas. Who is Eileen? His wife?" He knew Yarbrough had a burr under his hide, but it wasn't the Stone kid. He was just taking his hostility out on him.

"No, he's not married. That's the kid's mother," the captain replied.

Colonel Watson tried to take Yarbrough's thoughts elsewhere. "Hey, you remember the other night when they had that disturbance down on the hill and I sent Deputy Williams down there?"

"Yeah, and it turned into a family picnic!"

"Well, I'm going to collar him one more time. I shouldn't even give him one more chance, but we're hard pressed for blacks to cruise their section of town. The white men just refuse to go into that area. They say it's like entering a battle zone."

Watson was pulling at straws to take Yarbrough's mind off the incident earlier at the convenience store. "I warned him," the colonel continued, "if he didn't get tougher on some of those bums, I was going to pull him off the road. That would cool his heels."

"That's the trouble. When those black bastards get a little education under their belts, they think they have all the answers," Ray said, agreeing with him.

The colonel exclaimed "I guess we can't always expect to get a hold of men like Willy Murray!" They both laughed.

"Yeah, that fat, black bastard. Give him a little authority, and it goes right to his head," the captain said, still laughing.

"That stupid bastard never even completed high school. Getting his mark up on the department exam wasn't easy," the colonel added.

"Yeah, but he sure knows how to milk those niggers out of every cent, come pay off day. He talks their language and they don't put anything over on him."

"You know if it ever came down to a street fight and he had to choose sides, I'll bet that nigger would come over to our side, thinking we would need him, or want him."

The colonel started laughing again and Yarbrough joined him. "He sure as hell wouldn't last ten minutes among his own color. They frown on a brother selling them down the river."

"Yeah, old Willy sure does that. Every time we snap our fingers," the captain agreed. He had put the incident at the store out of his thoughts, at least until he had to make out his report. With the colonel's help it would go well. It always did.

"We were doing alright until that damn civil rights act started pushing us to hire more blacks. In fact, that was when I took Williams on, remember? He really had good credentials and excellent police training behind him. After working for the F B. I. he wanted to get into a small-scale enforcement agency. At that time we weren't as involved in the drug racket. He turned out to be a real asset to the department. He's a knowledgeable man, and he can't be bought. That's his biggest drawback. We can't afford anybody that honest. The only thing to do is try to discourage him into resigning," the colonel concluded.

"If the pressure increases, hopefully he'll seek greener pastures," Yarbrough said.

"Let's take a ride up by the Bock Lounge to kill some time. Who knows, maybe we can find one who'd sell his own mother for a fix," Watson told Yarbrough. "We're going to need some new recruits that are expendable for that freighter haul."

The captain turned north towards the bridge.

Within three minutes they could see the bright lights of the hottest, jumpiest watering hole north of the river. These places required constant patrol duty. When the roster was set up. The colonel chose carefully, always giving the duty to men he had control over. They had to know which areas contained turnovers in drugs.

Watson had his hand in the action at all times. Nothing transpired in the county that he wasn't aware of. At least that's what he thought.

Officer Earl Thornberry had the night's duty at the lounge. His object was to line up men who could be used for the upcoming shipment. They would have to be available at a moment's notice. They never knew the exact time of night to expect the next shipment.

"The department shouldn't be using civilians for stakeouts," the captain said, seeing the deputy sitting with a man in the cruiser.

"I don't like it either," Watson said, "but sometimes it becomes necessary."

"Thornberry has really latched on to a ding-a-ling for stakeouts this time," Ray said, laughing. "Yeah, he's got a few marbles missing, but it'll pay off when he's on one of his assigned stakeouts and he shoots someone. Who in hell would believe him if he told them he was working undercover for the department?" the colonel mused.

"It's not good for him to be so chummy out in public with Thornberry, Colonel."

"I know. I was just thinking the same thing. I'm going to have a word with him about it. Park around back, I'll just be a few minutes."

Yarbrough watched the colonel make his way through the crowd in the parking lot. He disappeared in a sea of bobbing heads. *My God, I've never seen such a mess of kids waiting to get into this place as there is tonight,* he thought. *What a waste of mental power; brains pickled beyond creative usefulness. What the hell am I thinking,* he reminded himself, *they are the bastards keeping me going. The stupid little pricks. If they haven't got enough going for them upstairs, I might as well cash in on it as the next person.*

Yarbrough pulled the vehicle around behind the building and doused the lights. He kept the motor running.

The department had a rule: never shut off the engine. The colonel always said it might be needed quick. Besides, the taxpayers were buying the gas. This place was a hot bed for drug trafficking and the authorities knew it. Once in a while they would stage a raid and make a good showing for the boss. People vital to the operation were tipped off so they could be elsewhere. After the judge fined those that were busted, it made them prime candidates for the expansion.

The colonel's ring was like a cancer. The more it was fed, the more it spread. The racket was like a stone cast onto the water. The rings kept spreading and growing. The hard users wouldn't turn snitch and eliminate their supply. The occasional user was too scared to talk. It was a dangerous game; drugs for the user, the dealer, and the pusher. There was always somebody trying to cut you off at the pass.

Ray Yarbrough only felt uneasy about one person in the whole organization: Billy Carter. He was a peculiar person, one he never could get inside. Ray had never seen such a loner, surrounded by so many people. He was deep and dangerous. Ray felt it. He never wanted Billy at his back.

The colonel came back and got in the car. "Carter's over there. Things are all set for the next shipment. Let's roll," he commanded.

"This place gives me the creeps. I can't stand to see these fools make asses of themselves. Carter has at least one new guy, maybe two. It always makes me edgy when he brings in new ones."

Yarbrough headed back across the river. "Don't worry, Colonel. Carter knows what he's doing. You heard him say he's too smart to kill the goose that lays the golden egg."

"Maybe so," the colonel answered, "but I know a goose that's going to be all over him, and soon!"

Chapter 9

Doty was at the computer adding to his long-running commentary on drug trafficking in Florida.

Marijuana is a Mexican-Spanish word for Cannabis Sativa. The substance is known by many names: A-Bomb, Ashes, Black Mo, Boo, Brick, Jive, Bush, Columbian, Congo Hash, Ditch Weed, Dope, Funny Stuff, Gainesville Green, Giggle Smoke, Gold, Golden Leaf, Grass, Hay, Hemp, Jadia, Joyweed, Juanita, Kentucky Blue, Kick-stick, Locoweed, Love Weed, Manhattan Silver, Marijuana, Mary, Mary Ann, Mexican Brown, Moocah, Nam Weed, Nickle, Panama Gold, Panatela, Punk, Ragweed, Reefer, Rough Stuff, Salt and Pepper, Shishi, Shit, Smoke, Splay, Stink-Weed, Straw, Stuff, Super Cool, Sweet Lucy, Tea, Thai Sticks, Tripweed, Viper's Weed, Wacky Tabbacky, Wana, Weed, Weed Tea, Wheat, Yerba, Zacatecas Purple, etc., etc.

It is grown and harvested from November through April. Sufficient rainfall will usually yield a bumper crop. Except for the harvesting, little care is needed to cultivate the plants. Trafficking is the heaviest during the winter and early spring months. However, it can be imported all year long.

The Florida shoreline is the dropping off point for at least eighty percent of the pot supplying the United States. In addition, it receives a high percentage of the harder drugs. This percentage rapidly increases each year through the actions of corrupt law enforcement officers and politicians.

Smugglers can carry much larger quantities of hard

drugs in the space occupied by large cumbersome bags of pot. They can also cut down on the time consumed in transferring the contraband from the ship to smaller craft miles off the coast. In all ways it is much more profitable to smuggle in the hard stuff, for the street value is astronomical.

Smugglers know they are only good for a few years, that eventually their luck will run out. If they are fortunate enough to get caught in an area where the law and courts are corrupt, they work out a deal. The judges will lower bail and only order a light fine. Within hours they can be back on the street. If they accidentally crash in the wrong area, they serve jail time.

The number of abandoned airstrips within Florida is surprising. Many are left over from the Second World War era. Several are the result of someone building a private airstrip to land for Florida fishing.

For every shipment that is confiscated, nine more succeed in meeting deliveries. The supply, demand, and large monetary value it returns for a few hours of gambling prompts many to make just the one run.

Smugglers usually make other trips, however, after finding out how easy it is. After a couple of good years of running contraband, a lucky smuggler can retire, go legitimate, and have money for healthier business ventures.

It all depends on how corrupt the law and the courts are in their areas. Their fate is often in the hands of the law: win, lose, or draw.

Doty stopped and read over the words. He'd soon have enough for a series of articles. That's what he wanted - a whole series exposing the rotten scum that traded in drugs and the even worse slime that gave them protection under the law. He turned his chair to see if Corky Corcoran had come in. Sure enough, he was walking toward his office. He grabbed his coffee cup and headed in Corky's direction.

"Morning Corky! I had an interesting interview last night."

"I know," Corcoran interrupted.

"How....You read my note didn't you?"

"Uh-huh," smiled Corky.

"You going through desks now?"

"Just looking for a match."

"You don't smoke," said Doty.

"I have friends who do." Corcoran sat down in his chair. "Tell me all about it. What did you find out?"

Doty recounted the entire episode for him, carefully omitting the part about being so scared.

"So what happened to the kid?"

"We talked for an hour more at the Waffle House. I took him to the Baron bus station and put him on a bus to Miami."

"Do you think it was bull or on the level?" Corky asked.

"I think the kid was being straight with me. Most of what he said about the smuggling I knew, or at least guessed at. But the information about the house on the beach and the wackos that are involved was interesting."

"Yeah," Corky agreed.

"Now, you talk to me. What's with the story on the front-page about the Seven-Eleven robbery?"

"It happened while you were out of town playing footsie with drug smugglers," Corcoran chided him. "Everything we know is in the article."

"Was there a news release from the department?"

"Not yet. We got our information from the clerk at the store, and a customer buying beer."

"It didn't say who fired the gun."

"Word is that it was one of two of your very favorite people."

"The sheriff?"

"Close. Captain Ray Yarbrough and Colonel Donald Watson."

"No kidding!" Doty exclaimed. "Since when do those comandos pull patrol duty?"

"Maybe they were on their way to a party."

"Yeah, sure," Doty responded.

"Incidentally, about the Manning shooting. You remember the missing two and half hours in the sheriff's news release. Has anybody mentioned the discrepancy? Did anybody notice it besides you and me?"

"Not to my knowledge. I was hoping at least a letter to the editor would come in questioning it, but nothing."

"I can't believe that somebody didn't pick up on it," Doty said, shaking his head. "Is everybody out there stupid, or do they just not care?"

"Beats me," said Corcoran.

"Well, I need some more coffee," Doty said, as he moved toward the door.

"And stay the hell out of my desk, Corky," he shouted over his shoulder.

Yarbrough was in his office early. The report on the convenience store robbery had to be turned in by ten o'clock. Lucky for him the sheriff was out of town. That meant the colonel would be handling everything. The department would be made to look as good as it had been in other cases. Through the years there had been many goof-ups. If it hadn't been for the colonel covering up for the men, there would have been a large turnover of deputies. *One smarter maneuver by the colonel to keep the men loyal to him,* thought Yarbrough. *No doubt about it, the man knows how to run an organization.*

Yarbrough wrote out the details, filling in blanks and spaces. This was the thing about police work he hated - the endless paper work that had to be filled out.

He had run a check on the black man he shot and found out he was an itinerant migrant worker. He had been fired for fighting in the fields over who got credit for picking a bushel of cucumbers. The migrant office had no address or information about him. Chances were good that no one would even report him missing. That made his report fall together a little easier. He made it as simple as he could.

A robbery in progress when we arrived on the scene. We saw the robber fleeing the scene, and when he failed to halt, he was shot. The captain neglected to mention that the man was shot in the back. Yarbrough leaned back in his chair, mulling over further details that perhaps should go into the report. He lit up a cigarette.

The colonel came in, not bothering to knock.

"Here," he said, handing Yarbrough the gun in his hand. "It matches the description of the one the clerk described the robber as having. She said she thought he was a dark-skinned or tanned man. Put in your report that he was possibly wearing a stocking mask. That will cover the fact that he was black. He made her face the wall as soon as he came in, so she didn't get a very good look at him and couldn't be sure about the description."

"Where did you get this?" Yarbrough asked, setting the revolver down on the desk.

"I got it out of the hot ones we confiscated last week at that hippie's house. He sure as hell won't complain if one is missing when he goes to trial. That is, if he doesn't take the plea before then."

"I thought there was another witness in the store."

"Yeah. A boozer buying beer. He swears he didn't see anything. He won't be a problem."

"What about the news release I saw the article on the front page of *The News Leader* this morning."

"I'll take care of the release. Just get the report finished and on my desk by ten. And don't forget the funeral at two. Another thing, I want you to wire Becky; she has an undercover assignment over at the courthouse."

"We've got a big day and night ahead of us," Yarbrough said with a sigh.

The colonel moved to leave. When he reached the door he turned and said, "Next time, don't be so damned trigger-happy. Look a little closer before you shoot a black. You'll have every nigger in the area on our asses, not to mention the N.A.A.C.P. and the damn A.C.L.U."

Yarbrough didn't comment. There was nothing for him to say. He'd just caught hell in the colonel's way of giving it to the people he liked. He finished up the report, and gave it to the stenographer on his way to the communications room. "Have this typed up right away and put on the colonel's desk."

Becky was waiting, and not happy that Ray Yarbrough was going to wire her. She had tried to avoid any close contact with him. It was a love-hate feeling, and she wasn't sure which was stronger. She was still attracted to him, but she couldn't stand him being close enough to touch her. Maybe it just reminded her of the great times they had enjoyed. Maybe that was it; maybe she really wanted more but knew she couldn't have it. She really didn't know what she wanted, but she was pretty sure it wasn't Yarbrough. Anyway, she was feeling a little more than nervous around him.

"So how's your big romance with the junior lawyer coming along?" he said, as he stood close in front of her.

"Fine," she answered coldly.

"Sounds like you got a little and like it."

His remark brought a rosy glow to her face. Her green eyes glared at him.

She'd like to have slapped his face, but he was standing too close.

"I think this will work better if we attach it to your bra. You are wearing a bra, aren't you, Becky?" He moved his hand inside her blouse and down and around her right breast. With his other hand he pulled her up closer to him.

She thought he was going to kiss her and she moved her mouth up slightly into position. Instead he bent his head down, rubbed his face through her hair and whispered into her ear, "You sexy red-haired broad."

His words made her furious at Yarbrough, but mostly at herself for getting suckered in. "You're not man enough, Ray. Not for me." Her words were sharp and cold as ice. "I've moved on to much bigger and better."

He withdrew his hand and finished applying the detection device. He leaned back against the table and watched silently as she buttoned her blouse and put on her jacket. She deliberately avoided any eye contact with him.

"Now, speak in a normal tone, so I can tell if I've got it set right," he told her.

Becky turned on her heels and stormed for the door. "How's this?" she asked sarcastically. "Is it set right? Go to hell, Yarbrough, on and the horse you rode in on!" Then she slammed the door behind her.

He smiled. He didn't care for the comment, but at least she was wired right.

Deputy Brock Williams had known this talk was long overdue. He'd made up his mind to overwhelm any adversity the colonel could throw in this path. He, like Deputy Gibbons, had police work in his blood. In fact, he'd made it his whole life. After a hitch in the Marines, as a M.P., he'd entered the university to obtain his B.A. A criminal law course sharpened his already keen senses. He came out in the top third of his class, ready to tackle anything the criminal element could throw in his way. The corps' rigorous training had prepared him and made him a natural for law enforcement. The Marines had toughened him to withstand and persevere over the obstacles he encountered at the department.

Williams had dreamed of one day belonging to one of the largest and most respected law enforcement agencies in the country. His dream was realized. He was appointed to the F. B. I. to serve throughout the Midwest. His family hadn't minded the hours he put in at first, for the prestige that the position held overshadowed the lack of his presence. But then their whole lifestyle changed. The dull routine started marital difficulties. Then came the divorce with the wife getting custody of the children. Then he began drinking. To top off his problems, his mother died and his father took sick. Williams resigned his post. He took the job at the Leeward County Sheriff's Department to be close to his father. When he accepted the job at the department, he didn't know about the shenanigans going on under Sheriff Myers, but it didn't take him long to find out about them. He thought he could circumvent the whole mess and outlast the corrupt machinery. He was wrong. Hank had been re-elected. Now here he was knocking on the colonel's door to get chewed out or maybe even fired.

"Come in," the colonel responded to the knock.

Williams entered. "You wanted to see me, sir?"

"Shut the door and sit down," the colonel said, motioning to the hard chair in front of his desk. Watson wasted no time in getting to the point. "Deputy, I told you before you'd have to change your attitude toward prospective prisoners. You have outright defied my warning. I have no choice but to take you off the road unless you feel you could use one more chance," the colonel threatened, then gave him a chance for a reprieve.

Williams was mad, but he held it in check. He needed the job. "I just cannot, when I have no reason, beat up on a man. There is nothing but animosity to be gained by it. sir, I feel my prior training has geared me towards a higher grade of ethics in the handling of prospective prisoners. It's just not in my make-up to beat the hell out of someone to put the fear of the department in his heart."

"Listen you black bastard. I run, rather, the sheriff runs this department, and things are carried out according to his wishes. It makes no difference what ethics you have. If I tell you to rough up someone, then you do it! No questions asked! Do you understand?" The colonel was on his feet, leaning over his desk and leering at the deputy as he spoke.

"I'm black, but I don't happen to be a son of any one other than a lady, a black lady. Perhaps you have me confused with someone else," Williams stated. His cut of character outshone the colonel's by far.

Watson was purple with rage. "On second thought, you go to records and receiving right now. I'm taking you off the road. To hell with it! Any more of your compassion antics and I'll see that you are looking elsewhere for work. You can go," the colonel shrieked. He was furious.

Williams maintained his composure. This was one time he'd like to carry out the colonel's orders and beat the hell out of him.

Without a word the deputy raised his tall, lean, solid frame out of the hard chair. He sauntered to the door and made his exit, joyous in his victory. He hadn't liked it on the road anyhow.

Doty had been on the phone all morning, trying to get a line on Billy Carter. Nothing. None of his contacts could supply a lead. At least he had so many lines out, maybe something would turn up. He decided he'd try to interview the clerk at the convenience store, then he'd drive down to the beach. *Who knows,* he thought, *maybe somebody would invite him to a party.* He started to get up, then sat back down. Jimmy Dale was coming through the door and heading for his desk.

"Officer Dale," he said, making an exaggerated welcoming gesture.

Dale laughed and stretched out his hand. "Hello, Mr. Doty." Doty shook his head and extended his hand at the same time.

"Steve, remember?"

"Hello, Steve," the deputy said, smiling.

Doty waved him toward a chair. "And what brings you to the glamorous pressroom of the great News Leader?"

"Another dispatch from the department," Dale said, extending a large manila envelope."

"Ah, ha. This is, no doubt, the press release on the convenience store shooting last night."

"Probably," said Dale.

"Answer the sixty-four thousand-dollar question for me, Jimmy. Who was it that pulled the trigger?"

"The rumor mill says Captain Yarbrough. But you didn't hear it from me."

Yep, Doty thought to himself, *I like this boy.*

"Say, do you fish much?"

"Every chance I get," Dale replied.

"Great," Doty said. "What about Saturday. Are you busy?"

"No. As a matter of fact I have the whole weekend off."

"Well, what do you say we do some fishing? Corcoran owns a nice little hideaway down in Baron County. Nothing fancy, but there's a dock and if you sit there long enough something usually jumps on your hook."

"Sounds good," Dale said, nodding his head.

"Are you married?"

"No," Dale answered.

"Steady girl?"

"Not really."

"Well, you see that sweet young thing sitting over at the desk in the corner?"

Dale nodded again.

"That's Alicia Babb and she just happens to be the nicest, cutest twenty-two year old in the whole county. I've known her since she was born, went to school with her mom and dad. And she can fry fish better than a Cajun queen."

"Are you trying to fix me up, Steve?" asked Dale with a smile.

"Absolutely. I've got more contacts than a Jewish matchmaker. Seriously, Jimmy, she's a really nice girl. I think you'd like her."

"Okay," Dale said, glancing at the clock on the wall. "I've got to run."

"Late lunch?" asked Doty.

"No. Funeral," Dale answered.

"Who died?" asked Doty.

"A friend of the sheriff."

"Jack Manning?"

"Yeah. The department wants to make a nice showing."

"Did you know the boy?" Doty asked.

"No, but I remember seeing him with the sheriff a few times last week," Dale replied. "As a matter of fact, until about an hour ago it looked like there wouldn't be a funeral, at least today."

"Why was that?" inquired Doty.

"Well, some Army officer showed up at the department this morning inquiring about the Manning kid's suicide."

"Really?"

"Yeah, the wheels were turning triple handstands trying to iron out all the wrinkles. Some problem about a missing two and half hours in the department's report."

"How about that." Doty had to swallow hard to keep from laughing out loud.

"Did they get everything straightened out?"

"Evidently. The funeral's scheduled for two." Dale turned to leave.

"What time for Saturday?"

"Let's make it ten. We'll meet outside in the parking lot and take my car."

"Great. See you then," Dale said, as he crossed to the door.

Doty watched him leave, then picked up his tape recorder and walked across the room walking toward the young lady in the corner.

"Alicia, sweetheart, did you happen to notice the young man in uniform that just left?"

"You mean the sheriff's deputy?"

"That's the one. His name is Jimmy Dale, and I think he's a really nice kid."

Alicia gave Doty a skeptical look. "Yea, right"

"No, honestly, I think he's all right. Anyway, I want you to go down to Corcoran's fishing hole with us on Saturday."

"Uncle Steve, are you trying to fix me up?"

"Have you got something better to do?"

"Well, I could."

"Bring your fishing pole and a good book. Meet me in the parking lot at ten sharp."

Before she could protest he was out the door and down the hall.

Heading for the parking lot, Doty passed Lou Share, one of the *News Leader* executives. They nodded to each. *That sure is a strange one,* Doty thought to himself. Share had been in town about a year. In that time, Doty hadn't known him to associate with any of the other employees.

When a large northern chain purchased the newspaper, the new owners had sent Share down to organize things the way they wanted. He had made some drastic changes that didn't make sense to Doty or to a lot of other long-time news people. But they had no say. It had been made perfectly clear that either they floated with the tide or they were out. It was as simple as that. Doty didn't like the new order, but he did like his job. And as long as Corky could hang in, so could he.

He headed toward the beach road. Doty knew he was on a wild goose chase, but what the hell. It was a great day and he could use a little sunshine.

Chapter 10

Everything was *go* on the shipment. The freighter had weighed anchor in the Gulf, fifteen miles off the coast.

The colonel had carefully prepared the roster for the night. He made sure that those patrolling that area were part of his group, leaving sufficient off-duty personnel to cover the delivery. He had chosen Deets to patrol the end of the island immediately connecting with the mainland. Pool would back him up in an area a short distance off the island. There Pool would be able to detect any unwanted activity coming from the city. A *legitimate* patrol had to cover that zone. He had assigned Sergeant Barry Sullivan, who normally worked narcotics division, to that detail. Sullivan's wife was the sheriff's secretary; if needed, a different roster could be slipped on the sheriff's desk to cover any questionable action. Captain Lawton Smith was covering the delivery with Corporal Larry Lemmon. Larry's brother, Jim, was waiting with a van on the old Negro beach that was seldom used since integration. Brown's Beach was nothing more now than a dump. Only the desperate parked there, because of the smell.

All the men had specially adapted walkie-talkies. Their communication couldn't be heard by others, as it would be were they to use the usual frequencies. Tonight's shift change looked no different than those of other nights. The men clocked in and disbursed to their scheduled patrol zones. The pre-arranged cars headed for the beach area. The patrols took the usual calls. Deets and Sullivan rotated back and forth, taking the routine assignments.

Carter waited at the house on the beach. He had been their original contact. He had worked out of many locales, and knew them from prior deals. Usually the same syndicate men weren't used twice in the same area. This practice was used as a precautionary measure, so the men wouldn't become familiar to anyone.

The colonel hung close to the city. With the sheriff out of town he was on call, should an emergency arise. In a little over two hours, the whole procedure should be over with, he thought, looking at the clock on the dash.

The weather was with them. There was a full moon and he'd had a report of calm seas. The boat wouldn't be hampered in the transfer at sea. The colonel remembered how rough seas had made loading difficult in the past. They had lost quite a number of bales of the illicit cargo in the Gulf, between the men getting seasick and the freighter's captain getting edgy during the delays in transfer. Once, when one of the smaller boats capsized and sank, Deets nearly drowned and Lemmon caught pneumonia from exposure. The colonel laughed to himself.

Lemmon, Smith and two men from Carter's group left in the old shrimp boat docked behind the beach house. Lemmon, being familiar with the waters, took the wheel. They pulled up alongside the anchored freighter within thirty minutes.

Working as an assembly line, they took twenty minutes to load their boat. Every available hole was filled, leaving them no room for comfort. The men all rode in the wheelhouse coming back in. When their task was finished, they immediately set out to meet with a smaller boat that was waiting a couple miles off the coast. They proceeded to meet with Lemmon's brother on Brown's Beach. The shrimp boat carried the remaining cargo further up the coast to pre-arranged meetings with other boats. It took a little time to load Jim's van. It was filled to capacity. Lemmon's brother drove back to town alone. Smith and Lemmon waited at the beach to be picked up by Carter.

"I hate this place. It's a filthy hole," Lemmon said.

"Hey, look over there," Smith said, moving the flashlight beam towards something on the ground.

"What in the hell is it?" asked Lemmon.

"Damn. We've landed in rubber heaven. Look at all the damn rubbers on the ground. Hey, look over here," he said laughing. "This bastard wasn't taking any chances. He wore two of the them things at once."

Lemmon walked closer to look at what Smith was raving about. Lying on the ground were two used condoms, one inside the other.

"I never saw anything like that before in my life." Lemmon then turned and faced the set of bobbing lights that had just turned off the main road. He watched them as they wound around the bushes and approached them.

"Hey, come on, Carter's here."

They both started to walk toward the approaching car.

"Jesus, shine that damned light over here," Lemmon shouted.

Smith directed the light's rays at Lemmon, who stood shaking his foot. Smith started to laugh, forgetting what a position he'd be placed in if caught.

Lemmon stood on one foot, trying to shake loose the used rubbers that had stuck to the bottom of his shoe. "It isn't funny, you bastard." He was still shaking his foot when their transportation back to the city arrived.

"What the hell's he doing?" Carter asked, not amused by their actions.

Smith tried not to show his amusement at Lemmon's predicament. "He's got himself into a sticky situation and can't get out."

Carter wasn't impressed with their hilarity. He said, "Hell, come on. Let's get out of this stinking nigger hole."

Smith opened the door and got in. Lemmon was left wiping the last rubber off his shoe. He hopped in the back seat just as Carter took off. He hadn't even closed the door yet, when Carter floored the accelerator, kicking up sand until he hit the black top.

Little was said on the ride back to the city. Smith finally broke the silence, only because of something he had just remembered. "Hey, the colonel told me you were supposed to have some new guy with you tonight. Where is he?"

There was a long silence, then Carter said, "After he cleared his head, and gave it some thought, he decided he didn't want to come after all."

"That's not too wise, having someone running around town who knows what's going down," Lemmon said, before Smith had the chance.

"Don't worry, he won't say anything to anybody. He committed suicide tonight. You'll find him out on Luckett Road. He's slumped over in his car and his hand is still on the gun."

Smith was speechless. He knew Carter was a cold bird, but this was the limit. The remainder of the ride was in dead silence.

The colonel was waiting on a deserted side road, south of the city limits. Carter pulled up alongside his car.

As Smith opened the door to get out, Carter picked up a small parcel from the front seat and handed it to him, "Here's a present for the colonel." he said. "Tell him it snowed real good in Columbia."

Smith barely had time to slam the door before Carter floored the accelerator. Lemmon reported to the colonel on the transfer, deliberately leaving out what Billy had told them about the suicide.

"Colonel, we still have some hours to pull. If it's all right with you, Lemmon and I will cruise around a bit."

Watson knew Smith had to unwind after a shipment came in. He'd seen him before tensed up like a banjo string, until he was sure the merchandise was put up safe.

"All right. I'll drop you off. Pick up a car. I'm going back in and do some paper work. I have to be in court tomorrow to testify on a pot case. The bastard won't take the plea."

When they arrived back at the station, the colonel backed his car in and shut off the motor. The two men got out without a word and walked toward a cruiser, while Watson opened the glove compartment and put the parcel inside. He locked it carefully then got out of the car and went into the station.

Lemmon started the cruiser and he and Smith headed for Luckett Road.

The night was still young as far as Becky was concerned. She had met Mark Sims for dinner at Fitzgerald's Restaurant, and was following him back to his apartment in her car. Her new assignment was going well; Sims was falling hard for her. Yarbrough was right, she was enjoying the no-stops romance with the public defender. Tonight she could relax and really get into a romantic interlude. She had already planted the listening device in the bedroom and the bug in the telephone. This was certainly a more enjoyable way to spend an evening than out on the street chasing addicts and pushers.

The roster was set up to appear as if she were rotating her shifts. If she needed to be with Sims her position was covered by one of the men at the station. She would work the days assigned to her on the roster that didn't interfere with her romance. That gave her a chance to catch up on the latest developments at the department.

She pulled up beside his new Corolla. He was waiting for her. She opened the door and he gently pulled her out and into his arms. *Oh, yes,* she said to herself, *I could really learn to enjoy this.* She raised her lips, and he kissed her lightly as he slipped his arm around her waist and guided her toward his first floor apartment.

"Next time," he said, "you come here first and we'll go in my car."

"All right," she said, sitting down in the corner of the sofa, stretching her arm out over the back.

"That's right," he said, removing his coat, and loosening his tie. "Get comfortable. I'll fix us some drinks." He disappeared into the kitchen.

Her eyes searched the room. She had been so preoccupied planting the bugs the other time she'd been there that she hadn't had time to mentally inventory the contents. Also, she reminded herself, she had spent most of the evening before in the bedroom. Tonight she had lots of time to enjoy the surroundings.

After only two dates she was learning his likes and dislikes. She figured he was fixing gimlets. She wasn't crazy about vodka, but then she wasn't difficult to please, at least in the liquor department.

The night before had been a nervous one, for her at least. She had been so worried about placing the bugs that she hadn't enjoyed the sexual drama as much as she would have liked. Even so, brief as it was, it was more than fulfilling. The junior public defender was no slouch when it came to sex. He had a great body and knew how to use it. She smiled as she anticipated another great match.

He handed her the long stemmed glass and sat down beside her. She smiled and took a small sip. He sat his glass down on the marble-topped coffee table, then reached down and slipped her shoes off. He gently pulled her legs up into his lap and began stroking her feet and ankles. He leaned over and kissed her knees, then worked his way down and around her calves.

What a technique, she thought, as she let herself sink down slightly toward him. He followed her left shin with his lips until he came to her knee again. He was caressing her right thigh in a long oval motion. She leaned toward him and rubbed her fingers through his curly brown hair. He looked up, smiled and gently pulled her in his direction until she was virtually sitting in his lap. It seemed like an impossible position, but he managed it easily. He kissed her softly for what seemed like an eternity, then moved his lips to her neck and around to her ear lobe.

She slipped the knot on his tie and pulled it from under the collar. Then she began unfastening the buttons on his shirt. That warm glowing sensation was beginning to take over her body. She let herself drift with the passion.

Yes, this was what she needed. This filled the need she'd felt since her divorce. She needed the softness of a man's touch. And this man was touching all the right spots. Even though she played the role of a tough narc cop, she had that need, deep inside, to be satisfied. Her job always came first, that's what had broken up her marriage. She had chosen the job over the man and he had walked out, leaving her to fend for herself and their three-year-old daughter. For the first time in years she was able to set her badge somewhere out in limbo. This was what she needed and to hell with anything else.

He picked her up and carried her into the bedroom. He stood her on her feet next to the bed and kissed her hungrily on the mouth. His arms moved from her shoulders down her back to her waist. He deftly unzipped her skirt and let it fall to the floor. Then he unbuttoned her blouse and slipped it off her shoulders.

She was returning his kisses now and bending and turning her body to maneuver it closer to his. He unfastened her bra and slipped the straps down and off her arms. He started to bend down to kiss her breasts but instead reached down and lifted her up to him. She instinctively wrapped her legs around his waist. Her whole body was tingling. She was ready, ready to be swept away in that wonderful ecstasy she adored. She kissed his neck and nibbled his ear.

"Oh, Mark," she gasped. "Please, Mark."

He moved his lips up to her mouth again and kissed her passionately, pushing his hard tongue against hers. He turned and lay her carefully on the bed. She stretched out her arms, beckoning him. He quickly pulled off his clothes and sat down on the bed beside her. She started to raise herself up to him to touch him, to pull him down to her. Before she could manage he was kissing her again, on her mouth, her breasts, her stomach. She could stand no more.

"Damn it Mark, give it to me!" she yelled as she reached her arms up to him.

"I thought you'd never ask," he said stretching himself out on top of her.

Chapter 11

The full moon's reflection shone brightly on the Gulf. Most residents took such beauty for granted, but visitors enjoyed it immensely.

Tonight, the occupants of one of the beachfront homes wouldn't care if the moon fell from the sky. They were celebrating the delivery of a new shipment. This house was always active, but never like tonight. An air of euphoria permeated the house and its occupants. The major partygoers were already present, but there would be late arrivals, if they could manage to get away.

Greg Sheppard had rented the house. Most of the time he shared it with friends. As each guest arrived, Greg went around the room introducing him or her to those present. The younger set preferred to be known by a first name. It was much easier to find someone on the street by a nickname or first name than by a given name. Guys and girls who spent nights together, later crawled out of bed, parted and still only knew a first name, or none at all. Not knowing a partner's last name didn't reduce their nights of fun with sex and drugs. Those who did know each other well had ways of handling their familiarity and its interfering with their wanting to remain anonymous to others.

After the guests had been introduced, they blended in with the present group, some taking refuge with those met at prior parties. Greg worked in the kitchen with a few of his close friends, filling glasses with ice and various liquids. They had been together for many years and had moved around from state to state following the drug scene. If they couldn't work something out with the cops, they got others to do the dirty work. All cops couldn't be bought. That realization put them on the move even faster.

"Take these in, Debbie," he said, handing a tray to the tall blond standing next to the sink. "I'll bring the wine coolers in a minute." He finished filling the glasses with ice and motioned to the others to pour the wine. A rap at the kitchen door startled him and he moved quickly to peer out through the screen.

"Hey....all right, baby. You could make it. Come on in and meet the crowd," he said as he swung the screen door out. Billy Carter stepped into the kitchen and shut the door behind him.

Greg placed his arm around Billy's shoulder and led him to the table, gesturing to the men pouring drinks. "You know Jake Thomas, Brian Rothchild, and Michael Gordon."

They all nodded and spoke out greetings. Billy went to each one, renewing friendships and grasping hands.

"And you know Chuck Charles, alias *Hollywood,* the DJ over at W A F M. Grab that bowl of pretzels and I'll introduce you to the kids in the living room," he said, picking up the large tray of drinks. He moved through the doorway into the middle of a sea of young bodies sitting and lying all over the floor. "Folks," Greg shouted, drawing their attention. "I want you to meet a very special friend of mine. This is Billy."

Everyone said "Hi" in unison.

Greg leaned over and set the tray on the coffee table, then pointed to each person, calling him or her by first names. Billy would nod his head, or occasionally give some verbal sound when he recognized someone.

"That's David, Keith, Donnie, Betty, and Dennis, Micky aka Michelle." When Greg would come to good-looking chick, Billy would give a little more than a nod. With Michelle he raised his eyebrows, gave her a smile and handed her the bowl of pretzels he was holding.

"Here's Holly. Now this you leave alone. She belongs to Brian," Greg quickly added. Everyone laughed, including Billy, for he knew Brian.

Sitting on the floor next to the kitchen door was Marian, Billy's contact from Texas. He grabbed her hand and lifted her to her feet. He put his arm around her waist and pulled her to him. With arms around each other, they followed Greg into the kitchen. The young people in the living room went back to whatever they had been doing.

They all laughed together, for they could feel that the evening was going to be a success. It was just a matter of time before the party would get so hot, no one would realize or care who anyone was.

Billy sat down on a kitchen stool and Marian stood close by, resting her arm on his shoulder. He watched silently while the others mixed more drinks. He knew everyone in the group well except Hollywood. Greg had been his contact up until now. It was time, Billy thought, to get to know more about the DJ.

Charles knew Billy was watching him and it made him uneasy. He sipped his scotch and tried not to look in Billy's direction.

Hollywood was a vital contact for the group. He was able to circulate among the local law enforcement agencies and pick up copy for the day's air releases. News data would include information about local busts, arrests, accidents, etc. Once in a while he'd relay a coded message to Greg from the department group over the air. He would work it into a comment or idle chatter, feats that disc jockeys are noted for. The media was used for their benefit rather than to keep the public informed. The sheriff's department only released items that made them appear efficient in the public eye.

Charles' appearance wasn't like the average hippy-type pothead. He was well dressed and had cultivated some impressive local contacts, including some of the more prominent politicians and the local assistant state attorney, Larry Stewart. His ties to the higher echelon made him feel secure.

He preferred to keep a low profile when he attended one of these get-togethers. He always stayed with the group in the kitchen until the party reached a peak. No one ever realized who he was. If they did, his name was never mentioned. It was an unwritten code among the revelers. Become loose lipped and be excluded from the next party. No one wanted to chance being cast out by one's peers. That was the ultimate mortal sin, dooming one to years of degradation.

It wasn't the pot or the booze that enticed him to the party, it was the sex. He loved the wild young girls, with their wonderful hard-toned bodies. He hated having to make overtures and small talk. He just wanted to enjoy himself and hump every giddy bimbo in the place.

Greg motioned to Brian to take the drinks into the living room and reached into the wall cabinet for a large circular tray. He emptied a huge paper bag onto the tray and arranged the *fixings* all around. "The gang's all here, and it's time to party," he squealed as he carried the tray to the living room and set it down. "Help yourselves, punks!" Everyone scrambled to the tray.

The general rule was that the host supplied the booze and the pot. If anything harder was needed or wanted, the person using it had to pay the cost. At a pusher's party, the rate was reduced, since the dealer would eventually reap future benefits from the user.

Billy got up and motioned for Marian to sit down on the stool. Then he walked across the room and quietly asked Chuck Charles, "You got your eye on the chick you want yet?"

"Hey man, I've been counting, and there aren't enough to go around."

Billy laughed. "Well, if you wait too long, you're going to lose out on the one you want, and have to end up sharing. That's usually what happens towards the end anyhow. There are a couple guys in there that can't handle the stuff. It puts them waaaay out." He smiled broadly and made a gesture towards open space with his hand. "So you won't have to worry. There won't be any competition when it comes to pairing off. That's the benefit of having them here. They bring their broads for us to use while they take their flights. Smart, huh?" They both laughed.

Billy continued to make small talk while Charles sipped his scotch. He'd heard a lot about Billy Carter and had hoped to avoid having to talk to him. He knew from Greg that he had a hair trigger temper and settled his grudges violently. He didn't want any trouble, certainly not with Billy. He enjoyed playing on the fringe of crime. It gave him a rush hanging out with Greg and his friends. Besides, he told himself, it was just a matter of time before they made marijuana legal. After all, he wasn't handling the stuff personally. He was careful to avoid learning any of the pertinent details. Hell, he didn't give a damn about drugs or smuggling. He was just there for the sex.

The voices from the living room were getting louder and the talk more slurred. Squeals of delight punctuated the roar of laughter. The action was about to start.

Marian moved across to Billy and nuzzled his neck. She reached up with her tongue and traced the outline of his ear. He moved his left hand from her waist to rub along her buttocks. Suddenly he pinched her hard. She drew back from the pain of the pinch and he pulled her to him and kissed her hard on the lips. She moaned and pushed her body closer to him.

"I really need to take care of this, Hollywood," he said, guiding Marian through the doorway into the living room. "We'll talk more later."

Not if he could help it, thought Charles. He was relieved that Billy was gone. He was anxious to get into the fray.

The living room was almost dark. All the lights had been turned off, except for a large shaded lamp on the corner table. The pungent sweet odor hung in the room. The smoke clouded so much that it took a minute for Charles to get his bearings. Bodies were together on the floor, the couch and the chairs. Rick was with Susan. Jake was with Debbie in the corner. Keith had passed out in a stupor on the floor. He posed no threat to anyone. Next to him sat the tiny brunette named Phyllis. She held a joint in one hand and her shoes in the other. Charles moved in the direction of her, stepping over the couples in between. He lifted her from the floor and carried her into the kitchen. He sat her on the table. She laughed loudly, dropped the joint and put her arms around his neck and pulled him down to her.

Brian and Holly were in one of the other rooms. They seldom shared each other; when they did it was on Brian's say so. She was strictly his property. They had lived together for several years and although she suspected he had cheated on her she never mentioned it.

David and Betty had paired off, doing their thing in the hallway.

Billy finished before Marian. He rolled off and sat up against the wall, smoking a cigarette.

"Come on, Billy," Marian pleaded. "Just a little bit more. Please."

He enjoyed the begging. He loved the feeling of control. Hearing a woman beg gave him a special kick. He enjoyed his sex but seldom was that selective. Knowing that he had left Marian craving more satisfied his sadistic streak.

Marian gave up finally, and crawled off to the center of the room to find another willing partner. Damn you, Billy!" she shouted back at him.

After the initial encounter with a first choice, the crowd melded together in one great ball of writhing flesh on the floor. The darkness didn't deter the guys from finding girls. The girls had been drugged to the point where they couldn't exert any effort to refuse. They were at the mercy of the drugs and the sex-crazed men. The party went on all night.

It was a little after four when Hollywood struggled to his feet. He adjusted his pants and buttoned his shirt as he moved toward the door, being careful not to step on the various bodies lying about.

"Hey, give me a hand," a voice said as he opened the screen to exit. It was Marian, holding out her hand. He pulled her up. She straightened her skirt and reached for her shoes, standing on the table next to the lamp that cast grotesque shadows around the room. "Are you going into the city?" she asked, following him outside.

"Yeah," he answered, walking toward his Mustang.

"Can you drop me at the Holiday Inn? I've got to catch a plane in three hours." She opened the car door and sat down.

Charles guided the car down the narrow street, turned right on the beach road and headed for town.

"Fun, huh?" Marian said, attempting to make friendly chitchat.

"It was all right," Charles answered. He was trying hard to remember if Marian had been one of his conquests.

"The only reason I came was to get close to Billy. What a dud."

Charles perked up at the mention of Billy. "Really?" he questioned.

"Yeah. The selfish prick. I think he's a psycho. I mean, I really think he likes hurting people."

Charles wanted to know more about Billy and how Marian fit into the picture. But he reminded himself that the less he knew about any of it the safer he'd be in the long run.

Marian babbled on about the heat and the damned humidity and how nice it would be to get back to Houston.

Charles nodded and agreed. He was glad when they finally pulled into the motel parking lot.

Marian leaned over and squeezed his thigh. "You were great. The best I had all night," she said as she opened the door, grabbed her shoes and got out. He watched her disappear into the lobby, then he turned on the way to home.

Airtime was 6 A.M. and he needed a shower.

Chapter 12

Billy came to life, slowly. He rolled over, letting his hand fall on the edge of the couch, and then he pulled himself up from the floor. When he moved fast it made his head swim, so he slowed down. He placed his other hand on the edge of the cushion to steady himself; then he raised up on one knee, hesitated a few seconds, and pulled himself to a standing position. He was wobbly, but at least he was upright. That was more than he could say for the rest of them lying around here and there. As he made his way around the room, he nudged with his foot the tangled mass of human flesh lying about the floor. Occasionally he would get a response, a moan or a movement.

Streams of light poured in through the windows. The floor glistened in the light rays. Those who had lain in one place for any length of time became momentarily stuck to the wooden floor because of the spills of the evening.

Within minutes, most were either sitting upright or lying on the floor with their eyes open. The conversation was light. The drug-induced sleep had fogged their senses. What had taken place the night before wasn't remembered by many. Even if it was, it was doubtful anyone felt shame.

Suddenly someone let out a squeal that attracted the attention of everyone in the room. Debbie was attempting to crawl away from her position on the floor while keeping her eyes on the motionless body that had lain next to her on the floor. The rest of the group gathered about her.

Billy walked over to the body lying on the floor. He had acquired more stability in his steps. "What in hell is going on anyhow?" he asked Debbie.

"She looks weird, Billy!" Debbie said, as she started to whine. A hysterical wave of emotion flooded across her body.

Billy looked down at the girl's body, then bent down and felt her neck for a pulse. The blue appearance of her skin should have told him that her pulse had ceased to beat hours before. She lay on her back, her eyes sunk in her head as if there were no eyeballs to hold the lids out. They appeared to be deflated, or never to have been there at all. She had vomited, and, not being able to help herself enough to roll over, had lain there and strangled.

"Who in the hell is this broad anyway?" Billy's anxious voice questioned, raising an octave. He looked around the room trying to spot someone's recognition of the dead girl.

The commotion had brought everyone in the house to the living room by this time. Billy's question drew their attention to the corpse on the floor. Several of the girls began to weep. Many others turned away or hid their eyes with their hands.

One of the guys hesitantly walked over to view the body. Curiosity didn't move him. The possibility of recognizing her caused him to take a good look at her face. "Oh, God! That's Amy. I think that's her." His voice trailed off at the end, as he tried to recall if that was really her name.

"Where in hell did she come from? Who brought her?" Billy demanded angrily. He wanted to know who had placed him in this compromising situation. He wasn't alarmed at problems he created, but he didn't like being faced with something he had no control over.

"I think some of the late arrivals brought her. They said she was someone they had run into on the beach. She was looking for a good time," Jake Thomas calmly interjected from the rear of the room. In fact, it had been he who had given her the cocaine-spiked drink. When he'd first seen her shapely body it had turned him on. He'd made up his mind right then that he would have her before the night was over. As it turned out, he was the first of several before she died.

The thought of possibly having screwed a corpse made Dennis vomit. He cupped his hands around his mouth and ran to the bathroom.

"Everybody get out in the kitchen," Billy yelled, taking command of the situation. He motioned Greg to his side.

Everybody was eager to comply with the directive.

"What the hell are we going to do with her?" Greg whispered.

He was stunned at having a dead body in his house, and had remained silent up to this point. He had been around bodies before, but the circumstances were different. "You know I rent this house; I sure can't leave her here and split. They would be on me as soon as the smell hit the street. It wouldn't take long either, in this heat."

Billy took a soiled sheet off the couch and placed it over the body. This gave him time to think the thing out. "We'll wait till after dark, then get rid of the body. She doesn't look familiar and she doesn't have much of a tan. I wonder if she's a tourist? She could be down here on vacation. If that's the case, somebody will be looking for her."

"How old do you think she is?" asked Greg nervously.

"Not old enough, buddy. She's definitely jailbait," Billy replied.

"Jesus!" Greg moaned.

Billy turned and walked towards the closed kitchen door. He opened it and spoke in a harsh tone. "Now, I want you all to listen to me and heed what I say. You get dressed and get the hell out of here. You are to tell no one about what happened here. Go about your business as if nothing took place. If you don't, it will bring questions on your head and me on your case. Forget you were ever here. Anybody asks, you spent the night on the beach. In other words, keep your big fat mouths shut!" He looked around as if memorizing every face. "If you don't, you'll join Amy, wherever she is."

Little was said as the groups gathered up their belongings. A few headed for the bathroom to wash their faces and give their hair quick once over. Most just made their exit. Considering the condition they had been in just ten minutes before, they were all amazingly wide-awake.

Greg waited until everyone left before he spoke. "Man, how in hell can you stay so cool when I have a dead body laying in my living room?"

Billy had a smile on his face as he turned to go and make a pot of coffee. He sat down on a stool, rested his cup on the counter and lit a cigarette. "I worked on the toughest police force in the country. I learned how to take care of sticky situations at a moment's notice. That's what you call thinking on your feet, my boy," he said laughing.

"My God, Billy!" Greg exclaimed. "You're like Dr. Jekyll and Mr. Hyde."

Billy didn't like the comparison. He squinted his beady little eyes and glared at Greg. "I can leave you to handle this nasty mess all by yourself if you'd like."

Greg apologized, "No man, I'm sorry if you took that the wrong way. I'm damned awful upset. No Billy, I didn't mean anything by it."

Billy enjoyed watching Greg grovel. "Pour yourself a cup of coffee, Greg, and put a double shot in it. That'll calm your nerves. We've got a busy day ahead of us, and an even busier night."

Greg shivered as he filled the cup. He turned slightly, hoping Billy wouldn't see his hand shaking.

The hot Florida day dissolved into a cool breezy evening.

Greg had been on edge all day, but kept himself busy cleaning up the house. Everything was done except for mopping the floor. He'd saved that until last.

In sharp contrast, Billy had been so relaxed he had taken a long nap. He'd fixed himself a sandwich, had a few beers and was playing solitaire.

Greg walked over to the window and looked out. Then he sat down on the overstuffed corner chair and lit a cigarette. He would have rather had a joint, but this was no time to cloud his mind. He was trying desperately to keep his nerves under control. He tried to concentrate on something beside Amy's body wrapped up in a blanket in his bedroom. He watched silently as Billy flipped the cards down on the coffee table.

He wondered how long after dark they'd have to wait to dispose of the body. He didn't even know the plan yet, making him all the more edgy. He didn't dare ask Billy what he had planned, for fear he would leave him like a cold mackerel, with a cold mackerel. *Oh what a mess this is to be in,* he thought to himself. He walked to the window and peered out to see if it was black enough yet.

"For Christ's sake. Will you get the hell away from that window? You're starting to get on my nerves."

Greg walked to the kitchen. "Do you want a cup of coffee?" he asked, trying to change the subject to cool Billy down.

"Naw," Billy answered, getting up off the couch. "You don't have time for one either. Come on; let's get this mess over with, so I can get back to town. I've got important business to take care of."

What the hell could be more important than this, wondered Greg, as he followed him to the hallway. Billy opened the bedroom door. The stench had started to build as the body was rapidly decomposing. That, combined with the sickening smell of vomit, caused Greg to gag. Billy gave him a dirty look. He'd experienced that smell before, and had learned to just tune his mind onto something else. Not much bothered Billy Carter. The things that did, no one around was aware of. Billy bent down and picked up the body, struggling to put it over his shoulder. The body, being slightly rigid, balanced there awkwardly.

"I'm damn glad I wrapped her in plastic first," Billy commented. "Otherwise, I'd have her fluids all over me."

Greg hurried out of his way, trying hard not to add to the already unpleasant smell.

"You sure as hell could open the back door," Billy said, as he strained under the body's weight.

Greg rushed to the door, opened it, looked out, and then motioned that the coast was clear. Billy carried the body to the car, while Greg ran ahead to open the trunk.

Billy tossed her in, letting out a grunt as he slammed the lid shut. "I'll drive. You get in the passenger's side," he told Greg.

Billy seldom rode with anyone. He always liked to know where he was going. He was ever alert to the fact that if he needed to cover his tracks he'd have to be in the driver's seat. If someone else made the mistakes, he knew he'd have to pay for them, but if he was the one who sidestepped, he knew he was quick enough to get out of it.

He'd had plenty of experience getting out of sticky situations. He was a prime candidate for this racket, knowing both sides of the law. Two years on the New York vice squad had presented him with the kind of challenge he needed. He loved living on the edge. It gave him a kick to know that he was walking a fine line between life and death every day. It was all a big game; which was smarter, whose mind was more devious. He enjoyed living by his wits. It was the ultimate thrill. He was king of the hill and he wasn't afraid of anybody anywhere.

They drove in silence to the far end of the island. There Billy found a deserted road that led off toward the beach. He drove carefully so as not to get stuck in the sand. *It would be a ticklish situation to have to get a wrecker to pull them out with a stinking body in the trunk,* he thought. He found firm ground to drive on, pulled to a stop and doused the lights.

"You keep watch, while I do the plant job," he told Greg, as he opened the trunk and pulled the body up over his shoulder once more. "By the way, give me your knife," Billy said reaching out with his free hand.

"What do you want my knife for?" Greg asked, stunned by the demand.

"We're going to play mumblety-peg, Greg, what do you think? Just shut up and give me the damn knife!"

Up to this time Greg didn't know what Billy had planned to do with Amy's body. He was glad to have the opportunity to stay with the car. Greg paced back and forth nervously, wondering why Billy needed his knife. He was just finishing his second cigarette when Billy appeared, walking backwards, using a palm frond to dust away his footprints.

The bastard thinks of everything, Greg thought.

"You drive the car back out to the road, while I walk behind the car," Billy told Greg. "And pick up those damned cigarette butts."

Greg responded to his command. When he reached the road, he waited for Billy to catch up with him.

When Billy arrived at the main road, he touched the palm frond to his cigarette lighter, then tossed the flaming stalk into the dry weeds. He hurried to the car and hopped in the driver's side, pushing Greg over rather than asking him to move. He threw the car in gear and took off at a high rate of speed. Glancing in the rear view mirror, he saw the blazing memorial he had left to Amy. His heart pounded with excitement.

In such a remote area it would take half an hour for fire equipment to arrive, if they bothered at all. There was no danger, with the lack of buildings in the area, and the underbrush would eventually burn off. With the fire able to burn only to the water line, it would soon be extinguished.

They drove back to Greg's house the same way they had come out, in silence. They both felt lighter, having rid themselves of their excess baggage.

Billy pulled in back of Greg's house and stopped the car. "I'm going back to the city," he said as he hopped out. "If you want to go in, you drive your own car." In a matter of seconds he was off down the street.

Greg was still shaken. He didn't want to be left alone, yet he didn't want to go into town either. He wasn't ready to go back into the house, not yet. He decided he'd go to the bar down the beach. Yeah, that was want he needed, a stiff drink. *Ugh! Stiff!* What a thought!

The bar was dimly lit, for which he was glad. He felt that what had taken place in the past few hours was written all over his face, for everyone to see. He was right. The drink did help him settle down. He sat, sipping his tequila, listening to the conversations around him. He had finally managed to put the horrible experience out of his mind, when he heard sirens go screaming by the bar. Greg quickly finished his drink, and headed for the door.

The phone was ringing when he got to his house.

"Where the hell have you been?" He recognized the voice as Hollywood. "I've been calling you for hours."

"I've been out," replied Greg.

"Well listen man, we may have trouble, or, that is to say, you may have trouble. There's a missing person's report out on a girl at the beach. Hold on a minute while I put on another disk." He left Greg holding a silent line for what seemed to be an eternity. "Okay, I'm back. We've been broadcasting a news bulletin all afternoon concerning a disappearance at the beach. She's here with her parents on vacation. Her old man's the president of some big business up in Michigan. I didn't think much about it until a deputy came by with a picture of the kid. Listen, Greg, she was there at the party last night. I recognized her right away. A small redhead in a peasant blouse. Her name is Amy Lesso. And she's sixteen years old." Charles paused for a minute, waiting for Greg to say something. "Are you there?"

"Yeah, I'm here."

"Well, do you know what happened to her? Did she leave with anyone you know?"

"Weren't you here when everybody left together?" Greg asked. He was puzzled.

"No, man. I cut out about four. I had to pull the early shift for Freddy Fry. I took Marian back to town and she caught a plane to Texas."

Greg hadn't realized that Hollywood wasn't there. In all the excitement he hadn't missed him. He was afraid to say too much on the phone so he waited for Charles to talk.

"They've asked for a broadcast every half hour on her description. Anyone knowing of her whereabouts is to contact the sheriff's department. They say that she'd had a fight with her parents. She ran out of the cottage after they wouldn't let her go to a beach party. At first they thought she was staying away to worry them, but then they found her shoes on the beach by the pier, and now they're afraid she's met with foul play."

Foul play isn't the word for it, Greg thought. He didn't dare answer Hollywood's questions. "Listen, man, everything's cool, don't worry. Why don't you come down when you get off? We'll talk about it, and I'll fill you in on all the details."

Hollywood could sense there was a problem from the tone of Greg's voice, but it was time to give a news broadcast, so he said, "Okay," and hung up.

Greg pulled his shirt off and threw it in the chair by the television. He sat down on the couch and put his legs up on the coffee table, lit a cigarette and put his head back. He still wanted that joint, but he'd wait until Hollywood got there. Chuck and he had always gotten along well; they had been together for a long time now. After first meeting in Anchorage, Alaska they had moved on and lived in other states together. Then last year Chuck had decided to take the DJ job at Fort Manson. He missed the excitement that Greg supplied, and talked him into following him to Florida. It didn't take them long to make the drug connection. Chuck liked to stay on the safe side of the dealing and kept his distance when the actual transactions went down. But that was all right with Greg, he knew Chuck didn't like to get his hands dirty, literally or otherwise. Until tonight things had gone fairly well with their setup. Greg had no longer felt threatened over the bank robberies he had pulled off in Alaska. He had covered his tracks well. Now, all of a sudden, he felt like things were coming down around his head. He had to keep a grip on himself.

Maybe the television would take his mind off the mess. He pushed on the switch as he crossed into the kitchen for a beer. The sound came on and he heard the voice of the local sportscaster. *Great,* he thought, *that'd take my mind of things.* He'd always had an inner desire to be a professional baseball player, but had lacked the drive to pursue it.

"We interrupt the sports roundup for this late breaking bulletin from the news desk. Details are sketchy, but it appears that there has been a murder at Fort Manson Beach."

The word murder and beach brought Greg running back from the kitchen.

"Sheriff's deputies report the discovery of the body of a young female at the south end of the beach. Attention was drawn to the area, when firemen rushed to extinguish a fire, which had apparently been set a short distance from the murder site.

"Officials refuse to verify if the discovery of the body is connected in any way with the reported disappearance last evening of a Michigan girl visiting the beach area.

"The missing girl, sixteen year old Amy Lesso, was last seen near the pier in the Long Key section of the beach. Her shoes were found in that area this morning, but no word as to her whereabouts has been received. Sheriff's officials ask that anybody who may have information about Amy Lesso contact their office immediately.

"We repeat, there is no known connection at this time between the body discovered this evening at the beach and the disappearance of sixteen year old Amy Lesso. Please stay tuned for further developments.

"We return you now to Floyd Richardson at the sports desk."

Greg sat back down on the couch. His mind was racing. *Damn that Billy,* he said to himself, *if he hadn't set that fire they might not have discovered the body for days, maybe never.* Now everything was coming apart at the seams.

He decided he couldn't wait for Hollywood to smoke the joint. He needed something to calm him down, now. That would do it. At least he hoped it would. Greg went back into the kitchen to get the makings, sat back down and rolled out the cigarette. He put his head back and inhaled as deeply as he could. By the time the Tonight Show came on he was feeling considerably better.

It was midnight by the time Hollywood left the station and headed for the beach. He needed to talk to Greg as soon as possible. He needed some answers to some questions.

It was bad enough to have been at the party where she died, but if what they were saying on the news bulletins was true, he could be dragged in on a big time murder investigation. If it were known that he was the least bit involved, his connection with the assistant state's attorney wouldn't do him a bit of good. They would throw him to the wolves as quick as any other bastard. *It was strange,* he thought, *the ethics of the dual-coded system.* Pumping dope into the area and ruining young lives seemed to be all right, compared to killing one of them through foul play. No matter what had happened or what Greg was involved in, he was going to protect himself and that was a fact.

He parked next to Greg's Olds and raced up the steps to the door. Greg was dozing on the couch.

"Hey, wake up! Rise and shine buddy! We need to talk."

Greg sat up fast. "Chuck! Boy am I glad to see you."

Charles walked into the kitchen. "I need a drink."

"There's some beer in the refrigerator," Greg yelled in to him.

"I need something stronger than that," Charles said, setting a bottle of Jack Daniels and two glasses on the coffee table. He poured himself half a glass and took a long swallow. "Have you been watching the news?" He didn't wait for Greg to answer. "They think the body on the beach is Amy Lesso."

"I know it's Amy Lesso," Greg said in a half whisper.

"Holy Moses, Greg. What happened?"

"I don't know myself. When we all woke up this morning she was dead."

"From what?"

"I don't know from what, I guess she was screwed to death. Anyway, we sent everybody home and then tonight Billy and I took her down to the south end of the beach and left her."

"I should have known that Carter was involved," Charles said, taking another swallow. "That bastard is crazy. He's got some major chips missing in his computer. It makes me sick to think about it."

"Well it sure didn't make you sick when you had your turn, Hollywood," Greg said defensively. "Besides, Billy handled the whole thing like a pro. You should have seen how cool and collected he was about everything."

"You're as sick as he is," Hollywood said, shaking his head in disbelief. "I really didn't think you were capable of anything like that."

"Like what? We just took her out and dumped her on the beach. What were we supposed to do, leave her here to rot on the floor.?"

"Dumping her I can understand, but the rest of it."

"The rest of what?" Greg wanted to know. "What are you talking about?"

"The mutilation," Chuck said, swallowing the word as he said it.

"The muti....What mutilation?" Greg's voice raised an octave. "There wasn't any mutilation."

"You dumb jerk," Hollywood said, realizing that Greg didn't know about how the girl had been abused. "She was carved up, like some satanic cult had used her for a ritual."

"Oh My God," Greg muttered. His mind was reeling. His mouth dropped open as if to say something, but nothing came out. He moved his hand up to his forehead and drummed his fingers over his left brow.

"Look you low-life bastard, you'd better not draw me into this mess. That sadistic friend of yours may have your hide in a wringer, but not mine."

"My knife," Greg said, as if everything was suddenly clear to him. "That's why he wanted my knife."

"Your knife?" Chuck said. "He used your knife to cut her up? Where the hell is it?"

"I don't know. He didn't give it back. I forgot all about it."

"Damn, Greg," Chuck set his glass down on the table and walked calmly to where Greg was sitting. He put his hand down and rubbed it through Greg's curly hair. Then like an explosion he drew back suddenly and knocked him to the floor, sending the bottle and glasses flying across the room.

Before Greg could get up Chuck was on top of him, his fists flailing wildly. Greg tried to fend off the blows but Chuck was astride him, using his knees to pin Greg's arms down. Chuck paused for a second, then slapped Greg hard across the face. The pent up anger subsided as Greg stopped fighting and went limp. He lay on the floor under Chuck's body and started to weep.

Chuck spoke in a low tone. "When you and I were up north we had a different thing going. Since Billy came on the scene it has become strange. It took me awhile to see it. Then at the party I sat back and watched him operate. I didn't realize there was more to him than the drug scene. He's one sick, weird dude."

Greg shook his head in agreement, then said, "Hey, don't ever let on to Billy how you feel. Since he's been under the protection of the sheriff's department, he's really extended his luck. He's done some pretty brazen stunts lately. I mean aside from the girl. The freedom he has just makes him that more daring." He tried to bring the discussion about Billy to a close. Even though he wasn't there, Greg felt in jeopardy just talking about him. "Hey, let's get a shower," he said getting to his feet. He reached his hand down and pulled Chuck up. They embraced for a long minute and went into the bathroom with an arm around each other.

Billy stepped from the shadows behind the shrub by the living room window. He had parked his car over on the next street when he'd seen Chuck's in the spot where he usually parked. He started to walk toward his car, then took off at a dead run.

Billy drove up the beach road, barely noticing the surroundings as they whizzed by. He had suppressed his inner turmoil as he watched the episode between Chuck and Greg. The conversation he overheard added to it. He could stand no more. He let go with a yell at the top of his lungs. Anyone hearing him would have thought he was in pain. He was in pain, but not the kind they'd have thought.

When he caught the light on Colonial, he squealed his tires. He was annoyed to think he'd had to stop. That was just one more thing that was against him tonight. When the light changed, he was off with a lunge. The Trans-am fishtailed up the street. He had to decelerate the gas in an attempt to straighten it out. He continued down MacGeorge, then turned right on Brahma. He turned off the dead-end street onto a dirt roadway known only to a few, that ran behind his house and led to the street. He'd often used it to elude someone. He may have a thing with the county Mounties, but the city boys didn't cut any ice for him. They knew about the corruption with the rackets, but were limited to city details. The county had it over them, especially with the state attorney's office backing their every move.

By the time he pulled up to the back of the house, he was furious. Some of his hostility was taken out on the car door, when he slammed it. His having to fumble with his house keys didn't help.

Finally he was inside and alone. He felt secure and safe at last. He walked straight to the kitchen to fix a drink, pushing the knob on the television set as he went by. It came on with a blare. He didn't care about disturbing the neighbors. He needed to take out his anger on someone tonight.

He wouldn't dare let anyone know what he'd heard at the beach.

Billy filed the whole beach scene in the back of his mind. His brain wasn't a dead-end, like everyone else's. In his brief span of years so much had taken place, there was no way his mind could hold on to it all. He kept only what was vital to his survival and let the rest go.

Billy plopped down in a chair, holding the glass of whiskey in his hand. He watched the late news as the reporter described the scene of the murder at the beach. "Believe me, buddy, you had to be there to appreciate it," he said loudly to the television. He chuckled to himself, then swallowed down the bourbon.

"Damn it!" He said loudly. He got up, turned the channel to MTV and headed for the bathroom.

An attempt had been made to modernize the room. The old-fashioned sink and tub were still there, but a prior tenant had tiled the walls and painted. Billy had added carpet to the floor, the kind that's cut to fit around the fixtures. It covered more than the floor in his bathroom. Billy sat down, reached over and pulled a corner up away from the wall, then back towards him, baring a portion of the floor. Doubling back the carpet on the floor he revealed a board that showed wears from repeated removal. Billy took a switchblade from his pocket, pressed the button, and the blade popped out. Using it on the crack, he opened the floorboard enough to get his fingers under it, then took it out, revealing a cavity. Secured to the sixteen inches between the joists, a tin box had been shaped and neatly nailed into place. It held several packages. Some were filled with marijuana. Others held a various assortment of multi-colored pills. There were several vials of crack and some packets of coke. Far more valuable was the white substance neatly piled at the bottom in clear plastic bags. The demand for heroin wasn't as great as with the other contraband, so it was kept on the bottom. That way it saved time when a caller came to make a buy. The ones who used smack wouldn't complain about the wait, for fear of being cut off.

Billy reached in and retrieved a pre-rolled reefer. *Yeah, I can use this,* he said to himself. He carefully placed the items back in their original order. Then he reached into his pocket and pulled out a small penknife. He dropped the knife in the box, laughed, and shouted loudly, "Your time might belong to Hollywood, Greg, but your life is mine."

He replaced the floorboard, and smoothed out the carpet nudging the sides with his foot. He leaned back against the wall and secured the joint in his lips. He lit it, drawing the smoke slowly and deeply into the lower cavities of his lungs. He held it there, savoring every last particle of stimulus from the intoxicating substance. When he felt his lungs would burst, he finally exhaled it into the room. The smoke mingled with the sweet smell that had accumulated from the lit cigarette. "Ahhhh... ." he sighed, resting his head back against the wall. The grass did its work well. It wasn't long before he was in a world of euphoria. Billy took two more long drags on the illegal weed, then pinched out the lit sparks on the end. His mind was too dulled to feel it burn his fingers.

He closed his eyes and floated out on a cloud of smoke. The trials of the evening were blocked out, at least for the time being. He listened to the music blaring in the living room. Every note had a different meaning, and he understood the message.

Chapter 13

Doty had seen a lot of things in his days of reporting, but nothing had ever matched the horror of the scene in front of him. He'd heard the call go out over the police scanner, grabbed his jacket, hollered for Ralph Jenkins, the photographer, and raced to the beach.

The deputy on duty at the scene tried to keep them away until the captain could get there. But while he was distracted with traffic they had slipped through. Now, Doty wished they hadn't. The fire department had set up portable batteries to light the area. The dim illumination only added to the already eerie scene. The young girl was lying naked on a mound of sand. Propped under her head were what appeared to be a skirt and blouse. Doty walked around the body making mental notes. He had trouble concentrating. The odor of decaying flesh filled his nostrils. The flies swarming over the body sickened his usually strong stomach. Anyway, he kept telling himself, he was there now, so he may as well make the best of it, get enough data to do the story, and get the hell away from the stench as fast as he could. Ralph wasn't happy about taking the pictures. He kept telling Doty that the paper would never print them because they were too graphic for hometown circulation. Steve told him it didn't matter about the paper; he wanted the pictures for his own purpose. A gut instinct; he didn't know why, but he had to have the pictures.

As they walked away from the body, Ralph crossed himself and said softly, "May God have mercy on her soul."

"Yeah," said Doty, "and the low life that carved her up."

They met Ray Yarbrough and the coroner Waldo Stone walking in on the sandy road. They acknowledged each other with a nod. Doty pitied those who had to handle this case, even though it was the sheriff's department.

Driving back to town, Doty could think of nothing but the naked young girl. She looked about thirteen or fourteen. About the age his own daughter would be, if she had lived. He thought about the girl's family. Memories of his own experience flooded in on him, and tears began to well up in his eyes.

"Who does something like that, Doty?" Ralph asked as they passed the city limits sign on Estero Boulevard.

The question snapped Doty back from the past.

"A real sicko. The worst kind of pervert."

"What was that stuck up her, you know."

"The word is vagina, Ralph; at least that's the nice word for it. I think it was palm frond. Your pictures should be able to tell us for sure."

"Did you notice that despite all the mutilation there wasn't much blood around?"

Doty hadn't noticed. What with the smell and the flies and everything else, he'd missed that. "You've got a good eye for details, Ralph."

"That's my business, details. But to tell you the truth I'd rather be snapping pictures of bathing beauties on the beach than dead bodies."

"Well, let's hope this is the last one for both of us," Doty said as he pulled into the *News Leader* parking lot. "Make me a set of the shots, will you, Ralph."

"Sure, Doty," he said, getting out of the car.

Doty swung the Ford around and headed east on Front Street. He pulled into the lot across the street from the sheriff's department, and shut off the motor. It wasn't really a vacant lot. It was what remained of the pump area of an old gas station that had been converted to a useful building years ago. The corner area in front of the building was a convenient place to park.

Often people employed by the sheriff to do undercover work would fill the lot. They would be carted to local bars and cut loose to entice unwary pushers into making a sale. If they succeeded, the pusher's hide would be grass, and the undercover agent would be the lawn mower.

Doty walked across the street and pushed open the star-affixed glass doors. Many men were proud of that emblem. They had lived and died for what it stood for. It meant a lot to the honest cop, but not much to those who sported it now. One day he hoped to be able to prove that.

Doty nodded to Larry Lemmon at the front desk. "I just came from the beach. Pretty grisly."

"That's what I hear," replied Lemmon.

"Any word yet about identification?" Doty inquired.

"Looks like it's the missing Lesso girl."

"Anything new on-" Lemmon cut him off in mid sentence.

"Listen, Doty, I know you're just doing your job, but I've got to do mine, too. The colonel finds out I tell you anything I'll be on his bed list for sure, then all he would have to do is kick the dirt in on top of me."

"Okay. Anyway, they can't say this one's a suicide." Doty noticed the startled expression on Lemmon's face.

"What do you mean suicide? What suicide?"

"You know the suicide out on Luckett Road. The young man in the car, with his hand on the .45. Didn't you read my article? I left a paper here this morning."

"Oh, yeah. That suicide," Lemmon said recovering his composure.

"Have you noticed how many suicides we've had lately? Damned funny, I say. And all of them young kids, too." Doty was fishing now, but Lemmon wasn't taking the bait.

"Well, anyway, tell the sheriff I was by, and I'd appreciate having his press release as soon as possible. Oh yeah, and it sure would be nice to have a copy of the autopsy report."

Lemmon looked around to see if anyone was watching the two of them. "Go a little easy on this one, Doty. The girl's brother is a deputy with the department."

"You're kidding!" The news hound in Doty was awake and hungry. "I thought she was from Michigan."

"She is. The family lives outside Detroit. They come down twice a year to visit the boy. They rent a condo at the beach so the kids can sun and swim. The department will go all out on this one, Doty, so try not to step on too many toes."

"The only toes I want to step on are tucked away in a pair of size thirteen cowboy boots," Doty said, as he turned and headed toward the door.

Becky stared up at the ceiling. She was so relaxed she felt she could float off the bed and into another dimension. She was totally and completely satisfied. It was getting more difficult to separate work from pleasure. The sex was better each time. Mark was an exceptional lover: gentle, considerate and thoughtful while at the same time forceful and domineering. His powerful hands did wonders for her body. Like it or not she was hooked, at least on the sexual part of the relationship. She was beginning to crave more and more of him. And there seemed to be a limitless supply. *God, he's good,* she thought. He didn't like to discuss work. She didn't care one way or the other. She would have been content to spend all their time together. But she knew the colonel would soon tire of hearing only about her encounters and would want some concrete information. Hell, she thought, it's damned strange not to put job first. When she was here with Mark the only thing she wanted to think about was fulfilling every erotic desire she could imagine. She looked at the clock on the nightstand it flashed one forty two. It was time to get up and going. She moved her legs to the side of the bed.

He felt her stir and reached his arm across her, holding her in place.

"Where you going?" He said.

"It's almost two; I need to get dressed."

"How about a nightcap?"

"I'm not thirsty," she replied.

"I wasn't talking about liquor," he said, pulling her over atop him.

She laughed as he began kissing her throat. *The colonel will just have to wait,* she said to herself, as she settled down next to the most glorious body she'd ever come up against.

Doty still couldn't get the beach scene out of his mind. He turned the car in the direction of the *Leader* office, but then, instead, headed left onto the parkway. He suddenly felt terribly exhausted. Maybe a tall whiskey and soda would help relax him enough for a few hours sleep. Funny, he used to sleep soundly six or seven hours at a time, now he was lucky to keep his eyes closed for three hours straight. Days and nights had gotten turned around the past year. Maybe he just didn't require as much sleep now as he used to. Or maybe he just wanted to keep on the go so as not to miss any of the colonel's shenanigans. *I'll bet that bastard never closes his eyes,* he thought contemptuously.

His thoughts flashed back to the shocked expression on Lemmon's face when he mentioned suicide. It was true there had been a lot of damned suicides lately. Jack Manning, the kid on the courthouse roof, the boy in the car on Luckett Road. Now the ritual type murder at the beach. Between the dope and the death rate, the youth of Fort Manson were certainly in jeopardy.

Maybe there was a pattern to it all somehow. He'd have to do some research when he had a few minutes; see if he could come up with a connection. Something was sticking in his craw, but he couldn't put his finger on it. He'd play with it in his mind awhile, and maybe he'd be able to figure it out. If he was barking up the wrong tree, so what? He'd run into dead ends before. One of these times he'd hit pay dirt. Then he'd be able to cash in on all the research hours, if he could only out-last the problems. The more he thought about it, the more his mind wandered.

Doty pulled up to his house and pushed the remote for the garage door. He used to leave the car in the driveway; the past year he'd parked it inside. When he got out, he locked the car doors. *Talk about overly cautious,* he laughed to himself. Hell, maybe he was getting paranoid. He tried to tell himself it was foolish, but he knew that a lot of newspapermen before him had run up against some deadly odds. It could be dangerous squaring off against the big boys. And the biggest boy he knew was Colonel Donald Watson.

He peeled off his clothes intending to head for the shower. He decided he couldn't make it. He crawled in between the sheets and immediately fell into a deep sleep.

Are you asleep?" Becky asked, as she stubbed the cigarette out in the ashtray on the bed table.

"Yep," Mark answered.

"What you thinking about?"

"About how I wish you'd give up those damned cigarettes."

"Ask me nicely."

"Pretty please, Becky."

"Not good enough. What will you give me if I stop smoking?"

"I'll love you four times a night for the rest of your life."

"Oh, hell, I'm already getting that."

"Okay, five times!"

"Does it really bother you?"

"A little. Mostly I want you to stop for you. You know the Surgeon General makes a pronouncement every other day about tobacco. I want you to live a long life, Becky."

"I know. I've been going to stop. YOU be my cure. Maybe with your help I can do it." *This could become as habit forming as cigarettes,* she thought, as she kissed his shoulder. She could tell he was drifting off. She needed to get something on tape, anything to placate the colonel. At least they would think she was making an effort to pump him for information. She would never have him in a better position. He could never suspect her of anything devious after a love session like that.

"You know, Mark, I heard something the other day that I thought was strange."

He made no reply, so she nudged him. "Hey, you sleeping on me?"

"Oh...no. I'm just resting my eyes. What were you thinking about?" he asked, trying to appease her and not leave her talking to herself.

Becky raised herself up on one elbow. "Well, I heard that the state's public defender's office is grooming someone to run for sheriff against Hank Myers in the next election."

He replied, with a faint, "Huh?" Suddenly he was sitting upright. "Who in hell told you that?" He was wide-awake and obviously concerned.

She didn't know whether to pursue it or not. But since she'd committed herself, she had better go through with it. She wouldn't dare bring it up again. That would surely arouse his suspicion. She laughed, trying to make light of it. "I said, there must be some mistake. Everyone knows a lawyer doesn't go in that direction. They usually head for the state's attorney's office. You know...the next rung up the ladder."

The comment hit a nerve and brought Mark to his feet. He turned on the light and reached for his robe.

Becky pulled up the sheet to cover her nakedness. Mark putting on his robe made her feel uncomfortable. Normally, she wouldn't care if she were covered or not.

Mark walked around the bed and sat down next to her. "Who's speaking rumors like that?" He asked.

"I don't remember who told me. I didn't place much importance on it. It really didn't register in my mind whom it was that said it."

"Oh, come on Becky." He knew she was hedging, and he intended to get to the bottom of it. "Who was it?"

She reached for a cigarette, then immediately put it down again. She was trying to stall for time, knowing all the time he wouldn't be stalled. His training as a lawyer would make him badger her until he got what he wanted. She was in a hell of a predicament, and wished she'd kept her mouth shut. "I think it was Eva, the Corporal on the desk. I'm not sure. Let me think a minute. In the meantime, can I have a kiss?" She put her arms around his neck letting the sheet fall around her waist.

He couldn't refuse. He had fallen hard for her. Even with her rough exterior, he'd found something about her he loved.

She tried to take his mind off the situation at hand and gave the kiss all she had. Before their lips parted, she said, "Yeah, it was Eva. The other day she was on the phone. When she hung up, she started to laugh, and I asked what was so funny."

"I wonder whom it was she was talking to?" he asked, deep in thought.

"Did you notice how I put the cigarette down? See what a good influence you are." She was trying desperately to take his mind off Eva and the election question.

He smiled, "I guess this means I've got to come up with number five!" He got up, walked around to the other side and turned off the light. She felt his robe hit the bed when he tossed it; then he crawled back in beside her.

"Becky, you sure do keep me guessing. I never know what you're going to come up with next. Maybe that's the reason I love you. Never have I met anyone like you....With so much to offer. By the way, that's the first time I've told you that I love you. You've never told me how you feel."

Becky remained silent.

"I don't mean to pressure you. I know we both said no commitments when we started this."

This time, she got out of bed, picked up a cigarette and lit it. "I don't know how I feel about you, Mark. I've got to give it some thought. You know that I've had a bad experience with what some would call a marriage."

She still preferred to blame her ex-husband for the break up. He never understood her need to express her independence in her career. Without her career she would never feel like a total person. She had always looked down on people who never went after what they wanted out of life. She had made up her mind that she could do anything she set her mind to, and that anyone else could do the same thing. The department was proof positive of that.

"I like the way things are going. It's been fulfilling for both of us, leastwise for me."

Mark added, "Me too."

"Then why do we have to complicate matters by having commitments?"

"I don't know, Becky. First I thought for a lark I'd go out with you. Then I started to fall for you. I tried to tell myself I wasn't, but tonight proved I was wrong. I'd like to occupy every minute of your time. In fact, I don't know how you manage to spend all the time with me that you do."

Becky could feel herself being backed into another corner. If she didn't give him a good explanation she'd overplay her hand. "I manage the work they line up for me days. Night shifts are a little more difficult, but I've worked out a way to be able to go in and take care of most of the work. What I can't manage, Barry Sullivan's wife helps me out with. When she offered to help, she hadn't thought it would be such a prolonged thing. She jumped me about it last night when I saw her. I had wondered how I was going to tell you that things have to change."

"You mean, we won't be able to see each other every night any more?"

"I'm afraid not," she said sadly. He'd accepted her story. Perhaps this would work out better than she had expected. She'd come up with the line just to get him off her back. Now it might help her to accomplish what she'd set out to do in the first place. Absence would make him grow fonder and it could play right into her hands. If that happened, she was sure to make points with the colonel.

"I'd better get going. I told Sylvia Sullivan I would be in tonight to talk with her." She stubbed out her cigarette and walked to the chair where she had put her clothes.

"I'm glad we discussed this, Becky. At least we know where we stand."

She started to get dressed. She'd abandoned her bra, at Mark's suggestion. Wearing only a bikini under her mini skirt, she didn't have much to put on. She'd loved seeing mini skirts come back into fashion. She liked teasing the men, letting them see just enough to wonder about the rest. Once in awhile, she'd deliberately bend over and exposes her posterior. Nothing serious ever developed from the few pats the men had given her.

"Hey babe, will you walk me to my car?"

He had put his robe back on, and with his arm around her waist said, "Sure thing," at the same time giving her a squeeze. He opened the door and they both walked to her car. She got in and started the motor. He kissed her one last time and moved back.

As she drove away, she saw him in her rear view mirror. He was standing in the parking lot, with both hands in the front pockets of his robe. *Poor stupid bastard,* she thought. *Wasn't it Eve who got the man to eat the apple? They're all just a bunch of pricks with ears, all of them! They strut around like peacocks thinking they're holding everything under their thumb. Women should band together,* she thought. *We could rule the world and have men at our beck and call. They'd have no alternative. Either homosexuality or us. Speaking of gays,* she said to herself, *it was strange that the law had never harassed them, by the sheriff's department anyhow. In other cities I've lived in, the law enforcement agencies put the poor bastards through hell. Probably just to reinforce their masculine ego, or to convince themselves they weren't leaning in that direction too. I bet there isn't a man alive who hasn't wanted to try the gay life at least once.* She thought of Mark, "It sure would be a shame to waste that on another guy," she said aloud.

It was true, she thought, *Mark was growing on her.* She was beginning to fall for the gorgeous slob. She could do worse. Becoming Mrs. Mark Sims would solve a lot of her problems. It would be nice to have her little Karen back. She was better off upstate with her mother, considering the wild hours she worked. But if she married Mark, she could. No, it wouldn't work. He'd eventually grow tired of her working at the department, and he'd pressure her to quit.

"Damned men," she said out loud, "the bastards are only good for one thing. And that's it!"

For a few minutes her thoughts took her away from the problems at hand. She pulled up to the red light at the corner. Instead of turning left, toward home, she turned right, taking her downtown to the department.

She entered the front of the station. Everything seemed normal. She waved at the girl at the front desk talking on the phone. She passed by Smith's office and heard him hunting and pecking on the typewriter. Becky stuck her head around the corner of his partly opened door and started to ask him how he was, but she could see for herself. He was white as a sheet. "Hey, Lawton, don't you feel good?" she asked with concern.

Her voice startled him, and he jumped.

"Huh...oh yeah. I feel okay. I'm just tired, and I'm trying to get this report done so I can go home and get some sack time." He then went back to his typing, hoping he wouldn't have to answer any more of her questions. He hoped she wouldn't ask about the murder at the beach. Maybe she hadn't heard about it yet.

"Hey, I'll do that for you and you can go on home." As she came up beside him, she read what he was typing. "It seems like there's been an awful lot of suicides lately. People seem so eager to take the easy way out. How old was this guy?"

Smith raised his eyes to meet hers, and she saw a look of genuine sadness in them. "Just twenty years old," he said, barely audibly. Then he returned his eyes to the paper he was working on.

He had ignored the offer, so she turned and headed toward the door. Suddenly she looked back and asked, "How'd he kill himself?"

Without looking up, Smith said, "With a gun."

She left his office thinking of the many suicides that had taken place in the city lately. She saw it was useless to stay around the department. Even Captain Smith didn't want her help. She decided she might as well go on home and take a shower. She suddenly felt very dirty.

Chapter 14

The sheriff's department was carrying on more than their usual investigation. One of their own had been touched.

The coroner performed more than the usual cursory autopsy at the sheriff's request.

As coroner of Leeward County, Waldo Stone had a fairly easy job. Not all cases compared to this one, or even came anywhere near it. This was one cadaver that was in need of true forensic medicine.

Stone worked closely with the sheriff's department. He felt cozy in his feathered nest. It was too late in life to demand changes, so he did what was expected of him. He didn't ruffle feathers and he didn't make waves. He had learned early that it was a lot easier to flow with the trend than to buck the system. And he was definitely a part of the Leeward County system. He marveled at what an intricate system it was.

Years before when he had first decided to run for the coroner's position, he'd had visions of being an exemplary medical representative serving the public need. The colonel made it clear immediately after the election exactly what his professional responsibilities included. He was to sign death certificates, and occasionally, when required, give a medical opinion that suited the department's needs. He was the legal rubber stamp needed to sanction anything the colonel wanted sanctioned.

Usually someone from the department phoned in the description of the death scene. He would give his consent for removal of the body to the morgue or funeral parlor. The type of death the victim met determined the attention he gave it.

Very little exertion was needed on his part. Most nights it was unnecessary to get out of bed. The normal procedure was for the department to have the body taken to the morgue. They seldom requested his presence at the scene of a crime. He realized that they had their own motivations, but he didn't mind. It took less effort on his part. It wouldn't make the dead any less dead, he reasoned, if he weren't there to officially pronounce them dead.

Being a tool of the colonel and a part of the system had its advantages. He was virtually guaranteed re-election every four years. He maintained a high degree of esteem in the community, and he was respected as the ultimate public servant. Even better was the envelope the colonel personally delivered to him the tenth of every month.

Sometimes it was thicker than usual. Often following a particularly heavy caseload. The sudden upswing in suicides, he reasoned, just might mean a fuller envelope. Two months before when he had filed the death certificate on a suicide at the county jail, the colonel had been particularly grateful. The prisoner had taken his life in a fit of despondency read the report. There was no mention of the fact that Captain Yarbrough had attempted to get the prisoner to cooperate by taking the plea bargain the state had offered. Things had gotten a little out of hand. The prisoner had refused and suddenly wound up dead. He had choked to death, as Stone's report stated, but not by the braided sheets from the inmate's bed. It was easy to falsify reports; no one disputed the county coroner's findings.

The Lesso girl's death would require more finesse on his part. Because of the sensationalism of the murder the sheriff himself would be directly involved. Stone had to use more discretion with the sheriff. He carefully wrote and re-wrote the official autopsy statement, using the precise language of the consummate medical professional.

He delivered the finished product to the colonel who read it through.

"All right," Watson said. "Now tell me what the hell it means."

"Well, in lay terms ..." Stone began.

"Lay terms, you're an idiot. Just spell it out in plain, unembellished words."

"Death was caused by involuntary strangulation. It appears that the decedent expired from inhaling and swallowing undigested gastric material."

"You mean she wasn't murdered?"

"Technically....No. There was a substantial amount of cocaine in the blood stream and a small amount in her stomach, along with traces of alcohol. My guess is she was given a drug-laced drink. The lung tissue showed a heavy concentration of marijuana particles. The vaginal canal contained a very large sperm count. I'd say she went to a party, was drugged, gang raped, got sick to her stomach, was too intoxicated to sit up or roll over and suffocated on her own vomit."

The colonel leaned back in his chair, and stared up at the ceiling. "What about the mutilation?"

"The knife wounds had nothing to do with the girl's death. They were done much later, probably twelve to fifteen hours after death. With the depth and severity of the wounds, the body would have been drenched with blood if she had been mutilated before or immediately after death. There was some visceral fluid from the intestinal area, but very little bleeding. Again, my opinion is that someone carved her up to mislead you into thinking the girl was the victim of some satanic cult. Or...it's possible that somebody did it just for kicks."

"Kicks?" the colonel asked.

"Yeah. Some perverted jerk, high on something."

"Did she die there on the beach?"

"No. She was taken there. Probably wrapped in the blanket and plastic sheeting your deputies found in the sea grass. Maybe forensics can turn up something there."

The colonel didn't bother to tell Stone that the lab had failed to find anything except a couple of smudged fingerprints on the plastic.

"So if we find the bastard that moved the body and slashed her up we probably can't go for murder one?" the colonel asked.

"The best you can probably do is manslaughter. That is if you can prove she was deliberately drugged. The rest of it is probably a misdemeanor - moving a body, desecrating a corpse."

The colonel was annoyed. This was the kind of case he despised. There was no way to satisfy the public indignation. If he did find the perverted maniac responsible for the girl's death, he wouldn't be able to prosecute and make it stick. One way or the other he had to go through the motions and make the investigation sound good.

"I'll give your report to the sheriff. He'll be very impressed. You'll probably get a lot of hassle from the media, Doc. Stay away from them the best you can. Give them the gory detail, which always satisfies their taste for the sensational. Don't mention anything about legal responsibility or what we may or may not be able to make stick on a conviction. If they want to play up the cult thing let them, don't offer your opinion either way. Do let them know that we are outraged and doing our damnedest to avenge the girl's death. Don't mention the drug connection, or that she was smoking marijuana. Let's make it sound like she was an innocent victim, through no fault of her own. She was drugged and taken advantage of, and we're going to move heaven and earth to solve the case and bring the culprit to justice."

"Sounds good to me, Colonel," laughed the coroner, getting up from his chair. "You know you can depend on me."

"You're damned right I know I can," he said as Stone moved toward the door.

Watson picked up the phone and issued his first directive in the new case. Every available full and auxiliary deputy was told to place all man-hours to finding the murder or murderers of the Lesso girl. Other cases would take back-burner status until the case was solved. Personnel would report to the squad room for briefing when their shift ended.

Sheriff Myers was up around the clock, making sure he personally talked to each of his men. He waited in his office before meeting with the last shift. He took advantage of the time, with the shift overlapping an hour, to revamp him. He sat elbows resting on the desk, holding his weary head cupped in his hands. After the second shift briefing the colonel had gone home. He'd be on relief when Myers finally finished up.

The sheriff looked at his watch. It had been over twenty-four hours since he'd been home. He thought about taking some No-Doze. If he did he probably wouldn't be able to sleep later. He gave up the thought, and placed his head back in his hands. It would only be a matter of minutes before the men started reporting in for their shift.

"Come in," he said, in response to a knock at the door. He looked up, chin still perched on the heels of his hands. He closed his eyes momentarily and wiped them with the tips of his fingers, trying to relieve the burning sensation.

Captain Yarbrough entered the room, looking rested. He'd gone home the same time as the colonel.

"Come in and sit down, Ray," the sheriff said, beckoning him to an easy chair by the side of his desk. The presences of the hard straight chairs were for men being called on the carpet. It seemed lately there had been more and more need to set straight some new deputy who'd stepped over his bounds.

"You look like you could do with a little rest, Sheriff," Yarbrough said, lowering his burly frame into the plush chair.

Myers pushed away from the desk, and leaned back in his chair, letting out a long sigh. "Tell me, Ray, do you have any ideas on the mess we've got at that beach?"

It wasn't unusual for the sheriff to ask for his and the colonel's opinion. Often solutions were worked out together. Myers depended on their advice and expertise to get him through difficult times like these. He felt at ease with them. They always managed to feed his ego at just the precise moment his esteem flagged.

"Well, Hank," he said, deliberately calling him by his first name, consciously using the leverage it afforded him, "I do know the people are up in arms. The switchboard's been lit up since the newspaper hit the street. And the TV station has been stirring the pot with news reports every hour. You know there's been so much in the news lately about satanic cults and rituals. Every time one of the talk shows has a program on Satan worship we get bombarded with calls. Now this so close to home has everybody nervous.

"You were down at the beach when they found the body, weren't you? How was it?"

"Pretty bad, sir. The girl was badly mutilated. It was definitely a sexual thing. It didn't appear to have anything to do with hampering identification of the body. It was just plain vicious, something you would guess a homicidal maniac would do."

"Do you figure that's what we're dealing with here? A maniac or maybe a serial killer?"

"God, I hope not."

"Incidentally, you went to the Manning funeral didn't you?"

"Yes, sir. The department was well represented."

"How was it....I mean it all went smoothly?"

"Oh, yes. It was really handled nicely," Yarbrough said, watching the tears well up in the sheriff's eyes.

Myers leaned forward in his chair and pulled a handkerchief from his back pocket, all the time keeping his eyes downcast, hoping Yarbrough wouldn't notice the moisture forming.

"He was a wonderful kid. I'll miss him."

"Yes, sir."

Myers was visibly shaken. The sleepless hours and the hurt over the Manning death were exacting a toll. He blew his nose hard, and quickly changed the subject.

"Now about this beach thing, have you heard anything from your contacts on the street?"

"Well, sir, I haven't had much time to get with my contacts. I've tried to help Deputy Lesso with whatever I could. He's taking his sister's death really hard. Trying to keep him under control and give support to his family too is dragging him down. I told him I felt sure you would want him to take off for awhile."

"Of course. What about the family?"

"The girl's mother had to be heavily sedated. They are all due to fly out this afternoon. Back to Michigan. They have their own Lear jet. I've scheduled a department escort for them from the beach to the airport."

"Good," Myers said, obviously impressed. I take it they are wealthy people?"

"From all indications. The father has his own business in Detroit."

"Well, what was the son doing here, working for us?"

I don't know. Scuttlebutt will probably fill in all the blanks. I... wouldn't be surprised if the boy resigns from the department." Ray rose from his chair and walked over to the window. He took out a cigarette and lit it, as he watched the fresh shift filling up the parking lot. "Here comes the next shift. Won't be long 'till you can go home and get some rest."

Myers stood up and sucked in his stomach, making his pants go slack around his waist. He tucked in his wrinkled shirt. He was very conscious of his appearance, and expected the same from his men. "You know, Ray, I'd give up a week's sleep to put this creep behind bars," he said, giving his shirt a final tuck. He took in a long breath, and quickly blew it out. "Well, let's get this over with. The county commissioners frown on paying overtime."

The squad room was alive with chatter. Even with a tragedy like the Lesso murder, they had found something else to talk about. The men seemed to have a knack for momentarily removing themselves from the situation at hand. Much the same as a plumber from plumbing or a bookmaker from betting. Being around crime-related incidents every day, tended to make them oblivious to the hardships and hurts present as a result of a crime. Probably more than anything else it was a defense mechanism. Compassion for their fellow man was not lacking, but the trials and tribulations of the occupation had toughened their exterior. This case was different; one of their own had been touched. It brought out a kinship similar to a fraternity, without the induction ceremonies. The department was their initiation rite.

The sheriff walked to the display table at the front of the room and rested his buttocks on the edge. "Men, I'm sure you've all heard about the murder at the beach." Each man acknowledged with an audible sound or a nod of the head.

"We have a very sadistic and deranged person or persons out there," he said, with a slight motion towards the window with his hand. "This is a hard enough case, but it has hit upon one of our own group. I personally promised the family I'd find the person or persons responsible for this atrocity. I need your help, men. Whatever contacts you have out on the street, use them to the fullest extent. Don't leave any stone unturned. The sadist responsible for this could strike again, and next time it could hit closer to home than to just one of your fellow officers. We all have wives and families. I don't have to tell you that the reputation of the department is on the line with this case. We need to wrap it up as soon as possible. You can make your reports to the colonel, the captain, or myself. The two of them will fill you in on the details of the case at a separate briefing. On your way out stop and pick up a fact sheet from the desk sergeant. That's all I have." The men rose and started to disburse.

The colonel entered the room, passing the men going out. Several spoke, while others nodded as they passed him. He shut the door, leaving the three of them alone in the room.

Myers was exhausted. He sat down fully on the table. He knew from Watson's manner in secluding them that he had something important to say.

"What is it, Don?" he asked wearily. He was anxious to get home.

"Hank, I feel if we were to get right at this, while it's still hot, and apply pressure, we'd get some results."

"What do you have in mind?" Myers asked, with renewed energy. He was spurred on by the possibility of soon getting this out of his hair. It would remove the pressure that the murder had already begun to generate. He'd seen the mechanics of the situation before. First the public becomes mute from shock. When the shock wears off, anger takes its place. Angry people make lots of noise and place pressure on the influential. Then heads start to roll. He didn't need the hassle. If the colonel had an easy solution, he was all for it.

"Well," the colonel began. "We have a lot of creeps out there that love doing their bit for the department. It could be from inner anxiety at being associated with the law, but as long as they keep coming across with information we don't care what thrill they get out of our contact. Let's cruise around today and tonight and see if there are any rumbles. If we have to apply a little pressure, we will, for the good of the community as well as the department. If anything develops, we'll contact you. I know you want this bastard off the street as much as anyone, maybe more."

The colonel always knew when Myers' ego needed a boost. Maneuvering the sheriff to do what he wanted was easy. If he didn't oblige, Watson would go ahead with the plan anyway. He'd done it before. If things went astray, the sheriff never knew about it. The report on his desk in the mornings never gave him the slightest suspicion the department was ever in the wrong. If one of the deputies stepped out of line, Watson would see that he was placed on the report. Fear for their jobs quickly brought the errant back into line. The colonel maintained complete control.

Without waiting for a response from Myers, Watson said, "I've prepared a special duty roster for this case, and I'd like you to take a look at it and give it your okay." He knew the sheriff was too tired to bother with it, when he drew it out of his shirt pocket.

Myers rarely looked at the roster, leaving it to the colonel to handle. "You go ahead with the names you have there. I'm sure you've picked the right people for this assignment," he said. Once more he felt relieved. The colonel would handle everything. He got up and started for the door. "I'm going home to bed. Make sure you let me know if there are any developments."

"Get some rest, Hank. We'll see you Monday," Watson said, turning his attention to Yarbrough. "Here, take this copy. You call those on the top half, above the line, and I'll take the bottom. If there's anybody on the list that's just gone out on patrol duty, get him a relief deputy.

Yarbrough glanced at the paper. The usual men and one woman were on the list. He smiled to himself. Don could have saved himself some time redoing the list; the names were always the same.

"Get going, Ray. I want everybody here in an hour."

Yarbrough left without a word. What could he say? The colonel had a plan. When the time came, he'd reveal it to him.

The men came into the squad room in every type of dress. Some still appeared to be half-asleep. They were aware they were being called for some type of emergency assignment, and they knew better than to keep the colonel waiting, especially the ones whose names were on the bottom of the list. The colonel couldn't stand delay and always gave the impression he wanted things done quicker than yesterday. The names from the top of the list hadn't taken the time to shave either, but the manner in getting them there hadn't been as crude.

Conversation was minimal. The colonel only had to step to the briefing table to gain silence in the room. The sheriff demanded their attention out of respect, the colonel out of fear. There was a great difference between the two in assignment success also. The colonel got what he wanted, period.

"You all know why we're here. The sheriff wants this Lesso killing wrapped up as soon as possible. I want every one of you with contacts, to get out, find them, and put the squeeze on. I want some information, and I want it now. These bastards who think they've been taking a ride on the department, are about to find out what protection costs. If anyone gives you a hassle, let me know. I feel there are a couple who, when put to the test to produce results, might balk. We want to separate the meek and mild from the true believers in one hand washing the other."

As the colonel called off the names, he placed a check by them. In undercover work such as this, he wanted to know each man's location when they were out with the scum on the streets. In case one of the snitches decided to call the scene quits and take their chances with the cops instead of their peers, he wanted their locale. Watson intended to make it very clear that cops were the worst of the lot to double cross.

At present, some of the men were void of contacts, so they doubled up. He would wait and see what the men could turn up. If the situation warranted it, he could always place Becky undercover. With her change of wigs, hippy clothes, and heavy makeup, she fit right into the scene at the dimly lit bars. He'd use her as a last resort, or to anchor someone under his finger where they would do their best for the department. As he checked the names, he asked for the general location that each man would circulate in.

This assignment had top priority, any business that came in unexpectedly would have to wait, or be handled by the regular crew. The detectives would practically control their own workload. He wanted results. It was important to get the department out of the limelight. He didn't like the close scrutiny that a sensational murder case could bring to the department.

"Now men, let's get with it. Make sure you take your portables. I want your progress and location checks every half hour." Watson started calling names. "Deputy Johnson, you and Deets go together. Pool, with Captain Kemp."

All the men held rank of some description, but he neglected to use it on some. It made its mark. Those who had earned rank felt it a privilege to have it tacked to their names. Rank was given to most of the men under the guise of achievement, if unearned. The only way the colonel could control the masses was through the authority rank stood for. "Detective Wally Thomas, and Thornberry, I want you to cover that bar out in the East End tonight. There are usually a lot of snitches there in the evening, looking for broads. Deputys Willy Murray and Jamie Hall, cover the hill. See if any of those low-life prostitutes on the street know anything. I've heard they sometimes pick up some interesting information while getting laid. It will look like a normal patrol. You'll fit right into the scene. Besides, if you can't get anything from the local whores, try that contact on the corner, down the street from the Red Rooster. He's always good for a bottle of wine." The colonel directed his comments to Willy, more than to Thomas. Both men nodded, they understood the order.

The colonel felt he had to spell everything out to them. He didn't give them credit for having common sense like he did most of the others. He used them. Their being black gave him an edge. They were important to his operation. But he never let them forget that they were expendable. There were always other blacks standing on the sidelines, ready to don the green uniform. Little did they realize they, too, were expendable. The colonel made a point of never choosing any with superior reasoning ability. It was all part of his master organizational plan.

The county school system had contributed to the colonel's employment stockpile. It was far from giving quality education. The classes were geared at the underachiever. Minds that were capable of something more became bored with nothing to challenge them. These wasted minds consisted of all ethnic groups. The colonel's supply was replenished at both ends: the lawless and the lawful.

"Corporal Lemmon, Paul Travers ..." he continued to call out names. "You two work the drug culture group. Someone should be ready for a fix and willing to talk. If you know for sure of one that's a heavy needle user, pick up on him. Cruise awhile in an isolated area until his last fix starts to wear off. Your proposition should look better then, and his information should flow."

Lemmon knew the first one to head for. It wouldn't take much time to locate him. Being one of the main suppliers for the drug market, Lemmon would head for the East End Bar, where he made most of his contacts.

The colonel continued to disperse his men. "Sullivan, Barry, you and Bert Dennison just float around. See what you can turn up."

All the men had finally been detailed. The colonel and Captain Yarbrough would go together, in the seek and find patrol.

"Okay, men, you can get started as soon as you check in the with the desk sergeant. He'll notify the dispatcher that although he hears us transmitting, we're working undercover and won't be on official call. I realize it's early in the day, and that most of your best contacts are made at night. But see what you can turn up. I want some concrete information by this time tomorrow morning.

Becky had sat quietly in the back of the room, expecting to be paired with one of the men. She'd been passed over. *Damn,* she thought, daring not to show her disapproval at being left out of the action. She'd psyched herself up for the detail she'd been briefed on. The letdown was devastating to her ego.

As the men filed out Watson turned to her, "Becky, I want to have a few words with you." His tone of voice let her know she wasn't getting called on the carpet for something. He walked to the back of the room and sat down straddle legged in the chair next to her. He rested his arms on the back of the chair. The men were gone, only Yarbrough remained, standing near the table.

"I haven't had the time to get back with you regarding your involvement with the public defender's office. How are things going?"

"Well, sir," she said, "I've been seeing quite a bit of him, but not getting much information out of him."

"Were you able to place the bugs in his apartment?"

"Oh, yes sir."

"Well then we should be getting everything on tape." He turned to Yarbrough for assurance. The captain smiled and nodded.

"I thought," Becky continued, "since I'm not getting much information that I would settle back into my normal work routine, and maybe just see him occasionally."

"No. I want you to stay with it. Full time if necessary."

She could see that the colonel was displeased, so she quickly changed her tact. "He's interested in me, sir, I saw to that. It shouldn't take much longer. I should be able to get him to discuss about anything soon."

"Make it now, Becky. It's Saturday, see if you can't set something up for today or maybe tonight. Who knows, maybe tonight's the night," he said with a smirk that was more dirty than encouraging. "I'll monitor the tapes as they come in. Let me hear something worthwhile." He stood up and she knew that he was finished with her. She walked to the door, passing close enough to Yarbrough to hear him whisper, "Get you're butt in gear, baby."

"Screw you, Yarbrough," she said under her breath.

"I wish you would, doll," he replied with a wink.

Damned men, she said to herself as she walked down the hallway. *That is all men ever think about is their sex. Well tonight I will give them something to make them sit up and take notice.*

Chapter 15

Doty sat at his desk, re-reading the front page. His article had come across well. The human-interest interview with the family by Sandy Mercer had just the right touch of pathos and sympathy. He was glad he didn't have to make the personal contact. He felt more comfortable writing the story details than dealing with the emotional element. The paper had wisely published a school picture of the victim. Ralph had been right; none of the pictures he took could be used. Doty opened an envelope on his desk and dumped out the eight by ten glossies. He studied them one by one, shook his head, put them back in the envelope and slid it into his top desk drawer.

He looked at the wall clock. The county coroner was due to make an official statement in thirty minutes. He'd have time to make that, then stop by the sheriff's department for the official news release. He should be back in plenty of time to meet Jimmy and Alicia for the fishing party. It was shaping up to be a really nice day.

At first the knock was so soft he couldn't hear it in his semi-trance sleep. The second set of raps opened his eyes, but he couldn't quite force himself to get up.

Brian Holcomb was annoyed. He didn't like to be kept waiting, and he certainly didn't like being ignored. He was sure Billy was doing both. He didn't know Carter well, but he didn't like him and he resented having to deal with him. He tried the knob, it wouldn't turn. *I know he's in there,* he said to himself, *his old Trans-Am is here. I know enough about the bastard that he never goes anywhere without his wheels.*

Shading his eyes, he tried to look through the window on the porch. The shade was drawn down tight. This time he banged on the door. "Come on, Billy, open up," he yelled.

The door opened. Billy rubbed his eyes, trying to focus on the figure in the doorway. A frown came to his face; it was Holcomb, the new syndicate contact. He made a sweeping gesture with his arm, inviting the visitor in. "Come in to my parlor, Brian baby," he said with obvious disdain.

Brian was furious by now. He knew Billy was patronizing him and he resented it. "Look, you weaseling little bastard, don't you ever keep me waiting again, or you'll be sorry."

The outburst made Billy angry. He didn't like being told what to do, and especially not by a sniveling little pampered brat like Brian. The last remnants of the high he had enjoyed earlier were suddenly gone, and his eyes glared. "What the hell you going to do about it, you cocky little prick? You going to tell Daddy? Well, Daddy don't cut any ice with me!"

When Billy got mad, he exploded with fury. His usual manner was to keep his cool. In rare instances his temper got out of hand, and the result was usually violent.

Brian decided he'd better back off. One more step backward and he would have been within arms reach of the doorknob.

Billy moved swiftly and with one well-aimed punch caught Brian on the chin, knocking him down.

Dazed, he lay on the floor, with Billy glaring over him. He was afraid Billy would pounce on him and he raised his left arm as if to fend off another attack. "Hey, man, cool it. Let's talk this over." The tone of his voice was much softer now. His jaw was beginning to throb, and he had a queasy sensation in his stomach. "I just came to give you a message, and I'll be on my way."

"You bet your sweet bottom you'll be on your way," Billy said, turning away and sitting down on the sofa. "You wouldn't have gotten in here in the first place if you hadn't been set up as the runner." That was the most degrading word he could think of to call Brian's part in the set up. Lighting a cigarette, he watched the boy struggle to a sitting position. Like a chameleon changing color, Billy's demeanor changed. The rage was gone. His usual cock-sure jaded attitude was back.

As much as he resented this jerk having a position in society, he wouldn't have traded places. The money wasn't the deciding factor for Billy; what mattered was the class people were born into. Society had long since placed a barrier down the center of the tracks, separating the wrong and right side. He used that barrier to his advantage. That way he never had to face what type of an individual someone was, where he belonged in society, or what he deserved to get out of life. With his warped set of values, Billy figured the world owed him something. And society was just another battle he was willing to take on.

"I'm waiting," he said impatiently. "Give me the damn message." He could tell that Brian was hurting and somewhat dazed by the pale expression on his face. He reached down and picked up a towel laying on the floor by the sofa. "Here, wipe the blood off your face," Billy said, tossing the towel.

Brian caught the towel and wiped his mouth. "I think you broke my jaw," he mumbled. "My God, you chipped one of my teeth," he cried as he spit it out with some blood on the towel.

"That's okay, your old man can get it fixed. I hear he can fix anything. He's got plenty of dough; I see to that. Just tell him you tripped over the tennis net." Billy put his head back and laughed. He enjoyed the thought of Brian having to put the pinch on his stepfather. The bastard with all his money and position, stuck with a mealy-mouthed little fart like Brian for a son. Maybe there was some justice in this screwed-up old world.

"Come on, Brian, give me the message," he said with obvious contempt.

"Well, Ruocco called, he's flying in from New Orleans tonight. He wants to meet with you, at my place." Brian tried to make it sound like a request and not a demand. "He set the meet for eight o'clock. Make sure you're not late. He doesn't like to be kept waiting. He has an eleven fifteen flight to Miami. He said he'd have to move on whatever resulted from your meeting, and you'd know what he was talking about." Seeing the look on Billy's face change suddenly, Brian quickly added, "That's exactly what he told me to say and that you would know what he was talking about." Brian had the feeling he'd better get out before Billy lost his temper again. He struggled to his feet and headed for the door. He paused, looking at the dirty towel he was still holding. A new wave of nausea was welling up in his stomach. With disgust he wadded up the towel and with a wrist flipping motion threw it across the room at Billy, hitting him in the chest.

Billy laughed loudly as he watched Brian hurry through the door. He reveled in being able to bring Brian down to his world.

The screen door spring stretched, then released, bringing the door hard against the jam. The bang was Brian's final protest.

"Bastard," Billy said, still laughing.

He sat there thinking about Tony Ruocco coming in a day early and wanting a meet. What could it be? Ruocco had said he would know what it was about, but he didn't. Billy mulled everything over in his mind, trying to remember anything unusual about the last shipment. There hadn't been any major hang ups, at least nothing the syndicate would know about. Everything was cool on this end. Maybe the colonel was responsible. As far as he knew, he was the only link between the department and the wise guys. He was careful to keep it that way. It was his protection from being squeezed out by the colonel. The syndicate must have found out about something they didn't like. Ruocco was either coming in to make some changes or to kick some butt. *Maybe both,* Billy thought. Whatever it was, he'd better get his act together.

"The hell with it," he said out loud, getting up from the sofa and heading for the kitchen. "Billy Boy needs a beer."

Chapter 16

The special assignment detectives mostly went through the motions until dusk. The contacts they needed to make were active after dark.

The night held terror for many people. For the names on the colonel's and his raiders' list of snitches, to be approached was the greatest terror of all. Being on the list in the first place was foolhardy. The colonel owned their hide. Ever present to his beck and call, one move out of line meant the end of freedom, one way or another.

Once hooked, it was better to make the best of it than to fight. Leastwise, that was the way Mike Gross felt about it. He was out of the slammer, able to have a drink and get a fix. That would have been more difficult if he were behind bars.

At Raiford getting drugs wasn't a problem, but he'd done his time in the Leeward County jail. They had made it very clear that he'd have a hard year. Taking the plea, he'd received just a month and three years probation. The judge had said it was to give him a taste of jail.

A month and three for receiving stolen goods, which, to begin with, he didn't know were stolen. Not that it made much difference, his buying the gun. He did feel it was a little ironic that he should be nailed for something of which he was innocent. He'd been involved with much more serious crimes, which could have brought him hard time. All in all, he was probably ahead of the game; except, now the colonel and his henchmen owned his soul and everything else.

Lemmon pulled into the Broken Bow Lounge. Parking under the sprawling oak in the back gave him the darkness to go unseen. He knew he'd found his mark when he saw Gross' old red truck parked in front. He didn't sell to him directly, but one of the larger buyers did. He'd realized he'd be losing out on sales to some of the small time pushers, but it took the heat off him. He still made the bucks, though not as many. The loss wasn't all that great, and he'd make up for it tonight, in two ways. When he finished with Gross he'd have the information the colonel wanted and the punk would be his.

Backing into position, he turned the lights off and left the motor running.

"You go in and bring out Mike Gross," he said to Travers. "You do know who he is, don't you?"

"Yeah, I think I do. Isn't he the one who drives that old red truck out front?"

"That's the one," Lemmon said, nodding his head.

"I pulled him over one night after he came out of the Bock Bar. He thought being a snitch for the department would protect him, and he got a little cocky with me. I soon put him straight," said Travers, getting out of the car. In thirty seconds he had disappeared into the side door of the bar.

Lemmon was glad he didn't have to go in. He wasn't all that crazy about the place. A share of his time had been spent there, making sale contacts. That was an unavoidable necessity in the pushing of the merchandise. Tonight he wasn't pushing...he was pulling.

Travers felt important going into the bar, knowing that every time the door opened, all eyes would turn to see who had entered. He felt special tonight anyway. The sheriff had given him a precise job to do. He always felt honored to do anything for Myers. This was the first real assignment he had given him since the night the Manning kid died.

The sheriff had managed to stay clear of him since then, except for brief conversations. Up to then he'd been the one who'd run all the sheriff's errands. Their relationship had been very special prior to the fateful night. He hoped the boy's death hadn't screwed it up. Travers knew Hank was taking it hard. He'd allow him time to get over it. He still ran errands and carried out regular duties at the office, so it was obvious Hank hadn't held him responsible for the kid's death.

He'd been right; when he opened the door, almost every eye was on him. Once they sized him up, the patrons continued on with what they'd been doing. As the door bumped behind him, Travers stood for a few seconds allowing his eyes to adjust to the darkness.

Scanning the smoke-filled room, he spotted his prey, sitting alone at a table in the corner. He strolled over to him and edged into a chair on the opposite side of the table, in order to look into Mark's face.

When he felt the movement of the table, Gross looked up with blood-shot eyes.

"What the hell do you mean?" he halfheartedly asked.

Travers rested his arm on the table, leaned frontward, and softly said, "There's someone outside who wants to talk to you."

"If someone wants me they can come in here." Gross tried to place where he'd seen the face before. "Who in hell is it anyhow?" Then it dawned on him. He remembered seeing Travers over the top of a flashlight. Its ray headfirst met him in the eyes with its blinding beam, then lowered to the ground. His recollection made his mouth go dry, and he reached for his beer. When he did, the build of Travers' hand went over the top of his and applied pressure to his thumb.

Travers spoke in a low, threatening tone. "Drink your beer and come outside with me. I said someone wants to talk to you now!"

Gross did as he was told, placing the empty beer bottle back on the table. He'd had difficulty swallowing the last part. Prior to Travers joining him, the beer had tasted good. He'd just used his last bucks for a fix, so he drank it slowly, making it last longer. Payday wasn't until Monday and he'd had to settle for the lesser mind-boggling drug.

Travers stood, then pushed his chair in to the table. He patiently waited for Gross to finish.

A barmaid approached him, stepping close enough for physical contact. "And what will it be for you, honey?"

"Nothing tonight, babe, but if you'll give me a rain check, I'll be back another night to collect."

"I'll take you up on that, handsome." she said, giving her hips a little sway as she walked away.

"Teaser," he muttered under his breath.

Gross had fortified himself for his encounter. "Okay, I'm ready. Where is this guy that thinks things are so damned important?" Gross tried to sound tough, but he was scared. The fix he'd had was wearing off sooner than usual. The adrenaline pumping full force into his veins watered down its effect, and fear set in.

Travers held the door open. They exited into the cool Florida night. The contrast to the stuffy bar sent a shiver down Gross' spine. He didn't see anyone in the immediate area and stopped still. Travers gave him a nudge toward the back of the building.

He had come within a few feet of the car before he saw who was in the shadows. His heart sank. Another hunk of his hide was about to belong to the colonel.

"Get in the back seat," Travers said as he opened the door. With his hand on his arm, Gross had no choice but to comply. He got in and Travers got in right behind him, closing the door.

Lemmon put the car in gear and pulled out of the parking lot, heading east. He waited until he hit the street to switch his lights on.

"Hey, where in the hell you going?" demanded Gross, as he made a lunge for the door handle.

Travers grabbed him and pulled him back upright in the seat. "Just stay put and you won't get hurt. We just want to talk to you, out of the earshot of nosy people."

Lemmon didn't speak, as he felt Travers was handling the situation well.

"Hey, man, I don't want to leave my truck there. They might have it towed away if I don't get back before they close," Gross said, in a vain effort to keep from being taken any farther out of town.

They kept heading east. The population began to thin out.

"Oh, your truck will be all right parked right where it is," Travers said, gripping Gross' arm tightly with his hand.

"Let go of my arm. I ain't going nowhere." Knowing all they wanted was information, he tried to get in a comfortable position. He was trying to relax; he wasn't having any luck. He'd tell them what they wanted, then go get his truck, and make tracks for home.

"Man, I hope this doesn't take long. I've got to get to bed and get some sleep. I've got a good job now. I make six bucks an hour on construction."

"Tomorrow's Sunday, Mike. You can sleep late," said Travers.

Lemmon finally broke his silence. He made a low whistle sound. "Six bucks and hour, that'll buy a lot of drugs every week."

Gross feigned ignorance. "Drugs? What the hell you talking bout? I don't use drugs. Oh...once in awhile I smoke a joint, but hell, who doesn't? I don't use any hard drugs...who said I did anyhow?"

"Lay off it, Gross. We know you're on the hard stuff. Look at the redness around your nose. You've burned the membranes in your nostrils sniffing coke," said Lemmon. "Besides, we aren't pulling you for using the stuff. That's your problem, you have to cope with it. We just want a little information, so stop your sweating. We need some help with a case we're working on. We figured you'd want to help."

Gross backed off when he heard the word case.

"Sure. But, hey, what do I know? I don't bother anybody. I'm staying clean. You know I'm on parole. I don't want to do hard time for violation, so I stay to myself. I don't know anything about anything." He was starting to panic. "Now, why don't you take me back? I'll get my truck and go home to bed." He'd been carrying on the conversation all by himself. They didn't mind. He was working himself into the frenzy they'd hoped for. It made their job quicker and easier. Soon, maybe, they could all go home to bed.

Lemmon had reached a remote area off Palm Beach Boulevard, on Orangewood. He pulled off the road and stopped, dousing the lights. This road was barely used. It dead-ended further down the road, making a good petting spot for the younger set. Fact was, this wasn't the first time Lemmon had used this road for meetings.

Lemmon turned around in his seat to eyeball Gross as he talked. "Now, why don't you have a cigarette to settle you down, then we'll talk." He held out a pack to Gross. With trembling hand he drew one out. "What the hell you shaking for, Mike? Travers told you not to worry about your truck. It'll be all right. If it does happen to get towed away, we'll see that you get it back."

Gross' nerves were going fast, "Damn it, what the hell do you want out of me?"

"Hey," said Travers, "Watch the yelling." He put one finger in his ear and shook it, as if trying to release sound waves that couldn't exit. "You might hurt my eardrums."

Lemmon switched to a more serious line of talking. "You've probably heard about the murder on the beach, and how she was wasted. We just thought you might've heard something, or that you'd like to wager a guess as to what happened."

Gross was really wild now. He leaned to the back of the front seat. "You creeps, you ain't going to pin that thing on me. I've got an alibi. Besides, I don't go to the beach. Only when the crew is working out there." He had to wipe the sweat off his forehead with his shirtsleeve to keep it from running into his eyes.

Lemmon was pleased to see his reaction. He knew it wouldn't take long now. "Think about it, Mike. Maybe you can remember some little thing...any little thing at all. No matter how it might appear to you, it could give us a good clue to work on." He tried to work on his sympathy. "You should have seen that poor girl's body, Mike. The things she had done to her shouldn't be done to a rattlesnake." Lemmon continued to talk, hoping it would give Gross time to think, but mainly to cover the dead silence in the car. "Well, Mike, what do you say?"

"I don't know nothing, man." He shook his head from side to side. "Come on, take me back to my truck so I can go home and get some sleep. I'm tired."

"Well, Mike, I guess we'll have to tell the colonel you just didn't want to cooperate. He won't be happy to hear that we found you in a bar, knowing you're still on parole.

The mention of the colonel caused Gross to shake twice as much. The wrath that these two men could ring down on his head was nothing compared to what the colonel was capable of.

"Wait a minute, you guys. I just thought of something. Now.... mind you, I don't know any names, but maybe it could help. I heard there was this place out at the beach that holds some pretty swinging parties. I don't know where it is, but it's on the beach somewhere. I don't know first-hand, it's just hearsay, remember."

The silence was deafening.

Travers finally spoke. "Now come on, Mike. You want us to believe that you've never been there? Plenty of dope and more females than you can handle in one night?"

"Look you guys, I've been staying on my parole and not getting into any trouble. I got my job, and I don't want to lose it. I'm finally getting a direction in my life. I don't need the trouble those parties could bring. All that jail bait makes that scene all the more taboo for me."

Thinking a minute, Lemmon said, "Well, I believe you, but I'm going to expect you to come up with a few names and a place, so we'll be in touch."

"Sure, sure." He'd been on a hook, and he was relieved to be getting off.

Lemmon handed Gross a cigarette. "Here, you need this." Gross looked at the cigarette and smiled. Then he took it and lit it on the match that Travers provided him. He drew the smoke in and sat back against the seat, relaxing for the first time since he'd been in the car. "Man, that's some of the best grade I've ever had," he said, as he exhaled the sweet-smelling smoke.

"Nothing but the best for our friends," replied Lemmon, with a smile on his lips. He put the car in gear, pulled the lights on, and turned around on the narrow dirt road. He glanced in the rear-view mirror at Gross enjoying the fruits of their labor, as he headed back to Palm Beach Boulevard and the old red truck.

"See what you can find out for us, Mike," Travers said as they pulled into the parking lot. "We need a name and an address, otherwise ..."

"Yeah, I know," Gross said, exiting the car and hurrying to his truck.

Both deputies laughed as he pulled away and accelerated down the street.

"Did you see that kid shake when I handed him the reefer? He's not going to give us any trouble," Lemmon said.

"Yeah, I sure did. I hope he can come up with something," Travers said, getting out of the back seat and into the front.

"You know, I think we should take a ride over on the hill and see what the black boys have turned up." Taking a right at the corner, he drove through the old part of town, coming out at a stop sign just past the city limits, in the middle of the colored section.

Lemmon looked up and down the street. "Do you see the cruiser?"

"Yeah," Travers said, pointing to an area off to their right.

Lemmon pulled up behind the cruiser and flashed his lights up and down to signal to the deputies. It was time for their half hour check with headquarters. Travers made the call while Lemmon got out and approached the vehicle. When he got close enough to see what was taking place in the back seat he stopped and exclaimed," Well, I'll be horn swaggled!" Placing his hands on the ledge of the rolled down front window he spoke to Hall in a subdued voice, "What in the hell is going on back there?"

"Willy's interviewing one of the local gals," Hall whispered back. "She needed a little persuasion, Corporal," he said, nodding to in the direction the action in the back seat.

"Is that what you call hands-on interrogation?" Lemmon said with a chuckle.

"I guess he's using his hands, too." Hall answered with a deadpan expression on his face.

Travers had walked up and was peering in from the opposite side of the cruiser.

"Is this what they mean by police brutality?"

"Yeah," laughed Lemmon.

"Talk about a lethal weapon," Travers howled.

Willy looked up from his prone position. "I think she's about ready to talk now," he said. With a final lunge he eased his movement and proceeded to dismount the shapely female under him. "Care to have seconds, Corporal?"

"No thanks, Willy," Lemmon replied. "I'll take a rain check." He was on Willy's ground now, and he didn't want to show animosity to him.

"Come on, Willy," said Travers, as he looked around, hoping no one's attention was drawn to the cruiser. "Put your neck back in your damned pants and get the broad out of the back seat."

"Dis here ain't no neck man, id be a chicken choker," Willy said in a thick drawl, as he stroked himself. "Thanks for the info, Delilah," he said, giving her a pat as she got out of the back seat of the cruiser.

"Any time, Willy honey. You know that...just anytime," she drawled back, giving her backside a pat with her hand as she drifted off into the darkness of the night.

The three of them watched as Willy undid the front of his pants and tucked his shirt in. He moved his body back and forth, shaking everything back into its normal position.

Lemmon's patience finally gave out. "Well? Come on, Willy, give. What the hell did she say?"

"She said there is this one white weirdo that comes down every once in awhile. He has no set pattern to his visits, but the actions he puts her through are a pattern. That's why he stands out in her mind." He paused, prompting Lemmon to bid him to continue.

"Well," he said, giving his pants the final okay by rubbing his hand over his crotch to make sure everything was in place. He gave a little sigh under his breath, still thinking about Delilah. It sidetracked his thoughts for a moment.

"Damn it, Willy, will you quit goofing off and get on with what she had to say?" Lemmon was annoyed.

Willy snapped back and tried to think of exactly what she did say. It was hard to make words sink in when the joy of the encounter with Delilah was still so fresh in his mind. "Well, she saw this weirdo in the area about a week ago. He takes her to her room and makes her lay on her bed. It has four posts. He has her spread eagle, then ties her to the bed. At first when he tried to do it, she threw a fit. She said she didn't know him well enough to let herself be placed in a helpless situation like that. Then he told her he wouldn't tie here up, if she'd let him do what he wanted to do to her. He told her he wouldn't hurt her, but when he brought out a broom handle about a foot long, she had her doubts."

Up to now, Lemmon leaned back on the car smoking a cigarette. When Willy mentioned the broom handle it brought him to a standing position. "Go on about the broom handle, Willy," he said excitedly.

"She asked what he was planning to do with it. He told her, use it in place of his joystick. Now I'll tell you, Delilah is a fine lay, but no way can she take a foot-long broom handle. No women's insides can conform to that kind of rigid stick. Well, finally Delilah and this weirdo dude decided on an appropriate sized object to put in while he went and did his business in the corner."

Lemmon slowly crushed his cigarette out in the sand with his boot. He looked up from the extinguished sparks at Willy. "I think we may have something here boy, and we have you to thank."

Willy didn't mind being called boy out of pure excitement at being credited with helping to solve a crime.

"Did she say anything about what he looked like?" Lemmon asked.

"Well, that's really weird too. Sometimes he would come around in different colored hair, other than his normal color hair. She said his real hair resembled straw with a kink in it, rather than the normal straight hair a white man would have. It was his own hair, though. She said she was sure it wasn't a wig."

"Did she give you any more details on what he looked like?" Travers asked. He had remained silent until now, with Lemmon beating him to all the questions before he could get a chance to speak.

"Yeah, she said it would be awful hard not to remember a creep like that. He was small, kinda prissy, you know, not real manly like. Someone who wouldn't strike her as going the whore routine."

Travers motioned for Lemmon to give him a cigarette as he said, "It doesn't sound like anything about him is routine. There are weirdos, and then there are weirdos."

"Anything else? What about the eye color, scars, things like that." The cop in Lemmon was coming out now.

"She said he had dark eyes, but that they were real small. Have you guys ever looked a gator right in the eyes?" Willy asked.

Lemmon scowled. He wondered what an alligator had to do with anything, but before he got a chance to ask, Willy said, "Well, she said his eyes reminded her of a gator's eyes, never blinking, just staring coldly at her."

"What does he drive?" asked Travers.

"Oh yeah, he used to come around in an old VW, but lately he had a different car. He always parked it out of sight. She said the last couple times they walked to her place. He would appear from out of nowhere, like he slithered out from under a rock. He's starting to get on her nerves, she said. It wouldn't be so bad if he'd pick on some of the other chicks, but he just wants her. She told me she really doesn't want to have anything more to do with him, but she's afraid if the word gets out that she's being choosy, it might hurt her business, and her old man wouldn't like that." Willy added that more as an afterthought that anything else. He understood the situation more than the white men did. He lived in this hellhole and knew the way it functioned.

"I think we just may have something here, men," Lemmon said. "You two keep up the good work and continue to scout around. And Willie, if you have to interrogate any more of these...ladies...get the cruiser off the street."

"Yes, sir," said Willie, with a smile. "From now on I'll do my interrogating down the alley behind the Laundromat."

Lemmon turned and quickly headed back to the car. Travers was caught off guard by his hasty departure and had to run to catch up.

Lemmon backed the car up about twenty feet and put it in park. He sat staring out the windshield. "When Willy was describing the weirdo... did it remind you of anybody, Paul?"

"I only know one bastard that would fit that description. But I don't know that even he would go in for anything as kinky as that."

"Did you ever see him drive a VW?" Lemmon asked.

"Nope. But there's a lot I don't know about the creep."

"He's just crazy enough to pull a stunt like that."

"I could see him playing games with some black whore, but why would he slice up a teenager?"

"I know, it doesn't make sense. But I'll be damned if he doesn't fit the make."

"If it is him, Larry, the department won't touch him. Not with the set up the way it is."

"I think we'd better get on the horn and set up a meet with the colonel," Lemmon said, as he pulled the car out and headed in the direction of Fort Manson.

Travers reached for the microphone. "532 to 555." He waited for a few seconds.

"555 to 532, go ahead."

"Go to channel 5, sir." Not waiting for a response, he reached down and switched his dial to 5, then pushed the switch that automatically scrambled the talking so it couldn't be monitored, even at the station.

"Go ahead, 532."

"What's your 10–20, sir?" Travers asked the colonel.

"I'm down at the south end of the old bridge. What's up?"

"We think we may have something on the beach case."

Before he could say anything more, Watson switched back. "Get on over to my location and tell me about it. I have to stay here to see that they fish some jerk out of the river."

"10–4," Travers replied.

Lemmon switched on the lights and siren and floored the accelerator.

Willie and Hall sat in the cruiser and talked. They didn't feel it necessary to go out on the road, at least until Willy could pull himself together. When they had the chance to goof off, which wasn't very often, they took it. There wasn't anyone around now to tell on them. The sound of their voice traveled out on the still night air.

"Willy, do you think Delilah will be able to finger that dude?" Hall asked.

"Sure, if they line him up without his pants."

"Naw, I'm serious."

"She ought to be able to; she saw him often enough. With a little persuasion she should be able to give the colonel a good description."

Willie was distracted by a rustling noise in the bushes. "Did you hear that?" he asked, staring into the shadows.

"Probably just a mangy mongrel. We'd better get back on the road," Hall said, starting the car. He pulled up to the stop sign on the corner, then turned right, heading down Anders Avenue.

"There's Delilah, waiting for her next john to come by. That gal's a real hustler." said Willie.

"In more ways than one, " Hall chimed in.

"Yeah," Willie said in a low growl, deep in his throat.

Delilah saw them turn the corner, but didn't acknowledge that she knew them. It wouldn't go down very well, her having an in with the fuzz. She liked Willy a little more than the rest of her customers. He always wanted to have her talk, but she didn't mind. She was used to carrying on a conversation while giving a man his desserts. It was only a job to her. The bucks that it brought in were few by the time everyone was paid off, with her being at the end of the line. Some weeks all she got was the sex, like a lot of the other prostitutes on the hill. By the time the husbands, boyfriends, and pimps got their money to support their habits, there was usually nothing left for the working girls. It was a vicious circle, and the sheriff's department was reaping all that flew off the top.

Willie was a refreshing break from the routine, and she really didn't mind the fifteen minutes he required of her time. Besides, she knew he'd make sure she was never hassled by the department. A freebee now and then to the sheriff's deputy added to her standing. A lot of the girls would have loved to put out to him just to claim they were choice merchandise. Besides, she never had to go through her routine to get his business. Her usual procedure was to stand on the corner, and give a little pat when a likely candidate approached. If she felt real daring, she would lift her short skirt up and give a sneak preview of what the customer could receive, for a small fee.

A car slowed down and pulled off the road just beyond where she was standing. It gave its customary sign, one flash with the right turn signal to signify he was her next trick. She ran up, opened the car door and hopped in. The car sped off into the night.

Chapter 17

Lemmon pulled up to the south end of the old bridge. The night was alive with flashing lights on police cars and emergency vehicles waiting at the scene.

Curious onlookers had pulled off the road, occupying every available parking area.

Lemmon gave up trying to find a place, and pulled to the far right of the pavement, putting his flashers on. "Hell, traffic is moving so slowly. I won't worry about the car. Let's go see what the hell's going on."

He and Travers ran to the familiar forms standing on the riverbank. Working their way through the crowd, they approached the accident scene. The situation needed no explanation.

Instead of turning either rights or left at the dead end Street, someone had gone straight over the bank into the river and landed upside down in the water. The wheels of the car still rotating were all that could be seen sticking out.

Lying on the ground was a man in his early forties. An ambulance stood by waiting to carry him either to the hospital or the morgue.

A medic shouted, "I have a faint heartbeat. Let's get him loaded."

They quickly placed him in the ambulance and it went screaming off into the night.

"Man, what a night this has been," the colonel said, running his hand over his forehead. He massaged his eyes, trying to soothe them. "My eyes feel like they're on fire. This is for the birds. Guess I'm getting too old for these late night hours."

"What the hell happened, Colonel?" asked Lemmon, looking around.

"It appears," the colonel said, "it's a D.U.I., but we won't be sure until the reports come through. We won't worry about that until we find out if he's going to make it or not. He's in pretty bad shape. The medic said it looked like one of his lungs had collapsed. If he pulls through, he'll be picking sand out of his ears till doomsday. He literally was buried headfirst in the sand." He laughed and shook his head. "The stupid jerk. If a passerby motorist hadn't seen him go in, he'd have probably drowned. Another guy had to jump in and help. If the tide had been in, he'd have been a goner for sure. They couldn't fight his weight and the water too."

The crowd began to disperse.

The colonel became annoyed when he looked around and saw his deputies standing idle. He blared, "Anyone that's not on special detail get you'r tails 10–8."

Deputies scattered, piled in their cruisers, and pulled out in all directions.

"Damn freeloaders," he said disgustedly. He then turned to Lemmon and Travers. "Now, what's this information you have on the beach case? Do you have a lead we can work with?"

"I think so, sir. I was talking with a black whore down on the hill tonight. She told us about a weird screwball that likes to do kinky things. The most interesting is, he likes to stick things up her, while he gets his own jollies in the corner."

The colonel stood silent in thought. Then he said to Lemmon, "It sure sounds like the same M. O. Do you think we could locate her again tonight?" He directed no conversation to Travers. He'd only been included tonight so the colonel could release Becky.

"Hey Colonel," one of the detectives yelled. "There's a call for you, from the captain. He wants to know if you can handle a signal 5?"

"Holy Mackrel, now a murder! What next?" the colonel said, as he ran for his car, slid across the seat and picked up the mike. "555 to headquarters."

Lawton Smith replied immediately. "Go ahead 555."

"Take this to channel 5 and scramble," the colonel ordered.

"There's been a murder down on the hill, Colonel. They found a woman in the ditch back of the Club 52. There's no doubt about her being dead. The man who phoned in the report refused to give his name.

You know how they like to remain anonymous down there."

"I'll take it," the colonel replied, "and I'll take most of the men here with me. They'll report in as they go on duty. Mark them up. The rest will stay on special detail."

"10–4," Smith replied. He began checking the numbers in, as the dispatcher acknowledged them.

The colonel called to Yarbrough, who was standing on the embankment talking to the wrecker crew. "Ray, come on. Looks like we've got ourselves another homicide."

Yarbrough scrambled up the embankment to the cruiser and slid behind the wheel.

The line of screaming departmental cars going down Palm Beach Boulevard was deafening, drawing the attention of the occupants in the houses they passed. Taking a right, all went through the red light at Seaboard. The oncoming traffic relinquished their right of way to the flashing lights.

It was difficult locating the scene of the crime when they arrived in the area.

"Damn. Everyone in nigger town's out," the colonel said.

"It's easy to tell which ones aren't involved. They always arrive ahead of us," Yarbrough added.

The squad cars pulled up, surrounding the bar like an army.

The colonel hopped out before Yarbrough could stop the car. He walked over to a deputy that was on the scene trying to control the crowd that had gathered. "Where's the body, deputy?"

The deputy pointed to the drainage ditch at the rear of the bar. "Out there, sir."

The detectives waded through the thick underbrush arriving at the canal; some reached it sooner than others.

Only the black men showed haste on the force. In most instances, the corpse was someone they knew. The community was closely woven and most of the residents knew one another.

Yarbrough reached the ditch first. He peered in. "My God!" He exclaimed. He turned around and looked away, just as the colonel reached his side.

Watson's eyes spotted what had made Yarbrough turn away. "Man! What the hell's cut loose in this town?" He said under his breath. He turned and yelled out, "Keep those people away from here, and someone gets a blanket or something to cover this woman up!"

Willy was having a difficult time getting his oversized frame through the thicket.

Hall had already seen the body in the ditch and started back to the cars. He tried to stop Willy from going on. "Come on....stay here," he said, taking hold of Willy's arm. But he was too big and strong and broke away from Hall's grasp. He ran the remaining feet to the edge of the ditch. Without a word he dropped to his knees, sliding down the slope.

The colonel saw what was happening and shouted to no one in particular, "Get him the hell out of there!"

Yarbrough and Hall slid down the back. They tried to move Willy out of the filth from the ditch.

"My God in heaven, who in hell would do a thing like this to Delilah?" Willy's anguished voice pleaded.

"Come on, Willy," Hall said, as he tried to pry Willy's arms from around Delilah's neck. He was smeared with her blood.

Hall knelt next to Willy. "Come on out of here, Willy. We can't do anything for her now 'cept find the animal that did this horrible thing to her."

Hall's soothing manner worked. Willy let Delilah's head slowly slip from his grasp back to the ground. Yarbrough and Hall finally got Willy to his feet and they started back up the slope. The blood from the body had mixed in with the slime and they had difficulty keeping they're footing.

Willy was being led out through the trampled weeds just as Lemmon arrived.

They passed him without a word.

Lemmon looked puzzled. "What's Willy crying about?" he asked, as he walked up to the colonel.

Watson gestured into the ditch.

Lemmon looked down, did a double take and then focused on the body. "Oh, my God!" he exclaimed.

Delilah lay on her back, clothed only in a blouse. Her wide-open eyes still exhibited the horror of her death. A piece of cord bound her wrists together and her legs were spread wide apart. Someone had used a knife to cut her from anus to navel. The intestines had spilled out of the abdominal cavity. Clots of blood and tissue, making it difficult to make out what other things had been done to her, held those that weren't on the ground, in.

"Better go call the coroner. He'll have to come out on this one," the colonel told Lemmon.

"He won't be happy;" Lemmon answered, as he headed back to the car.

The colonel shouted after him. "Get a K-9 unit in here." Then he added in a softer tone, "I don't think we'll get anything with all this garbage around."

Lemmon wove his way through the crowd and back to the car. He called the dispatcher and relayed the colonel's messages. The dispatcher acknowledged and proceeded to notify the proper officials.

Lemmon walked back to the ditch and stood next to the colonel. "Sir, I need to talk to you about the woman in the ditch."

"Did you tell the dispatcher to step on it?" Watson asked.

"Yes, sir. And I requested an I.D. unit also."

"Good," the colonel replied.

"Sir, I really need to speak to you."

The colonel was annoyed. "All right, let's go over there away from the stink. The garbage smell is bad enough, but all that blood and guts is a little bit much."

Lemmon was also relieved to vacate the area.

"Well, what's so damned important, Larry? Make it quick. We have to make sure no one does anything stupid. We have to be extra careful in this area and make sure nobody's civil rights are tread on."

Lemmon wanted to scream at the colonel to shut him up. "She's the one I told you about earlier," he said, pointing to the ditch. "The one we were coming down here to see."

The frown on the colonel's face turned to surprise. "No kidding? It'll be interesting to see what the coroner turns up. I hope the bastard's sober," he muttered under his breath. "Tonight we really need his expertise. We've got to find this butcher fast."

Sirens could be heard at a distance. They pulled to a stop close by.

A large hulk of a man emerged from the crowd and calmly walked over to the ditch. He stood there peering down at the body. No one tried to stop him. Most thought he was part of the sheriff's retinue.

A deputy had found a blanket and descended the bank to cover the body.

As he did, the man turned away from the ditch. When he faced the crowd, tears were streaming down his face. He made his way back into the crowd and disappeared.

"Who the hell was that?" Yarbrough asked.

A voice from the crowd said, "That was her man."

The ambulance crew made their way through the crowd. Following behind them was Waldo Stone, the coroner.

The silence that fell on the crowd was hard on the nerves. The detectives found it difficult to talk. This increased the already strained atmosphere.

The coroner took a quick look at the corpse and said, "Let's get this thing wrapped up and back to my garage. Be sure you pick up all the entrails." The corpse was placed in a body bag and carried up the embankment to a stretcher, then to the waiting ambulance. It sped away without benefit of the siren.

The K-9 dogs were trying to pick up a scent with no luck. The scattered garbage hampered them from finding a trail. They led their handlers from one pile of decaying rubbish to another, and then always back to the ditch where the body had lain.

One of the K-9 handlers hollered to Watson. "Hey, Colonel, we can't get anything out here. It's no use with all this garbage around." Without getting the official okay, he motioned to the other handler to load the dogs' back into the pen on the wagon.

The colonel nodded his approval, not caring that they had proceeded without his say so. He didn't blame them for wanting to get away from the odor.

They hastily loaded and left.

The coroner came up out of the ditch, rubbing his hands on his pants legs. He reached to the ground, picked up a dirty rag and finished wiping his hands as he walked to the group of deputies. "This sure is a nasty one, boys," he said, throwing the rag down.

"I want a full report as soon as possible" said the colonel." These people won't let this lie long, Doc."

Yarbrough crouched low on the ground, pulling aimlessly at some weeds, his mind deep in thought.

The colonel paced from the ditch to the bar, watching as the deputies took statements from individuals in the crowd.

Now he had two murders to trigger the public's furor. Oddly enough they couldn't be farther apart, yet they had something very much in common: a deranged person was killing women. Murders on the hill weren't unusual, but they were normally simple shootings, knifings or strangulations. And they were usually committed in a moment of passion or because of gambling debts or jealousy. Nothing had come close to what he had seen tonight. This had the smell of premeditation and he couldn't even make an educated guess as to what the motive might be.

The colonel assessed the strengths and weaknesses of the deputies still on the scene. Willy and Hall weren't of much value generally, but in this instance they could prove their worth. He was sure they could acquire information he needed faster and better than any of the white deputies.

Willy was sitting slumped over in his patrol car with the door open, his feet planted on the ground. Hall stood by the door smoking a cigarette.

The colonel walked over and stood in front of both of them. "How are you feeling, Willy?"

"Better, sir. I feel all right now."

"I take it you knew the dead woman?"

"Oh, yes sir. That was Delilah Short. She may have been a prostitute, but she was good people."

"I'm sure she was. We're going to need some deputies to inquire and take down statements from individuals in the area. Ones that didn't give information over by the ditch. Are you and Hall up to staying?"

"Oh, yes sir. That'll be fine," Willy said.

Hall nodded in agreement.

The colonel looked at the blood and mire on Willy's shirt and pants. "If you'd like to go home and change clothes, go ahead. We'll hold things here until you get back."

"No, Colonel. Maybe seeing Delilah's blood on me will make people more eager to talk. Besides, we don't want to waste no time on this."

"Good thinking, Willy. I'll leave another man to help you." He walked over to Detective Thomas. "I want you to stay here with Willy and Hall to help with some statements. I don't think you'll get much. But make a first class effort anyway."

Thomas's face expressed his discomfort at being left on the hill.

The colonel looked around and asked, "Who are you riding with tonight?"

Thomas recognized a chance to be reprieved at the last minute. He quickly said, "Thornberry, sir," pointing in the deputy's direction.

"Hey, Thornberry, come over here!"

The young deputy hurried over to the colonel. "Yes, sir?" he asked.

"You're to stay here on the hill and help Thomas take statements. Willy and Jammie Hall will be helping too. I want every possible lead followed up," he told them as he walked away.

The men who were wise to the colonel's procedures were smart enough to leave as soon as they surveyed the scene. The newer men on the squad hadn't yet tasted his tactics. Normally, the chain of command dumped all the garbage on down the line until it got to the end of the pole. Tonight, Thomas and Thornberry were low men on the totem.

The colonel turned back to Willy and Hall. "I'm counting on the two of you to get us something we can move on. Whoever this nutcase is, we've got to get him off the streets before he hurts somebody else. Help me solve this case and there'll be commendations and promotions too."

Willy knew that this was his chance to make some points with the colonel.

"Detectives Thornberry and Thomas will stay to help you gather information. Do what you can in the next few hours, and then knock off for the rest of the night. Keep the patrol car and bring it back in tomorrow. I want you both at the ten o'clock meeting with anything you've been able to dig up."

"We'll be there, Colonel," Hall said.

Willy nodded.

The promise of the rest of the night off, and the use of the patrol car, spurred the two men into motion.

Most of the sightseers and curious had gone back into the bar, to commence where they had left off. The majority hadn't seen the ghastly sight in the ditch. Those who did needed to get drunk, damned good and drunk.

The two detectives let Willy and Hall take care of questioning the patrons on the inside, while they mingled outside. So far all had struck out.

Beginning to feel uncomfortable, Thornberry said to Thomas. "Hey, Wally, what say we call it quits? We aren't getting anywhere here. I'd much rather come back here in the daylight. These bastards sure do look menacing in the dark."

Thomas was eager to oblige. He walked to the bar door and opened it, hoping to get the attention of one of the deputies.

Willy was writing something down on a piece of paper. He caught Hall's eye and motioned to him to come out front. Several minutes later the two deputies exited the bar and walked over to Thomas and Thornberry waiting by their car.

"Did you get something in there, Willy?" said Thomas, noting the paper in the deputy's hand. His question lacked enthusiasm. He frankly didn't care one way or another. All he wanted to do was get the hell out of there.

"Hey man, we didn't get much of anything. All I found out was the last time she was seen alive she was running to get into some john's car. They weren't sure of the make or the color. Down here, with so many prostitutes on the streets, they don't pay no 'tention."

"What a night this has been," Thornberry exclaimed.

The rest nodded in agreement.

"I'll take back the information you got." Thomas said, taking the paper out of Willy's hand, "and give it to the colonel."

All Willy could say was, "Okay." The paper was already out of his grasp.

They bid each other good night and parted.

"Man, this is unbelievable," Thomas said, leaning his head back on the seat and shutting his eyes.

After a couple of minutes of silence, Thornberry asked, "Hey, you sleeping?"

"Naw, I was just thinking. Both of these murders have been so sadistic. They both parallel, with the disposals of their bodies. No one's been able to locate anyone that knows anything about who called in the original report. With the black woman, it could have been anyone connected with her profession: disgruntled customer, an angry suitor, or maybe that guy that someone said was her man. Though it's not likely he'd go back to the ditch and expose himself."

"I don't think he did it. He looked pretty distraught when he passed by me. I didn't know who he was, or I'd have stopped and questioned him. Even the colonel was surprised by how calm he was. It's not normal for a person to see a loved one in that condition, and not go all to pieces."

"This whole damned place is not normal, if you ask me." Thomas said, shaking his head. There is something sick about having your woman out selling herself to get money for your next fix."

"It's quite a place all right," agreed Thornberry.

They parked the car in the station lot, got out and opened the plate-glass star-decaled door. The well-lit room was in sharp contrast to the atmosphere they had just left.

"Well, at least we won't have to make out a long report before we can go home." Thomas said.

Larry Lemmon pulled in the parking lot of his apartment building, turned the motor off and sat there thinking. He wondered if he had done the right thing in not giving the colonel the description of the weirdo with the broomstick. Oh, hell, he thought, there probably wasn't any connection with the other murder anyway. He got out, and started up the stairs to his apartment. He noticed that his brother's van was parked in one of the woman tenant's reserved space. *There will be hell to pay tomorrow when that old lady complains to the landlord,* he thought. He unlocked the door and quietly entered. Jim was sprawled out asleep on the couch.

Lemmon was exhausted. He wasn't even going to take a shower; he was too damned tired. He headed for the bedroom. A knock on the door stopped him short.

"Oh, Damnit!" he said disgustedly, as he turned back to answer it.

He opened the door and motioned the young man in. He quickly shut the door, not speaking word until it was securely closed.

"You fool; this is a helluva time to be coming around. I told you before, I have to keep a working man's hours. I need my sleep."

The young man, in his early teens, stood just inside the door. He tried to alibi his late arrival. "I've been by four times tonight, and I couldn't catch you home." He pointed to Jim on the couch. "Your brother wouldn't sell to me without your okay. If you'll get it, I'll be on my way."

Lemmon knew with the service he conducted, he had to expect this type of thing. He had laid down stringent rules at the very beginning, and not many had deviated from them. "Okay, how much do you want?" he asked, in a more controlled tone of voice.

"I'll take two fingers' worth." the kid said sheepishly.

"What! You bothered me in the middle of the night for a lousy two finger?"

"All right, make it an ounce. If I get busted for having that much-"

Lemmon interrupted him. "Hey," he held out both hands, palms up. "I told you kids not to worry about getting busted. We take care of our own. If the city boys get you, you'll end up at the county jail anyhow so don't sweat it."

Lemmon left the room. A few seconds later, he came back with a small plastic bag. The annoyance he felt earlier came back. "Give me the money, and get the hell out of here," he said, handing the bag to the young man.

The teenager handed him the wadded-up money and started for the door.

"Hey, wait a second, till I douse the lights." Lemmon said, rushing to the door.

The boy stopped until Lemmon turned out the light. Then he quickly departed without a further comment.

Lemmon didn't bother turning the light back on. He felt his way into the bedroom and collapsed on the bed.

Chapter 18

Delilah's body had been placed in the coroner's garage. There were no lights, so Stone had gone in and lain down until the sun came up enough to do his work.

The clean but cramped morgue at the hospital was adequate for the autopsies necessary for an institution, but not for the detailed legal work required of a county coroner. The messy autopsies, referred to as stinkers by the knowledgeable, were done in Stone's dirt-floored garage. A hose attached to an outside spigot was the only water. He and his three medical assistants had worn the bloodstained floor to a smooth patina. The dissections, the human waste, the remnants of blood and tissue had dyed the floor a mauve rose, resembling something from Egyptian times, when berries were used for coloring.

The mess and the smell didn't bother Waldo Stone. The only corpses that got to him were those of children who had died mysteriously, usually as the result of abuse and beatings.

The body that lay before him was just another cadaver. Black, white, male or female, they were all the same basically. He proceeded with the autopsy before any of his attendants arrived.

May as well get this thing over with, he thought, as he wrapped his rubber apron around his protruding belly and tied it in back. He pulled on his gloves and moved the bucket of water nearer the table. "Might as well start at the bottom, so I can get your legs back together. The undertaker will have to cut holes in the side of your box," he said aloud. He often talked to his specimens, feeling confident none would reply or complain, either about his technique or his humor.

Cupping his pudgy hands together, he gathered some water from the bucket and sloshed it over the pubic area. It dislodged some clots of blood, but others still clung to the pubic hair. With his hand he used a raking motion, pulling the majority of them loose. He then bent down picked up the bucket, and poured the remainder of the water in the bucket over her. Before it had completely drained off, he turned and left to refill the bucket.

"Morning, Doc," said Budd, approaching across the back yard. He noticed the coroner was covered with blood up to his wrist. "Got a messy one, huh?"

"Yes, I do. If this damned county would break down and build me a decent medical examiner's building to work in, it would make things a hell of a lot easier," he said, as he drew the bucket full from the hose.

Budd followed him in the garage and made himself ready to assist. Budd was an unusual young man. Instead of occupying himself with live people, he hung around Doc Stone learning about dead ones. He had decided years ago that he wanted to be a forensic medical examiner-hopefully in a larger, more conscientious county than Leeward.

The coroner went to the back of the garage to gather up his tools.

Budd turned, and for the first time saw the corpse lying on the table. "Damn. Someone really did a number on her, didn't they?"

Curiosity prompted him to bend down and look into the now greatly enlarged, gaping hole. A scowl came across his face. He looked up. Stone was busying himself at the rear of the structure. Budd reached over on a shelf for a flashlight. He turned it on and directed the light into the knife-enlarged cavity.

"Hey Doc, what the hell do you suppose this is in here?"

"What?" the coroner answered with little enthusiasm.

"Come here a minute, and take a look at this. It looks like something jammed in what used to be her vaginal tract."

Stone's curiosity was aroused. He walked around to get a better view. He looked where Budd was projecting the light on a foreign object injected into the gaping hole. He reached in for it but had difficulty keeping a grip on it. It had become encrusted with intestines and blood.

"Damn," he cursed each time he lost his grip. Finally, he said, "There I've got hold of if. Keep that light on it so I can see. He pulled with some force until he felt it give way.

"What the hell is it, Doc?" Budd asked, as he stood fascinated.

"I don't know yet. I'll have to get it cleaned off," he said, as he threw it in the bucket of water beside the table. "We'll finish here; by that time it should've soaked enough."

"Where do you want me to start, Doc?"

"See if you can pry open her mouth enough to get out whatever that is stuck down her throat."

Budd forced open the mouth and retrieved a pair of fancy red satin panties. "Do you think they were trying to strangle her?"

"Probably not, most likely trying to keep her quiet while they went to work with the knife," Stone said, holding the article up to the light and then tossing it on the work table.

They ran the usual test. When they had finished placing the entrails back inside the body, Stone secured them with some stitches. "That ought to hold it," he said under his breath. "Well, my boy, I would say this is a classic example of a tormented soul. She must have died one helluva death." He pulled off his rubber gloves with a snap. "Let's have a look at that thing we found inside her."

The water was bright reddish-brown color. Stone took an old wooden spoon off a shelf and swirled the water. Slowly the object rose to the top of the bucket. He reached in and lifted it out of the water. He stood there holding in over the bucket, letting the fluid drip back into the water. "I'll tell you, I've seen everything from coke bottles to doorknobs inside women. Most were self-inflicted, but I doubt that she did this to herself."

Budd stood watching, repulsed by the horror of it all, yet intrigued, too.

"Looks to be a piece of broomstick. What would you say Budd, about fourteen inches long?"

Stone turned and gestured to a shelf fastened against the wall. "Hand me that yardstick from over there." He held the two together, gauging the length. "Yep, pretty close. Fourteen and three-eights." He handed the yardstick back to Budd who replaced it on the shelf. "Now, hand me that rag over there. I'll wrap it up and take it down to the sheriff."

Budd responded to the demand, then said, "Well, I guess I'll go, if you don't need me any longer."

Without looking at the boy, Stone said, "Sure go ahead. All I'm going to do is run some water over her, hose down the floor, and call the funeral parlor. I'll write up the autopsy report, then call it a day."

Budd made a speedy departure. For the first time since he'd been assisting the coroner, he was glad to get away.

Sheriff Myers entered his office, walked slowly to his desk and sat down. His basket was full of reports from the 3–11 crew. He thumbed through them, noticing they were mostly accident reports, with an occasional D.U.I. and two drug busts. There were a few early arrest reports from the 11–7 shift. It wasn't unusual for the men to work on the sports when they had a slow period.

A manila folder at the bottom of the reports marked Florida Sheriffs Association reminded him that, as the newly elected treasurer, he had letters to dictate. He'd put those off until later, he decided.

He started to buzz for his secretary, then remembered it was Sunday. He pushed the button for the dispatcher. "Find Travers and send him in here, please."

He leaned back into his chair. He didn't know why, but he felt uneasy today. He would have rather been at home, but things were still difficult with Betty and he felt more comfortable away from there. Normally he would have been at the camp, but it would be a long time before he could go there again.

Now that he was here, he might as well do something productive, he thought to himself. He pulled open his bottom desk drawer. First, he lifted off the top layer of papers. He'd have to clean it all out soon. It seemed that all the junk mail had been tossed in the bottom drawer. He leafed thought the papers, digging further down. His hand touched something cold and hard. He pulled it up and out. When he saw what it was he froze. It was the framed picture that had once graced the corner of his desk. He set it down in front of him and studied it. It reminded him of happier times. His eyes moved across the picture, resting momentarily on each of the five men, decked out in hunting gear. He stood between the colonel and Ray Yarbrough. Lawton Smith and the Manning kid knelt on the ground in front of them. He remembered the occasion well. Jack had had difficulty keeping the pose, and kept falling forward. Being in back of him, Hank had placed his hand on

Jack's shoulder to steady him. They'd all had such a good time that weekend. Damn! If it hadn't been for the newspaper jumping the gun on Manning's suicide, he'd have let it go as a hunting accident as the colonel suggested. *Damn, I loved that kid,* he said to himself. The day had gone so well; he hadn't shown any sign of being despondent. He was due back at the base the very next day. *God,* he asked himself, *will the hurt ever go away.*

The buzzer rang on his desk, breaking his train of thought. "Yes?" *He paused, listening.* "What type of special detail last night? Oh, yes, I remember. What time is the colonel's meeting this morning?" *He paused again.* "All right, I'll see Travers then." *He put the phone back. He hoped they had been successful in uncovering something. The colonel wouldn't let him down. He'd see to it that the men turned up something. He shoved the picture back in the bottom drawer and walked to the door.*

He swung it open and stood face to face with Becky Gibbons. They were both startled, but only she jumped.

She had heard he was in the building and had just approached his door and put her hand up to knock. "Oh," she said, as he stepped back out of his way.

"Did you want to talk to me, Corporal?" he asked her.

"Well, yes sir, I did," Becky said. Suddenly losing her courage, she glanced towards the floor. "But it can wait, sir...it wasn't important." She turned and quickly walked away.

I wonder what that was all about, the sheriff thought as he approached Yarbrough's office. He rapped lightly on the door. Without being beckoned in, he turned the handle and entered.

Yarbrough, seeing him come through the doorway, quickly hung up the phone.

"Good morning, sir," he said, trying to regain his composure. He would have been better off to have casually hung up. He'd done the wrong thing, and the guilt was written all over his red face.

"Am I interrupting anything?" asked Hank, not really caring if he had.

"Oh, no sir. Just taking care of a little business," Yarbrough said, trying to muddle through the awkward situation. "We didn't expect to see you until Monday?"

"Well, I wanted to see if anything had tuned up on that special detail last night. Were you out on it?"

"Yes," Yarbrough said, nodding his head.

"Anything worthwhile?"

"Well, we thought we'd hit on a good lead, but that abruptly ended, with the second murder." As soon as the words left his mouth, he regretted them.

"What do you mean, second murder? I didn't get a report on another murder."

"I know, sir. It occurred so late last night that the report hasn't been prepared yet." He hoped to smooth over the fact that neither he nor the colonel had turned in a preliminary report on it. They hadn't expected the sheriff to turn up for another twenty-four hours.

"The colonel went home to rest and I've been here all night, coordinating the reports from different squads. Even the coroner had to show on this one," Yarbrough continued, trying to smooth over the sheriff's ruffled feathers.

Myers' interest was aroused. "Who was it, and where?" he asked, as he lowered himself into the chair in front of Yarbrough's desk.

The captain detailed the lead they'd stumbled upon. He quoted Lemmon's words verbatim, leaving out the part about Willy using the back seat of the patrol car to pay off Delilah.

The sheriff shook his head, and let out a sigh. He was thoroughly dismayed by the new developments. "Do you think the two are tied in together?" he asked Yarbrough.

"I doubt it, sir. She may have had information that could have helped us in the case, but saying the two are tied in...no, it's not likely. He probably met up with a rejected lover, or maybe she didn't comply with some john's request." Yarbrough was trying to convince the sheriff, but he had doubts himself. Delilah had a reputation for being one of the best lays on the hill. She had the body, looks and personality to please any client. She was a consummate professional when it came to her part of the contract, and Yarbrough doubted that any irate client had killed her.

"Well, I know we'd better display some concrete evidence pretty soon, or the public will be clamoring for our heads," Myers said, as he walked to the door. "I've got paper work to go over. You keep me posted on your progress. On second thought, if you've been all-night you need some rest. Go on home! I'll hold down the fort until the colonel gets in."

Yarbrough drew a sigh of relief as the sheriff closed the door. He scribbled a note to the colonel, attached it to some papers, and shoved everything into a departmental envelope. He grabbed his coat off the rack and headed down the hall to the dispatcher.

"Give this envelope to the colonel when he comes in. Tell him I'll try to make it back by ten for the special detail meeting." Yarbrough pushed open the door and headed for the parking lot. He started his vehicle and headed toward Cape Corrine.

Even though he and Jane were no longer married, they still remained friends. They had to. They had a common interest: their fourteen year old son, John. In the beginning they had been happily married, but about the second year things had started to go sour. Being in contact with so many women, he was tempted to occasionally stray. Jane couldn't take it and had asked for a divorce. He was glad they'd only had the one child. Since the divorce, the boy had become a disciplinary problem.

After he had remarried, he was glad that this new wife had let her ex-husband have custody of their six-year-old boy. At least he didn't have the responsibility of any other children; John was enough of a headache.

He was happy enough with Rose, but often he'd regretted remarrying. At the time it seemed like the wisest thing to do. They had fallen hard for each other. She was married, and they couldn't carry on the affair. When she divorced her husband and gave up the child, it seemed to be an easy solution for everybody. With his being a captain in the department, they couldn't risk the publicity a divorce battle could bring. Their marriage had been reasonably happy, so he thought things had worked out of the best. At the time, everybody at the department thought he would marry Becky. Their affair had been torrid and tempestuous. They had been absolutely crazy about each other. Yarbrough thought about the spunky redhead; actually, he thought about her a lot. Seeing her at the department every day awakened a lot of the old feelings he had for her. I would be easy to fall back into old habits with Becky. She had been a dynamo in bed, and as fulfilling as any female he'd ever had.

Not that he hadn't strayed in his second marriage, but nothing important or lasting. One night stands, generally, when he'd gotten carried away, or when Rose was out of town. The AIDs thing had scared him sufficiently to keep his wandering to a bare minimum.

Yarbrough pulled in the driveway next to the stucco-covered house, got out, slammed the car door and headed for the front door. He wanted to resolve this problem, and the sooner the better. Before he could knock, the door opened.

"I heard you drive up," Jane said.

He walked into the all-too-familiar room. Looking around he asked, "Where the hell is he?"

"In his room. He found out I called you. The door is locked," she said with a sigh.

Ray headed for the bedroom at the end of the hall. He knew it well. It had been his and Jane's. After the break-up she had switched rooms with the boy. She said it held too many memories. He knocked on the door. When he got no response, he knocked again, harder and louder.

"You unlock this damned door, or I'll break it down," he yelled.

Almost immediately he heard the lock unlatch. The knob turned, and the door opened. Instead of the timid, scared boy he expected to see, he saw a defiant, belligerent teenager. He hesitated for a second. He was used to handling this type of kid every day of the week, but this was his own.

The blue haze that hung in the air, with the familiar sweet odor to it, sent Yarbrough into a rage. He shouted at the boy. "You dare to do that in my house?"

"It's not your house anymore. It's mom's," the boy yelled back.

He spoke the truth. It did belong to Jane; he'd signed it over to her. "Don't you have any more respect for your mother than to bring shame down on her like this?" Ray quietly asked his son.

"Why should I?" the boy shot back.

"What made you turn to this, John?" he asked the boy, sounding as if he were trying to undo something in minutes that had taken months to build. Then the detective instinct took over. He walked to the dresser on the other side of the room. He yanked open the drawers, started pulling everything out and throwing it in on the floor.

"You aren't going to find it in there," John said arrogantly. "Why don't you just ask me for it? I'll give you some."

Ray could take no more. He moved to the boy and started to slap him with an open hand. When he saw the boy wasn't frightened, he became enraged and began hitting him with his fists.

John fell backwards on the bed table, knocking over the lamp. He was determined not to cry, to take his beating like a man.

"Why marijuana?" Ray pleaded.

"Would you rather I go on booze or coke," the boy asked sarcastically. "There isn't any difference, is there?"

Ray clenched his fists as he stood over the boy. He was trying to hold himself back from pounding any more on the battered face looking up at him.

"Why in hell shouldn't I smoke it?" John asked defiantly. "You put it out on the street for sale, don't you?"

Ray was stunned. His eyes opened wide. He hadn't bargained on his son knowing about his involvement in the drug trafficking. Suddenly he felt like a brute. He wanted to leave...to get out of the room...the house.

Jane stood in the doorway, tears streaming down her face. "Is it true? Are you involved with drugs? Was it going on while we were married?"

Ray couldn't answer. He couldn't even look at her. He just lowered his head, pushed by her and ran for the door.

The chickens had come home to roost. The one thing he'd never anticipated was this mess touching his own son.

He had to have time to think. He drove down by the river's edge and stopped the car. He sat there, staring out at the water through the car window.

Two shrimp boats were tied to the city docks. They rode each wave, as it washed under them, then splashed against the seawall. The boats had been confiscated as evidence. The men on board had been arrested and taken into custody. They'd managed to have their bonds reduced and had been released. Most were already involved with the next shipment from Columbia. It had been arranged in advance. The men, after the pretense of a trial, would be allowed to go free on a minor technicality. They had been boarded, arrested and their cargo had been seized beyond the statute mileage limit. It had been out of the department's jurisdiction to board. It also suggested that they were on the ball and living up to the sheriff's pledge to fight crime.

The poor unsuspecting slob, thought Ray. *He actually gave himself a pat on the back for a job well done. He'll sure holler in protest when he finds out the limit was violated.* Ray smiled to himself. Those two boats had just replenished the local drug supply.

When the sheriff had ordered it burned, hay and sweet clover had produced the needed aroma. It was done so quietly and in such a remote area that the public was unsuspecting.

His mind wandered from the sheriff and the boats back to his son. He'd send out the word, any one caught selling to his kid would never sell again...to anyone. He could apply enough heat to...who was he kidding, he thought. There were suppliers all over. He couldn't stop any particular sale; there were too many open channels. The boy could be getting it from a hundred different sources.

It was revenge. He was sure. The boy was doing it for revenge. He was simply lashing out at Ray for leaving him and his mother. Maybe now that he had vented his anger, he would be all right. *I won't have to worry about him any more,* thought Ray, deliberately shoving the boy and the confrontation out of his thoughts.

Oh hell, he said to himself, *I'm going home and get some sleep.* He started the car and pulled away from the river dock, where the two boats still rocked on the incoming tide.

Chapter 19

Billy Carter knocked on the door of Brian Holcomb's apartment, as he smoothed out his shirt that he'd just pulled out of his pants. He didn't like coming here, but he had no choice. Holcomb was his syndicate contact and Ruocco. The syndicate's man was in town and wanted a meet. Ruocco just flew around the country. He'd make a touch-down in a city long enough for a meet and hop on the next plane out, whether it was headed in the direction he was going or not. It made it hard to pinpoint him and he was as unpredictable as they came. Carter stood there thinking while he waited. They had two prior meets, both in different places. This time he'd chosen Holcomb's pad. Why, Carter wondered. Maybe because Brian hadn't lived there for long. Not long enough to draw attention to himself.

Billy stood looking around. The apartment complex was nothing but a den of sex, sin and drugs. He knew, for some of his best customers lived here. He had thought of taking a place here himself, to be close to the action. He could pick any apartment, and by midnight there would be at least ten people laid out on the floor, doing one sort of thing or another.

He listened with his ear to the door, then knocked again. This time he heard movement. Before the door opened, he was viewed through the peephole in the center. Carter hated those things. He didn't like to be seen first, or spied on. He would have stepped to the side of the damned thing if this meeting hadn't been crucial, but if he had, the door wouldn't have been opened to him. The syndicate didn't play games, so this time he tolerated it.

The door finally opened, and Holcomb greeted him with a brother hand slap. "Come on in, man. What do you say?"

Billy wouldn't give him the satisfaction of pretending they were friends, and overlooked it. He walked to the center of the room, while Holcomb shut the door and bolted it. That was a tip off to Billy; they didn't want a chance of his leaving in a hurry. He pretended to ignore it, and flopped into the closest chair. He was sitting in direct line with the syndicate man. He always liked to put people at a disadvantage. He knew it was rare for anyone from the syndicate to be placed on the defense.

"Billy, you remember Tony Ruocco?" Holcomb said, gesturing to the slender, wiry man in the corner chair.

"Sure I do," Billy replied, nodding to Ruocco. "How was your flight in?"

"I didn't come here to discuss airplanes." Ruocco growled. "Look Carter, when we started working through your area, we only brought you in because we needed your contacts. They're in the right places. We worked out a deal, this being the logical port to bring in a boat. We gave you and your group a good cut, for letting us unload when the other coast needed a rest for awhile. We never expected to turn this place into a permanent delivery zone. It has turned into such a lucrative... well, it's been less trouble than we had thought it would be. The fact is, we've been able to move more out of this area than we had planned." He leaned back in his chair and adjusted the paper that lay on his lap. "The pick-ups come down here for their deliveries now, instead of us having to move them north. The heat is on in Mexico....so we've decided to move to Fort Manson on a permanent basis."

Billy flew into a rage. He realized he was being eased out. He wouldn't be needed as the middleman any more. They'd call the shots after they set up, without a struggle. Who'd tell them they couldn't? Not the sheriff's department. Not after they'd condoned their actions in the past and benefited through them. This was just what the colonel wanted to squeeze him out.

"You want to take over the area, huh?" asked Billy, "What in hell makes you think you'll be allowed to, without our agreement? You don't just have the sheriff's department to contend with. There's also the state patrol, the feds, and the coast guard, all of which don't get a cent, and aren't on the take. In fact, if you didn't have our protection, you wouldn't be getting in here at all."

Up to this point, Ruocco had control of the situation. Now that he was losing it, he began to lose his cool. "Are you telling me to relay the message that you aren't giving your consent to our coming into this area any more?"

"Hell no. I'm telling you that you can go back to that boss of yours and tell him we aren't letting him muscle in any more than he has already. If he doesn't like it, he can find other waters to pull his contraband into. Then how will he distribute his stuff?" Billy was calling their bluff; without them he would be out in the cold too.

"I ought to drill you right where you sit," said Ruocco, slipping a gun out from under the paper on his lap.

"You low-life scum," Billy said, squinting his eyes to narrow slits.

"I would say you are in a rather precarious situation to be calling names," Ruocco said, happy to be in command of the situation once more. He turned slightly toward Brian. "How long before dark?"

Holcomb pulled the shade aside and looked out at the setting sun. "I think another hour will about do it," Brian told him with a sound of triumph in his voice.

"We'll just wait till dark. Then we'll take a little ride out to Highland Hills." Ruocco said, glaring at Billy with hard, cold eyes.

Billy's mind was racing faster than any bullet could travel. How did he know about the remote areas in Highland Hills? They had this all planned. That bastard Brian had set him up from the start. He knew what Ruocco had come for and he had helped plan it. He had to think of something to throw Ruocco off his guard. He could wrestle him for the gun, but he'd get off at least one shot before he could get across the room to him. Still, he might not want to chance the sound of gunfire. Billy still had an advantage over Ruocco. This was his territory and he knew the scene. Ruocco didn't know the tenants in the building like he did. They didn't pay any attention to noises, or what others did. It was doubtful that the sound could be heard over the loud rock music being played in most of the apartments.

Holcomb was still off to the side. If he would stay that way he'd have a better chance. His mind changed gears and zeroed in on a noise. The air conditioner had just clicked on. Yeah, sure. It's worth a try, he thought. "Do you mind if I have a joint, man?" he asked Ruocco. Beads of sweat stood out on Billy's upper lip. He wiped them on his shirtsleeve. "I mean, when someone tells me they're going to waste me, I need something to cool me down."

Billy motioned to Ruocco with his hand for a reply to his question, making a gesture with his fingers as if holding a cigarette. Brian had better have some matches in his kitchen, Billy thought. He would need them to have a chance.

Ruocco gave his approval with a nod of his head.

Billy slowly stood up and got a joint from his sock. He put it to his mouth, holding it more with his teeth than his lips.

"Hey, Carter, don't get any funny ideas and try something there," said Ruocco, waving his gun at Billy.

"Hey, I'm only looking for a match!" Billy said, as he patted his pockets. "You got a match?" he asked, looking at Holcomb.

"Sure," Brian walked to the kitchen and returned with a book of matches. Keeping his distance, he handed them to Billy, then backed off to the kitchen doorway.

The last thing Billy needed to complete his plan hadn't happened yet. He stalled for time. Without it, his plan would never work. He tried small talk, but Ruocco wouldn't buy it. Billy was good at playing the waiting game...he'd been trained by professionals.

Then the waiting ended. It happened. He knew he would only have the one chance, or he would be dead. Either way, he would be dead. He had to try it. The cigarette hung from his mouth as he struck the first match to light it. It went out. He was standing directly under the air conditioning vent, and the draft blew out the match. "Damn," said Billy. He turned to light another match, shielding it with his back from the cold blast of air. It was a normal reaction to have made, so his movement didn't alarm Ruocco. He barely moved, except to be lighting his cigarette. Then, with his right hand, he reached under his shirt and down the front of his pants. With the smoothness of a cat, his hand touched the cold steel. He grasped it and drew, hitting the floor at the same time.

The quickness of Billy's movements brought Ruocco to his feet, but too late to realize that it made him a larger target.

Billy fired two shots in rapid succession, both hitting their mark.

Ruocco fell dead, without getting off the first round.

The swiftness of Billy's movements caught Brian off guard and he fell to the floor in fear. He lay there cringing.

Billy cautiously approached the body. With his foot he kicked the gun from the reach of Ruocco's motionless hand. Then he bent down and with his left hand felt for a pulse in the neck, while still holding the automatic in his right. He looked at Holcomb, who was trembling uncontrollably.

"I ought to kill you....you bastard," Billy yelled as he narrowed his eyes to a squint. "You led me in here like a lamb to the slaughter."

Holcomb turned white with fear. He began to whine and cry. "Hey, I didn't know what he had set up, or what the meet was about. In fact, he was a day early."

Billy tucked his gun back under his belt, and said, "Help me drag him in the bathroom and I'll think about what we have to do."

"We?" said Holcomb, with a quiver in his voice. "How in the hell am I going to explain a dead man in my apartment?"

Billy then went around to Ruocco's head. Ruocco was lying on his back. The force of the bullet had knocked him over backwards. Billy straightened out the body, "Come on, stop your sniveling and help me get this in the bathroom."

Brian reluctantly approached and helped lift, carrying Ruocco's feet. "Holy cow, we don't just have the law to worry about. This is the syndicate!" He was suddenly placing other priorities over the advantage Billy held over him.

"You said he was a day early, didn't you Brian?"

"Yeah, he never keeps a tight schedule. Kept, I mean," Brian said, glancing down at the limp body in their hands.

They had barely reached the bathroom when Brian lost his grip and the feet dropped to the floor. He hastily left the room, leaving Billy to manage in the small area.

"You are a twit," Billy said, disgustedly. He had to step over the body to leave the bathroom. When he tried to shut the door, the body blocked its closing. Billy used his foot and rolled the body over to free the door.

"We'll just wait till after dark to get rid of him," said Billy coming back in to the living room. "Don't you pull any stunts, or you'll find yourself right in there beside him," he threatened, looking at Holcomb.

Staring at the large red stain on the rug, Brian dropped into a chair. "You don't have to worry about me. You have the mafia to answer to," he told Billy, gesturing toward the bathroom. "Oh," he said as an afterthought, "it happened in my place, so they'll come after me too. Oh," he moaned, "We're both dead." He put his hands up to his face, as if trying to hide from an unseen enemy.

Billy said, arrogantly, "Listen, punk, I've been handling people like this for years. You just have to outsmart them, that's all. Our main concern is getting him out of the city and into the county. I have to use your phone. Where is it?" Holcomb pointed to the bedroom.

"Listen to me, Brian, listen carefully. If you're not sitting there when I come back out here I'll find you and I'll kill you. I'll cut you up so your own mother won't know you."

"I'll be right here, Billy. I won't do anything without your say so." There wasn't a doubt in Brain's mind that Billy meant every word he said.

Billy closed the bedroom door, so he wouldn't be overheard. He dialed the number. It was picked up on the second ring.

"Yeah," the voice said.

"I have a disposal problem, Colonel," Billy said lowly.

The colonel listened, trying to place the voice. *It's that crazy Carter,* he thought.

"What the hell are you talking about?"

"Well, I just had to waste a man, and I've got to get him out of the city."

It hit Watson like a ton of bricks. "What the hell is the matter with you? I told you never to pull any of your dirty business in the city. If you have any eradication problems, it is to be done in the county. We can't afford to have the city sticking their nose in." He suddenly became more curious about the victim than concerned about the city. "Who in the hell did you have to waste?"

"Nobody you know. It's only syndicate blood," Billy said gleefully.

Watson couldn't restrain himself. "You stupid freak. It isn't bad enough you do our dirty work in city territory, but now you've taken on the syndicate." He paused to catch his breath and then hurled more reprimands. "I don't even want to know what you do with the body, but I'll tell you this: if the city gets wind of anything, and they start poking their noses around, you'll have more than the syndicate catching up with you...if you get my drift." He didn't wait for Carter's reply, he just slammed down the phone. Watson unlocked his desk drawer and took out his little black book. He leafed through the pages, letting it lay open, then made a check on one. With an air of satisfaction, he placed it back in the drawer and locked it.

Billy didn't like being cut short. One day he'd put the colonel in his place for treating him like an underling. But right now he needed him and his influence. Billy put the phone down and went back to the living room. Holcomb was still holding his head. At least he'd have him to show who held the upper hand. "Let's have a cup of coffee," Billy demanded more than suggested. "We'll wait till the building clears out, and settles down for the night, before we chance it."

Brian limited his movements while they waited, leaving Billy to fix his own coffee. He consumed a pot and watched the late night news.

The closer the time came for moving the body, the more nervous Brian got.

Finally, Billy stood up and stretched. "Well, it's time," he stated. "I want to get to bed sometime tonight. Get me a blanket and some rope."

"I don't have any rope," Brian said timidly.

"Oh, damn, Brian!" Billy cursed. "Well, get me a knife and cut the electrical cords on the lamps. Wait, on second thought, I've got some rope in the trunk of my car. Go down and get it." He tossed the keys to Brian, then disappeared into the bedroom. He pulled the spread, blanket and top sheet off the bed. He used the corner of the sheet to wipe the phone clean. As he left the room, he wiped both sides of the doorknob. He dropped the linens on the floor in front of the bathroom door. In the kitchen he washed the coffee cup and wiped the pot and everything else he had touched with a kitchen towel. He crossed back into the living room and wiped the television set and remote control, along with the arms of the chair he had sat in. He spotted Ruocco's gun by the wall where he had kicked it. He leaned down, picked it up and examined it carefully. "Yes, yes...this would have made a really big hole in ol' Billy Boy!" he said aloud.

A sudden noise made him whirl around, and he instinctively pointed the gun.

"Hey, take it easy. It's just me," Brian said, handing him the rope.

Billy shoved the gun in his pocket, and headed for the bathroom. Ruocco wasn't a big man, and Billy thought of how much smaller he looked, lying there in the pool of blood. He placed the bedspread on the floor, than the blanket on top of that, then folded the sheet double. He managed to roll the body over on it, then pulled the entire parcel out into the hallway where he wrapped it, unaided.

When he moved the body, there was more blood than he had expected there to be. "Damn, I'll have to clean that up before we go," he said aloud. "Just one more complication to slow us down."

After Billy tightly secured the body with rope, he grabbed the towels off the rack and proceeded to sop up the blood off the tile floor. "You'll have to use a brush on these cracks when we get back," he told Brian, after he looked up and saw him standing in the doorway watching him. "I wiped up all I could get with the towel."

Brian didn't like the thought of that, but he kept quiet. He had no choice but to comply. All that Brain was concerned with was getting rid of the body, and the sooner the better.

"You go unlock the car. Drive it to the back entrance and leave it running, with the trunk lid up. If there's any way to get that light off in the trunk, do it."

Without a word, Brian left.

While he was gone, Billy washed the blood off his hands, being careful not to touch the fixtures or faucets. He walked through the apartment, checking and re-checking to make sure there was nothing with his fingerprints. "Hell," he said, spotting the book of matches he had used lying on the floor next to a chair. He reached down, picked it up and stuffed it in his pocket.

Brian rapped on the door as he opened it. "Come on," he whispered. "The coast is clear."

"You'd better be sure, or you get left holding the bag," Billy said, as he strained to hoist the body and put it over his shoulder. He was able to descend the stairs without being seen. He tossed Ruocco's body in the trunk, letting it roll off his shoulder. "I'll drive," he said as he closed the lid.

"Maybe I should follow you in my car," Brian said. He didn't want to be caught with a dead body in the trunk.

"No. You come with me."

Brian didn't argue. It was probably just as well, he thought; he was shaking so bad, he might not be able to drive.

Billy drove east, toward Highland Hills. He searched and found a deserted road that showed no sign of being recently traveled, then turned onto it.

It seemed to Brian that Billy had driven for an eternity. He was anxious to get rid of the cargo and back home.

Billy pulled to a stop, got out and opened the trunk.

Finally, thought Brain. He could hear Billy rattling around. Then he felt the car jerk, as the body was lifted out. He stayed in the car. Billy hadn't told him to get out, and he'd rather not have anything more to do with the body.

Billy dropped Ruocco a short distance from the road. He saw no need to strain himself carrying it very far. He returned to the trunk, took out a gas can and closed the lid. He walked back to the body, released the spout and emptied the can over it. He took the book of matches out of his pocket, struck three together, and threw them on the bundle. It ignited immediately. Billy ran back to the car, threw the can in the rear seat, and took off down the road to the city.

As they left the area, Billy looked back in the mirror. From a long distance off, he could see the trail of smoke spiral in the air. He didn't torch this one for the thrill. It had to be done to confuse identification of the body.

"Now, Brian, did Ruocco make any phone calls while he was here?"

"No. I picked him up as soon as he got off the plane. He didn't call anybody. We went directly to the apartment."

"He didn't make any calls from there?"

"No."

"What name was he traveling under?"

"I don't know. He never used his own, I know that much."

"What about fingerprints at the apartment, did he touch anything that you need to take care of?"

"I don't think so. The only thing he handled was the newspaper he kept on his lap to hide the gun."

"Was it a local paper or did he bring it with him?"

"It was one I had at the apartment."

"Well, get rid of it, just in case. And you'd better tear out that living room rug; you'll never be able to clean up that blood."

"What about the gun?" Brian asked.

"I've got it. Nice thing about the wise guys, they always use clean, untraceable hardware. It'll make a nice addition to my trophy case."

"What'll I do if somebody comes looking for him?" asked Brian.

"You haven't seen Ruocco. You went out tonight for...a drive. If anything comes up about where he was, you don't know anything about it. Got it?"

"Yeah, sure, I got it. Do you think I want to get killed by the syndicate? Hell! They'll come looking for him, you know. That was stupid to kill him."

Billy's fuse was lit. "You little bastard, what the hell did you think I'd do, let him kill me? I knew it was either him or me when he aimed that gun at me. You would have done the same thing I did. So you better get your story straight when they contact you. Have it down pat, or they'll hang you and your balls out to dry."

"I hope I can pull it off."

"You'd better," Billy threatened. He'd reached the city and was heading down Brian's street when he suddenly pulled into a driveway and turned around.

"Where you going now?" asked Brian.

"Take a look back there, and tell me if you want to go home," Billy said, moving his head back toward Brian's apartment.

Brian turned around. "Holy Moses! Why are the cops crawling all over the place?"

"I don't know," said Billy. "I hope you have some money. With your apartment in there, you'd better lay low till we find out what's going on. We don't dare take a chance, and it might take some time to find out what's going on. They could hold the story back if they need to catch somebody. They're cagey bastards, those city cops. Them you don't screw!" First he thought of getting Holcomb out of sight. He could take him to his place... no, that wasn't a good idea. He was beginning to regret not leaving him out in Highland Hills with Ruocco. That would have been the smartest thing to do, leave him to the mosquitoes and the vultures, Billy thought. Too late now. Anyway, he'd better keep an eye on him, he told himself, and he is squeamish as hell. Billy drove around until he found a telephone that was isolated. "You wait in the car," he told Brian. "I have an important call to make."

Annoyed, Brian asked, "Why in the hell don't you have a phone in you car like everybody else?" He could feel the fear rising in his throat. "It would save a hell of a lot of time running around."

Billy feigned surprise at Brian's question. "You don't know the reason.....and with your old man the assistant state's attorney? It's because phones can be tapped, you dumb jerk!"

"Well, with the people you've got working with you, you shouldn't have to worry."

"Those you don't trust, of all people," Billy said, getting out of the car and shutting the door. He dropped a quarter in the slot and dialed the number.

Yarbrough answered on the first ring.

"Captain, can you tell me why the city cops are crawling all over Maple Oak Apartments?"

Yarbrough yelled into the phone. "You stupid weirdo!"

Billy was annoyed. "Hey, don't call me names. Just tell me what is wrong?"

Ray swallowed his anger and tried to speak in a calmer tone. "Listen, you jerk, this time your luck's run out."

"What do you mean?" questioned Billy.

"Well, for openers, the colonel's spitting half dollars. He said you called him tonight and told him you had a disposal problem."

"Yeah, that's right. It really upset the old bastard, huh?"

"Listen, punk," Yarbrough could feel his blood pressure rising. He swallowed hard. "Don't you ever call the colonel again...about anything! You call me...just me!"

"Okay, okay. Now tell me about Oak Apartments. Why all the cops?"

"Some dude named Jackson went into his bathroom to take a leak and found blood dripping through his ceiling. Who in hell is dead anyway?" asked the captain.

"Damn," Billy said. He was annoyed to think he'd been so careless.

"Hey, are you there?" Yarbrough shouted.

"Yeah, yeah," answered Billy. "Go ahead."

"Well, he called the city and they're over there investigating it. There's blood all over the apartment, but no body. They know who the place was rented to. For Christ's sake, tell me who got killed."

"It's syndicate blood."

"Holy Christ! Now you've taken on the syndicate! You're going to get us all killed," he shouted.

"Screw off, Yarbrough. I haven't taken on the syndicate. It was self-defense. Besides, I saved your hide. They want to muscle in and take over the whole damned set-up, dealing you out. I did you guys a favor. I should leave town and let you try and figure this out all by yourselves, being you're so damn smart." He was trying to get Yarbrough to view it rationally. "At least this way you're aware of what they're up to, and you can be prepared. Also, so far as they know, their man was never here. He came in a day early, so we're covered there. What you'd better do is go out to Highland Hills and bury the body. I torched it, but under the circumstances, it's better to be disposed of entirely. That way you won't have to come up with a name, when and if the body is ever discovered.

Yarbrough agreed, and wrote the directions down on paper. "Where is Holcomb?"

"I have him in the car. He's scared stiff. If anyone gets to him, he'll have diarrhea of the mouth."

"Get him out of town. I'll get hold of his stepfather, so he knows what's happening. Give him some money, and when he gets settled somewhere his old man can send him enough to get out of the country."

"It'd be a lot simpler if we just wasted him, too. He's been nothing but trouble," Billy said.

Yarbrough yelled back, "Hell, no! Don't go and do a crazy thing like that. We've got enough problems as it is with the state attorney's office. You just get him out of town. Take him up to Punta Gorda and put him on a bus." As an afterthought, he said, "I don't think his stepfather knows he's tied into the syndicate. Just see that he gets out of town and doesn't come back, period. There's a long shot chance that the city boys may think it was Holcomb's blood."

"Yeah." Billy caught the captain's train of thought. "If Brian disappears, they might figure he was the victim and chalk it up eventually as an unsolved mysterious disappearance," chuckled Billy. "And if the syndicate can't find Brian, they'll never be able to find out what happened to their boy. Yeah, Captain, I think this just may be the solution to our problem."

"You'd just better hope you didn't goof-up and leave something at that apartment that will tie you and Holcomb to the syndicate."

"Don't worry, Captain, I took care of that. Everything is cool, or it will be after you cart you're hindend out to Highland Hills and bury what's left of the you-know-what," Billy said sarcastically, then hung up. He had control again, and he was enjoying it.

Yarbrough hung up the phone. He sat there for a minute thinking. Then he stood up, drew in a deep breath, held it as long as he could and emptied it through clenched teeth. He sat back down and leaned over the desk to push the buzzer.

Corporal Eaton, at the front desk, acknowledged the intercom. "Yes, sir?"

"Is Travers in the station?"

"Wait a minute, Captain, I'll check the roster."

Yarbrough didn't like making decisions without the colonel's say, but he had no choice. He had to act fast on this.

She came back and told him, "No, sir, he's on the road, in zone one."

"Have the dispatcher call him and 10–45 me," Yarbrough told her.

"Yes, sir," she replied. *I'd like to know what's so damned important that he needs a landline,* she thought, as she pressed the dispatcher call button.

Yarbrough walked to the window and peered out between the mini-blinds. "Another hour till daybreak," he said under his breath.

The phone rang. He crossed to the desk and grabbed it before it could ring again. "Travers?" he asked. He hesitated a second. "Are you still checked out to fly the chopper?" He waited for the affirmative reply. "Pick up a couple of shovels, and meet me at the copter pad in thirty minutes. And, Travers, don't call in where you're going. I'll take care of it for you." He hung up the phone and walked to the door. He stopped, pushed the lock and closed the door behind him.

At the front desk he stopped long enough to tell Eva Eaton to have the dispatcher replace Travers in zone one; he was now on special duty.

"Will you be coming back in, sir?" she asked, more out of curiosity than anything else.

"I should be back in by nine."

He turned to the front door and was startled to see Doty coming in.

"Morning, Captain. It's going to be a great day. How about a paper?" Doty extended a newspaper. Yarbrough ignored it and kept walking.

Travers was waiting for him when he pulled onto the field. In less than five minutes they were airborne.

"What are the shovels for, Captain?" asked Travers.

He replied, quickly, "Treasure hunting. Head for Highland Hills."

The copter banked to the right, towards the glimmer of light that signaled another hot, humid dawn in southwest Florida.

Chapter 20

Doty had felt pretty good this morning, until he looked at the date on the calendar. It was the anniversary of the death of his wife and daughter. Damn, he missed them. Each year that passed burned the detest larger and more bitter to the sheriff's department. The accident that took their lives happened years ago, but he felt that if the department had been on the ball, had called and gotten them medical attention, they might still be alive. That was only the first screw-up that had contributed to their deaths. The man that hit his wife's car head on was drunk. He'd been stopped for D.W.I. an hour earlier. He was a prominent businessman, so the deputy had called a taxi to take him home. After the taxi driver had driven around for an hour, unable to find the man's house, he'd taken the man back to his car. He'd then given the drunken man his keys and they'd both gone their separate ways. Minutes later, the drunk's car careened over the median and hit Doty's wife's car head on.

The first young officer on the scene had found her wandering around, babbling incoherently, and had mistaken her for being drunk.

Her little girl couldn't be seen, as she had been thrown off the back seat to the floor, and was bleeding severely. She'd gone unnoticed, and bled to death while the deputies were trying to put his wife through a sobriety test. In her dazed and shocked condition, she kept trying to tell of her baby in her car. Finally, when a passing motorist who had stopped glanced inside the car, he saw the crumpled body on the floor in a pool of blood. Immediately help was summoned, but too late. His daughter was D.O.A. at the hospital. His wife died a few hours later of shock, after first lapsing into a coma. She was such a frail little thing anyhow, Doty recalled.

Later, the drunk that had hit them was charged with vehicular homicide. The state allowed the six months needed for a speedy trial, to expire, and the judge had no alternative but to throw it out of court. The only bodily injuries the drunk sustained from the accident were a few cuts and scratches. The stupor he was in, people stated, kept him relaxed enough to keep from being injured worse.

Vengeance and prosecution of the man wouldn't have put Doty's life back together. But the mockery of justice that was done definitely added to the ache already in his heart and head.

The man was remorseful about the deaths, but the influence he had allowed him to escape punishment. Also later, Doty confidentially obtained information from the motorist who had discovered his little girl: the deputies who were putting his wife through her perception exercises, toyed with her as a cat would with a mouse until he'd made his presence known.

Doty had spent the better part of the day working on a special article to be printed in next Sunday's paper. It covered crimes, death, laws, and punishment in the county. But once his family crept into his mind, he couldn't do the articles justice. *Oh to hell with it,* he thought. *I'll wrap it up for the day and get home to bed.* He didn't even take the time to smooth out the cover on his typewriter. He'd always taken special care of it, being the means of his livelihood. This morning, it was just a repetitious act he carried out after years of practice, for his mind was elsewhere.

Colonel Watson pulled into the parking lot just as Dr. Stone was getting out of his car. Seeing him, the colonel waited for Stone to gather his briefcase and other paraphernalia. He was anxious to hear what he had to say about the black woman's autopsy. Not because she lived on the hill, where the population was mostly black, but because he hoped it might shed some light on the murder of the young girl at the beach.

As the coroner walked toward him, the colonel wondered if he'd slept in his clothes, as he looked as if he'd just crawled out of a goodwill box. His short stocky body added to his unkept appearance. His hair was tossed by brisk gusts of wind. The colonel doubted he'd even combed it to start with; it always looked that way. The full growth of hair on the sides made up for the complete lack of it on top. Recently had he started to grow a full beard, which contributed to his already eccentric look.

"Hi, Doc. You got anything for us?" Watson asked as the coroner arrived at his side.

"That I do, my boy. That I do. Right here," he said, showing him the rag-wrapped item in his hand.

"What is that?" the colonel exclaimed, as he looked at the filthy article.

"Come on and I'll show you." the coroner said excitedly.

They entered the department's back door and went into the colonel's office.

Watson closed the door behind him. "Now, what the hell you got in that damn dirty rag, Doc?"

Doc Stone didn't say a word. He unwrapped the rag, like a little boy toying with a friend about a secret.

The colonel stood anxiously waiting to see what the rag held.

In the doc's hand lay a stick of considerable size. "That, Colonel, is a piece of broomstick, fourteen and three-eighth inches to be exact."

"What in the hell does it have to do with the murder case on the hill?" Watson asked, a little annoyed.

"I found it inside her vagina," Stone said, as if disclosing some great discovery. The coroner continued to talk, not minding that the colonel had gone to use his phone. "Who ever did this used her own pants to stuff in her mouth to keep her from screaming out. She probably would have suffocated on them if he hadn't done her in with the knife first. She must have died a hell of a death," he concluded.

"Thanks, Doc. Leave your report with the sheriff on your way out and I'll get back to you."

The coroner didn't notice he was getting the bums' rush. He didn't have anything else to report to the colonel anyhow. He wasn't much on small talk; he only bothered with it if someone was knowledgeable in his line of work. As he left, he heard the colonel talking on the phone.

"Get Lemmon, Hall, Willy and Travers in here as soon as you can locate them," the colonel told Becky. Finally, he felt, they had a break. Waiting for the summoned men was difficult. His anxiety built.

The men soon entered the room. Watson told them to shut the door and grab a chair. Then, directing his question to Lemmon, he asked,

"Didn't you tell me about a house on the beach that holds wild parties." Not waiting for an answer, he went on. "You find out everything you can, and get back to me as soon as possible." He then looked at Willy, and gruffly demanded, "Tell me every thing that black slut had to say about that weirdo who was wanting to put things up inside her."

For the first time, Willy balked at someone degrading his race. In defense he said, "Sir, she may have been a prostitute, but she was good people." He'd like to have said more, but didn't know what to say, or how to say it.

Watson realized he'd hit a raw nerve, and attempted to smooth it over.

"Willy, I didn't mean to speak ill of the dead."

Willy accepted what he thought to be an apology. He then finished telling his version of the meeting between himself and Delilah. Colonel Watson came around from behind his desk. He walked over to Willy with the dirty rag-wrapped article. He then flipped open the rag and exposed the sawed-off broom handle.

Willy's eyes widened and he gasped.

"Like this one, Willy?" asked the colonel, as he shoved it closer to him to view.

Willy's face grimaced. "Good, Gobaloo" exclaimed Willy. "No wonder she wouldn't let him do that. She couldn't have taken that. It would have killed her."

"Yes, Willy," said the colonel sarcastic. "He did get it inside her, and it did kill her."

Willy hung his head.

The colonel turned to Hall. "Is there anything you want to add to what Willy has told me?"

Hall slowly shook his head side to side.

"As soon as I can get with Captain Smith, I'm giving a briefing to the rest of the squad in civil. You already know about the creep we're looking for, so you have a head start. Has anyone got any questions?"

No one responded.

"Travers, I want you to stay a minute; the rest of you can go back on duty."

They heeded his command and left.

Watson waited till they were alone, then asked Travers, "Have you heard any rumors floating around the station?"

A look of puzzlement came over Travers face as he looked at the colonel. "What type of rumors?" he asked.

The colonel hesitated, wondering if he should pursue the topic. Gathering more time for his thoughts, he rose to his feet and walked over and straightened the plaque on the wall, then continued. "I was told there's a little discord in the C.I.D. unit."

"I haven't heard a thing to that effect around here, sir."

Watson let it drop and changed the subject. "Have you been in to see the sheriff yet this morning?"

"No, I haven't. As soon as I got in, I was told to report to you. I'll head that way now, though."

"If he has any type of problem, let me know." The colonel motioned for Travers to leave.

Once outside the colonel's door, Travers hesitated. *I wonder what that's all about,* he thought. He sure had something up his sleeve.

Becky came out of Yarbrough's office and shut the door, a little easier then she would have liked. "That bastard," she said under her breath. She definitely didn't feel like a day's work. The more she saw of him, the more contempt she felt. *Just like a damn man; he takes all the good out of a woman, and then turns her back out to pasture.*

She had once felt so serious about him. She thought that one day they'd be married. Their dates had been quite serious. She knew she'd not taken things for granted. Everyone around the station was surprised that she wasn't the lucky girl when he announced he was getting married. She was crushed, but had to act as if he was just another one of her flings. Having to spend every day at work by his side had just added to her hurt. They'd always made such a good team, on the job and off. She'd divorced her husband and he and his wife had broken up shortly after they started to date. This gave her good cause to believe she might fit into his plans for a replacement. He'd been so nervy as to ask her to the wedding. She had gone with some of the other personnel. If she hadn't, the torch she carried would have shown. She had never wanted the truth to be known. He'd told her he never wanted to marry a cop; their affair had merely been fun. He had found a love like he'd never experienced before.

Lately in work, it seemed as if they'd been thrown together. He still joked with her, as if they'd never meant anything to each other. She knew now that she'd been used.

Now, another flame was lit under her. She'd noticed that things around the department weren't being taken care of according to rule. It probably had been going on before, too, but she'd been too blind to see it. She'd never thought Ray could do any wrong; her love for him had run deep.

She'd just finished a couple months staking out a job, then turned in the report. Ray said he wanted to hold off on it; maybe they could nail the guy with something more. She'd thrown it back at him. It hadn't been an authentic stakeout after all. Ray had just wanted to gather things to use as leverage against the guy. Ray had just smiled one of the devilish smiles she had once loved. That's when she had gotten up and left.

Her affair with the assistant in the public defenders office had taken on a peculiar twist and was still being tossed around in her mind. She was able to find out enough information to pump back to the colonel to satisfy him and his old cronies. She had herself to blame for the twinge of conscience. If she hadn't been so willing to place herself in the position where she would know everything that was going on, she wouldn't have had to cope with the battle inside here now. What to do with the warning that Mark had given her was tearing her apart. She had very few close friends, only a few acquaintances. She'd never had time to make friendships. Her life had been taken up with the men in her career. Now there wasn't one she dared trust. She would have to go with her gut feelings.

Chapter 21

His job was exceptionally quiet tonight. There were some nights like that. The dispatcher lit up a cigarette, just as a call came in.

It was Willy. His voice was unmistakable. "Car 274 to headquarters."

"Go ahead 274." Dispatcher Brown said.

"Give me a 12–28 on 18 plain 35531," Willy said.

Brown turned to the computer, punched out the data requested, and read it back off to Willy. "It should be on a 1974 V.W., blue, registered to William Carter, 1426 Liberty Bell Court, Fort Manson," Brown said.

"10–26," Willy replied.

The black man wrote down the information on a piece of paper. "Hey, thanks brother," he said, tapping Willy on the shoulder. Then he walked off in the darkness.

Willy pulled out into traffic, proceeding on his beat.

Doty was sitting at his desk, trying hard to work, but the words just wouldn't come.

He took advantage of the time, reminiscing about the past few weeks. They'd been some of the happiest since he'd lost his family. To think a trip to the sheriff's department had provided him with a companion that actually helped relieve some of his inner anxieties. He and Jimmy Dale had gotten to know each other quite well. They had also struck up some in-depth conversations. Dale didn't seem to have much association with his co-workers. It was as if he needed someone to relieve a deep feeling, and he'd found Doty to fill the bill.

Doty was reluctant to submit to the young man's friendship. It all appeared genuine enough, but Doty couldn't be too cautious. Even the chance meeting with Jimmy at the desk of the sheriff's department, Doty had felt, could have been a play by the colonel to have Jimmy befriend him, then after they got well-enough acquainted, to report back to the colonel on stories before they broke in the paper. Doty had worked overtime on that one, but fortunately, he didn't find that to be the case. He found Jimmy's company to be quite authentic. It replaced what his life had lacked in the years he'd been alone. He'd laughed, for the first time in years, when Jimmy had gotten pulled into the river by a runaway fish, averse in getting caught. While busy talking, Jimmy was thrown off guard when the fish started to fight. They both laughed until they cried. Doty had found once more how to enjoy life, and get something out of it other then constantly chasing a story. Oh, he still wanted the all-important expose', but he felt different now. His feeling of resentment and revenge had slowly faded away. Now, he was working towards the expulsion of the guilty ones in the department, and the dismissal of those who held higher seats in the political machinery of the county and state.

He also realized that his work output was of much better quality. The stories were flowing easier and better. He didn't have to work as hard for them. He'd really grown to admire the young deputy. He never thought he'd ever have anything but repulsion for that green uniform. Now he knew it was who was in the uniform that mattered, not the material itself.

Doty knew, as a result of their friendship, that the kid had even suffered. He'd spent a lot of time trying to convince Doty of his sincerity. He had, in fact, been called into the colonel's office for the single purpose of questioning him about his friendship with the newspaperman.

Jimmy was a good cop. He was a cops' cop and went by the letter of the law. He held the book in reverence, and used it as a strict guideline to follow, with no variations. He had compassion and was fair. He never used his authority to lean on a suspect. He believed that if you broke the law, you should be punished for it, but believed also that each instance had extenuating circumstances. It had been said of him that he'd arrest even his own grandmother if he found her breaking the law. His ethic code was high. If he continued to maintain a good record, he'd go far in law enforcement.

The thing that had clinched their relationship was when Doty had to interview Jimmy after the *News Leader* had selected him as the years' outstanding policeman. Jimmy had been credited with talking a jumper down from the span over the river. He could have been pulled to his death if the man had chosen to grab him as he jumped or fell. Jimmy had spent a couple of hours high over the super highway talking to the black man. Other black men had watched from the ground, while he risked his life for one of their own. Jimmy seemed to always go out of his way, leaning towards helping the black man, though Doty never knew why.

Doty wasn't quite old enough to be his father, but the feeling he had for Jimmy resembled the love and admiration most fathers had for their sons. They enjoyed each other like brothers, laughing about nothing in particular, and just having a good time. But their closeness didn't prevent Jimmy from having a personal life of his own.

Jimmy had been dating one of the girls in the department. She hadn't wanted to get into anything serious, and neither had Jimmy. They were perfect company for each other. She was an outdoors girl, and the three of them would go out when they could all manage to be off the same days and would often go on camp outs. The men would usually catch some fish and she would do a tasty job of pan-frying. The atmosphere was quite relaxed; they talked very little shop.

Doty had sat the better part of an hour daydreaming.

"Hey, you loafer," Corcoran yelled across the room. "Am I going to get any work out of you today?"

Doty looked up and smiled, then turned back to his typewriter. He started to peck away, soon getting lost in his story.

Jimmy stood there for a few minutes, watching him type and wondering how all those words could be locked inside his mind. It appeared that Doty got them to flow automatically off his fingertips onto the paper.

Doty stopped for an instant, thinking how to phrase a sentence.

This is when Jimmy spoke. "Amazing," he said, with a touch of sarcasm in his voice and a smile on his face. His dark, wind-tossed hair was in need of combing. Lines wrinkled up at the corners of his sparkling dark eyes when he smiled.

Doty looked up from his typewriter and saw him. He met Jimmy's smile with one of his own. "What's amazing?" he asked.

"Oh, I was just thinking of how you're able to sit there putting things on paper."

Doty pushed the typewriter stand aside. "My boy, they're sure not the words that I'd like to be putting on paper."

Jimmy didn't pursue that any further. He knew what Doty was referring to.

"What the hell you doing out of work anyhow?" Doty asked him.

"I've been changed to the night kick for the next sixteen days. I thought I'd come down and see what you're up to."

Doty rose from his desk and walked over to Jimmy. Putting his arm around the young man's shoulder, he said, "I'm sure glad you did. I needed a coffee break anyhow."

They walked off to the coffee room. "What will you have, Jimmy?" Doty asked, as he reached into his pocket for change.

"Oh, just coffee, I guess."

Doty fed the machine the coins and retrieved two coffees. He said in a joking manner, as he placed Jimmy's in front of him, "That's graft."

They both laughed.

"I know when I covered the feature story on you, you stated why you had gone into police work, but what really made you want to go into police work? Why would you pick "this" sheriff's department? All other law enforcement agencies in the state are just crying for men. With the marks you had, and fresh out of the academy, you probably could have named your own salary. Here, I know the salary is fixed, and the raises a long time in coming."

Jimmy looked into his coffee cup. He'd finally been confronted with the question he knew he'd have to face.

"How long we known each other now, Doty?" he asked.

Doty thought for a few seconds and replied, "Oh, I guess about seven or eight months."

"You know me well enough to realize I've been using you. So now I can talk to you in confidence, and you'll have a better idea about a lot of things."

"Yeah, we trust each other." Doty said.

"Well, " Jimmy said, "back about four years ago I had cause to experience one of the most formative, yet challenging, ordeals in my life. I made up my mind that I would change courses in my life. I did, and here I am."

Doty smelled a story and he wouldn't let it lie; not like that. "Come on, Jimmy, what happened?" He could tell Jimmy was unsure of himself, as he was hedging. He wondered if he should pursue his course. He'd built an emotional bond with this news item, and he didn't want to read on thin ice. Personal ties made a big difference.

Jimmy carried on the conversation in his own vein." Would anyone here mind if I used your library to look up back-clippings?" he asked.

This really surprised Doty. He was positive he sensed that Jimmy had more than that on his mind. "Sure, they are open to the public. The girls in there won't mind helping you. How far back do you want to go?"

The deputy sat his coffee cup down. A broad grin came across his face. "About four years."

Doty knew he need ask no more questions on the subject. "Do you want to start getting yourself acquainted with it while I'm here?" Doty asked.

"Yeah, I'd like to, if you don't think Mr. Corcoran will mind."

The reporter picked up his empty coffee cup and motioned for Jimmy to follow him. Doty threw his cup in the receptacle, as did Jimmy. He stuck close to Doty, as he was led to the library.

"Hey, girls," Doty said, entering the library. "I have a young man here who would like some help getting started on some research."

The girls looked up. After seeing the handsome young man, both girls were eager to help. "Sure," they both said unison.

Leaving Jimmy in capable hands, Doty went back to his typewriter and began his story with new vigor. He knew deep inside that he'd finally found the answer he'd been searching for for four years. Yep, things were about ready for a change and he knew it. His typewriter hummed in harmony with his singing. He'd not been so happy in years.

Becky knocked on the sheriff's door.

His "Come in" gave her the right to turn the doorknob and enter his office.

"Hello sir," she said as she entered the room.

"Hi, Becky. Come over and sit down. What can I do for you?" the sheriff asked, as he motioned her into a chair.

"Well, sir, I want to discuss something that I feel should be brought to your attention." She felt very uneasy, and now wished she hadn't sat down.

He slid forward in his seat and leaned his elbows on the desk, waiting for her to speak.

Becky charged ahead. "There are things going on in the department that are not according to regulations." She'd planned to start out with some small things, to get his attention, then proceed to the larger incidents. She could tell from the way he looked at her that she had better use caution. She'd known that the colonel had done a good snow job on the sheriff, but this was ridiculous, she thought.

"I see," Sheriff Myers, said. "What, for instance?"

Becky was grasping at straws now, and she could feel the heat creeping up her neck from under her uniform. That was one of her traits. Whenever she was mad or nervous, her neck got red. Right now it was nerves. She'd like to get up and run.

"Well, come on, Becky," he said, his voice showing agitation at his time being wasted. His fuse was short and it didn't take much to set it off.

"Well, sir, I have known...Did you know that C.I.D. has used money out of confiscated gambling money to purchase drugs? Some of the reports that cross your desk are falsified, to lead you to believe that things are going all right." Becky hastily continued to speak out. "There have been narcotics raids without search warrant, and/or the doors kicked down to gain entrance. I, as well as other agents, have been told to falsify reports."

Hank sat there listening to what she had to say, a look of disbelief clearly written on his face. "Well, Becky, I keep in constant contact with all the department heads - Captains Yarbrough, Smith, and the colonel. Now all three men confirm the same thing. There are no wrongs being perpetrated here in the department...I'd heard lately you were not able to get along with your co-workers."

Becky hung her head.

He continued. "Do you have some type of problem that you're having difficulty solving? If so, do you want to talk about it? I know about the thing you've had going, with one of the men at the public defender's office."

She looked up quickly. "That's another thing, sir...They asked me to have an affair with Mark Sims. When I did, they told me to secure information on selected clients who were being charged; they wanted to know how they were going to plead."

Her charges brought the sheriff out of his chair. "Now look, Deputy Gibbons! I feel for all those concerned that it would be wise to transfer you to a different department for awhile, till things can be resolved in your relationships."

Becky knew she had the shaft as soon as he referred to her as "Deputy," not Becky. She queried, "What do you mean, sir? That I won't be given cases to work on in the detective division any more?"

"Well, I feel, with your emotional problems, it would be better if we reassigned you to auto thefts. Now you understand, it's only temporary, just till things work themselves out."

It would do her no good to complain. He'd do nothing, for he believed the lies the men had told him. Naturally he would, for they actually controlled the department. She saw no use in even trying to argue. Sure, she thought, this would all blow over; then she'd be placed back on the nark squad, her first love. She'd play their silly game, and go for the transfer. They'd expect here to throw a fit, giving them cause to fire her. Well, she'd fool them. She'd play along, be gracious about it, and make the best of it.

"I'll have one of the men tell you tomorrow what your task in the department will be," Sheriff Myers said, as he sat back down and started leafing through the papers on his desk. He'd heard enough, and that was her signal to leave.

She got up without another word and left the room. "Those bastards," she said aloud, as she walked down the corridor. Becky helped out with the desk duties. She knew it would be futile to get involved in a case report.

The following day she was told to take care of auto thefts. The other women deputies never did have much involvement with her. They weren't the same breed of women. They were too polished. They'd never had to get dirty with the filth. They didn't know how it was to live with the scum in the streets.

Becky couldn't imagine how they could go for a whole week with a hair-do undisturbed. Sure they looked better, but she was smarter, more street-wise. The men liked women with brains. All that fluff and frills wore a little thin after awhile. She knew, for hadn't the men occasionally turned to her for consolation, sexually and mentally? They must have felt her far superior over the rest. Otherwise, why was she the only female narc? *The rest just couldn't cut it, that's why,* she thought. Becky worked with Sylvia Sullivan, but their conversations were limited.

Sylvia's husband worked in C.I.D. unit, so she couldn't commit herself. Besides, the other women probably had turned Sylvia's mind against her. Not every one knew of the skullduggery going on.

Grudgingly, Becky threw herself into the task of trying to solve the auto thefts. She figured they'd come around, wanting her to come to their aid, once they were faced with a case that only she could help clinch. They always had need for an undercover chick they could depend on to pull their fat out of the fire, on evidence.

How wrong Becky was; they had already begun to groom another to take her place. Being in another part of the department, Becky didn't even know of her replacement's existence.

One day, the news broke. One of the biggest land fraud scandals in the history of the United States was happening right here under her nose, in Leeward County, and the surrounding areas. There was a rash of unhappy people, clamoring for justice to be done for them. They had invested their lives' savings, only to find later they had nothing to show for their money invested.

Almost immediately, the local state's attorney, John Costello, assigned Becky the task of taking statements from the flood of people who claimed to be victims of fraud. She felt compassion for the old people who made up the larger number of those who streamed into the office. Some had genuinely been duped. There were others, though, who had figured it a good "get-rich-quick" scheme, so they hadn't minded dipping into their life's savings to reap a few thousand dollars over a short span of time. Those, she felt no remorse for, as they wanted something for nothing.

Becky was allowed free reign as long as she made periodic reports back to the state attorney's office. Acquiring the depositions, and filing them for action, took all her time. The auto thefts had to be assigned to others. The importance of the land frauds far outweighed an occasional joy ride in an unauthorized vehicle. Even when it was a pure case of auto theft, the state bargained, and re-classified the case as joy riding. This increased the ring of snitches at the disposal of the sheriff's department.

Becky had accumulated a large pile of reports on her desk, along with cases pending, for the state's filing against the companies responsible for the fraud.

One morning a knock sounded on her door. She thought it was another old couple who had finally gathered enough courage to file, admitting they had been cheated like thousands of others. "Come in," she said.

When the door opened, she saw the assistant state's attorney, Larry Stewart, entering her room. She thought *he wanted to pick up the latest reports she had made out, but had not yet had a chance to deliver to his office.* "Hey, I'm sorry, I haven't gotten these over there yet," she said, reaching for the stack. "Did someone come in you hadn't received a report on yet?" she asked, while hastily gathering up the folders.

"No, Becky, I don't need the cases." he said, while closing the door.

Mentally, she breathed a sigh of relief. She wasn't on the carpet. "Then, to what do I owe the honor of this visit?" she asked him, while placing the folders back in his basket.

He sat down in the chair that had been occupied by so many crying elderly people.

Then he unbuttoned his sports jacket, reached into an inner pocket, removed a cigarette, and lit it up, ignoring the fact that she smoked.

"Well" he said, "I have to talk to you and work something out." He drew in on the cigarette, then blew the smoke upward into the room. "The directive has come from the state. They'll supplement funds with national aid, for the investigation on these land fraud companies." Being a paid political figure on a fixed income, his overtime used on the investigation seldom increased his paycheck.

"I want you to let up on the investigation, so the state and federal governments will have the pressure applied to them. It will then fall into my lap. I'll be given the opportunity to control the funds needed for the investigation."

Becky was flabbergasted by his frankness. "Do you mean to sit there and tell me to stop this investigation? Let those people down whom I have given my word to help? Just let them fall by the wayside, in the red tape. Is that it?" She was furious.

"Listen, if it's a matter of money, I'll be more than glad to compensate you for your help in this matter. Together, we can really handle them as the Governor wishes. First, I have to get you to stop this full-scale investigation. And, Becky, I could put it like this: if you don't let them fall by the wayside, it could go very hard on you, job-wise."

She took this as the threat it was meant to be. Outwardly, she cooled down and leaned back in her chair. She asked," Have you talked to the colonel about this, or the sheriff?"

At the hint of a threat, he reacted, saying, "I could call the colonel in here right now to set you straight on your stability with the department, if you'd like?"

She caught his intended aim of having her detached from the department if she didn't cooperate.

He rose from the chair and walked in the direction of the door.

Before he opened it, he turned and made one last comment. "As for the sheriff, he doesn't need to be bothered with trivia like this." Mockingly, he continued, "He has too many important things, that only he can handle." He then made his exit and closed the door.

Becky sat dazed for a few minutes. Finally, she gathered up the complaint files from her desk and threw them in a bottom drawer. She replaced them on her desk with a word-puzzle book, and slammed the drawer on all those false empty promises.

Chapter 22

Travers and Lemmon had been hot on Mark Gross's trail to produce some information. So far, he'd come up against a blank wall. He wasn't able to secure any type of lead for them. Colonel Watson had told the two deputies to lean and come up with something, for he'd been receiving heat from the sheriff and the state's attorney.

The only hard core facts they had were that both women had been done in by a sadist. Tonight, they spotted Mark going down Palm Beach Boulevard and pulled him over.

"What the hell did I do this time?" Mark asked disgustedly. "Can't you guys leave me alone? I don't owe my soul to you." He was tired. Working in the hot sun all day had drained his strength, and he wanted to get home, shower, and have a cold beer. Since the night they'd first approached him, he hadn't dared stop for a drink in a bar.

"Come out of the truck, Gross," Lemmon commanded, ignoring Mark's plea.

Mark dragged himself out through the opened door.

"Assume the position," Lemmon barked.

"Oh, come on guys. I don't have anything on me."

Lemmon pushed him up against the truck.

Under protest, Mark placed his hands on the hot hood of the truck, which added to his anger.

Lemmon then kicked his legs back in a wide arc position. He now had him leaning at such an angle that if the truck hadn't been there, he'd have fallen on the ground.

Mark said under his breath, "That's not necessary."

Travers did a fast, sloppy job frisking him. He then motioned to Mark, "OK, you can get back into your truck now."

Mark climbed back into his seat.

Lemmon placed both his hands firmly on the truck windowsill and started to shut the door.

"Oh no, you don't." said Mark, putting his foot out to stop the door from closing. "Get your filthy hands off my truck." When he reached out to lift Lemmon's hand, a small pack of marijuana fell to the ground.

Lemmon looked down. "Well, I wonder where that came from?" he exclaimed. The sarcastic grin on his face added little more to the fake element of surprise in his voice.

"You rotten bastard. You were going to plant that on me, then run me in." His mounting anger gave him courage. "I happen to know your tactics. I'm wise to the fact that it's easy to plant pot in a car, just by leaning with your hands on the window opening. Sure, I've been in trouble with the law, but I'm straight now, and you can't stand it." Mark threw caution to the wind. "You bastards better leave me alone, or else!" He was tired. He was fed up with being stopped. He knew to buck the system would be treading on thin ice. Nonetheless, he had to chance it, or they'd never leave him alone.

Deputies Lemmon and Travers had remained silent, waiting for Mark to finish his courageous outburst. They had seen this type of thing before, and knew what to expect next. Drug users' courage paralleled the content of their spine: both were made of jelly.

Mark saw he was getting nowhere, so he decided to appeal to their better nature, though he doubted they had one. His courage was waning. He pleaded, "Look, my wife's expecting. She's been having a hard time of it. If she has any upset, she could lose the baby. Common, can't you just think of her and stop making it rough on me? If I get picked up again, she couldn't take the strain."

Lemmon looked Mark right in the eyes, with a serious expression. "Just think, Mark. It could be your wife next that the butcher goes berserk on. How would you like to have him cut that kid out of her belly, while she lay there still alive? Assuming she would be alive after he did a number on her sexually.

The thought made Mark shudder, and the hairs stood out on the back of his hot dirty neck. Still, he had to safeguard against the hint of a threat. "If you do anything to my wife," he said, returning Lemmon's hard stare to his eyes, "I'll kill you."

Lemmon looked at Travers and said, "I think that was a threat against a police officer, don't you?"

Mark was out on a limb, but it felt good. He started his truck and said out the window, "No, that was a promise, sir." Then he quickly pulled away.

They both stood motionless, watching the truck travel down the street. Someone had actually bucked up against them. It wasn't normal, and was even rather embarrassing.

Rather then add to it, Lemmon said, "Well, come on. I think we shook him up enough, so he'll make a little extra effort finding something."

Captains Smith and Yarbrough sat in the colonel's office talking. They'd met in the hallway, and stepped into the closest office to talk. Smith said, "You know, with all this public pressure for the solving of these murders, it's hard to get anything done on other cases." Yarbrough lent little to the conversation.

"Did you see the letters to the editor in this morning's paper?" asked Smith.

"Naw, I don't read it that much. I don't have the time. My workload has been too great."

"Yeah, it's been hectic around here lately. Not to mention the added effort needed to keep the troubles within the department on a low key," said Smith. "Becky wasn't too happy when the assistant came over here and told her to lay low. She was just beginning to forget the raw deal we dealt her too."

Yarbrough added, "That's the trouble - we don't have control over the way they play ball. Sometimes I think they control us more then we do them."

"I know what you mean. I guess we should be thankful they allow us to function as we do."

With emotion, Yarbrough commented, "Damn, they should. Costello just sits up there on his duff, rakes in all the benefits, and never gets his hands dirty That stupid four-eyed assistant of his don't have sense God gave a louse. He does all the running around and neck stretching, then accepts the scraps Costello throws him."

Smith didn't like him, so he didn't have feelings for his predicament. "He must be satisfied. He never appears to be unhappy," he said with a slight laugh. "In fact, he seemed elated when he found out his wife's kid was missing, even with the presence of the blood. I figure the kid must have been like a burr in his side. The kid had more authority then he did. He probably got paid better, too."

They both laughed.

Ray said, "It's too bad the mother had to be led to think the blood in the apartment was her son's."

"Yeah, but with women talking like they do, she'd have to tell one of the girls. Before you knew it, we'd have had that one in our laps. As it is, we make a show of a half-assed effort of looking for him."

Ray said, "We have to make the effort of solving his mysterious disappearance for Hank's benefit too. I had to laugh when I gave him the investigation report. Like everything else that crossed his desk, it'll soon get lost and forgotten, like the Manning thing. He carried that a hell of a lot longer, but for good reasons. He lives to play sheriff, especially when the news media wants statements from him."

Smith added to the mounting criticism. "Yeah, he has to get the information from the colonel, before he arrives."

Yarbrough looked at Smith with a strange expression. "What's the matter, Ray?" he asked, concerned.

Ray didn't answer. He clutched his chest with both hands, and toppled out of the chair onto the floor.

While Smith stretched Ray out on the floor and ripped his shirt open, he yelled for someone to help. His shout brought those within earshot running.

Upon seeing Ray on the floor, Pool picked up the phone and called for an ambulance, while Smith started to give him mouth-to-mouth resuscitation.

No one dared to ask questions, for Smith, being the only one who could explain, was trying to aid his comrade.

Within minutes siren could be heard approaching.

Quickly, the unconscious Yarbrough was loaded on the stretcher and rushed to the hospital. Only then was Smith able to relate how they'd been talking, when all of a sudden, without warning, Ray had clutched his chest and fell to the floor.

At present, Smith, being the superior officer, took command. He told everyone but Pool to leave, so he could call Ray's wife at her place of employment. He turned to Pool. "You be on your way with a car to pick her up and take her to the hospital. You'd better stay there with her, too. As soon as I'm relieved, I'll be down. Make sure to let me know his condition, especially if it changes. He didn't look too good."

Captain Smith was alone. He picked up the phone, then remembered he didn't have the phone number where she worked. He started searching Colonel Watson's desk drawers for a phone book. He tried the drawers, finally coming to one on the right that was locked. At first he thought it was stuck and gave it a little extra tug. It still didn't give. He finally realized it was locked. As he dialed information, he wondered what could be so important in there.

Yarbrough's diagnosis: stroke.

Several days later, when the doctor made his visit, Ray sat up in bed.

He asked Ray, "How you feeling today?"

"Pretty good, Doc. In fact, a hell of a lot better."

"That sounds like someone who's trying to get out of here and back home," he chuckled, as he glanced over Yarbrough's chart.

"At least back to work," Yarbrough suggested.

"Oh, you won't be able to take that on so quick. You've got to give your body a chance to rebuild. By the way, having a stroke at your age is not ordinary." The Doctor sat in a chair at the side of the bed. If he'd known how up set he was making Ray, he never would have pressured him. "Suppose you tell me just what type of pressure you've been under at work to cause you to have a stroke?"

"Just normal police work, Doc." Ray's heart rate increased.

"Well, after you recuperate, and are able to resume work, you are going to have to take work less seriously. It's just a job, you know. It's microscopic, in comparison to your life. I mean it, too, Ray. 33 years old is far too young to be facing serious problems. This was just your body giving you a warning to slow down." The doctor got up and walked to the door. "Well, I'll see you tomorrow," he said as he went out the door.

Yarbrough broke out in a cold sweat. What the doctor had just said kept reverberating back and forth in his mind. He laid his head back on the pillow. Oh God, what would he do now? He had to work. Police work was all he knew. He was too young to retire. The workload could be lessened, but what he knew couldn't be. That's the pressure he was under. He'd kept it bottled up inside for quite some time. He'd never expected this type of repercussion. That was another thing Becky was good for. She was a good listener. All the gory things didn't get to her the way they did to Rose. He was able to relieve a lot of tension through Becky. It was ironic how once he took such solace in her, and now she was the main person causing him his aggravation. Ray wondered how he could be relieved of part of the heavy workload when he was one of the colonel's main cogs in the whole operation. Things would be better after he got back on his feet. The doctor was wrong. Ray had his age on his side. Hell, 33 is still young. He'd be able to revamp himself and be good as new.

In another section of the city, Jim Lemmon, detective Lemmon's brother, was preparing for the long trip back to his small hometown in California. This had been his first entrance into the drug world on a big-time basis. He hadn't been drawn into it until he was made aware of the risks. Then his brother hadn't given his final approval, until he knew the setup was safe enough to bring his kid brother in. They scheduled a harmless run to California with stops along the way. Jim had been in Fort Manson six months and had grown to like the place. He lay on the couch in the living room, thinking about the trip back home.

Detective Lemmon entered the front door. "Hey, what you up to today? You about packed?" he asked his brother.

"Yeah, I'm ready to go, except packing the merchandise tonight after dark. I sure dread the thought of that long drive ahead of me."

"Well the drop-off spots along the way should help break the monotony," the deputy said, as he flopped down in a nearby chair.

"I've grown to like it here, and I wouldn't mind staying, permanently. Man! I've never seen things run so smooth and out in the open like they are here. This is drug heaven," he laughed.

"Jim, don't get no lingering notions! You're pulling out tonight! Besides, you wanted in; now you have to take a little unpleasantness with the payoffs."

"Yeah, yeah, I know. Don't get your scivvies tied in a knot. I was just daydreaming. Someday I'd like to take up residence here, permanent. Maybe join the force like you."

Right now, all Lemmon wanted was to get him on the road to California. "We'll consider that in the far future. Right now, we're trying to get you established in the delivery system. Take one thing at a time." He got up and stretched. "I'm going in and lay down a few hours. You'd better get some sleep, too."

"Yeah, I'll crash here on the couch and, come dark, I'll be on the road." Jim rolled over, and Deputy Lemmon walked into his bedroom.

The workload was heavier in the department with Yarbrough out. It placed extra work on each man. The colonel was still able to keep abreast of activities. As usual, Captain Smith spearheaded the investigation in the Criminal Investigation Division. The men under him gave their normal efforts in solving the crimes. Their crime-solving rate, though, was far below last year's. Their failures finally brought a letter of concern from the Governor. It seemed like there were more dead ends than customary. They played on the theory that in time, the public would forget both murders. Chances were good of a more violent crime taking up their thoughts. The unsolved beach murder brought even more pressure then usual. By now the colonel's corruption had managed to infiltrate the two major divisions of the department: felonies and misdemeanors. The other petty crimes would be shuffled around to one who had the smallest workload. Their main intention had always been to recruit more men in their group. Yet, either they didn't get around to it or they could never find people who completely filled the bill. Yarbrough's having a stroke proved how taxing and demanding of your physical and emotional makeup it was. Watson guessed the time was right. The thought had been prominent in his mind for some time. Now was as good a time to act as any, and probably better. The colonel called to have Smith come meet with him as soon as he was free.

Smith knocked on the door.

The colonel was anxious and annoyed to be kept waiting for his arrival. "Come in," he said, with obvious disgust in his voice.

Captain Smith was the type who didn't balk at his antics. He knew his position in the setup was secure. They didn't have the usual power struggle that went on in the underworld activity. He offered an excuse. "I came just as soon as I finished a briefing with the sheriff. He needed reassurance that the department wasn't suffering as a result of Ray's absence."

Smith sat down without being asked. He carried a slight chip on his shoulder, but he had a build to support any mood he cared to show. He felt his reason was legitimate and that he shouldn't have to make amends to the colonel.

Ray's attack had made everyone up tight. It had made them all aware of the pressure they placed themselves in. It also had removed from their circle a very efficient and functional man. His absence left a visible void that was felt by everyone.

The colonel threw the question right out to Captain Smith. "What do you think about bringing another man into the operation?"

Smith wasn't sure of the colonel's rash suggestion, and ventured a querying of his own. "I think it's a little risky. Don't you?"

Watson said, "He wouldn't have to be brought in on all the things. And, of course, he'd have to prove himself first."

Now Smith knew the colonel had thought this through, and it wasn't just an idea off the top of his head. He questioned, "Who do you have in mind?"

The colonel knew his choice would alarm Smith. "I thought that Dale kid."

Captain Smith came right up out of his chair. "What the hell's the matter with you? My God! You know he's been going down to the News Leader, talking with that reporter, Doty, who by the way would love nothing better then to stick one up our backside."

The colonel's mood was calm in contrast to Smith's excitement. "Damn it, settle down. I know all about the kid going down there. I also know he's had the hots for a girl in the copy room too. Plus the fact that his goes out fishing with the paper man. I can't think of a better patsy than him. He'd have access to first-hand information, which could put us one step ahead of them with their news scoops. They'd never again get to jump the gun and release a story, like they did on the Manning kid. And, you forgot I said he'd have to prove himself first."

The captain paced back and forth. Then his step slowed, and he came to a stop right in front of the colonel's desk. He leaned down on the desk and pointed his finger at the colonel in agreement. "You know, you might have something there after all....Yeah...I do believe you're right." He straightened up. "Shall we bring Pool in on this?" he said with his hand pointing to the door.

"Not now. You and I will lay the groundwork first, then you can fill him in. If he's brought in now, we'd have to brief him with all the things we've just covered. I don't see any need in that." He then dismissed the subject of Pool and went back to Dale. "Feel the kid out as a recruiting prospect, and get back to me."

With that settled, Smith started to depart, then stopped and asked, "Just how do you propose that he prove himself?"

"How does murder grab you?" replied Watson.

Shaking his head, Smith let out a sigh of exasperation, then said, "Man, that's something we haven't had to demand of ourselves." He thought the colonel was overstepping his luck now.

"Yeah, I know." the colonel argued. "But a lot of time would be saved, without wondering and worrying about his being on the level." He hoped to reassure Smith and remove the look of doubt on his face.

The captain was reluctant, but went along. "OK, we'll start feeling him out and I'll get back to you." He went out the office door, convincing himself that Watson had always known what he was doing. *I guess he does now, too. It's also his neck on the block if it falls apart now.* As he walked away from his door, he heard the phone ring.

Colonel Watson completed the connection coming in on his private line. "Hello."

The callers' voice was unmistakable, yet he knew there had to be a good reason for his calling on the phone. Up to this point, he hadn't involved himself. His assistant ran interference so he didn't have to be soiled. His image in the public's eyes was that of a fine, upstanding crusader for justice in the state of Florida. His eyes were on the Governor's seat.

The colonel was compelled to show respect. "What can I do for you, sir?" he asked, with sincerity in his voice. Without the help of the state attorney, he'd be unable to pull off his mockery of justice. Then the only income he'd have would be what he earned in the role of crime fighter in the department.

Costello was annoyed. "Tell me what's being done on the beach murder case. I've had pressure applied to me and I don't appreciate it. I've had calls from congressmen from the Lessos' home district. They're upset about their daughter's murderer not being found yet. They've been applying the pressure to him. Now Colonel, there's no need in my telling you if the political angle enters into this mess, what the consequences will be. I mean solve that damn case, if you have to intimidate someone into confessing. Do you understand?"

The lump in the colonel's throat kept him from saying anything else but, "Yes, sir." He was left with a dead phone in his hand. He'd just been chewed out. After the initial shock subsided, he put the phone down and immediately put his mind to work, for a solution to satisfy the Lessos. With a name like theirs, he was sure there had to be more than a political element involved. Damn, now he had heat coming from another angle. Costello never gave him the chance of telling about the new evidence in the case. Good thing his ticker was in good shape, or he'd be in the same boat as Yarbrough.

He pressed the buzzer and asked to have Lemmon check in with him before going off duty. He looked at his watch. Ten minutes, he thought, would give him time to collect himself. He shut his eyes and leaned back in his chair.

The knock on the door startled him. He had dozed off.

Wiping his eyes, he said, "Come in."

Upon entering, Lemmon saw him rubbing his eyes. "Have a rough day, Colonel?" he asked.

"Uhh, oh yeah, I have."

Lemmon shut the door.

"Come over and sit down," the colonel said, pointing to a chair. "So far our investigations have turned up nothing. Even the snitches have come up empty. It's as if it's right there." he said, holding up a fist, "and we can't touch it. I have that feeling, and I don't know why." Watson looked at the deputy. "Have you had any luck getting anything out of that guy out on East End? I know you've leaned on him a couple times, but we've got to get some leads from somewhere."

Lemmon chanced catching hell, and put out a suggestion. "Sir, Pool and I were talking about bringing in the Dale kid. Do you suppose with his contacts at the News Leader, he might be able to pick us up some information? Sometimes the paper has a lead, but doesn't dare move on it until the facts are released from you. Often they hear things, you know, bits and snitches of information. They don't know what story it pertains to until something breaks. Then they discover they had a portion of it before it ever broke." Lemmon followed the colonel's changing facial expressions with each sentence. He continued, "Now would be the opportune time to bring in Dale, too. He'd never have the slightest suspicion you had bigger and better things cut out for him later."

Colonel Watson didn't appreciate the fact of someone else's planting the idea and giving directional signals, but this was not time for him to split hairs. He was desperate.

"Lemmon, you may have something there. I like it when I make the right decision and bring someone in, then he substantiates my move when he comes across with the scheme I've been thinking of myself." He'd managed to pat himself on the back , and boost Lemmon's ego at the same time. With enthusiasm, he said, "Send that Dale kid in when you have the opportunity."

Lemmon was elated to think he could add further to the colonel's jovial mood. "You're in luck, sir. He's out there filing an accident report now. He's about ready to go off duty, too."

"Good, send him in before he goes home." The colonel paused to recall the duty roster he'd made out. "If I remember right, he had the next three days off too, so he'll be able to give it more time." He assumed he already had Dale in his grasp.

They both laughed as Lemmon made his exit.

When the door shut, Watson leaned back in his chair and placed his hands behind his head...*Damn,* he thought, *this is going to turn out better than I expected.*

Lemmon approached Deputy Dale and flashed a big smile.

Doty was busy at his typewriter, as usual. Tonight he was working against a deadline. The time limit was running out with an abundance of material yet to be typed.

When Jimmy saw the look of frustration on Doty's face, he knew he was too involved to be disturbed. He'd become close enough to him to know his moods. He hated to be interrupted when on a train of thought. Instead, Jimmy walked to the room where he knew Alicia was working. He stood in the doorway watching her. She was also busy. He was near giving up the idea of talking with anyone here tonight, when she looked up.

Alicia, being more perceptive than Doty, could feel someone looking at her. She smiled. Then her eyes moved from his face to his form. He was still wearing his uniform. He'd never worn it in the building before. People were aware of his being employed at the sheriff's department. Those who knew him personally, placed him in the category of the good guys. But the uniform still made them uneasy, for they knew what it stood for in this county.

"Hi, honey," she said in a low voice.

Jimmy returned her greeting with a broad grin, but he had no control over his blushing face. He knew she'd drawn a bead on him, for Doty had told him. But he'd never committed himself; he had too many things in his life to accomplish before he settled down with a wife and family. She was sweet and nice to be near. Best of all, she wasn't a conniving female, so he could let his guard down, and relax around her. A few times he'd thought, when the day did come to settle down, he'd like it to be with her, and he secretly wished she'd still be available. At present, they just dated, and enjoyed each other's company. She'd been indispensable in helping him on the articles. Doty hadn't been able to go into detail. Alicia had sat for hours, filled in gaps, and answered questions.

"I see you're all working hard," he said, not acknowledging her word of endearment to him.

"Not so hard that I can't stop and go have a cup of coffee with you," she purred, as she pushed her chair away from the desk. Alicia rose and approached close enough to touch him. She gave his hand a squeeze, tugged at it, and said, "Come on, fuzz, we'll go get a cup of coffee." She expressed how proud she was of his being in law enforcement, though she wished he'd picked the city. She said if he'd not come to this city, they would never have met, and she couldn't ever think of their not getting together.

They purchased their coffee from the machine and sat down.

Alicia sat across the table and watched him fix his coffee. She asked, "What are you doing here tonight, anyhow?" She knew it would have to be of some importance for him to come in wearing his uniform, as he was aware of the uneasy feeling everyone had around it.

In seriousness, Jimmy said, "I have to talk to Doty, and it's quite important. How long do you think it will be before he'll have a few minutes to talk? I don't want to interfere with his work schedule, so I'll wait, if no one minds."

Alicia chuckled and looked at her watch. "He shouldn't be very much longer. Anyway, he'd better not be; he has 30 more minutes to meet a deadline. I'll sit with you, if you don't mind my company," she said, as she reached over and took his hand in hers.

"Hell, no, I don't mind your keeping me company." He returned her squeeze with one of his own, then looked into her eyes. "Won't you get into trouble taking this time?"

She shook her head. "No, I'm due my meal break anyhow."

Jimmy got out of the chair and walked to the vending machines covering the wall. He drew coins out of his pocket and asked. "What do you want to eat, honey?" It had slipped out before he realized it. The look he saw on her face now made him realize that with that little word he'd just committed himself. *Oh, what the hell,* he thought. "Honey, I asked what you want?" It sounded good, he thought, and he felt even better when it caused her to smile at him.

"Just get me a sandwich. I have to watch my figure."

With his eyes, he gave here the once over, and said, "Babe, there isn't a damn thing wrong with your figure."

Jimmy was retrieving the sandwich as Doty stuck his head around the corner of the door.

Seeing Jimmy, he entered the room. "Hey, I heard you were in the building. I checked Alicia's desk, and when I found her missing, I knew right where to start looking."

Jimmy smiled at him. "Oh, you did, did you? Think you're smart, don't you?" He enjoyed seeing Doty nearly as much as Alicia. He'd never realized till now that Doty took a back seat to her.

Alicia quickly finished her sandwich, for she knew the men were just keeping themselves busy with small talk and wouldn't carry it any further until they were alone.

Doty realized there had to be something important to bring Jimmy in while still in his uniform.

"Well men, I'll leave you two to talk! Call me tomorrow, will you, Jimmy?" she added, as she looked at him. She didn't wait for an answer. She left the two men alone.

"Now, what's up?" Doty asked in earnest.

"Well, you'll never believe this, but I've been approached about joining the choice group. I've been given a job that will show my worth to them for bigger and better things to come."

Doty listened intently, then came back with, "They're using our friendship, aren't they?"

His approach made Jimmy feel a little shitty. It had placed the first blemish on a pure and beautiful relationship. "Doty, I don't see it that way. There's nothing that can hurt our friendship," Jimmy said smiling. Trying to make the situation lighter, he said, "Except my getting married."

Doty had to return the smile, for he knew that was the truth. Doty had the ability to pick on feelings and knew when something was genuine or not. He knew if he was never sure of anything else in his life, he could be sure of the feelings they shared for each other. "You know, kid, that might be just exactly what we've needed." He'd added that without realizing the burden he was placing on Jimmy's shoulders.

Jimmy had the same thought, but had hesitated to say it. "Well, it's like this. I'm supposed to find out what, if any, information you have on cases that haven't broke yet. Then fill them in, so they can use them with their investigation data in the solving of the crimes."

Doty interjected, "They're right. We have our informants too."

"Right now, I'd say the pressure is being put on for apprehension of the beach murderer." Jimmy hesitated a moment, then said, "I heard the Lessos' are from prominent and influential families."

"They sure as hell aren't going to have their daughter done in, and sit by without a conviction on the animal that did it," Doty said.

Jimmy continued, as if Doty hadn't said a word. "They probably called the political angle in. I know when regular channels can't solve something, strings can be pulled in the political machine that bring pressures home to bear."

When Jimmy had finished, Doty sat back, folded his arms, and said, "Damn it! You're a smart little bastard. Where in the world did you learn all that strategy in your few years of living?"

Jimmy smirked, "I told you I went to school, and I took advantage of the books they had in the library. Law books have some interesting reading material in them, you know."

Doty knew well. For he had once started into law and then gone into journalism. He had received enough legal knowledge to help him with his stories. It made him aware when cases weren't handled as they should have been.

"Doty, I have a couple days off before I have to go back on duty. I'd like to put some more time in the library here to read back clippings. Thus far, I've been taken my time, 'cause I didn't feel there was need for any haste. Now in order for me to ward off their element of surprise, I have to know what I'm up against."

"Sure," said Doty, "You can come in a go through the library anytime you like." His eyes focused on Jimmy's uniform.

Jimmy noticed Doty's concern. "Oh, don't worry, I'm going home to shave, shower, and change my clothes before I get started. Didn't you know the sheriff frowns on our wearing the uniforms other than in an official capacity?" the deputy said, winking.

"You mean, you're going to get started tonight?" Doty asked with surprise.

"Yeah, I am. I have lots to read before I'm thrust headlong into what I think I'm getting into."

Doty shook his head, as he got up from the table. "To hell with that, I'm going home to bed." Doty knew too well what the stories contained; he had written them. "You know how to run the film machine. The stories will be self-explanatory, so you won't need me."

They both left the room together, and bid each other farewell as they parted. Doty went right back towards his desk, while Jimmy went out the rear entrance.

When Doty arrived the next night, there sat Jimmy, at the film machine. His eyes red and blood shot.

"My God, son, you been here all night?"

Jimmy welcomed Doty's arrival as a chance to remove his tired eyes from the countless strips whizzing by. He'd been looking for a special news story that didn't necessitate his reading the whole paper. He'd made several notations on the pad in front of him. Wearily, he said, "I wish you newspaper people would stop using such misleading headlines, and get right down to the nitty-gritty. It'd save me a lot of time." He'd neglected to even greet Doty.

Doty saw in him the determination that he'd possessed in his youth. He still had it, but it wasn't foremost in his mind anymore. "Sensationalism in the headlines; don't you know that's what sells papers. If the topic banner wasn't misleading, there wouldn't be many papers sold."

"How long before you have to go to work?" Jimmy asked.

Looking at his watch, Doty said, "Oh...not for another hour yet." He had deliberately come in early. He had an inkling Jimmy would pull this stunt.

"I have some questions to ask you about some of these stories. Do you mind?"

The paper man pulled up a chair. "Hell, no. I don't mind. Shoot. I have an hour; it's yours."

Jimmy turned off the machine, and Doty got up.

"While you tuck that stuff away, I'm going to get us some coffee. I'll be right back."

When he returned, coffee in hand, Jimmy waited with an eagerness he'd never seen in him before. "I want just an hour of your time. Then I'll go home and sleep all night. Tomorrow too."

Shrugging his shoulders, Doty said, "All right, let's get on with it."

Jimmy leafed through his papers. "First, I'd like to know about this story on the bank robbery in the south end. Has it ever been solved?" He looked up at Doty, waiting for his response.

"Not yet. From what I've heard, there's not a lead. Another source told me he knew who did it, but the thief was being allowed to walk the streets. The cameras are supposed to have picked up beautiful pictures." He quickly added, "And there was more than one...But the sheriffs department only gave a report of a lone gunman."

The deputy jotted down a few things on paper, then fired the next question. It was as if he were the reporter, instead of Doty. "How about the robbery at the bank in Bond Springs, south of here? The one that was hit after the dog track receipts had been deposited."

Doty had forgotten about that one, and had to think a minute. "You really have been digging, haven't you?"

"Come on, quit stalling for time." said Jimmy.

Doty knew he meant business. "Ahh, that one's never been solved either. A hole had been sawed in the roof, but the initial cut wasn't made until after the bank held the receipts from the dog track. Scuttlebutt was, it could have been an inside job. It held the largest receipts ever taken in. It was as if they had waited to pull the heist, perhaps until after someone tipped them off about the money. Upon examination, the hole in the roof showed it had been severed for quite some time. The sun had caused the tar to melt over the previous cuts...Nope, it's never been solved," Doty said, almost in disbelief.

Jimmy touched on one case right after another. After Doty talked he'd make notations on his paper and go on. "Now," he said, "let's go to the murders. There was one at the beach. The woman raped, then murdered."

"Jimmy, I really don't think that will fall into the category of what you're looking for. She picked this hitchhiker up and gave him a ride to the beach. He then forced her to drive him to a secluded road, where he raped her and left here dead in the car. That very same day, he'd walked away from the stockade. Twelve hours later, when he was caught, he was still wearing prison garb. That must have been a thorough manhunt they put on. He wasn't even spotted while hitchhiking back into town with his prison clothes on. The cops finally caught him, and he was sent up after the trial. Negligence. Pure negligence." Doty added.

Jimmy pushed on. "Then I read of an elderly lady who was raped and murdered in her own apartment. They ever catch that one?"

Doty shook his head.

"All right, there was the sex murder of the little boy, in the eastern area of the county."

Doty's facial expressions changed with that query. His feelings went deep on that one. Any crime that had to do with the kids, hit him below the belt. His voice was soft as he spoke. "That was really a sad thing. The little boy was waiting for his school bus in a rural area with a group of other kids. This guy approached them, asked him if he'd show him the way to something. No one's sure what he did say to the little tyke. The eight-year-old boy went with the man. He was never seen alive again." Now Doty's voice gained volume. "There are several things about that case that are appalling. Some of the public out there wouldn't receive good conduct medals for their actions taken, or should I say not taken. It was reported the kid either hollered or screamed. The other kids waiting for the bus had a couple of their parents with them. The kids and the parents stood by and never did a thing to go to the aid of the poor little guy. I suppose it's that old thing of not wanting to get involved. The kids can be excused, but the adults ..." Doty's voice and head lowered.

Moments later he was spurred on again. "Then when the investigation got underway, the sheriff's department pulled all known sex offenders for questioning. Without sufficient evidence, they were released. Well, it so happens that the same thing happened in Virginia a few days later. When the news came out, it was thought the one who committed the crimes up there was the one they suspected of doing it down here. They had the weasel right here, and they let him go. Although they knew of prior records as a sex offender to children and a patient in a mental institution, the department didn't follow up the data. Instead, they let him go. Fact was, he'd walked away from the mental institution in Maryland after a mandatory self-admittance, which, thanks to plea bargains, was a reduction from the twelve charges originally against him. He should have been placed under stringent detention. If he had, two little boys would be alive today. The department could have spared the second boy's life, if they'd not been so inept. Maryland did catch him, tried, and convicted him. He's locked up for a long time, I hope. Unless some half-assed judge sees fit to grant him another trial, because his civil rights have been tread on." Doty was fuming. "That's what the laws of this country have turned into, favoring the criminals instead of the law-abiding citizens." Doty was wound up like and eight-day clock. "Another thing, you'd be surprised at the stories that never make the paper."

"Yeah, like my brother's ..." Jimmy made a slip.

Doty looked astonished.

Jimmy was too tired to cope with that now.

Apologetically he said, "Doty, I can't go into that now, but I will later, OK?"

"Sure kid." He respected Jimmy enough to abide by his wishes. He then glanced at his watch, making Jimmy aware he'd taken a great deal more time then he'd anticipated.

"Just one more question, then I'll get out of here and let you get to work. This robbery at the Purolater Company. Why did we lose a man.?"

He'd hit a nerve when he used the word *we,* unnerving the newspaperman. Doty hesitated with his answer, then threw caution to the wind. He told himself he was being over cautious, that Jimmy was speaking in a broad sense of the word.

"After this, you've got to go home and get some sleep. The armored car burglary took place on a Saturday afternoon. The kid that got killed shouldn't have had a scratch on him. The manager, who just happened by while on an afternoon motorcycle ride, discovered the robbery. He notified the sheriff's department, and the call went out on an armed robbery in progress. The two lawmen closest to the scene responded, one city and one county. They rushed to the scene, approaching from opposite directions. The deputy, instead of standing to the rear of the car, where he couldn't be reached, walked right up to the door of the car. The correct training would have made him realize he was placing himself in jeopardy. He was killed with a single shot to the heart. The city policeman fired and hit the one who'd shot the deputy. By this time, cops were crawling all over the place. The deputy who was killed was related to a local judge."

"I thought I recognized the name," said Jimmy. "I was going to ask."

"That's a little ironic too; this particular judge has another relative, who he keeps having to go to bat for. Seems like he has a thing for little boys, and every time he gets caught, the judge throws his weight around and gets him off. That's one of those tips, again, we have to sit on, for the incidents are never made public."

The reporter rose from his chair and took hold of Dale's arm. "Look, kid, I think I know what you've got in mind, but you have got to take it slow. You also have to get some sleep."

Jimmy was too tired to say anything to the contrary. Besides, he agreed with him on both statements. he had to get to bed before he fell asleep on his feet. "Yeah, I'm going, and thanks a lot for your time. I'll have more for you later, OK?"

"OK," Doty said. "Look, though, you'd better have one little bit of news to carry back to your colonel. On the Manning suicide. I got my tip from one of the guys who works at the service barn."

"Thanks again," said Jimmy. "If I don't come around as often tell Alicia that I'm on special detail, will you? I wouldn't want her to think I don't care."

"Sure, sure. Go on home and don't worry about her. She's hooked." The smile he had turned slowly to a frown. "Worry about yourself," he said, seriously.

Again, Dale left by the back entrance. He headed straight home to bed.

Chapter 23

Willy sat in his car on a secluded side street, listening to the sounds floating on the breeze. The talk on the radio was faint, for he had it turned low. His trained ear could still pick up on the coded messages. He'd been given the word that he was to meet with someone tonight, who might shed some light on one of their cases. The caller hadn't given any indication as to which one. Willy didn't mind what the information was about. He'd do anything to get in the good graces of the group, instead of always being on the outside. For once he'd like to say that he contributed. Willy knew the hill, and there were places here he'd rather not be in alone. This was one of them. This area was known for its coarse way of life. The majority of its inhabitants sold their own women to obtain their next high, whether from booze or a fix of the hard stuff. Their women were precious to them. Without their supply of money for feeding their habit, they'd never survive. Their women had to be equally dependent and weak to go the length of selling their bodies to fulfill their own needs.

Delilah had been snuffed out, and the girls were leery about going out on the street; even when prodded by their men. If their anxieties weren't relieved soon, the whole hill would go sky-high. Their livelihood was being threatened, and their men's habits were being all but extinguished. Neither could take much more. In addition to the explosive atmosphere, one sole male that had meant something to her, had more than the general ailments of the rest of the community on his mind.

Willy's mind was preoccupied with thoughts of his having to be present in this territory. That's when his car was approached. He didn't hear the man until he was standing by the window. Willy jumped at his presence.

"Hey, brother. What you scared about?" said the black man, laughing.

"You just startled me, that's all," Willy said. "Man, I was thinking and my mind wasn't here." His increased heartbeat continued.

"What 'ya thinking 'bout, brother?" queried the man in the shadows.

Flippant, Willy answered, "Nothing special," wishing he could cover his true feelings. "What you up to tonight?" he asked, trying to change the subject.

The man walked closer, then bent down to the car window, until Willy finally was able to view his face.

Willy recognized him. "Hey! You're the one that asked me to check a license number fo' ya...Did ya get it straight with the guy?"

The black man gave a slight laugh and stepped backwards. "Hey man, what makes you think I wanted to get something straight with the dude, huh?" Raising his voice slightly and with another slight laugh, he asked, "Did I give you the impression I was after the dude?" He gave his body a little twist, as if he was dancing to a tune no one else heard.

This put Willy more at ease, and he relaxed some.

"Well, brother, I got to go. Hey, you know what I mean?" the man said, as he slowly sauntered away.

"Yeah, I dig, brother. Have one for me too."

Finally, Willy pulled back out into traffic. He increased the radio volume, then reported back on duty. He was amused about the meet not going down, but was disappointed at not being able to take some news back to the captain. When Willy passed the corner, he saw the man he'd talked with earlier. He was standing in a phone booth with a woman, while she was talking on the phone. A smile broke across Willy's face. *Well, he's got his for the night,* he thought.

The phone booth was hot with the both of them in it, but it was necessary, as he had to hear what was being told to Sheila. She was a black with polish and finesse. She didn't have a drawl. He wrote on a piece of paper what Sheila heard, then repeated it aloud. She finally thanked the woman and hung up. "Hey baby, I sure do appreciate the favor," said the black man, as he gave her a small pat on her behind.

"Maybe I can return the favor sometime." Then he was gone.

Sheila stepped out of the booth, smoothed out her short, tight skirt, and slowly swaggered down the street.

The sheriff arrived early at the office that morning. He'd been tipped off. The roof was ready to blow, and he wanted to be there when it did. State Attorney Costello had called Hank that morning, and said he'd been given the word on the grand jury convening to investigate his department. Hank was shocked, and he intended to find out if the information told him was true, or not. He slipped through the rear entrance and went into his office unseen. He tidied his desk and asked to have Travers come in.

A short time passed until Travers knocked on the door.

"Come in," said Hank.

Travers entered the room. "Good morning, sir."

"No it's not," Hank said gruffly.

Travers was caught off guard. "I don't understand, sir."

"Paul, I need a friend, and when you call me sir, I feel you are placing me in an authoritative position above you. Please refrain from it."

"You know we're friends, Hank, and always will be. We've gone through too much together to let anything come between us now. What seems to be your problem?"

"State Attorney Costello called me this morning. He said the department is going to be put through a grand jury investigation. One of the main things they're placing emphasis on is Jack Manning's suicide." Being so engrossed with his own bewilderment, Hank didn't notice the change in Travers color and facial expression once the Manning kid was mentioned.

When he was able to compose himself, Travers asked, "But, Hank, why are they bringing that up?"

"I'll let you know as soon as I can get Becky in here."

Travers looked shocked.

Hank summoned Becky. A few minuets later, she arrived. By that time so had Captain Smith, and they all sat waiting on her. When she entered the room, Becky knew this was the blow she'd been expecting ever since she reported the wrong doings to the public defender's office. They had filled fifty-five legal-sized pages with her testimony about situations she was both knowledgeable of and suspicious about. As a result, the public defender had taken her testimony straight to the Governor. He in turn had ordered a thorough investigation. It hadn't yet been made public. The sheriff's knowing about it only proved her suspicions. There had to be someone on the inside, keeping them abreast with the action.

"Becky, what made you do such a thing?" asked the sheriff, trying to keep his cool.

"Sir, I tried talking to you about the things that are going on in this department unknown to you."

"That's a damn lie," he shouted.

It was rare for people around the department to see him lose his cool. Those that did had covered up his violence. His quick outburst brought Travers and Smith to their feet, more for her protection than his.

Hank continued in anger. "To tell the truth, I don't want that excuse for a female around me, or my department." he said, pointing at her. "Get her the hell out of here," he shouted.

His voice carried through the whole department and people that heard couldn't understand why.

Becky came running out of his office and through the front door. She was crying hysterically. Her car could be heard squealing as she swerved off around the corner.

It took a considerable effort for Smith to restrain the sheriff. Finally he decided he'd go home.

When the colonel arrived, he was briefed on the days' happenings.

The sheriff remained home until the colonel reported to work; then he came in to talk with him.

Colonel Watson showed disbelief in what he was being told. "I didn't think it was good business to bring her in. I hate the thought of women being involved in this business. They're too emotional when they come up against the detail part of it. Don't worry, Hank. I'm positive we'll get a no bill from the grand jury. I'll see to it, in fact."

Hank looked at him in amazement. "How can you make a statement like that?"

Colonel Watson had overstepped his bounds, and he was going to have to do some fast-talking. "Sir, the young kid, Dale...Remember the one that I told you about?"

The sheriff didn't. He wasn't aware of three-fourths of the men's names, but he didn't want it known.

Watson continued. "He's planted in the paper with a good connection. He goes with one of their office girls. I'm sure if there's a rumble, he'll be the first to pick it up; then he'll tell us." Watson was aware that Hank wasn't too convinced of what he was saying. He'd always been able to manipulate and maneuver, so not much fallout came down on the heads of the department. That's what he was paying on. Hank's trust in his ability.

"Do what you have to, Colonel. She's blackened this department, and now it needs to be white washed. I have to go home. I don't feel well. I just can't bear the thought of all the poking that's going to take place." Hank appeared like a whipped dog, with his tail between his legs.

"Don't worry, Hank, it'll be all right. We'll see to that," Watson said confidently.

Sheriff Myers left his office and the station by the back door, and went home.

"My God! If this is any indication as to what the day has in store, I'd better fortify myself," the colonel said disparately.

Neither Travers nor Smith, still present in the room, said anything.

The buzzer sounded and added to the colonel's irritation. "Oh, damn." He picked it up, expecting it to be for the sheriff.

It was Ruth. She'd seen the sheriff exit, and knew where the colonel would be. "Sir, Pool is here and he needs to talk to you. Do you want to see him, or do you want me to tell him to come back later?"

"He worked last night, didn't he?"

"Yes, sir, he did."

"Send him in. I'll find out what he wants."

Pool didn't knock as he reached for the doorknob, as he'd been allowed the rare privilege of entering without it. "Good morning, Colonel," he said, not meaning it literally. The expression on his face reflected the sour tale he was about to unfold.

"What's up?" asked Watson, in a disgruntled voice.

"Well, we had a rather sticky situation last night. It all happened so fast, there was nothing to do but go with the city."

Hearing the city mentioned threw the colonel into a rage. "What in the hell's the city got to do with us?"

Pool was very uncomfortable. He started to gesture with his hands while he talked. "Well, this guy got beat up by our friends in the Manor. His parents live in the city, they called the city cops. They had to call us, because it took place in our territory."

The colonel threw his head back and rolled his eyes up in his head and exclaimed, "Ohhhh, unreal!"

Pool continued. "Well, we were called to go down there and get this other kid out before they killed him."

Colonel Watson scowled at him.

"Yes, I said killed. Then, the mother called city headquarters and had them radio us while we were en-route not to go in; a friend had just called. He'd gotten out."

Exasperated, the colonel said, "Let's hear the rest of it."

"Well, we all went back to the kid's house. The one that had the number done on him came down here and filed a complaint. He named the dudes as just Jake and Bruce, he didn't know their last names. Anyhow, he swore out a warrant for their arrest."

"Then the city isn't in on it anymore? They left it all up to us?" asked the colonel.

"Yes, sir. It's all in our lap," Pool was happy to reply.

"Well, that isn't so bad then. We'll just use the excuse of not being able to learn the last names. Then that will be that. Things have a way of getting lost between the state attorney's office and here." With that problem solved, he went on to the next. "Get Carter to get on their case for leaning so hard on people. He seems to have control over them."

Pool had hesitated telling what he thought to be the worst thing. "It was all because ten pounds of pot got ripped off."

Colonel Watson came up out of his chair. "Those sonsabitches should know better than to bring amateurs into this business."

Pool thought a little humor might lighten the matter. "The kid even told us he'd help us if we wanted him to. That he knew a lot of names and places."

"That's lovely...Get a hold of that deputy's brother. The one that works for the phone company. Tell him I want a tap on that kid's phone. Man, if he talks, he's had it," Watson commented.

Pool made no attempt to leave. He was wondering why his planned humor didn't work.

The colonel said, "Well, get going," and Pool immediately left. "My God, it seems like everything is coming down on our heads all at once. Becky isn't going to give us too much trouble, though; we have people in the state office that will see to that...It's not knowing what the damn potheads are going to do next that throws me. I supposed they're the risks when we run them for distribution....Hey, anyone heard how Ray's doing lately? I haven't had a chance to see him, I've been so busy."

The colonel had changed the subject so abruptly that everyone was thrown. He was confident he could solve the problem, and had gone on to other things. Meanwhile, it left everyone else still worrying.

"No," Lemmon was the first to speak. "I haven't seen him, but I talked with him on the phone a couple of days ago. He said he's planning on coming back to work in the near future."

"That will be great, getting him back in the department. We sure could use him." Watson was elated.

"Lemmon, while I have you here, I want to ask you about your brother. Did he make it back to California all right? I hope he didn't run into any hitches making the house calls along the way."

Lemmon replied, "Sure, he did just great. He'd like to come back here to live."

"God, I hope he doesn't do that right away. He's far too important for out-of-state contacts. I'd rather have our own, than have to depend entirely on that Carter. He gives me an uneasy feeling." The colonel hesitated, then continued, "Yet, he's so vital to us."

He felt they'd spent enough time talking. Glancing at his watch, he said, with a ridiculing air, "The sheriff needs reassuring. The next time he comes in, he'll see no discord, 'cause we'll have things under wraps. It's fortunate the grand jury doesn't convene for awhile. It will give things time to cool off."

They all just sat and listened while the colonel did all the talking. Somehow it seemed to relieve them of any phobias they might have built up.

Jimmy had spent the better part of his last day off in bed. He hadn't slept, just lounged and given thought to a multitude of subjects. Things had been moving fast, and he hoped he wouldn't get caught up in them. It gave him a leery feeling, every time his thoughts went back to the mess he'd committed himself to. Once in awhile, he'd catch a lump rising in his throat that resembled the same one that had accompanied his experience four years ago. Time had given him wisdom. He had grown aware of the local occurrences and the man who gave out the directives. They weren't the ones that surface appearance would have one believe. There remained no doubt in his mind that the sheriff's department was in the state attorney's hip pocket. No wonder they were able to cover up so well, giving the department such a good appearance. Jimmy shuddered when he thought of the life he'd been headed for. Strange how some people's misfortunes had way of changing others lives.

Jimmy lay there looking up at the ceiling and wondering. Alicia cropped up...She definitely was a threat to his single status. He hadn't planned to get involved with a female, for they had a way of screwing up your thinking. Right now, Jimmy thought, he needed all his wits about him to even stay alive. Right now he was playing with fire and he knew it. He could end up getting the same thing his brother had. Once in awhile, a shadow of depression and inadequacy flooded over him...Who did he think he was to think he could overthrow the well-planned organization that was maneuvering and manipulating the people, things, and events to suit themselves? His task seemed monstrous. He already felt defeated. Jimmy took hold of himself and sat up in bed. He said aloud, with determination, "I am going to do what I set out to do. After I saw what they did to Joe, I made a commitment in my brothers' name, and I will do it, if it kills me!" Hearing his own voice fortified him against the doubts and fears that kept creeping in.

He hopped out of bed and went in to take a shower. *Hell, I'm going in and going through some more newspaper,* he decided as he lathered up. Besides, he'd get a chance to see Alicia. Funny how the importance of that paper had changed priorities from Doty to her. Jimmy laughed to himself. Yes, she sure was a threat to his remaining single.

After Jimmy had consumed the knowledge of certain articles over the past four years' news paper, he thought of looking farther back just to pass the time until Doty arrived. The more articles he read, the more he searched for the original story. He sat and read, completely consumed by the story of the automobile accident that took the lives of the little girl and, eventually, of her mother. Jimmy sat, staring at the screen. What a horrible waste, he thought....Now I have the motive of Doty's private war. He must have gone through hell...Strange how we're both spurred on to the same goal, and each coming from different directions, thought Jimmy. He snapped out of the fixed stare and rolled the film back on its spool. "I've seen all I need to," he muttered. As he was placing the microfilm in its canister, he noticed Doty approaching from the far side of the building.

When Doty came within talking distance, they greeted each other.

"Hey. I'd like to talk to you," said Jimmy. With nothing else said, they stepped into a nearby room, Doty leading the way, where they wouldn't be overheard. Jimmy shut the door after them.

"What's up?" asked Doty.

"Now, don't think I'm pumping you, but I have my reasons for asking you the question."

Looking at Jimmy with a smirk, Doty said, "OK, shoot."

"Have you heard anything about some rumor of an investigation going down with the grand jury?"

The newspaperman's ears perked up. "What did you say? I think you mentioned the grand jury, and my boy, if you did, I sure do know what you're talking about. This happens to be one of those bits and pieces your buddies referred to when they said we news people pick up tidbits, not knowing what they pertain to and file them for later. I had a tip from the courthouse something was in the making, and I wondered when it would surface. Do you know who's putting the heat on?"

"No, but I've noticed a strained atmosphere around the front office in the past few days." Jimmy paused. He rubbed his chin, as he tried to bring to mind something that plagued him. "Hey, I know who's missing. I haven't seen Becky Gibbons around the office in a few days. I thought she just may be on days. Now that I think about it, the same crew always works when they're up to their dirty antics. They seem always to pull off these busts, heists, and raids on the 3–11 shift. With the same ones always in on it, too. I'm scheduled to go on an upcoming raid pretty soon too. The colonel told me today, when I stopped in to pick up my paycheck."

Doty didn't like the sound of that at all, and he didn't hesitate saying so. "That sure is fast work, letting you in on a raid. Make damn sure you're not being set up. What else did he tell about the raid?"

"Well, it seems like they've had this house under surveillance for quite some time. They detect the trafficking of drugs. Isn't that a laugh?"

"Like I said, please be careful."

Jimmy looked at his watch and got up. "I've got to get to work. I have the night shift, and I have to shave and shower yet. I have the patrol all alone tonight, out in the East End." He was at the door and ready to exit, when Doty spoke.

"Hey kid, watch out...OK?"

"Hey, you do too much worrying. What in hell could happen out in that part of town anyhow?" He gave Doty a broad smile of reassurance, and left.

It didn't help. Doty had felt uneasy since Jimmy had told him he was being taken into the group. He sat down at his typewriter and started on the night's work. He hoped it would take his mind off Jimmy and the peril that could befall him.

Chapter 24

Jimmy had gone into work early to have a look at the duty roster. He was still thinking about not seeing Becky Gibbons in the past couple of days. She was so dedicated to her job, she usually came to the department even on her days off. With the shifts not ready for changing, the briefing room was empty. He could look at the paper without raising anyone's suspicion. Her name wasn't on the list. The previous week's roster was tacked under the new one. Her name wasn't on that one either. Why wasn't she working any more? He'd overheard talk among some of the men that the grand jury was going to give the department a good going over. He'd kept his mouth shut and pretended not to hear. Now he couldn't ask questions. *I wonder,* he thought *if the two things are related?* He decided to sit down and have a cigarette while waiting for the rest of the shift to arrive.

With the overlapping of shifts, it wasn't long before the squad room was busy. It would take about an hour for the men to get on the road, or on the way home. There'd been only a short briefing tonight. The colonel had made only one major announcement. He was putting Deets in the dispatcher's job, starting tonight. He was going to train him for a few weeks. When vacations rolled around, he'd be able to work relief. With the large crew of dispatchers in the department, someone was always on leave or vacation. The logical time to train him was now, when things were slow and the colonel had the time to give him the supervision.

So far the night's duty had been routine. Dale had only had to give one traffic citation. He usually tried to be fair, and listen to the other side of the story. In some cases, however, the law could only be stretched so far.

The traffic was light, as he patrolled the Orange Boulevard area. Suddenly he spotted an old red pickup truck run a stop sign. He pulled out of the side street and followed the truck. He called headquarters for a registration check. "Car 77 - headquarters."

The dispatcher acknowledged, "Go ahead 77."

Oh boy, thought Jimmy, *I would have to get Deets. He's sure been pulling some boners tonight.* Dale asked, "Give me a 10–28, all the way, on 18MK2347. My 10–20 is approximately three miles off Palm Drive on Orange Boulevard."

"10–23," Deets replied.

Dale looked around at the area. The houses had thinned out.

Deets turned to the computer console and glanced at the colonel, who stood close by, arms folded.

He gave the dispatcher a nod, and smiled ever so slightly.

Deets punched out the data and pressed his button to talk. "Headquarters to 77. That should be on a red Ford pickup truck, 1978. It was reported stolen. Overcome and apprehend. Approach with caution. I'll call in a back-up unit in your area."

"10–26," Dale acknowledged. *Why in hell would anyone want to steal that old truck?* Jimmy wondered. Maybe Deets had made a mistake. No, the colonel was there. He surely wouldn't make a mistake reporting something as serious as a stolen car. That's fed into a computer. It couldn't be a mistake. He put the question aside and acted. He hit the lights and siren to signal the truck. It pulled to the side of the road. Dale pulled in behind it, drew his weapon and slowly approached. He stayed back far enough to be out of the driver's direct view. Loudly he said, "Step out of the truck with your hands in full view!"

The man didn't acknowledge the command. Dale took one step closer toward the truck. He repeated his command, only louder. "Come out of that truck with your hands in full view!"

The man moved suddenly, leaning toward the opposite side of the dash.

What's he doing? Jimmy asked himself. *It looks like he's getting something out of the glove compartment. Maybe it's a gun!* The cruiser's headlights supplied the only illumination in the area, hampering Dale's vision. His pounding heart kept pace with the car's pulsating colored lights. Suddenly his pounding heart jumped into his throat. The words Deets had said echoed in his brain - approach with caution! The man suddenly sat up straight.

Dale tensed and took the stance. His sweating hands gripped the pistol tighter. As the man turned in his direction, Jimmy's finger squeezed the trigger.

The approaching sirens of the back-up unit drowned out the sound of the gunshot. Dale was still standing in place when Officer Jerry Johnson came running up.

"What the hell's going on, Jimmy?" Johnson asked.

"Go check out the truck. I'll keep you covered," Jimmy said, not moving from his position, the gun still posed and aimed.

Johnson unholstered his revolver and approached the rider's side of the truck. He slowly made his way to the window and cautiously peered into the black interior, illuminated only by the truck's dashboard lights. When Johnson saw the man slouched on the seat, he told Jimmy to call on the radio to demand the colonel to get out there.

Dale relaxed his aim. Johnson's voice didn't sound right. "Why, what is it?"

"Just do as I tell you and get on the horn!" Johnson shouted.

Dale didn't heed him; instead he ran to the other side of the truck and peered in.

There'd been no error in his aim. It had hit its target, and the young man's motionless body lay on the seat.

In his right hand was a cassette tape. He'd reached down to take it out of the player, and Dale had thought he was reaching for a gun.

"Oh...my God!" Jimmy cried in anguish. "I thought he was going for a gun. The truck is stolen, and I thought he was going for a gun!" He started to open the door to render the man aid, but Johnson yelled at him.

"Leave that alone! Don't touch anything! He's dead! You can't help him! Get the hell back to your cruiser and call the colonel, like I said."

Jimmy was too shaken to move, so Johnson ran to the mike. "409 to headquarters," he shouted. These circumstances were unusual, and he needed help, fast.

"Go ahead 409," Deets answered, just as the colonel exited the room.

"Go to channel five and scramble," demanded Johnson, then he quickly related what had happened. Deets assured him that the colonel would be there in a few minutes.

"Get Dale under control. Make sure you don't touch anything," said Deets. He released the lever on the mike with a trembling hand. He nervously proceeded, acknowledging other calls from the patrols.

The colonel sped to the scene. He knew it was vital to get there and calm the men down before he radioed for the coroner. He arrived on the scene and approached both men sitting in Johnson's squad car. "What happened, Dale?" he asked.

"Sir," he replied, his voice quivering, "When I phoned in the license number, the dispatcher told me it was a stolen vehicle and to approach it with caution. Twice, when I ordered him out of the truck, he didn't do it. Then he moved to the right side of his truck, and I thought he was going after a gun, so I fired." Dale hung his head. What he said was barely audible. "He was only taking a tape out of the player." He raised his head and looked into Watson's face. "Sir, I wouldn't have shot, if it hadn't looked like he was going for a gun, and if the truck hadn't been stolen."

"Come on. Let's see what we have here." The colonel's authoritative manner prompted Jimmy to regain control of himself, and he once more assumed his role of deputy.

All three approached the truck. The colonel reached the window and looked in. It seemed like an eternity to Dale before he finally spoke.

"Dale, you go call the coroner. Johnson, put that tape back in the player, while I get something out of my car."

Jimmy had his wits about him enough to know that tampering with evidence was bad business, but the colonel definitely had something on his mind other than correct procedure. He notified the coroner, and rejoined the two men. Johnson had replaced the tape in the player.

As Jimmy approached the truck, he saw the colonel put a gun in the dead man's hand. Bewildered, he stared at the colonel. Watson met his look with a glare.

"Listen, Dale, this is for your own good, and I don't want to hear any comments," he said as he pointed to the dead man. "This bastard has been on parole for sometime. He didn't know what was good for him, and didn't have enough brains to keep his nose clean, though he'd been warned often enough." Then he continued in a normal tone, "There'll be no one to argue whether he did or didn't have a gun. So placing it in his possession is keeping you from the ordeal of an investigation that neither you nor the department need."

Dale knew what the colonel had done wasn't right, but he was in no position to argue.

"You go home for the remainder of your shift. Go ahead and take the cruiser. Bring it back when you come in tomorrow morning to make out your report. I'll be there when you go in to give the details to Sheriff Myers. In fact, I'll tell him what happened. You just keep quiet, unless he asks you something."

Without a word, Dale walked to his cruiser. He felt queasy as he opened the door and leaned on it for support. He broke out in a cold sweat, but the night air helped to revive him somewhat. Then, once more, he was overcome with an uncontrollable urge to vomit. He ran to the side of the road and heaved until his stomach was completely emptied. The realization that he had just killed for the first time brought a new onslaught of dry heaves. He thought his stomach would turn inside out. He stood for a few minutes trying to compose himself. A slight breeze had started to blow, giving him a chill, and he shuddered. Every stitch of his uniform was wet with perspiration. He could feel the water running down his back. He made it back to the cruiser and sat down.

Deputy Johnson came running over. "Hey, are you going to be all right to drive home?" he asked as he shut the door.

Jimmy weakly shook his head, but even that made him woozy. He started the car and Johnson stepped away, allowing him to pull out on the road. He barely remembered the drive home. His mind was occupied with the sound of the single shot that had killed. He could smell the gunpowder, the sulfurous, gritty aroma. Killed, *MURDERED!*

When Jimmy stepped in the shower the water snapped him out of his shocked stupor. For a long time, he stood facing the water, letting it hit him square in the face,. He wished he could wash all the filth he felt was on him down the drain. It didn't work, so as soon as he lathered up, he rinsed off and got out. He wrapped the towel around him and sat down on the bed. He leaned back and shut his eyes. He felt as if the whole world was sitting on his chest. A tear rolled out of the corner of his eye and disappeared into his ear. He turned on his side and drew his knees up to his stomach. He lay there, whimpering ever so quietly until a restless sleep finally overcame him.

Jimmy woke with a start, and sat up on the bed. Beads of sweat broke out all over his body. He'd gone through the nightmare of killing the young man again. Once more he walked to the shower and stood under the water. This time it helped relieve him of his nightmare. All he had left was the remorseful anguish of the actual deed. The brisk drying with the towel brought a glow to his skin and got his blood pumping faster. At least he was wide-awake, he thought. Driving down the street past the newspaper office, he watched the sun approach the horizon. Its rays spread light all over the city, casting a magic spell just before the fiery red globe could be seen. He looked but didn't see Doty's car. *What will he think?* Jimmy wondered. He felt dirty. Maybe it was due to the fact that he knew the colonel had covered up his crime. His reasoning ability returned. The worst he could have been charged with was justifiable homicide. He remembered the colonel saying that neither he nor the department could take the heat of an investigation. The grand jury was being brought into action at Becky's prodding. Now Jimmy understood the need for the colonel wanting to cover up. It all made sense. Jimmy noticed the colonel's car as he pulled into the parking lot. He was glad he was there. For the first time, he was going to depend on the colonel to pull his hide out of the fire. He wondered how many more times he'd have to rely on him.

Headquarters was quiet. He headed right for the colonel's office. He knocked on the door and was told to enter.

"How are you feeling, Dale?" asked Watson.

"I'm all right now, sir. I had a little difficulty getting over the fact that I killed my first ..." his voice trailed off.

Watson's face took on a cold and calloused look. "Young man, it may have been your first, but it definitely won't be your last. This is a violent business, and we deal with dangerous individuals. If you can't hack it you'd better get the hell out right now." Dale reeled from the impact of the tongue lashing. Watson's manner toned down, and he said, almost compassionately, "Look, kid, everyone has the same feeling when they make their first killing. After a while, it won't get to you so bad."

That's what I'm afraid of, thought Jimmy. Then he said, "I know, sir. I'll be all right. I definitely want to stay in law enforcement."

Watson handed some papers to Jimmy. "Here, read this. See if it matches the sequence of events as they happened. Then we'll be ready to see the sheriff when he gets in. I saved you the trouble of making out your report. I knew how much it affected you, and I didn't want to chance your leaving anything out."

Jimmy started to read.

"Of course, you'll notice a little variance from the actual details."

Once more Dale started to read, and once more the colonel interrupted, "You'll also notice, I included in there the fact that you called in and were told to commandeer the vehicle and its occupant. After I saw the vintage of the truck, I checked out the report. It's a heart-sickening situation."

Dale didn't understand the remorsefulness in Watson's voice or what he was leading up to.

"The license plate had belonged to a stolen car back a few years ago. The number was never removed from the computer. Last year, when the tags were re-issued, the numbers were fed into the computer. That's when the numbers joined up with the same number that had been fed into it years ago as stolen." Watson shrugged his shoulders, and extended his arms, palms up. "Hence, the command for you to stop the truck, when you called in."

The colonel had barely ceased talking when Jimmy blurted out, "You mean to tell me that the truck wasn't stolen that I killed an innocent man in cold blood?"

"I wouldn't say that. You were misinformed, that's all. You can't be held responsible. Besides, the sheriff isn't the type of individual that could cope with the unpopularity. It would place the department in, let's say, a less-than-favorable light."

Dale was dumbfounded.

Watson continued. "Considering the facts, I think we should keep that part of the report to ourselves. I've already removed it from the computer, so there's no official record. The only ones who know about it are the four of us: Johnson, Deets, you and I. So, let's keep it that way."

There was no mistaking his words for anything but a direct order.

Watson rose from his chair and glanced at his watch. Sheriff Myers should be in by now," he said as he started to the door. "Come on, let's go get this over with."

Dale followed, still speechless. He dreaded facing the sheriff about anything, but especially with this concocted lie. What made matters worse was he was helpless to do anything about it.

Watson knocked on the door, opened it, and entered without waiting for the sheriff's invitation. "Good morning, Sheriff," he said in a jovial mood.

Myers acknowledged his greeting and nodded to Dale.

"Sit down, men. What can I do for you this morning?"

The colonel placed the report on his desk. "Well, sir, we have a slightly nasty situation. This young man is on the verge of quitting the force over it." He gestured toward Dale.

That's a damned lie, Jimmy wanted to say. But he knew better than to open his mouth, or allow his face to show any emotion.

Myers looked at him and spoke in an understanding tone of voice. "Tell me about it, son. What did you say your name was?"

"It's Dale, sir. Jimmy Dale."

"You're new here aren't you?" the sheriff asked.

"I've been on the force almost six months, sir," Dale replied.

The colonel eased the conversation away from the present direction. It would only confirm the sheriff's inability to be concerned about his men.

"Well, Sheriff, this deputy was on patrol last night. He radioed in a license check as he pulled over a truck. It was all routine, until the man reached for a gun. Deputy Dale here," he reminded the sheriff he was one and the same man they were talking about, "Deputy Dale had to shoot the man in self-defense. It's all in the report, sir. Just like it happened." He gestured at the paper he had placed on the desk.

"Were the proper officials notified? What about the man's family? Who was he, anybody we knew?" Myers asked.

Patronizingly the colonel answered, "Oh, yes sir! The proper authorities were notified, and the family consists only of a wife. He has no other family." In a flat, unemotional tone, Watson added, "The unfortunate thing is, she's expecting a baby."

Dale cringed, realizing that the man's widow, after having to cope with the husband's death, would next have the burden of a new baby to contend with all by herself. All because of a stupid computer mistake.

Myers broke into his thoughts. "This is indeed unfortunate, Dale. But don't let it deter you from the life you want in law enforcement."

"Sir, I just don't know."

Watson cut him off, "I think I have him convinced to stay with the department. I told him time would ease the pain."

The sheriff assumed the colonel's comment to be fact. The deputy would be staying with them. "Dale, you go on home now. Try to get some sleep. It'll help you forget what has happened."

"Yes, sir." Dale could say no more. He left the office. Just as he shut the door he heard the day's workload being discussed by the two men. *How in hell can they dismiss all this just like that,* he asked himself. He quickly left the building. Suddenly he felt very unclean under its roof. Jimmy wished he could discuss the whole episode with Doty. For the time being though, he didn't have the courage. He hated to admit, even to Doty, what he had done. He drove in the direction of the river. The riverbank was a place that could bring him the peace and solitude he needed right now.

He sat for an hour, mulling over all the happenings of the past months, and the events leading up to his present situation. Now he was beholden to the colonel, and he knew it. He suddenly understood the colonel's concern for an investigation, coinciding with the grand juries. Dale was more clear-headed now. His reasoning powers were coming back. He knew there had to be a greater motive for the colonel's cover up. He had to laugh when he thought about Watson having to protect the sheriff. *Damn,* he thought, *Myers shouldn't even be sheriff, if he can't stand the heat and the pressure.* Jimmy's mind wasn't clouded any more, and he was beginning to feel better. He thought he would be able to sleep now. The killing still gnawed at him, but he had sorted things out in his mind. Now he felt he would be able to stand the pressure a little better. At least he hoped he would. As he drove home in the blinding sunshine, he asked himself how in hell a city this beautiful could support such corruption, and still maintain its beauty.

Billy woke with a start and glanced at the clock. He'd overslept again. On the way to the bathroom he reached down and gave Debbie's bare butt a hard slap. She didn't move.

Man, he thought, *she must've been bombed out of her skull last night not to respond to that.* He ran the brush through his medium-length, dingy blond hair, then brushed his teeth.

Getting dressed, he got his foot stuck in the leg of his jeans, causing him to hop to keep from losing his balance. "Oh, damn!" he said, as he hopped his way around the room, trying to dislodge his foot. The more he tried to free it, the more tangled up he became. As he started to plop down in the chair by the window he glanced outside. Something caught his eye. As fast as his entangled legs would allow, he got back up and looked out the window. He leaned on the chair for support. He needed to study the front yard. He thought he'd seen someone near the rear of his car. Now, when he looked, there was no one. *Damn,* he thought, *I've had so much on my mind, I'm beginning to see things.*

A chill went up his spine as he sat back down in the chair. He remembered what his mother had always told him as a little boy: that it meant someone was walking on his grave. Funny, what stories his mother thought up. She'd sure been credited with more than her share of tales. *Damn,* he said to himself, *I ain't going to have my old lady upset me today. I have enough on my mind.* He was still trying to resolve the problem of too many fingers in the pot.

The colonel, via Lemmon, had expressed his view on the matter, which was triggered by the near involvement of the city police, in a simple reprimand by a couple of his gang. He didn't like pressure, so Billy had to make a decision. He didn't want to have Greg leave; he liked having him around, especially when Debbie wasn't feeling up to par every month. Greg gave his life a little extra zing, with no questions asked. If possible, he'd try to keep Greg around and get rid of someone else. Donnie maybe; he was a little warped anyway, a wacko screwing up the works. Billy hesitated before going outside. Looking around, he descended the steps and got in his car. He started it and headed for work, never noticing the pair of eyes peering at him from behind the hedges.

Doty checked the messages on his desk. It was strange, he thought, that he hadn't heard from Jimmy for several days. He reminded himself to ask Alicia about him when she came in. He turned on his computer and began to compile the story on the shooting of the young man in the pickup truck the night before. He noticed the name of the deputy had been omitted from the sheriff's department release. He was hoping Jimmy could shed some light on the story. The paper had sent a reporter to the dead man's home to interview his widow. What she could tell them was very sketchy. He was on parole, but had never owned a gun in his life. She said he didn't like weapons. She'd been distraught over what she claimed was a senseless murder. Being pregnant with her first baby made her feel even more helpless. She wasn't able to shed light on any of the meager details given out by the sheriff's spokesman. Maybe tonight, Doty thought, he'd get a chance to see Jimmy. He could probably fill him in on the details. Anyway, he hoped he'd stop by; he missed his cheery smile.

Doty turned his attention to the letter he'd received from a vice president of a Baron County Bank. He asked that his name be withheld for obvious reasons. Clipped to it was a copy of a note that was self-explanatory. It read, "Dear Mr. Trent, Please help me. I am being held in the Leeward County Jail on trumped-up charges and I need your help. I have money in the Potters National Bank in Fort Manson. My attorney is trying to get me to give him my power of attorney, so he can draw the money out. He says he needs it for my defense or to buy my freedom. I want you to transfer my money, and put it in your bank. No one is supposed to be able to draw it out, unless it is my mother or my brother.

Please help me, for I have no other person to turn to." The letter had been signed, but the bank withheld the signature.

Doty read the note and filed it away in his desk drawer with other tips he was unable to use. If he printed the note, it could get the man in worse trouble. If the story ever surfaced, he'd definitely use it. Maybe someday, he thought, as he closed the drawer. Just maybe the grand jury would make it possible. Doty hoped they'd get the sufficient data together before the next session. To postpone would allow time for memories to go blank, hands to be crossed with long green, or witnesses to get scared and split. *Time surely does have a way of healing all wounds,* Doty said to himself.

He looked up from his desk in time to see Lou Share pass by. He nodded to him, and went back to his computer. *What an odd duck,* Doty thought.

Ray Yarbrough pushed open the back door to the department and started down the long corridor to his office. It felt great to be able to get back in the swing of things.

There was something here that made his adrenalin pump. The excitement he achieved being able to wield authority really put him on top of the world. The doctor had wanted him to stay home another week, but he had been out of commission long enough. He needed to get back in harness. Hearing of the possibility of a grand jury investigation had convinced him that he was needed at the department. He was sure the colonel would exhaust all efforts to prevent it from materializing. In the past he'd been able to stave off several threats of internal investigation. Ray was confident he'd be able to do the same thing this time.

"Hi, Ray. It's great see you back," said a familiar voice.

Ray turned to greet the outstretched hand of Captain Smith. "How are you, Lawton?" he said, shaking Smith's hand. "I'll tell you, it's great to be back, too. How's everything at C.I.D.?"

"Same old jazz. You look good, Ray."

"I should. You don't know how I've been pampered. Those hen clutches were starting to get to me. You can't believe the things I had to submit to because of my wife."

"Really?"

"She put me on a strict diet, took away my cigarettes, starting pumping vitamin pills into me, even got a friend of hers in to do my chart."

Smith looked puzzled.

"You know, my horoscope."

Smith started to laugh. "Hey, you don't believe in that garbage, do you?"

"Who, me? Hell no. You'd be amazed at the things I had to do to humor the little woman." He couldn't admit that the astrologer had impressed him. The reading she gave him had hit home in more ways than he would have believed. It was hard to understand how so much information had been derived from a mess of figures, lines and symbols on a circle. She had assured him that things would not go as bad with Becky as he'd anticipated. True or not, it helped to relieve his anxiety. "Anyway, the togetherness thing was beginning to wear a little thin." He wanted to get to a more comfortable subject. "Enough of that. What's been happening here, anyhow?"

Smith looked around, then motioned for Ray to follow him into his office. He closed the door, and said, "You read about the man getting shot in the truck?"

Ray nodded.

"Well, the new kid the colonel brought in shot him. And, you'll never guess who the guy was." He was like a kid with a secret not waiting for Ray to answer.

"He was the one Lemmon has been leaning on. The last time Larry roughed him up he got cocky and threatened him back."

Ray's mouth curled into a half smile and half grin. "That should send a message to the rest of the snitches that we mean business. When we want information, they'd better produce, or else. I'll bet the rate of cooperation increases one hundred percent from here on in. Did the Dale kid know who he was wasting?"

Smith scowled at Ray. "What! Are you kidding? That's the colonel's way of getting the edge and knowing he has him sewed up. You should've figured that out."

Ray laughed. "I guess I've been gone too long. I'm out of practice and losing my perspective."

They both laughed.

Smith prodded, "Hell, anyone who has to consult an astrologer to find out if the sun's going to favor you or not isn't too smart. All you have to do is look outside and see if the sun is shining."

Ray let it pass with a laugh. He only knew that somehow his chart did reveal past and present happenings. The future predictions he'd have to wait for. *Too bad the damned department didn't use one,* he thought. *Maybe they wouldn't have so many screw-ups.* "Well, let's get busy. Where do you need me?"

"Becky really threw one into us, and we can't afford to let her break it off, so we've really got to have our stuff together for this grand jury thing. Do you feel up to working on that?"

Of all the things to have to start back on, Ray thought. He would rather not have to tackle that, but he didn't dare say so. One who was no longer useful, was expendable. And he could be considered a weak link in the department chain. "Sure, why not?" he said, feigning enthusiasm.

Smith handed him a folder of papers. "Here, these will help you get started."

Chapter 25

When Jimmy walked into the newsroom, his visit was long overdue. He had finally faced the fact that he had to tell Doty it was he who had murdered the man in the truck. When Doty saw him coming across the room, he knew there was something wrong from the look on Jimmy's face. Doty finished the copy he'd been working on and rang for the delivery boy. He didn't want to leave now, after not seeing Jimmy for so many days.

"Take this to the copy room now for me, will you, Fred?" he asked the young man, without looking at him. He couldn't remove his eyes from the approaching deputy. At last Jimmy was close enough to speak to him without having to shout over the noise of teletypes and typewriters. "Hey, I thought you'd curled up and died," he said, as the copy boy went hurrying off.

"I wish I had," was Jimmy's downhearted answer.

This threw Doty. "Hey, kid, what's the matter? You sick?"

Jimmy shook his head. "No, I'm not sick, leastwise physically."

Doty got up, stepped to the side, and looked into an empty nearby office. "Let's step in here and talk about it, kid."

Jimmy wasn't looking forward to it, but he couldn't prolong it any longer. So he followed the reporter in the room, and Doty shut the door. The deputy looked for a chair to sit in, and flopped.

Doty walked over to him, bringing a folding chair. "What's the matter, Jimmy?" he asked as he sat down. "I've never seen you like this the whole time I've known you."

Jimmy hung his head, and the tears started to well up in his eyes. He felt like hell, and he didn't care who knew it.

Doty reached out and touched his hand; it was trembling. Doty's instinct gnawed at him. "Holy Moses! It was you, wasn't it?" The light had suddenly dawned. He knew what was bothering the kid. "Why has it taken you so long to come and talk with me?"

Jimmy had difficulty talking, for the lump in his throat choked him. "I killed a man, Doty. I didn't mean to. It was one of those mistaken things...well...you know how it goes."

Doty had heard what Jimmy said, and he had a hundred questions he'd like to ask, but Jimmy's condition now was of greater importance. "Do you want to tell me what happened?" Not giving him a chance to answer, he said, "You don't have to...if you don't want to, you know?"

The deputy wiped his face on his shirtsleeve. "I've got to tell someone. You're the only friend I have, and the only one who'd believe me."

Jimmy looked more serious than Doty had ever seen him when he said, "Doty, what I tell you has to be between friends, and not a story."

The reporter shook his head in agreement. "Sure kid. You know if you ask me, I'd put your wishes ahead of a story."

"Doty, they own me. I no longer have any control over situations, and I'm just sick. I don't know where to turn. It seems like the men I should be able to tell are as corrupt as he is."

Doty knew he referred to the colonel. He allowed the kid to keep talking, while he listened. He'd truly thought he'd heard everything there was to hear, but when it came from one he loved as his own, he had his doubts. It sounded different and its impact was harder. After Jimmy ceased to elaborate on what happened, Doty knew he had to tread slowly. But he had to ask one direct question: "Jimmy, are you actually telling me that he literally covered up the fact that you accidentally shot the man because you thought he was going after a gun?"

"Yes," Jimmy answered.

Doty's investigative qualities took over. "Now let me get this straight. He or the dispatcher told you the truck was hot, so you approached it with that in mind, right?"

Jimmy nodded, never raising his eyes to Doty. "Yes, afterwards they told me the computer hadn't been cleared from the previous ownership of said number. That's why it printed out stolen. With that in mind, I proceeded with caution, after I stopped the truck. Honest, Doty, I would never have shot the guy had I known he was only taking a tape out of his player."

Doty looked at him in amazement. "What did you say?"

"I said I wouldn't have shot him-"

Doty interrupted, "Never mind that. How in hell did he get the gun, if all he had was the tape?" Doty was bewildered, for this was the first mention of a gun. Jimmy neglected mentioning the gun, for he was more distraught about shooting the man then their covering job. "Are you telling me the colonel concealed the fact about the man not carrying a gun? Let me guess. I'll bet he got one out of his car and placed it in the guy's hand."

Jimmy looked up for the first time. "How did you know that?" he asked. With red-rimmed eyes, he searched Doty's face for the answer.

"Well, kid, if you'd been around the lawmen that have walked both sides of the law like I have, you'd be able to figure out the particulars also. I've always felt it took a special breed of men to become cops. Most have had to wander over that thin margin between right an wrong. They've devious minds, and they know the mind of the criminal. The majority popped back to the right side. Those that didn't became colonel's. Part of the luck in solving crimes is learning to outfox the crook knowing what they would do if confronted with the same predicament." Suddenly Doty dropped the subject and told Jimmy, "You sit here. I'll be right back." He made his exit and Jimmy was once more alone in his misery.

He would be glad when Doty returned; his presence replaced the hurt that had resurfaced.

The door opened up and Doty bounded in, gliding into the chair. "My boy. Sweet, sweet Jimmy. You've been had." With each word his voice rose in volume till it was practically a shout.

Jimmy looked at him in wonderment. How could Doty be so jubilant when he, Jimmy, was in such a mess.

Doty calmed down when he saw the confused look on the deputy's face. His outburst needed an explanation to clear up the kid's thoughts before he scared the hell out of him...Calmer in manner, he spoke, "Jimmy, I've just checked an article I remember seeing back when they first installed that computer system. They'd stated its innovated memory bank automatically erased all the prior years' numbers, as new ones were fed in their place." He proceeded to try to enlighten the deputy on the intricate mechanism of the computer. "It's just like when the telephone company obtains an inactive number. It's put on ice, so to speak. The license tags go through basically the same process. They're shelved for a reasonable time. Jimmy, you were set up...I haven't figured how they did it yet, but I do know you were deliberately put on the hook. The reason is obvious. They're getting you ready to be put into action. That's what you wanted - it's just too bad the young man had to be wasted in order for the colonel to get a hold of you. He'll figure you'll be beholding to him now. Let's not let the man's death be for naught."

Jimmy couldn't believe his hears. He'd known of their calloused tactics, but now that he was the basis of the action, he finally realized how corrupt it all was. He got up and put one hand on his hip, while using the other to rub his hair back and forth. "Damn, damn, damn," was about all he could say. Then his anger set in. "Those rotten bastards set me up."

Doty hastily shut the door. "Look kid, I don't know for sure, but I think someone here has to be watched out for, too. So we have to be exceptionally careful. They've started a cancer, and it's spread. Only the Lord knows where."

The deputy clenched his jaw and looked at the newspaperman. "Doty, I've never told you what changed my life and directed me into police work. I think it's about time I disclosed it to you. When I was a young and stupid kid, I felt the world owed me a living. The world was my oyster and all I had to do was take what I wanted from the weaker ones. I never got caught." He hesitated, and drew in a long breath of air to fortify him. "One night, I needed some money and I decided to drop in on my brother, who lived here in the city. I hung my hat mostly on the other coast, though I bummed around for awhile. He was always the more stable of us two boys. That's all there has been; our parents died while we were still small." His face took on a sad look, and his eyes took on a far-away stare for a few seconds. Then he continued, "He was a good brother. I'd always looked up to him. No special reason, I guess, unless he was all I had. He'd helped raise me, while he himself had no one to maneuver him through his pit falls. He was a quiet-type person, except when he had a few beers. Then he got loose-lipped. In fact, I feel that's what was his undoing. One night he'd had a few beers and he disclosed, to all who could hear his big mouth, where a large stash of pot was being baby sat for. Well, the owners of the pot beat the hell out of him. He went down and swore out warrants for their arrests, but he never did find out their last names. But he did do a positive I. D. on a mug shot of one of the guys. Then the department prolonged the whole thing with weak excuses, like they couldn't find the last names, but they were still working on it. Then they had to turn it over to the state attorney's, who dragged their feet.

"Now, back to the night I blew into town, unannounced, for the loan. I'd known about the prior beating, for he'd come over to my pad to recuperate. What a mess he was. The doc says it's a wonder his jaw wasn't dislocated and some teeth knocked out. The only thing that had saved him from that was, while he was getting the hell beat out of him, the other guy held a gun on him. All he could do was clench his teeth and take the beating. The clenching of his teeth saved the jaw and the teeth until later." Jimmy's' emotions were getting aroused with the length of his tale.

Doty didn't move a muscle. He just sat and listened to the ghastly tale being told to him.

Jimmy continued. "When I opened the door to his apartment, I felt something was wrong. He didn't answer me. The radio was blaring away. So I started to look for him. Finally, I found him. He was hanging from an old ceiling light fixture in his bedroom. I ran because I was scared. I couldn't do anything for him. In the next day's paper, the coroner ruled it suicide. I saw him, Doty. He didn't take a jump off nothing. His battered body hung like a limp bag of broken bones. The bastards beat him so bad his eyes were cut and swollen shut. Taking the beating he suffered, he probably wished he were dead before they finally killed him. This time they'd managed to shut him up permanently. They buried him with little fan-fare. Hell, they wanted to get him in the ground before he got cold. What could I do? All I could do was make a silent vow to my brother to one day be able to avenge his death. To someday meet them face to face. After he was buried, I tried to get a copy of the report he'd filed, but none could be found. Things have a way of getting lost at the department. I did remember once he told me three names of those who were heavily involved in trafficking. Billy, Brian, and Greg. Last names never came up. But I feel someday, somehow, they'll surface. Then I'll know the last names of those who are also responsible for his murder."

The room was silent. The sound of the teletype floated through the adjoining partition.

Jimmy was mute and still deep in thought.

Doty was digesting all that Jimmy had told him.

The deputy was first to speak. "You were right when you stated a cop has to walk that narrow line, to dip far enough to the other side to get that taste of fear in your mouth, and the smell of it in your sweat. Did you know you have a different smell about you when you're frightened?" As an afterthought, he said, "My God, do you realize, there have been two men killed on account of me?"

Jimmy concluded the prior discussion and again gained Doty's interest. "I found I could accomplish nothing by staying around here, so I headed back to Miami and the police academy. I changed that night I saw him hanging there, Doty. It took me seeing my brother killed in cold blood to make my life take on a meaning. That's hell...They've got to be stopped, Doty, but what in hell can we do? We have no one to which we can turn. No one we can be sure of, who isn't on the take. My God, we'd be wasted without them batting an eye."

He finally stopped talking long enough for Doty to say his piece. He hadn't wanted to give Jimmy the idea he wasn't willing to hear him out. He was aware of the burden that Jimmy had carried around for years. Now he could see Jimmy's relief at getting it off his chest. Jimmy needed encouragement and support. "Look, we have to keep on like nothing has happened. You might as well prepare yourself; they're going to give you a chance to commit yourself to them fairly soon. Prepare for it. When you're directed to perform something that isn't to your liking or according to the book, you're on your way. So be always alert to the situations. Either go along with them, or you might as well get out now; they can't be overthrown. We haven't gathered enough data. It will take time."

Jimmy listened to the advice. "Well, as I am responsible for a man's death, I might as well stick it out to see that justice is done."

Doty thought a minute, then said. "You may not like the things they ask you to do, but you'll have to make yourself do them."

"But what if it's something so bad that I'm not able to do it? There are things where I'll draw the line."

"We'll cross that bridge when we get to it. Always remember, I'm in it with you; you're not alone. Maybe we should bring someone else in on it." He hesitated, then said, "No, I don't think we'd better."

Jimmy had been doing some thinking while Doty mulled the matter over. "You know, Doty, this may be bigger then either of us can imagine. You're risking a lot if you get involved. Maybe you shouldn't. For years you've built your status. I would be a shame to throw that all down the drain."

"Listen kid, you've been honest with me. Maybe it's time to tell you the stake I have in seeing the final downfall of the sheriff and his raiders."

Jimmy interrupted, "If you're going to tell me about the incident with your wife and daughter, I read it in the clippings."

Doty was surprised. "You have done your homework, haven't you?"

Jimmy nodded.

"Then I guess we've got a deal," said Doty, as he extended his hand to Jimmy.

Jimmy's grasp was firm and sincere. "I feel like a criminal talking about deals."

They both laughed.

"Except for one thing, Jim. There is no honor among thieves, and there is between us."

Dale made up his mind as he walked out of the paper that he'd have to become hard as nails, or he'd never be able to deal with the colonel. Even if he were able to revert back once the deed had been completed, he was certain its effects would remain with him. He would no longer be the same sensitive person he now was. Was it all worth it? He asked himself. Was he going to wallow in the slime and filth? Become the same thing he despised? *Yes,* he thought. *It is worth it.* Then he said a silent prayer. God, give me the strength to do what has to be done. Forgive me if I should sin in your eyes, for only through your will can it be done. Jimmy never considered himself religious. He believed they're to be a Supreme Being, but he had never done much praying. Now, suddenly, he felt he was going to be doing a lot of it, from here on in.

Shifts changed the next day.

The colonel approached Jimmy as if he were playing into the game that Jimmy and Doty had devised.

A drug bust was planned on a house that had been watched for months. Its involvement in the drug scene was known for sometime. The ring was allowed to flourish as long as it benefited the department's sales, then it ceased circulation.

Deputies used force and roughed up the men to the point that police brutality could have been charged. Jimmy was sick to be involved in the rough tactics used, but for the sake of being convincing, he didn't show it.

Deets and Lemmon conveyed Jimmy's performance to the colonel. They were told Jimmy would have to perform one more task for him before he would be convinced.

By the time supper was consumed and papers prepared, the sun had set. Then the three men, Deets, Pool, and Dale, headed for the car.

The downtown areas were the main haunts for young people who'd turned informers and snitches. Most were paying the department back for favors received, while the rest enjoyed the advantage it gave them over their peers. Some proposed informants were reluctant and had to be persuaded. They were usually the ones with the most informative tidbits.

The trio had already hit both bars where the young set hung out. So far they weren't able to turn up anything.

Pool said, "For Saturday night, there doesn't seem to be much action."

They entered the Broken Arrow bar parking lot out in the East End. Then Pool backed the car under a tree and doused the lights. "Lemmon, why don't you go in and have a look see? Maybe we'll hit pay dirt here." He was getting tired. Of not reaping any rewards.

Lemmon was gone about ten minutes. When he returned, a man in his early twenties, with shoulder-length blonde hair accompanied him. The deputy's hand gripped his arm.

Pool beckoned to Dale. "Come on, we'll give you the first lesson on getting information."

It was Dale's turn to play the role. "It doesn't look like he was too anxious to help us," he said, as he got out of the car and slammed the door with a bang. He knew the first impression he had of his companions was important. He also knew he was under scrutinizing eyes, so he had to act as they wanted him to.

Pool tucked his shirt in his pants, acting out his roll.

Lemmon brought the young man over to where the men stood by the car then pushed him, so he hit the car with a thud. "Things would go a lot easier on you if you'd come around once in awhile. We wouldn't have to come looking for you if you gave us what we want," said Lemmon.

Pool motioned Dale closer.

This was the moment Jimmy had dreaded. Now it was facing him.

"Why don't you tell the kid about the judo you learned at the academy in Miami," said Lemmon, pointing to the visibly shaken young man.

It was apparent to Jimmy that the man had been pressured for information before. He approached to within a foot of the boy, and they stood face to face. "You got anything to tell us tonight?" said Jimmy gruffly. "My colleague here and I need some vital information. I hear you're capable of giving it to us. Is that right?"

The young man's eyes had a defiant look, which made it easier on Jimmy to do what he had to do. It was vital to him and Doty. He brought his knee up with such a quick thrust that it thoroughly surprised the young man and the other two men present.

The blonde doubled over in agony.

Jimmy had tried to make it appear more brutal then it was. It was almost impossible to keep from hurting him to some extent. "Now, maybe that jarred your memory a little bit," said Jimmy, leaning down to the man who was now crouching on the ground.

What happened next, Jimmy wasn't expecting. Therefore, he had to use some tactics he'd not wanted to use.

The man reached out, grabbed Jimmy's legs, and brought him to the ground. Then the young man landed on Jimmy.

Temporarily, Jimmy was at a disadvantage. He again needed to gain the upper hand, and, in order to do that; he'd have to hurt the kid. He resorted to his knowledge of judo and had the young man on the ground within a split second. Then he pounced on him, and proceeded to beat him about the head and upper body with his fists.

The young man tried to fight back, getting in a couple of lucky punches. But he was far over matched, so it didn't take Jimmy long to out maneuver him.

"Hey, Dale, we don't want him unconscious," said Lemmon. "We want his mouth to work."

Jimmy pulled his fist to a stop in mid-swing. "You got anything at all? No matter how stupid or unimportant to you it might seem? Come on, damn it, talk, if you can. If you don't, I'll give you a little more, so you won't be able to talk to anybody for a while."

The blonde raised his hand, and said through bloody lips, "All right! All right! Just don't hit me again, I don't know that much."

Jimmy started to raise his fist.

"No, I mean I'll tell you all I heard, but I don't know all that much."

Jimmy relaxed his clenched fist. "Ok, then talk, damn it. We haven't got all night. I want to know all you've heard or been told about a B&E in the city. Some expensive jewelry and weapons were ripped off. It would be stuff you'd never see broads in these dives wearing, unless it had been ripped off. They don't have that much class. Tell us anything you've heard or seen."

"Well, I heard this guy was trying to push some hot guns. You know, pistols, and his girl was trying to sell some jewelry at the Bock Lounge. I was going to go take a look at them," he added hastily. "But I never got there. There were quite a lot of people...you know...looking. This guy gave rings and other pieces of jewelry to this girl."

Jimmy took the initiative. "Can you describe him?"

The blonde tossed his dirty, mud-matted locks from side to side. "Nope. I never saw him, but I was told to ask or look for a kid called Don."

Jimmy directed his eyes in the direction of Pool and Lemmon, who had remained on the sidelines. "Is there anyone in the bar now who might know this guy? Perhaps someone who may have received a piece of jewelry?"

"No, I don't think so....Wait! There was some girl earlier, who had jewelry all the way up her arm. But she was only in they're a minute, and she appeared to be looking for someone. I don't know anything else.

Honest!"

Jimmy looked at Pool, who nodded his approval. Then he said to the young man. "Okay, you did real good. Man, I won't forget it, but you better get something done with that face. It looks like hell." Jimmy felt bad for having to do such a number on the man. One day, he might be able to give him an apology he hoped he'd understand.

"Hey," the blonde man said to the departing deputies, "Don't tell no one where you got the information. Please. I hear that guy's a weirdo. He's crazy. He carries a gun down back of his pants loaded and cocked. He told everyone if they talked about his loot, he'd find them and blow them away. He isn't bull-shitting either. I tell you, he's crazy."

The men proceeded to the car.

"Don't fret, man. Mum's the word on where we got our info," Pool said out the window of the car, as he pulled out of the parking lot into traffic.

Then he directed his comments to Dale. "Hey kid, you really did a number on that dude. He'll be hurting for a long time to come."

"Well, did I do the right thing, or did I over-do it?" Without asking, Jimmy knew. He'd done just as they wanted, and he'd given a class "A" show on his aptitude.

"Hell, you did ok as far as I'm concerned," said Lemmon.

"I just hope he doesn't decide to leave town. He's been a wealth of information. It seems like he knows when or where everything goes down," Pool said. He added, "Why not turn on the radio and let's see what's happening."

Lemmon complied.

The numbers sounded over the radio, giving the coded instructions to other patrols on the road.

"Hey, listen to that," said Pool, drawing the two men's attention.

They stopped talking and listened.

"Car 185 to 188, what's your 10–20?"

"I'm coming in at the end of the street to your left now," car 188 answered back.

"We'll catch them in between us, if you douse your lights when you turn the corner and come in towards me."

"10–4," 188 acknowledged.

Lemmon said, "Evidently, they're trying to catch someone in the act of something."

"185, where are you now?"

"I'm coming down the street toward you ..."

The air went blank, and a rackling noise was all that could be heard.

"What the hell went wrong?" asked Pool. He picked up the mike. "501 to 185 or 188."

A weak voice from the other end broke the silence. "188 to 501."

"What in the hell happened?" asked Pool.

The silence lingered so long, he was about ready to call again. Then the voice came back.

"501 take it to channel 5 and scramble." Both did this. Pool, concerned, asked for an explanation of the preceding events.

Sheepishly, the reply came. "Well sir, we received a tip on a pot party taking place in this vacant lot. We'd planned on approaching it from different directions. We could have had them with the goods, plus prevented them from being able to split in their cars, if we had had both ways blocked."

"Well, did you catch them?" asked Pool.

"No, sir," the voice said.

Annoyed, Pool asked. "Well, what happened?"

"We were running with no lights, and we ran into each other... head on, sir." The reply was barely audible by the time he had finished.

"Jumping Jesus, and all the saints. You mean to tell me you hit head on?"

188 answered back. "Yes, sir. It looks that way, sir"

Angrily, Pool demanded, "Call the wrecker, and get those cars back to the barn before people see the idiots we've got on patrol out there."

"10–4," was the final reply.

"Sonofabitch. This makes five vehicles those clowns have wrecked this month. What in hell kind of rubber jockeys we got driving anyhow? Man, the colonel will go through the roof, not to speak of the sheriff. He'll make the colonel's hole look like a bb hole."

The conversation amused Lemon and Dale.

The deputies cruised around the remainder of the night. They had made their initial score.

The impact of the report on the beating Jimmy had given the young man was lessened when it accompanied the demolition derby report given to the colonel. He was pleased to hear that Dale fulfilled his expectations, but when he learned that two more cars were wrecked, he went through the ceiling. Capable as he was, he covered it up to the sheriff, saying that the deputies had been closing in on a speeding car, which had suddenly pulled to the right. The deputies hastily maneuvered to keep the car from crashing into them, and hit each other. They didn't mention the fact that they were running with no lights. The sheriff was annoyed, but nothing compared to what he would have been had he known the complete truth.

With the ever-increasing probability of the grand jury's convening and reviewing the charges brought by Becky against the sheriff's department, tension mounted, especially with the department heads. They were the ones whose heads she was after, and who would feel the impact of the charges.

Doty disliked the Sunday paper. The extra news items had to be worked in that had been missed all week. He was working later then he expected. It was early morning, when he liked to head home for bed.

Jimmy saw Doty's car, and stopped. The change of pace Doty offered him was refreshing. Today he needed a friend to cheer him up.

Doty was just coming out of the copy room, as the deputy approached his desk. "Hi kid. You look like you've had a rough night." He sensed the low morale in the young deputy. "Something you want to talk about or just tough times?"

Jimmy walked into the empty office without saying a word. Doty had picked up the right vibes. He wanted to talk about something.

When the door shut, Jimmy started to talk. "Man, I sure hope this pans out the way we hope it will. I hate to lower myself, beating up defenseless men, like I had to do last night. They're barbarians! I roll right in the filth with them. It's a wonder there're any honest cops left in this country. The lousy rotten bastards! They really take the shine away from the good cop."

Doty knew Jimmy was mad. He'd never heard him cuss as he was doing now. He contributed some of it to nerves.

"Sit down here, kid, and tell me what's making your collar hot."

Doty remained silent a couple of minutes after hearing what Jimmy had to say about his encounter hours earlier. The he said, "Well, you knew it'd be nasty. The worst is yet to come. You felt you could take it."

Jimmy, more fortified, looked back at Doty. "I still do and I am." He got up and left the room without speaking another word to Doty. He walked over to Alicia's desk and, without a word to her, bent down and gave her a quick kiss on the mouth.

She was stunned, and wasn't able to say anything before he was gone.

Doty stood in the doorway of the room they'd just occupied, grinning at Jimmy's actions. He knew it was Jimmy's way of fortifying his own convictions.

Poor Alicia, he thought. She didn't know what was going on, but Doty did.

That's all that mattered for now.

Chapter 26

While he pondered the thought of staging another dope raid, the colonel sat at his desk. The department was losing prestige in the public eye. Something needed to be done to boost it back up. He knew of a house his men had been watching for a long time. Its occupants weren't choice, so it didn't matter if they were roughed up a little. The colonel rang for Smith. "Come in here, will you?" He didn't wait for an answer, and left Smith talking to himself.

Smith rapped on the door, then entered. "What's up, Don?"

"Haven't you guys had a house of potheads under surveillance for sometime?"

"Yes, we have," Smith declared.

Watson informed him. "We need some warrants, so tell Stewart to have some make up. We'll hit it tonight. They're always having one more fling on Sundays to fortify for the weeks' work."

Within an hour they were knocking down the door at a Market Street apartment building. Entering unexpectedly, sent naked bodies running all over the place. Taking advantage of the situation, heads got banged and feels were copped.

"I wouldn't mind fifteen minutes with that little thing there," said Pool.

"I'll hold her for you, if I can have seconds," Lemmon added.

"To hell with that. I'll hold her for you, if I can watch," Sullivan commented, eyeing the young girl's bare body, as she unsuccessfully tried to cover herself with her hands.

"Your wife wouldn't think too much of that, Barry," Deets remarked.

They all laughed.

"To hell with it all. Load her with the rest of them. She's probably got crotch rot anyway." Smith's comment sounded futile.

Thornberry, reluctant to give away a chance, said, "Yeah, but I think it's worth the chance from what I saw when I kicked in that bedroom door. What do you say, Dale?" Deets asked.

Up to this point, Jimmy had kept from contributing to the conversation. "Naw, I don't believe I want to take the chance."

"Oh, that's right , you're getting all you need from that sweet little number at the *News Leader,* aren't you?" sneered Lemmon.

The reference to Alicia being that type of girl made Jimmy mad, but he said, "You bet I am, and I don't need to stray."

The contents of the raid, human cargo and drugs, were rounded up and taken downtown. The confiscated drugs were catalogued, and taken to the back room, where they substituted their contents in the plastic bag for powdered milk. The drugs were destined for the street, via the colonel's own delivery service. Up to now, Lemmon had been the main courier, but the colonel had different plans for tonight's bounty. He was going to get one more hook into Jimmy.

Colonel Watson had waited till everyone had written up his reports, then he made his move. He called Deputy Dale into his office. "Jimmy, I have something I'd like to have you do for me. Tonight's haul of smack was choice. I have to have it delivered. Will you drop it off on your way home?"

Jimmy's palms started to sweat. He tried to act casual, as he answered, "Sure. Where do you want it taken?"

Watson wrote down the street and number, then gave it to Jimmy. "You sure you don't mind?" he asked the deputy before releasing it from his grasp.

"Yeah, I'm sure," he said. Then he put the paper in his shirt pocket, without showing concern over its contents, bid the colonel good-bye, and left the room. He was dying to see the paper, though he refrained from removing it from his pocket until he had stopped at the red light on the corner. "Holy Moses! River Grove Apartments, "he exclaimed. He thought about calling Doty. No, he'd better wait. He might be watched.

He arrived at the apartments just as a paper man was delivering the paper. He spoke as they passed, and Jimmy returning his greeting. The deputy made sure the man was around the corner before he knocked on the door. He knocked again. This time, he heard stirring in the apartment.

The door opened.

There in the doorway stood one of the biggest shocks Jimmy had since he'd hit Ft Manson. It even prompted him to take a second look at the paper in his hand, to make sure he'd not made a mistake.

"Come on in here," the man said, "and stop looking so damn dumbfounded. What's the old saying? Comrades make strange bedfellows, or something like that." His voice trailed off in a slurred effort to recall. His cocky, flippant attitude did not befit the type of character he was.

"I'm giving you a message to take back to your boss. You tell him, I want a bigger cut. I won't accept anything other than a positive answer."

Jimmy didn't add a word to the conversation. He just shook his head, then took the money handed to him by the man. If he'd had to speak, he doubted very much whether he could have.

"You tell him, if I don't pass it on in the gay bars, he'll lose all their trade. Therefore, I want a bigger slice. Also tell him, I saw his boss the other night. We've become very good friends. I'm sure his boss would be interested to know who supplies me."

Mr. Share's comment jolted the deputy. *No wonder Doty never knew of Shares's socializing with any of the other employed,* Jimmy thought. *Wait till Doty gets a load of this one.*

Jimmy's observant eyes saw a door ajar across the room. It slowly closed.

Share took hold of Jimmy's arm and casually escorted him to the front door.

Just his touch made Jimmy's skin crawl. For two reasons: the dope involvement, and he knew he was intentionally touching his body. Jimmy didn't need persuasion. He left gladly.

Once outside, the air cleared his head. He was hoping to catch the colonel before he had a chance of leaving headquarters. He was sure the colonel would be interested in what he had to say. Luckily, he located a phone booth on a nearby corner. He had just been given the private unlisted number, but he had to look through his billfold twice before he located it. The phone rang three times. Jimmy was about to hang up, thinking he'd missed the colonel when he answered.

The relaying of Mr. Share's message was done quickly and concisely.

The colonel's anger caused him to blurt out a command, giving no mind to the caller. "I want you to waste that bastard at the earliest possible convenience, and I don't care how. I can't afford him. I won't have any trouble getting some one to replace him One monkey won't stop the whole show."

The colonel hung up before Jimmy could say any more. This was one of the colonels traits; he was fast learning many of them. The major thing Jimmy was aware of was that he was in now, and in for good. It scared the hell lout of him. For the first time, he knew he'd bit off more than he could chew. He scoured his pockets for another dime.

"*GOD DOTY!* Be there," he mumbled under his breath as he dialed. The phone rang five times. Jimmy's heart was pounding. "Oh," he muttered.

The sixth ring was interrupted by Doty's sleepy voice. "Hello."

"Doty," was all Jimmy had to say.

Doty's first call from Jimmy brought him wide-awake. "What's the matter, kid?" Doty asked with concern.

"My God, Doty, now I've been given the instruction to murder a man. What in the hell am I going to do?" The idea of murder far outweighed the importance of who was to be murdered.

"Can you get over here without being followed?" asked Doty.

"Yeah, I think so," he replied, as he looked around. "I'll be over soon. I'll make sure I'm not being followed. See you in a little while." He hung up the phone, went back to the car, and sat. Watching the rear view mirror for movement, he noticed none.

Several detours on the way to Doty's further assured Jimmy that he wasn't being accompanied. Doty's garage door was up and Jimmy pulled the car in. Then he pulled the door down and entered the house through a connecting entrance.

As soon as he saw the lights turn in the driveway, Doty rushed to the door to meet him. "Jimmy, you look like hell."

Jimmy went into the living room with Doty close behind. They both sat down. "I feel like hell," stated Jimmy.

"Will you tell me what in hell's up?" Doty asked anxiously.

"Man, I never thought I'd have to go through what I went through tonight. I sure got fooled. It only proves were aren't playing games."

Doty was getting irritated. "For crying out loud, will you tell me what the hell you are talking about?"

Jimmy started to explain.

Suddenly Doty's face took on a most peculiar look. His facial expression didn't change until Jimmy had finished telling him the events of the evening.

"I'm glad to see it hit you the same way it hit me. At least I don't feel alone anymore," said Jimmy.

Doty made a half attempt at a whistle. "Wow! That sure is a blast.... No wonder he never fraternized with the other personnel personal."

"Hey, that's the same thing I thought," said Jimmy.

"Man, what the hell am I going to do? I'm sure as hell not going to waste that dude...no matter what." Determined, he said, "I'm not committing murder, for anything. The only way I'm shooting someone is in the line of duty...and I hope I never have to do that ..." He added, thinking about the truck incident, "again."

"Hey, don't worry about that. We'll cross that bridge when we get to it. Our time now is of the essence," said Doty.

"Just don't worry," Jimmy mocked. "Hell, that's easy for you to say." Then, noticing the distant gaze in Doty's eyes, he asked, "Doty, what the hell are you thinking about now?"

Doty snapped alert to Jimmy's question. "Remember when I told you we had to be careful, because I felt that someone in the office was tipping our hand?"

Jimmy agreed. "Boy, you aren't kidding there, man. We could be wiped out," he clicked his fingers together, "just like that...Just like the colonel told me to waste Mr. Share. He's playing for keeps. He just calls for an extermination, and that's it." Jimmy was astounded at his own words. He had thought it, but hearing it aloud almost made him disbelieve what he'd been ordered to do.

"Hey, I keep telling you, we'll take one thing at a time. We'll cross that bridge when we get to it." He was talking, but Jimmy wasn't listening. Doty wanted to relieve him of his frustration. "You'd better get home, and get some sleep. You work tomorrow night, don't you?"

He'd distracted Jimmy again.

"Huh...Oh, yeah." He departed without further talk.

Doty understood. With Jimmy being so engrossed in his thoughts, a mere good-bye would have interrupted his concentration.

The paper completed, Doty headed home to bed. He was concerned for Jimmy's welfare. The mess he was in, or could get into, was serious, even to a seasoned reporter, let alone a green kid. Sure, he had his own dangers. He would print the damn story, but Jimmy had to live it.

Doty slept most of the day in a fitful rest. He was as tired when he awoke as when he had gone to bed. As he prepared himself for work, his mind was not on today's news, but on Dale. His skin crawled when he thought of the consequences. It was of the utmost importance that he appear confident. Without himself for support, he knew Jimmy would never be able to pull off his facade. Doty had to masquerade as a pillar of strength for Jimmy's sake.

The department had just entered the two-week shift. The colonel and his bandits had the night trick, and all had to adjust to the late hours. On the 3–11 shift, they rarely were able to leave on time, with all the reports they had to write out and with covering the goof-ups.

Colonel Watson knew damn well the fagot from the paper had to be silenced, and right now. He wondered if he'd done the right thing in demanding it of Deputy Dale. It was too late, now. It was done. He'd have to keep tabs on the kid, though. To make sure he didn't goof-up the job. He'd appeared as if he were getting adjusted to the routine. But the smoothness of Jimmy's approach to the action didn't curb the cautious element in the colonel. Rather, it kept him even more aware.

Jimmy had to force himself to get out of bed. He wanted to arrive at the department with enough spare time to check out his zone. He had been moved around from area to area, and never knew where they would be needing him next. He would acquaint himself with an area, then shifts would change.

Hours remained before he was scheduled to clock in. Being restless, he couldn't do anything, so he decided to head out. Maybe he'd get a chance to see Doty before he went on duty, although there wasn't really anything to talk about. It was the first time since he'd known Doty that he'd felt that way. *Damn mess,* he thought. His relationship with Alicia had tapered off also. *Sure hope she doesn't get interested in another man,* thought Jimmy. *That'd be about the worse thing that could come out of this whole mess, except losing my life.* He tried hard not to think of that, but most of the time he didn't succeed. The idea seemed always to creep into his thoughts, taking all the joy and fun out of the things that had once given him pleasure. Now the thought of having to go into work brought an added pressure, for he knew if he wasn't constantly alert, he'd slip up and tip his hand. He often found himself examining his ability to undertake this dethroning of the political corruption in the county. At least he wasn't alone; he had Doty, who was an inspiration to him. Each time they met, Doty reinforced his confidence. His not having the knowledge of how far up the ladder the corruption reached made it even more dangerous. Doty had given him the needed thrust to propel him onward. Even now, as he thought of Doty's comments, they gave him the strength and determination to vanquish bewilderment and doubt. If it weren't for America, he wouldn't even be given the opportunity to try, or Mrs. O'Hare either for that matter.

Doty had said, "It took just one woman to take the religion out of the schools. She had to overcome much adverse public opinion. Her life must have been sheer hell, bucking odds that large. Yet she succeeded in doing what she set out to do. Not that Jimmy or Doty agreed with her philosophy, or beliefs. It was Doty's way of proving something could be done by just one person. Jimmy had been doing a lot of praying. It was ironic; he'd been doing the things she fought against. He'd be using all the strength and power God could give to get him through this.

He truly believed he had to commit all his efforts to expose the corruption to the public. What they did with it was another thing. There were many county residents who didn't like the actions of the political machine that functioned in their county. They wouldn't exert themselves to work out a solution, so they became part of the problem. Many chose to turn their backs, hoping it would go away. It didn't. That's the food that fed the corruption and allowed it to flourish and spread, consuming everything it touched. Until the public faced the true facts, it would continue to spread and feed. It had to be obliterated, and the only way to do that was to fight. At least Deputy Dale would give it the college try. Then he'd know he'd done his best. Jimmy didn't feel like a soap box preacher, but he felt he'd been chosen. He knew he was fighting for his very existence, and the future of the young kids coming up. Some day his kids, if he expected to stay in Leeward County. The county didn't have much future, if the fact wasn't made known soon. The public had to look long and hard. He'd overheard conversations about reform having to start at the top level of government before it could be dealt with. Jimmy didn't believe that to be the case. He wanted to see it start locally, at the source. Doty and he had had quite an in-depth conversation that night. Each time Jimmy thought of it, it gave him the added burst he needed to go on. Doty's support affected him like a pep rally. Added to his own ideals, the doubt dissipated. Jimmy took a long breath, ready to charge headlong into the problem.

He stood under the shower for at least a half hour, spending most of his time thinking. Water strangely affected him. It worked like a purifying agent on him, spiritually and bodily. He turned for one last splash in the face, then turned the water off. After rubbing his body vigorously with a towel, he moved it up to his close-cropped, curly black hair, and rubbed it to remove the water that remained.

Just as he hung the towel over the shower rod, the phone rang. He walked casually to the bedroom to answer it.

"Hello," he said.

There was silence at the other end.

His heart leaped to his throat.

At last a soft, feminine voice said, "Jimmy, am I interrupting you?"

It was Alicia. The heart in his throat now beat faster. "No, you're not. I just got out of the shower."

He could sense she was uncomfortable about calling him.

"You know, Jimmy, I wouldn't have called you, except I hadn't seen you lately and thought perhaps you were not feeling well.

Jimmy thought that to be as good an excuse as any for her to call him. He was aware she knew he was all right, for she'd asked Doty several times about him. He tried to make amends. "Every time I'm at the paper, you're not working yet. Lately I've had such off-beat hours. Nights that I'm off I'm dead tired, so I sleep. I'm sorry, honey, I haven't gotten back to you in so long." His tone of voice made her like putty in his hands.

"Gee, Jimmy, I'd hoped maybe we'd be able to get together for a movie. We could just sit and talk. My mom and dad would love to meet you."

"I didn't know they knew about me." He was shocked to find she'd discussed him with her parents.

"Yes, they know about you. I hope you don't mind my telling them. I'm all they've got, Jimmy, and we're relatively close knit."

"What do they know about me?"

"Oh, only what I've told them, which wasn't derogatory."

He was more relaxed, and talking came easier. "When this shift changes in four days, we can take in a movie if you'd like."

"That sounds super," she said. "I'll wait to hear from you then. Okay?"

She wasn't giving up on him. He was glad to find that out. Intentionally he'd slighted her, not wanting to cause her anguish. He'd not intended for his feelings to go so deep, but they had, more than he cared to admit. Knowing about Share being the inside man, he'd rather his chance of having Doty involved not include Alicia also.

"Yeah, I'll give you a call, or I'll stop in. I definitely want to spend some time on my days off with you."

With the promise as proof she'd see him again, Alicia allowed him to go get ready for work.

After her call, he leaned back on the bed and stared up at the ceiling. "Damn! That's one hell of a woman." He bounded off the bed and went about getting dressed, all the while humming a little tune.

As he was putting his time card back in the rack that held some

150 other cards, a voice that was unmistakable summoned him. With repulsion, he turned around and faced the colonel. He had taken his one step back; now he was prepared to charge. "Yes, sir?" he asked.

The colonel motioned for him to come into his office. Then he disappeared into the room, waiting for the deputy to join him. "Come in. Shut the door," he said, as Dale appeared in the doorway.

It was difficult to tell what was on his mind, so Jimmy trod lightly.

"Come over and sit down."

Jimmy did as he was told.

"Jimmy, I've been thinking," started the colonel. "Are you sure you're capable of handling the job I gave you last night?" Not wanting to sound reluctant to use him, he hastily added, "I mean, do you need some help?"

The colonel made a poor attempt of trying to offer aid. Needing assistance was the farthest thing from Jimmy's mind. He squirmed on the hook. "Oh, no sir, I don't need any help. I figure the less people in on a job, the less chance of botching it up. Don't you agree, sir?" Jimmy had to take the chance and he hoped he hadn't overplayed his hand. He couldn't risk the interference of a tag-along. How he would pull it off, he hadn't figured out yet. He hoped Doty would come through, like Doty had led him to believe. The only cohort he needed was Doty. Definitely no departmental representative.

The colonel, not wanting to feel outfoxed, quickly agreed with the deputy, "You have something there, Dale. Have you figured how you'll do it yet?"

Jimmy was on the spot. He replied with the first thing that popped into his mind. "Well, sir, I think suicide is out. There have been too many of those lately. As for a crime of passion or robbery, there aren't too many of those ways to bump someone off and make it look authentic. We don't need any questions asked of the wrong people."

The colonel was satisfied with the answer. He only added, "The quicker, the better."

With the colonel's instructions, Jimmy took the opportunity to exit. His knees went weak with the thought of Doty's plan nearly shattered. As he shut the door to the colonel's office, he breathed a sigh of relief.

One of the seven patrols zones within city limits was assigned to Dale that evening. He spent most of the night just circulating the area. It was senseless to have patrols in the city, he thought. The city police did a superb job of patrolling and protecting the city. Dale was sure one thing the city would hesitate to do was secure a back-up unit from the county.

The onslaught of heavy downpour made his patrol easy, for the city police handled accidents. Jimmy cruised the city and noticed the clean appearance it had after the rain. Essentially, it was a beautiful city. Since he'd moved here, it had grown by leaps and bounds. As he passed under a street light, he looked at his watch. He'd float around the south of the city, he thought. The bars would be closing about now, so he'd stop in at Rivers Bend restaurant soon and have a bite to eat.

The restaurant was packed. Usually a cop positioned himself in the back of the room facing the door. It wasn't possible tonight; he had no choice but to sit in a side booth near the door.

When the waitress came to clean off the table, she asked, "You alone?"

Jimmy answered, "I am right now, but probably not for long."

Rarely would a fellow deputy, hearing that one of his own in the area was on break, fail to join him. They liked to eat with their own, feeling there was strength in numbers.

Chapter 27

Doty's dislike of the morning newspaper was because by the time the paper hit the street, the news was old. Radio and television, on the other hand, gave quite good coverage at day and night.

Doty obtained the department's press release after going to Highland Hills. It was skimpy and didn't say much, which was par for the course. He felt they didn't know much, so they couldn't make up for something they lacked.

Published with the story was their general composite lone gunman had held up the bank, but he'd been seen in the get-away car with two other men. The car used to flee the scene belonged to a young woman, who was completely without knowledge of the robbery. So ended the sheriff's quotes. Doty thought the colonel had probably prepared it. *Everything usually is,* he told himself. *I'll bet the sheriff can't even take care of bathroom duties without the colonel's being there to wipe him.*

It took all of five minutes, and it wasn't much of a story, but Doty was helpless to improve it. He had so little to go on. Disgustedly, he pondered the condensed words. Hell, this would probably fall by the wayside of unsolved crimes, as the bank robbery in the south of town did. The department would use it to produce great headline publicity. Gradually, the case would be moved to the back of the file cabinet, as others took its place.

"Oh, damn," Doty said, as he tore the paper out of his typewriter and rose. "I might as well take this one to the copy room myself. I need a cup of coffee, after this farce ..."

The evening was also upsetting for others that night.

The colonel had just received the assistant attorney's call, which informed him of the need for another supply to replenish the sources that were running low. It would take time to set up a raid, Colonel Watson explained, but he'd take care of it as soon as possible. Stewart mentioned hearing of a disgruntled man in the fold who wasn't content with his cut. He told Colonel Watson the boss passed the word to shed the excess weight. The man had become a hindrance to the operation. Stewart also told Watson of hearing from his stepson. The young fellow was adjusting to living in South America. He'd had to disclose his involvement in the operation. Now Watson got the impression that Macomb's participation wasn't as hard felt as they had anticipated. He'd become quite vital to the operation in South America. At least they felt more secure knowing one of their own men was in on the beginning of things. Hopefully, it would prove to be more advantageous.

"Don't worry about the greedy one. You tell the man that I've already taken action to lighten our load," Watson told Stewart.

Stewart replied, "We were notified that the governor has ordered a grand jury investigation into the alleged accusation on Becky's sworn 55-page statement."

"Bullshit! That won't make the sheriff too happy. Does the state think they can handle it without making us look black?" asked Watson.

"One good thing, we hand picked the jury, and it'll be held in closed quarters. One of the witnesses giving testimony has the favor of four judges. You might say, he has them in his pocket," added Assistant Stewart.

"Must be damned awful crowded in there," the colonel quipped. But it didn't work. Stewart ignored the comment.

"I'll be calling you within the week and hope to have more information. You tell Sheriff Myers I called. Tip him off about the grand jury's investigation. He'd better get busy and improve the department's image in the public's eye, before they get wind that one is on the way. We'll try and play it down. But you know the man has appearance to contend with in an investigation of any wrong doings."

"Okay, will do." The colonel got the message. "Be in touch later." He hung up, and sat there, pondering his next step. He'd have to talk turkey; reassure the sheriff that things would work out, without leaving a black mark on the department. Hell, it could wait till morning. He was going to get a few hours of sack time before he faced Hank with that. The sheriff always felt *his* department was lily white, the stupid fruitcake. If he'd ever stop to look, he'd realize things were going on right under his nose. He was only interested in appearance, and being the figurehead of one of the biggest sheriff's departments in the state.

He had a lousy rapport with his men, and his ability to be re-elected shocked numerous people. Especially when men in his own department campaigned for his opponent. Few actually knew the real reason behind the tactics for the deploying of an opponent. Perhaps it was for the reassurance, that whoever acquired the post, would not interrupt the deals and corruption. If the public had been made aware of the relationship of the opponent to Billy Carter, the corruption would have been easier to expose.

Watson checked the locked position of the top drawer on his desk, then he surveyed the room with his eyes before dousing the lights. He left by the rear entrance, after placing his peg on the out-of-service column on the duty board.

Doty tore his report out of his typewriter just as Corcoran stuck his head in the door.

"You about done?" he asked Doty.

"Yeah, I just finished up. Why?"

"I was wondering if on your way home you'd mind stopping by Mr. Share's. I've been trying to reach him on the phone, and I can't get any answer. He's got a report at home that I need. I'd go get it myself, but I've a scheduled meeting that I can't put off."

Doty started to clean up his desk and cover his typewriter.

"He probably didn't hear the alarm go off and overslept," Corcoran said.

"Yes, I'll stop by."

"I'd sure appreciate it, Doty. I could use that report at this meeting. Tell him if he can get here with it as soon as possible, I'd appreciate it."

Doty finished tidying up his desk and reassured Corcoran, "Sure, consider it done. I'm going that way anyhow."

Corcoran said, "Thanks," and was gone.

Doty headed out east, and turned down River Drive. Mr. Share's apartment complex contained six apartments. His was on the far end of the building. Doty drove in the parking area and followed the walk to the end of the building. People hadn't yet begun to stir. The early risers had gone to work and left their sleeping families behind. School being out, the majority of kids were sleeping in. Their activity didn't start until later in the morning, after cornflakes and cartoons.

Doty knocked on Share's door and waited. He knocked again. "Come on, come on," he said under his breath. He knocked once more... only louder. He didn't care if he did wake other tenants in the complex. He was getting annoyed. "Hell!" he grumbled. "Maybe he's on his way to the office already. I could have passed him, or he just took another route." He stood there wondering what to do. He knew Corcoran needed that report. He didn't know why, but he suddenly reached for the doorknob and tried it. It turned. The door was ajar. Doty paused, then nudged it about four inches into the dark room. "Mr. Share," he called through the crack. No answer.

Then he sounded his name again. This time a little louder. "Hell!" he said. As he was about to shut the door, the thought passed through his mind that it wasn't normal for Share to go away and leave his door unlocked. So he pushed the door open and entered the room. He groped for a light switch on the wall. *They're always on the wall by the doors,* he thought, as he ran his hand down the wall. His hand ran across something rough and hard. A shiver went up his spine. His fingers lingered a second and continued on for the switch. Finally with his left hand he found it, and closed the door with his right hand at the same time.

Doty scanned the once dark room. It was very attractively decorated. Nothing compared to the way he'd thought it would be, though. It didn't look macho enough. He walked to the kitchen area and peeked around the corner.

No Mr. Share. The only other rooms left to check were the bedroom and of course the bathroom. Doty went in the direction he suspected the bedroom to be. He got to the door, and it was ajar. He stopped. *If he didn't hear me come in, I'd better try to raise him once more, before*

I go barging in on him. He rapped on the bedroom door. No response. Then he opened it and stood there looking at the bed. "Holy mother of Christ!" He said in exclamation. For a few seconds he didn't move. He remained still, gazing at the scene on the bed.

There was Mr. Share, trussed up hand and foot. He was on his stomach. His hands had been tied behind his back. Cord had been wrapped around his feet, then brought up his back, and looped around his neck. It appeared that when he could no longer bear the strain of his legs from dropping, the rope had tightened around his neck, and he'd strangled himself, very slowly from the look that was on his face. His eyes were open, very wide. In fact, they looked like one more little tug, and they'd have popped right out of their sockets.

Doty finally moved toward the body. He knew Share was dead, but he felt his cold skin for a pulse. There was none. He moved around the room, searching for a phone to call the police. He finally spotted one on the nightstand by the wall opposite the bed. He lunged for it. *Damn!* He thought. *This place would have to be in county territory.* He started to dial their number, then he stopped and put the phone back. He stood there a couple minutes, deep in thought. Quickly picking the phone back up, he dialed a number. The phone rang on the other end. "Come on, answer it. You got to be there," he muttered.

On the fourth ring, the voice said, "Hello."

Doty said, "Jimmy, I don't have time to explain right now. Just do as I tell you and do it quick. I think we have a solution to your problem."

Jimmy was caught off guard. "What problem?"

Doty was annoyed with him. "Damn it! Will you do just this one thing without questions? Please! Just this one time?"

Jimmy heard the anger in his voice, but he thought he recognized something else in it too. "Sure. What do you want me to do?"

Doty was relieved that he didn't have to go into detail on the phone. "Get in your car and come out to Mr. Share's apartment."

"He lives in the apartments on River Drive?"

"Yes, on the end of 'C' building. Come in plain clothes, and park down the street. Walk around the back of the building when you come in. Knock lightly on the door, and I'll let you in. Please hurry, Jimmy," he pleaded. "It's imperative. Do you understand?" Not giving Jimmy a chance to reply, he added, "Oh yes, and don't wear anything that resembles cops." Then he hung up.

Jimmy put his shoes on, then double checked his attire, making sure he didn't have anything on that would suggest the law. He did, however, put his gun in the shoulder holster he carried when off duty. He drove as fast as the traffic would allow. He drove to the right section of town and parked his car down the street from Share's place. He walked quickly to the apartment. He didn't dare break into a full run, as Doty had told him not to draw attention. He was eager to see Doty, to find out about the mystery. It wasn't the best idea for him to be going to Share's place, after receiving the directive from the colonel. He knew Doty was aware of the dangers connected with his being seen there, but Doty's pleading gave Jimmy no choice. Jimmy walked around the end of the building and knocked on the door of the end apartment. It opened immediately, and Doty yanked him inside the room.

"What the hell is going on Doty? Your crazy, having me come here, after what the colonel told me?" Jimmy said in a whisper, for fear of being overheard.

"There's no need to whisper. He's not going to hear you. Better not talk too loud, though. Someone might overhear you."

Jimmy looked at him in a weird way. "Man, you sure do talk in riddles."

Doty took Jimmy by the wrist and led him to the bedroom, without saying another word.

Jimmy stood in amazement at the rocker-shaped, lifeless form. "What in the hell happened?" he asked.

"I don't know. Jimmy, I dropped by to see why he didn't come in to work....I found him like this." He gestured toward the bed. "I started to call the sheriff, and then happened to think this could be the thing we need to pull you're meat out of the fire."

Jimmy looked at him in amazement. "What in the hell are you saying? Tell them I did this to him?"

Doty pulled him off to one side, as if to keep from being overheard. "Look, this is the thing that the colonel wanted done, isn't it?" Doty tried to sell Jimmy on the deed. "Well, hell, he'll cover it up for you. All you have to do is drive Share's car to the boondocks." Doty tried to convince the deputy the plan would work. "Out there in back of the airport, you let the car roll into one of the canals. It will never be found. When the rain season hits, the water rises in there waist deep to a tall Indian. No one in his right mind would go out there to battle that army of mosquitoes. You won't have to worry about his car being found for a long time, if ever. It will appear as if someone robbed him and left him like this."

Jimmy thought, *Here we're talking about how to cover up this man's murder, while he's right here.* Though Doty was convincing, Jimmy still had the colonel to contend with. It was the choice of the worse of the two evils. He continued to think as Doty began to talk again.

"You take his car and deep-six it, while I make the place look like it was ransacked. It will cut down on the time. Then I'll call the sheriff's department, and report what I found. You call the colonel and then he'll be able to lay the groundwork to cover it up. He has to! He told you to do it. Now get going, and I'll get back with you later. Don't worry! After you get rid of the car, walk back out to the highway; then call a cab to bring you back to your car. It's parked far enough away so as not to draw attention to it for a few hours."

Finally, Jimmy looked at Doty and said, "You know I appreciate your doing this for me, when his is one of your own. His death though should be vindicated."

Doty said, "Go," giving him a nudge toward the door. He'd said all that needed to be said.

After Jimmy left, Doty wasted no time in making the apartment appear disheveled. Then he calmly rechecked everything, making sure the place was as he wanted it. He allowed time for Jimmy to call the colonel, and then he took a long breath and dialed the sheriff's department.

Meanwhile, the private line on the colonel's desk phone lit up.

Watson pushed the button and picked it up. "Yes?" he said. His facial expression soon changed from a blank stare to a smile. "Good! I'll take care of everything. Right now you just get his car gone, and I'll hold off sending a *Bolo* out on it. I can give you time to get back into town." He hung up, leaned back in his chair, and smiled. His eyes lit up with a twinkle. Then he placed his hands behind his head and waited.

Not much time passed before the sheriff's department was notified of finding Share's body.

"It was Doty, the reporter, the one who brings our paper every morning, sir. He found the body," Corporal Eaton told the colonel.

"Boy! That's sure to go into print first. Dispatch the nearest unit now. Tell them to let no one touch anything until I get there. I'm on my way. Also, call the sheriff. He should be in on this one. It'll probably make one hell of a loud outcry from the paper. There sheriff should be prepared from the outset."

Without giving Corporal Eaton a chance to answer him, he was gone. He felt she would carry out his orders.

That she did. The sheriff beat the colonel to the scene.

"Get you out of bed, sir?" the colonel asked him, as he casually approached.

"No, I was up. Planned on getting an early start on some paper work this morning. That damn treasurer's appointment to the sheriff association has been a pain, and the added work I don't need."

Their conversation was casual, as they walked toward the murder scene. Additional units were fast arriving.

The coroner didn't hesitate staying away from this one. He looked like he'd slept in his clothes and just crawled out of bed. His hair could have used a trim and his unshaven face gave him the appearance of a skid-row bum. But he seemed unscathed by what others thought of him. He lived in his world of the dead. His appointment in his official capacity was beyond defending. There wasn't need for his having a degree. Although his assistant was required to do so. Doc Stone once had his eyes on greater goals and finally did acquire his doctorate.

As the sheriff and colonel entered the apartment, the sun had risen well above the horizon. The bright day's sunshine sent rays streaming through the wide-open doorway. The coroner, with no emotion, stood and looked at the body. Then he asked the colonel, "Your men got all they need? I'd like to get some preliminary ideas, before I send him to the morgue."

The colonel looked at the crime lab personnel that had been busy lifting prints, making notes, and taking the usual pictures.

One extra picture-taker had been added to the usual. It was Doty. He took his pictures at different angles in silence, almost as if he were taking them for reasons other than reporting a story. He swiftly covered every angle that the police photographer did, and some besides. Then he was gone.

"Well, I guess he's all yours, Doc," Sheriff Myers said. It was the first display of his authority since he'd been on the scene.

The colonel had withdrawn into the background, wanting to make sure that nothing suspicious would direct anyone's' attention toward Jimmy and the cover-up.

The Doc drew out a pocketknife from his pants pressed the button, and the blade popped out. In a blasé' manner, he then reached down and cut the window drape cord from the dead man's ankles.

"Damn! I sure hate them in this condition. It's harder than hell making them lie flat....That's one hell of a way to have to be laid out, too. He'll appear as if he's trying to peak over the top of his casket," he said, laughing to himself.

No one else could grasp his morbid sense of humor. Doc Stone reached over and pushed the body over on its side. He then took the towel away that had been wedged between the dead man's legs. "Holy cow, what do we have here?" he said, as he leaned closer for a look at what had been the man's penis. "I should say, what haven't we got here."

His comment aroused the other men's curiosity, bringing them closer to the bed.

Hank gasped when he viewed the sight on the bed.

By reflex, all the viewing men placed their hands to the front of their trousers to reassure themselves that their penis still hung there.

Docs Stone stood erect and rubbed his hands together. "Well men, I would say our Mr. Share has died in what you might call a crime of passion, sometime during the last twenty-four hours. I can be more explicit in time, after I do the autopsy." He then motioned for the ambulance crew to take the body.

Everyone reached for cigarettes. Colonel Watson didn't bother with reaching for a light. He waited till all the others had theirs lit then asked Lemmon to light his.

"Well, I think we'd better wrap it up and get back to the office. It looks like we'll have a full day," Sheriff Myers said.

Colonel Watson knew he was referring to the other men; he was aware he'd be the one to fill out the report and give the news release. That would have to be accurate, for Doty had probably gathered all the details needed to write his story. Time would tell. The colonel silently hoped that Jimmy had retrieved his car by now, and been unseen by anyone. *I sure didn't think Dale had it in him,* he mused, *to do what he's done to Share.* The colonel thought he'd make a personal visit to Doty, and find out how he had happened to find Share. If he showed Doty he was concerned about one of his colleagues, he might be able to chalk one up for he department's side. It wasn't too often he could do that, and he needed all the points he could collect.

The phone rang. Doty cursed under his breath, but answered it. "Yeah," he said, and kept typing. He listened. Suddenly, he stopped clicking away on the keys, and asked, "Hey! Tell me what happened?" He listened again, then breathed a sigh of relief. "Hey kid, I hope this is going to go okay. You're sure the car won't be found?" He was silent for the third time. "Have you seen the colonel yet?" He paused, then said, "That should be an interesting conversation. I would like to be a fly on the wall. All right kid, keep me posted. Good-bye."

Mr. Share's remains should be sent to Rochester after cremation here. That would cut down on the freight costs, Doty thought. *Good God! I'm getting as morbid a sense of humor as the Doc.* The way Mr. Share met his demise hadn't been revealed to anyone, or even hinted at in the article that was to be printed. *What a hideous way to meet the end!* thought Doty. As his eyes scanned the account, he concluded that it was sufficient. The article would lead people to believe he'd been trussed up, and, when he struggled to get free, he had choked himself to death. The fact of his having been a homosexual was never mentioned. The Doc had passed it all off lightly, Doty remembered. The sheriff was the only one who had been visibly shaken by the ghastly scene.

Doty shouted for a copy boy, and tore the paper out of the typewriter. Now he was glad he had a few minutes to think. He was more relieved now that Jimmy had called him to tell he'd made out all right. *It sure is a risky situation that kid is playing with,* Doty thought as he leaned back and folded his arms. *I hope he can carry it off. It's not so hard to cover up something once you plan it, but to be quickly thrust headlong into it makes it difficult to keep up with what's happening and not to trip yourself up.* Something still bothered Doty about the call from Jimmy, but he didn't know what. *Well,* he thought, *I guess I'll head for home and get some sleep.* "Damn!" He said aloud. *I may be getting little sleep today, but old Share will have lots of it. Too bad his murderer won't be caught. Maybe in the long run, his murder will be vindicated, with the exposure of the corrupt law enforcement in the county. Share's family up north will at least be spared the publicity of it all.*

Chapter 28

The colonel had a task to perform, but he'd had lots of practice at carrying on a routine investigation and not being able to uncover anything. He'd put up a good front, fooling everyone, including the sheriff. That meant more needless paper work.

The prick would have to demand a larger cut out of the operation, thought the colonel. The thing that had gone undetected by the colonel was that Share knew the sheriff. The story would state that the person who murdered Mr. Share would have had sufficient time in which to make his exit from the city. In the long run, he'd completely eluded the police. That would be the final story. Sheriff Myers would have to be stuck with it. Colonel Watson had sent two deputies he could trust to cover the routine questioning of Share's neighbors. If anything came back incriminating Jimmy, he'd misplace it. He wanted no suspicion thrown on Deputy Dale. A lost or overlooked report wasn't out of the ordinary.

A knock came at the door. Watson thought, *what the hell could it be now? Damn, it's hard to get a breather.* "Enter," he said.

The door opened. Will Wood of the telephone company security department walked in.

"Hell, I never expected to see you again so soon," said the colonel.

"Well, I didn't realize you'd have to end up having so many of your men's telephone conversations taped. I was getting one hell of a bundle, and I thought I'd bring them over," he said, as he took them out of a brown bag and handed it to the colonel. "When will you have time to listen to all of them?' he asked the colonel.

"I don't listen to them unless the need arises, say like with the case Becky's' trying to build. If it doesn't die, I'll be ready for her. Listen," he said jokingly, "if the government can have their Watergate, I could have my tapes, too." Seriously, he asked. "You've never told anyone about these, have you?"

"Hell no, I haven't" answered Woody. "You know it's strictly illegal. If I got caught, I could kiss my career in any phone company goodbye. In fact, I probably wouldn't be able to get a job in a place that even had a phone."

"What I pay you for this is handsome enough to make up for that," the colonel threw out to him.

Woody ignored the payola comment and continued. "Your men only know about an occasional wiretap, right?"

"Yeah, that's right, and I want to keep it that way."

"Well, the highly technical way this is set up, there is no chance of having it detected, unless someone requests wire tap check of their lines. With this gadget we use, it only kicks in as the conversation starts, and halts when it stops, which cuts down on the needless waste of tapes. And with the search mechanism they use for detection of wire taps, this system I am using immediately senses the probe and disconnects. It is highly secretive but it works great in situations like this. Not many around the country are being used. I have a connection high up and was able to acquire one. It gives out only faint clicks, nothing to make anyone suspicious."

The colonel didn't miss his chance to belittle Woody's place of employment. "Hell, with the condition of this phone company and the lousy service it gives that click wouldn't be anything to draw attention. It's always full of clicks."

Again, Woody ignored the colonel's comments. He felt uncomfortable. "I have to get along. I was gathering quite a supply, so I thought I'd run them over to you. I have trouble finding places to keep them. Where the hell do you, anyhow?" he asked the colonel.

"Oh, I manage to find room."

"Well, see you Colonel," and Woody was out the door.

Colonel Watson reached into his pants pocket and took out his ring of keys. Leafing through them till he found the one he was looking for, he slipped it in the keyhole on the right desk drawer and unlocked it. When he pulled the drawer open, he paused and surveyed the large stock he had accumulated. He'd been having tapes made only for the past year, and he'd already had to transfer the drawer twice. Each time he purchased new tapes, he thought someday the pay off would be worth the investment. The drawer was about one-third full. He rearranged them in order. He took the rubber band off one small pile. Dale was written on a piece of paper under the band. This time, there was one tape for his pile. Watson hadn't been receiving tapes of him, so he drew the conclusion Dale didn't have much phone conversation. The colonel once had listened to one. It was so boring listening to Dale's conversation with an old Miami classmate that the colonel gave it up, and shut off the recorder. *That kid sure was a bore in his social life,* Watson thought. He hastily added tapes to the other groups in the drawer, lingered over Becky's accumulation, and thought. *I'll have to get busy on Becky's tapes pretty soon to pin her to something.* Then he closed the drawer and locked it.

The men's incoming reports would have no bearing on the final outcome of Mr. Share's murder report, so Colonel Watson worked on it. He couldn't chance the female deputies knowing its contents, so he typed all three himself. He alone would be knowledgeable of its content, in comparison to the incoming reports of the investigation. He wanted this off the docket as soon as possible. Naturally, no evidence would ever surface on the stolen car; everyone would suspect that Share's murderer had used it to drive out of town or the state.

The main disturbance for the colonel came from the almost constant phone calls. The phone rang again. This time he answered it with annoyance in his voice. "Yes," he said harshly. The annoyance changed when he recognized the caller.

"Yes, sir, we are looking for the newsman murderer!" Watson said. He then ventured a question, which he usually didn't. "Has someone issued a complaint that we are shirking our duties, sir?"

"Listen, I've been subjected to enough pressure out of that girl's murder at the beach, that you have yet to solve. Her parents are exhausting all the influence they're capable of wielding. For your information, I don't like being on the hot seat. That is what I pay you for! All I need now is to get the pressure started from the press. Once the wire service picks it up, the whole damn story will be publicized all over the country. That will be very detrimental to my political career. It won't do much for your health either, my dear Colonel," State's Attorney John Costello asserted.

The colonel took its meaning. In doing so, he also took offense. "You have a hell of a lot of nerve, sitting up there doling out the directives to keep your hands lily white, while the rest of us have to wallow in the mud. You keep all the benefits, and do nothing for them," Watson shot back.

"Don't forget I had my choice on which side I wished to favor. I'd have been further ahead to cooperate with the syndicate, who is more experienced in carrying out their orders than your group is. I might add, if it weren't for my being in my influential position, your advantage over the unsuspecting victims you have on the hook would be nil. If the syndicate ran the whole works, which I alone have been able to placate, you wouldn't have a snowball's chance in hell. You'd better pull in your horns and look at the situation at hand. Do something about it, and quick. Have I made myself clear?" Costello asked.

"Yes, I believe you have." Things weren't going to well. "I do have to tell you, though, I've had a lot on my mind. I hope you take that into consideration." Having to apologize went against Watson's grain. "We've always been able to work things out in the past with no hitches. I hope we can continue to do so." The colonel's tone changed from what he had used moments earlier. He hoped to smooth Costello's ruffled feathers. He wielded a lot of power and could control almost any situation, and the colonel knew it. But with the pressure and the many hours of sleeplessness, the colonel's fuse was short. He had allowed his raw nerves to become irritated. He formed his words apologetically, but he wasn't sure whether Costello accepted them or not. It was difficult to tell.

Costello said, "I have urgent business to transact, so I'll have to get back with you later." Then he hung up, leaving the colonel with the dilemma he'd so often left others with, a dead phone.

"That bastard," the colonel said. *He has Stewart do all his dirty work. Stewart does his running, playing errand boy, and then Costello has the audacity to put me on the carpet, to throw his weight around. It sure would be interesting to have his phone bugged.* He hadn't yet dared, for Costello was too wise and would detect the tap. Then Watson's' life wouldn't be worth a plug nickel. He sat at his desk, holding his head in his hands. He tried to sort things out in his mind. That was the trouble, having so many things going at once, so many obliging men at your disposal.

With the new electronics communications system at the department, Watson could summon each man with a different frequency so that no two would ever know what the other men's involvements were. They were a loyal lot, this group he had at his command. They knew to keep their mouth shut about their actions. Watson did know, however, that he had to produce something that would suggest that he and the departments were securing results. He knew that the most pressing at this time was finding the murderer of the Lesso girl. Given the similarities of the murders, he knew he was looking for a perverted man who had an attraction to the female sex organs. The murderer gave both a final addition to the already horrible crime he had perpetrated. This person had to be evil through and through.

If Watson could only find that man, it would get the state off his back. He would be allowed to get back to the routine business of the department. *Damn,* he thought, *I've never had words with Costello before. I sure didn't need them now, either. I hope he accepted my apology, after considering the fact that I've been under extreme strain lately. Oh to hell with it! He couldn't do anything to me and not expose himself too.*

Confident and secure, Watson settled back in his chair, pleased with himself at solving that problem so soon. Now, if he could only solve the girl's murder, he'd have it made. He, of course, would go to all extremes to find her murderer. If he ever would run up against some wise guy who needed to be put in his place, he'd pin the crime on him. That was one way of eliminating his problem children and solving the crime at the same time. With the help of the assistant attorney, putting together a case would pose no threat. If things ran according to usual procedure, Watson wouldn't have to wait long for a patsy. Someone was always cropping up who had a big mouth that needed silencing. He had found there was no better way to make them lose their train of thought then to have to defend themselves on a trumped-up charge. After being charged, whether they were cleared or not, their word didn't have much credibility. They came off looking like the jerk, no matter how the trial ended. He had all the angles covered. Once more, he was in search of an angle to get the state man off his back. Deep in thought, a knock on his door caused him to jump. "Come in," he said in a much less gruff voice then he had used at prior times.

Yarbrough entered the room. Closing the door behind him, he said, "I just got word there's another small shipment coming in at the abandoned army barracks tonight." Saying this, he sat in a chair.

"Why in hell don't they give us more notice than this?" asked Watson.

Yarbrough shook his head slowly. "I don't know. Unless they're uncertain themselves about being able to get through."

"Weren't you supposed to stop smoking after you had that stroke?" asked Watson.

"Yeah, the Doc told me to stop, and I tried, but I couldn't find anything to replace the habit of always having something between my fingers." He didn't dare tell the truth. He had to revert back to smoking for his nerves. He didn't want the colonel to know that he was capable of cracking under pressure. The excuses he had given were the quickest one he could think of.

"Back to the shipment," the colonel said. "I think I'll send Dale tonight to retrieve it."

Rubbing his chin with his left hand, Yarbrough gave the appearance of deep thought. "Don't you think that is a little early to give him that sort of involvement?"

The colonel looked at him and smiled. "He performed beautifully on his last assignment."

The captain took a last drag on his cigarette, then crushed it out in the ashtray. He asked," And what was that?"

"You heard about the newspaperman, didn't you? I'm sure you realize there's a good reason for my not having put an all points-bulletin on his car yet." Mockingly, he stated, "We have to allow time to check with all his friends. Maybe one of them will have knowledge of it. By that time Deputy Dale will have been able to cover his tracks.".

Captain Yarbrough sat looking at the colonel, then spoke in an astonished voice. "You telling me he did that?"

The colonel nodded.

"Well, I'll be a sonofabitch. I sure didn't think he had it in him to pull off something like that."

"To be quite frank, I didn't either, but he proved me wrong. Now

I think he's capable of picking up the shipment, don't you?"

"Hell, yes, I would say he is too. And he could probably use the extra money that comes to the retriever of the shipment."

As far as the colonel was concerned, the conversation was at an end. He wanted to get on with other things, so he started to straighten and shuffle papers around on the desk.

The captain took the hint and rose from his chair.

"Get a hold of Dale and tell him I want him as pickup man, will you?" Watson said. I'll assign him special duties tonight. That will take him out of the demands on patrol. Oh, yes, also give him a state map, detailed and outlining the abandoned air strips and drop points. You have an extra one, don't you?" The colonel asked the captain.

"Yes, I'm pretty sure I do, in my desk. That reminds me, I'd better get some more made up, too. A couple of the guys have complained that theirs are getting a little tattered and worn."

The colonel looked up from his desk and said, "Make damn sure you get one back for every one you give out, too. I want them all back. That reminds me of the call from City Detective Harl. He told me about a woman who brought him in a map last week. She found it blowing in her front yard. It appeared awfully suspicious to her. He said the markings on it were like someone was using it for flying a plane, instead of a directional land map. He told me to be on the look out for any suspicious cars in the outlying areas while on patrol. Naturally, I assured him we would, and thanked him for the information." He laughed in a mocking manner, then, seriously added, "That map definitely showed the landing areas that have been used. Some half-wit jerk probably let it blow out of his car. He probably didn't realize it was missing until he tried finding the location of the next incoming shipment."

"I'll bet he was spitting nickels, looking for that drop zone," the captain said, then proceeded out the door. "I'll take care of that as soon as possible." He shut the door behind him.

Dale didn't show much concern when he was handed the map. He folded it and stuck it up over the visor, leaving his study of it for later, when he would have uninterrupted attention to give it. At present he was heading south, toward the airport road. When he turned onto the road, he headed toward what used to be the old World War II army base in Buckingham. It took him into a deserted remote area. He still had what he thought to be a reasonable length of time before the plane was to fly low and drop the sacks of contraband. He was told there was no fixed time the plane was due in. No set pattern was formed. It kept the chance of detection and getting caught slim. Often, the plane would not even make a drop. If when flying over the site things didn't *feel* right, the pilot pulled up and proceeded on.

Dale pulled the unmarked car to a halt, at the end of an overgrown dirt road. He'd have to walk the rest of the way in. This location hadn't apparently been used for deliveries for some time, as it didn't show any sign of wear. Only a small area of the entrance was used as a necking spot. There had been no need to venture farther down the road, when only the first clump of bushes was sufficient to obscure young lovers.

The deputy took a small pen light out of his pocket and directed it at the unfolded map. "Oh Man," He said, as he took his first look. It was a regular road map, one that could be picked up at any gas station. With one exception: its alterations were to accommodate a pilot using it in flight. On the lower left-hand corner was a latitude and longitude insignia, with due north printed above the arrow, pointing the northern direction of the map. Also on the map were circles drawn around small insignias that designated airstrips or flat areas suitable to touch down, located in various areas of the state. "What a set-up!" he said aloud. "These bastards have a regular network all over the damn state." He tried to imprint the southwest areas drop zones in his mind. He was hoping he'd be able to redraw them on a fresh map for Doty. Jimmy put the light out and folded the map in the dark. He'd better start the trek into the weeds, he thought, in case he wasn't able to locate the area right away. Besides, if possible, he wanted to get a look at the men who actually did the dropping. He'd come too far to pass up an opportunity like this.

He was able to shut the car's door by pushing it hard, after its initial contact with the jam. It hooked, but not tight. That was sufficient, he thought, as he headed into the undergrowth. What a mess. He could feel his shoes sink into the soft sand. Wallowing through the weeds, he felt stick tights cling to his pants. Once in awhile one reached his skin. He dared not holler out, so he bore the irritation for the time being. When he passed through the last thicket, he emerged into clearing, and concrete sheets stretched as far as he could see into darkness. Occasionally, the moon floated out from under the cloud coverage, and allowed him to see more blocks of cement extending farther to the south and east. He stood on the very edge of what used to be a practice and training base during the Second World War. He hadn't yet finished taking a complete survey of the area, when he heard the drone of an aircraft off in the distance. He looked skyward and saw the lights of a small aircraft blinking off and on, and approaching his area. It appeared to be heading in from the southeast and banked, straightened up, then headed for the runway, coming right toward Jimmy from the east. He had been so engrossed at the complex set up that had undoubtedly taken men months to organize, that the plane's approach and landing took place before he realized it was on the ground. It had barely touched down when bundles began tumbling out of the black gap in its side. The DC3 never even stopped rolling. By the time the last bundle had been tossed out, the plane was already airborne. Within seconds, it was high in the air, banking around into the wind and heading north.

"Damn," Jimmy said. He started walking toward the bundles on the cement pads. He looked around, checking to see if he was the only one present. Then he took off on a run. He reached the first bundle and looked around for the distance of the next, which lay about six feet away. There were six bundles in all. All were neatly wrapped and secured with twine. He gathered and stacked them together. With the first bundle just beyond the overgrowth, he started a pile. Retrieving the remainder and loading them in the trunk of the car took about an hour. He had worked up such a sweat that he would have preferred to sit there and cool off before leaving. To be on the cautious side, however, in case the low-flying plane brought concern from area residents, he thought better of it. The cool air blowing through the windows felt good on his body. He took his time driving, to allow himself time to digest the sight he had seen an hour earlier. "Amazing, just amazing," he said aloud.

He drove the bales of pot to the prearranged rendezvous point in Sugar Manor. The development's only occupants now were mostly living in the houses on the main drag. The remainder of the houses had been left to go to ruin.

He had description of the van to be used for the pick up of the contraband. He was told to drive to the rear of the van, get out of the car, unload the pot, and then walk around to the front of the van. The persons would hand the money out the window to him, and he was to bring it back to the colonel.

There sat the van, with no lights on and the motor running. Jimmy ran his vehicle around to the rear of the van. While unloading the bails, he glanced at the license tag. *Crafty bastards,* he thought. They had covered it up with a rag so it couldn't be read. He finished unloading. As he walked around to the side of the van, someone had hopped out of the opposite side and hastily loaded the pot. The hand was already out of the window gripping the money. Jimmy reached up and took it, then backed off. His police training had taught him never to turn his back on an unsure situation. This was one situation he was very unsure of. He arrived at the rear of the van and he noticed a dent in the side of the left rear taillight. He continued to the car and got in. Just as he was closing the door, the van pulled out, with no lights on, at high speed. It and its cargo disappeared in the darkness.

"Man those bastards are fast," Jimmy said to himself. "What a night! What an experience! Man, I sure would like to have gotten a look at that license number," he said, as he pulled back out on the highway. "Oh well." Immediately he went home and called the captain, complying with the colonel's orders. "I have the mission completed, sir. And all went as planned."

"Good," the captain said, then hung up.

"Weird, man, real weird," Jimmy said as he placed the phone on the hook. "Damn, I've been talking to myself lately. I sure hope I'm not losing my grip." He walked into the bathroom, turned on the shower, slipped out of his clothes, got in, and washed the dirt of the day off.

The colonel pulled his spotless white Lincoln into the parking lot across the street from the Yacht Basin. He was annoyed and irritated enough to break the neck of whoever it was pulling this scam. He intended to get some answers and then, if necessary, bash some heads. Five minutes past seven flashed the clock on the dash. He didn't like to be kept waiting.

A rap at the rider's side window attracted his attention and he automatically flipped the lock button.

"I figured it was you," said Billy Carter, sliding in and settling down in the cushy leather seat.

The colonel was trying hard to hide his surprise. "What the hell is this all about, Carter?" It was obvious he was annoyed, and Billy was enjoying every minute of it.

"At first I thought it might be the sheriff. But it didn't figure, because he was crazy about the kid."

"What the hell are you talking about, Carter?"

"Manning, Jack Manning. *YOU* swatted him, Colonel. It had to be you. You didn't have it done, you did it yourself. I admire that in a man. I always say, if you want something done right...do it yourself."

"You're crazy, Carter," the colonel said disgustedly. "Why would I want to snuff Jack Manning?"

"Cause he was putting the squeeze on you, or at least trying to."

Watson didn't say anything; he just stared at Carter, letting him talk.

"The dumb fool thought he could shake you down, then run back to the Army for protection. I must admit I was a little surprised that you just didn't pay him off. Was it because he threatened to tell the sheriff about your little sideline? You could have probably bought him cheap. I told him to ask for fifty thousand. But I figure you could have talked him down to a couple hundred. You are good at that, screwing people. "

"How can you be sure it was me?" Watson asked.

"Easy, I only sent out two other invitations for this little get-together, and neither of them said when. You were the only one that showed."

The colonel's curiosity was getting the better of him. "How did you know Manning?"

"We met a few months prior to his going into boot camp at a bar in North Fort Manson, had a couple drinks, exchanged a few tall tales, smoked a little grass, and swapped a little info. He was wanting to spread his wings one last time before being anchored into that Army.

Imagine my surprise to find that we had some mutual friends. I was frankly shocked. I thought you and your boys had a little more brains than to let your dirty business be known to those beyond your circle. He surely wasn't in your nest. Granted the kid had a sweet chance to collect from you, but nothing was worth trading dying for. What did he do, stumble into your little racquet? Did he threaten to tell his buddy the sheriff? "

Billy's sarcastic humor was driving Watson's temper to the boiling point.

"What did he do, tell you that he found out about the plane you buried in the Corkscrew Swamp? He had to have done something bad to make you wack him," Carter threw out at the colonel just to see how much of a rise he could get out of him. "Yeah I think you did the kid in to keep his mouth shut," Cater continued to prod the colonel.

"Listen, Carter ..." he started to say." He didn't like having old actions brought back up.

"No you listen, Colonel." Billy's eyes went cold, beady and staring. "I know you're angling to ice up outer rings of your operation. I know you hate my guts and it thrills me. Back off....Back way off. Give me room. And keep Lemmon off my tail."

"Or?" the colonel asked.

"Or I'll have my own little pow-wow with the sheriff. He might forgive you for the dope running but there's no way he'll protect you if he finds out you whacked Jack Manning."

The colonel was silent. He was backed into a corner and they both knew it.

"And another thing, the next time we have a shipment, we're going to divvy the spoils my way. You've been getting much too much of the good stuff for yourself. You and your cronies are on short rations as of now."

"Listen you piece of low-life scum, who do you think you are? Nobody tells me what I will or won't do."

"Face it, Colonel, you're screwed. It's like I keep telling you," Billy said as he opened the door, "you never kill the goose that lays the golden egg. You've got to keep me around; I'm the prick with the Midas touch." Billy slammed the door and disappeared into the bushes.

The colonel could hear Billy's sadistic laugh as he walked away. "Just amazing," he said aloud.

Chapter 29

When Sheriff Myers entered his office that morning, he didn't expect to be greeted by the news that the state was proceeding with the grand jury investigation. He knew Becky's accusations were a lie. Her claims about his men's involvements couldn't be true. He would have known, or the colonel would have told him if trouble were brewing.

Hank was troubled. He couldn't stand it any longer, and he had asked the colonel to come to his office. He was losing his patience waiting for him. He knew he'd have to contact the state attorney's office, but he would like to have details first. When the rap sounded on the door, Hank's annoyance at being kept waiting was at high pitch.

The colonel didn't hesitate to enter; for this office, he never did. "Morning, Hank," he said in a casual tone and sat down.

"I sure wouldn't say it was good," the sheriff snapped back.

"Why do you feel that way, Hank? It sounds like you have a burr under your hide."

The sheriff rose out of his chair and walked around the desk. Sitting on the front of it, with his hands folded over each other on his knee, he stepped into the colonel's face.

"Perhaps you'd better inform me about the validity of Becky's accusations," he said, trying to keep high cool.

Colonel Watson had no alternative but to sit in the chair and listen. The way the sheriff was sitting prevented him from rising out of his chair. "You...Ahh...we have nothing to worry about. I'm sure she'll never be able to prove anything, for there will be nothing she can put her fingers on."

The sheriff sat up and stared coldly into the colonel's face. "You mean there is a possibility that there is some truth in what she claims has been going on around here? Where in the hell have I been, and why haven't I known about all these things? Have you known about them?" he threw out to Watson, never giving him a chance to answer the first question.

Watson was getting hot under the collar. He'd like to have told him why he wasn't aware of department functions and problems. Why he didn't know three-fourths of his men's names. He was so interested in his re-election slogan of crime fighter that he'd forgotten to perform like one.

Before Watson spoke, however, he gathered his cool, which was difficult to do. He didn't have the time to gather his composure. But finally he started to talk, guarding every word, and treating the sheriff with kid gloves. "I've realized you've been under considerable strain. You've taken on other duties, and the need of your being troubled with details around here has been minimal. I've seen that you had all reports on your desk. You've issued orders to the men, which I have carried out." The colonel continued to play the sheriff like a fine violin with his lies. "You've given your attention to every important case that has come into this department. Sir, I can't think of one case where you've been kept in the dark. I will admit, I have taken the liberty of doing some minor details that were needed in some cases. I didn't see any point in bothering you with them. You always did end up with the detailed final report on your desk. So, even though I did proceed with some of the objectives on my own, I had only your well being at heart. You, yourself have done nothing, but rely on me. I have fulfilled my duties, and I don't feel I should be chastised for it. Hank, I can understand your being upset about the investigation. I have been informed that it will be swayed in our favor, so you don't have to worry about a thing."

The sheriff looked stunned. "You mean you know for a fact that it will go in our favor? Who told you that?"

He moved away from the colonel and allowed him to have breathing room. Watson felt more confident now. "Well, I have a fairly good rapport with the assistant state's attorney, and he told me there was a good chance they could be convening, while looking into Becky's accusations. I didn't bother to tell you, for I felt that you'd had enough to worry about, with the extra duties placed on you. Until it was a sure thing, I didn't see any need for your being prematurely upset."

The sheriff drew in his horns when he found he was being protected. Maybe he was being a little hasty jumping on the colonel. "We have nothing actually she can put her hand on to give the grand jury, do we?" he asked of the colonel.

"Hell no! That I'm sure of. She's just blowing smoke, trying to trump up charges, to make all those who are running for reelection look bad in the public eyes." Watson told the sheriff what he wanted to know, and hear. "If that's all, sir, I have a meeting this morning with a deputy who needs straightening out on a couple of procedures in the department. Unless you'd rather handle it, sir?" he quickly added, knowing he'd decline.

"No, you go ahead. I know you have full command of the situation. That was why I made you second in command, to take some of the pressure off me." He had mispoke. "I mean, to free me up so I can have more time to handle more important details."

Watson rose and stretched, "Oh yes, Hank, I know what you mean." With a smile on his face, he headed for the door. "I'll get back to you later, all right?" He walked out the door, leaving the sheriff to answer his last batch of mail.

The colonel entered his office to find Dale there waiting for him.

"Good morning, sir," said Dale.

"I was just exchanging the same words a few minutes ago myself, but I won't give you the answer that I received. Yes, it is a good morning." He shut the door securely. "How did you make out last night? No trouble, I hope," he said, as he walked around and sat at the desk. He placed his feet up on the top, after leaning back in his chair and placing his hands behind his head in his favorite conquering position.

"No, sir, I didn't have a speck of trouble. I have the money right here," he said, handing the envelope to the colonel.

Watson took it, looked in, and counted the money without taking it out. Then he looked up at the ceiling, fixing his eyes on a stain. He was figuring what cut he should give the kid. "Well, Dale, I figure like this. You haven't really been in the group, or the family as I'd prefer, to call us. For we are like a family. As I was saying, you've been in for only a short time. Those that are in for such a little length of time have to work up to their pay. But I feel you have done an outstanding job; therefore, I'm going to give you a bigger cut then I usually do for the men in your position. Here is 100 dollars," he concluded, reaching into the envelope, taking out two fifties, and handing them to Jimmy.

The deputy took them out of the colonel's hand. "Gee, thanks a lot. I can sure use this. I need to get a gift for Alicia. Got to smooth over a lover's quarrel we had a while ago." He got up and started for the door, then turned around and said, "I'm real glad you're pleased with my work, sir. I will strive to continue doing well...and better, if it pays off this good." He waved the fifties in the air.

"You'd better put those in your pocket before you leave here. There are some that don't make out so well," said the colonel. "By the way, I've been meaning to tell you how impressed I was with the job you did on the newsman. He was really giving me a fit. I didn't think you had it in you to pull off some thing like that. It sure was ingenious, making it appear that a sex crime had been committed. How did you come up with the idea of doing him in that way anyhow?" the colonel asked, inquisitively.

Jimmy was ready to open his mouth and give some hint of an answer when the door opened.

The sheriff walked in, "Oh, am I interrupting something?" he asked.

"No, we were just finishing up. You can go now, Dale." the colonel said, anxious for him to leave.

"Is that the one you had to straighten things out with?" Not waiting for an answer, the sheriff added, "I thought he was doing so well, too. They'll all backslide, I guess, once in awhile."

She pulled up beside the Corolla and rushed to the apartment door. She pushed her fingers into the bell button and held it until the door swung open.

"You bastard...you dirty ..." she stopped in mid-sentence as Mark quickly put his fingers to his lips and whispered, "Shush."

"I don't want to go for a-" Suddenly it dawned on her that he needed to talk to her outside in the open air, where there wouldn't be a chance of someone overhearing.

"I know you're upset, and I don't blame you. This is rotten business we're in. But you know you love it as much as I do."

"Why, Mark, why?" she asked.

"For the same reason as you. Think about it, Becky. It's the same silly game, just reversed."

He guided her to the pool area, where deck chairs and tables had been grouped together. "We can talk here," he said, motioning her to sit.

"I really thought you cared for me." She couldn't hide the hurt she was feeling.

"I did, and I do care for you. And I don't want you to get hurt. And I'm not talking about your feelings, Becky."

"You knew from the very beginning, didn't you?"

"Yes," he said, nodding his head. "I was sent in here to make a contact, and you were the most likely candidate. It was either you or one of the other sheriffs' deputies, and I'm not about to cuddle up with one of those hairy chest bastards."

"All the time I thought I was suckering you."

"We were suckering each other."

"And you knew about the bugs in your apartment."

"Of course, with yours and ours the place is covered from top to bottom. Incidentally, so is your car, so be careful, and your telephone at home, as well as your cellular phone."

"My God." Becky gasped. "What were you trying to find out?"

"Whatever you knew about the sheriff and the department."

"But what did I give you?"

"The same. I gave you nothing. It was obvious fairly quickly that you weren't part of the colonel's hit squad."

"But that's who ordered me to set you up."

"I know. But you're not part of the inner circle, Becky. Like it or not you're just the token broad for the department. ."

She knew it was true, but it still hurt her pride. "Do you do this a lot?"

"It's my job. It's what I do. I'm sort of an undercover trouble shooter."

The word undercover struck them both funny and they laughed together.

"Then you really do work for the state's attorney's office?"

"Only I work out of Tallahassee."

"And you're here to expose the colonel?"

He shook his head. "No, Becky. I'm not one of the guys in the white hats."

"But then... ." Becky was puzzled.

"Let's just say it's....expeditious for the bad guys to know what the other bad guys are up to. In this business, nobody trusts anybody. My job is to find out what the other hand is doing."

"If you're one of the bad guys, why are you telling me this?"

"I'm telling you so you can protect yourself. You've put yourself into a dangerous position with this grand jury investigation. There's no way they will let you testify, Becky. These are important toes you're treading on and their connections go way past Tallahassee. To them you're just an insignificant little pawn. They'll sacrifice you."

"How?" Becky asked.

"Easy: a special assignment, coming out of a grocery store, in your apartment; taking you out wouldn't be a problem."

"You mean they'd actually ..."

"In a heartbeat."

She was having trouble grasping everything he was saying . It seemed so impossible. She realized she was creating some friction at the department. But to kill her? It was mind-boggling.

"Now here's what you have to do. Get together what ever you can't do without, I mean really do without, pack a suitcase and get out of town. Leave everything else, furniture, personal mementos, whatever. Go up to your mother's and pick up your little girl. The two of you get out of the state. Don't look back, and for God's sake don't tell anybody you're leaving or where you're going, not even your mother. On the way to wherever, get rid of your car. Sell it outright and buy one from an individual. Pick a state where the license plate goes along with the car. You know how that works. You're already so far into this thing you'll have to look over your shoulder for the next couple of years. You're smart and as familiar as you are with going undercover, you've got a good chance to beat this. But remember, don't trust anybody. And watch every step you take. Get yourself relocated, and stay out of police work. If necessary get yourself a job slinging hash at a drive-in. Anything to make yourself untraceable. Then find yourself a really nice guy and let him take car of you." He reached over and stroked her hair. "It might be a good idea to get rid of this gorgeous red hair too. Blondes are supposed to be having a lot of fun." He smiled as he moved his hand from her hair down to her arm resting on the table.

"I can't go, I've only got a couple hundred dollars. I couldn't get past the state line."

"When Costello came to see you today didn't he give you an envelope?"

"Oh, yeah, with some very explicit nude shots."

"Save 'em, and sell 'em to Playboy. I've seen them. They're dynamite. But I like the videotape better," he said with a wink. "Anyway," he continued, "wasn't there another envelope, probably white?"

Becky searched her memory. "Yes, I think there was."

She remembered Costello showing her a white sealed envelope and then slipping it in with the pictures. She had been so angry it hadn't registered at the time.

"There should be twenty grand in there."

"What!" she said, disbelieving the words.

"That should be enough to get you out, relocate and see you through some hard times till you get settled."

"I can't take blood money. If I take their money, I'll be as guilty as they are."

"Don't be so damned self-righteous, Becky. We're talking about your life here. Besides, taking the money will convince them that you won't be a problem in the future; that you're as sleazy as they are."

"But... ." Becky stammered, then nodded her head up and down in agreement. "One thing I have to know. Was it all act...I mean the ..."

"The sex? No. If it had been I would have cut it off as soon as I found out you weren't in the game. No, darling Becky, it was as real and sincere as I could make it. I loved every minute of it, and I hope you did to."

"Are you married?"

"Hell, no," he laughed. "There aren't many wives that let their husbands screw other women for a living. In this kind of work you can't afford to get bogged down with entanglements."

"When are you leaving?"

"Tomorrow morning. I'm packing now."

"Were you going to say good-bye?"

"Of course, I wouldn't have left without seeing you."

"Then, this is it." she said wistfully.

"I'm afraid so. Unless...I mean we still have tonight. We can go back to the apartment and pick up where we left off the other night. Nothing would give me greater pleasure than to replay every moment we've spent together."

Becky threw back her head and laughed till tears came to her eyes. "Are the bugs and the video camera still set up?"

"Yeah, they won't remove them until after I'm gone."

"I think it's a great idea. We'll give them a helluva show. Besides, what girl in her right mind could pass up one more night in your bed."

"I'll make it a night to remember."

"We both will," she said smiling. She started to get up from the table.

He pulled her back down and looked her squarely in the eye. "Promise me you'll do what I said, about getting out."

"All right," she said, "I promise."

"Be gone by Thursday." The tone of his voice was harsh.

"But why?"

"Don't ask me, Becky. Just be sure you're gone before Thursday."

There was something urgent in his voice. She didn't speak, only nodded her head.

His mood lightened immediately, and he smiled, the same wonderful smile she had flipped for the very first night. He rose, pulled her to her feet, and put his arm around her waist as they walked back across the parking lot to the apartment.

"I just happen to have the most fantastic bottle of champagne in the refrigerator. If you get hungry we'll order pizza."

"Who needs food?" Becky laughed.

"You're right," he said. "If we get hungry we'll just nibble on each other."

This was going to be the most ecstatic and erotic night of her life, she was going to see to that. She intended to have one last glorious fling.

Jimmy could barely wait to get to Doty with his newly-acquired loot. He knew he'd be able to catch him when he spotted his car in the parking lot. Jimmy pulled around the back of the building and stopped. He got out, and entered the building, floating on air. Now they had their first evidence to start building their case.

Doty was at his desk having coffee. He saw Jimmy walking across the room. "Hi, kid. You look happy about something. In fact, you look about ready to bust. What's up?"

Jimmy smiled and didn't say a word. He reached in his pocket and pulled out the two fifties. "Here they are, and I'm sure you'll find the serial numbers fit the ones that we recorded off the money. It never left my sight. He paid me right out of the envelope."

Doty smiled as he took the money. Then he directed his attention to the numbers and compared them with a list he pulled out of the desk drawer. "Hey! We got-um now. I'm sure glad we decided to bring Corcoran in on this before Watson paid you."

"Who in the hell would have thought he'd have taken me in so fast? I wouldn't have. I'm glad Corcoran 's in too. I won't talk to him, though. It's too risky. You'll have to keep him filled in. By the way, I had a disagreement with Alicia. I need to get her a makeup gift, so think of something to get her and I'll buy it. See you later. I'm going home and hit the sack. I've had a hard night."

They both laughed as he walked toward the door.

Doty knew when Jimmy mentioned the gift, it was a cover-up for something he had to tell the colonel. This had already been discussed between them. They had an unspoken code that both would recognize, when either talked of something out of left field. They were to play along, as if it were reality.

"Before you leave, I have a bit of news that I can't quite figure out yet," Doty said, changing his joyous mood to a more serious vein.

"What is it?" asked Jimmy.

"Would you believe me if I said I didn't have anything I could put my finger on, except the fact that it's the first time there's ever been a gag order on an autopsy finding? With Share's case, the final release will have to come through the sheriff's department. It's highly unusual that I can't find out something, in spite of the orders they have given. I've always been able to get around those before, no matter what."

"Oh, I wouldn't worry about it, Doty. It's probably only because you're one of his colleagues."

Doty shook his head. "I don't think so. I have a funny feeling, and I've learned never to go against my feelings. You just be on the alert. Remember, they won't release the findings of the autopsy."

Jimmy sat on the corner of his desk. "Can't you go through the courts and acquire the findings?" he said.

"Sure we can, and that's probably what Corcoran will do. But in the meantime, they know something we don't and you should. Now, do you get my drift?"

For the first time, Jimmy realized the severity of the whole thing. "Now I know why the colonel was leading me toward that line of conversation this morning. When the sheriff entered the room, I was more or less dismissed and the conversation ceased."

Doty was even more sure of there being a deliberate cover-up of something. "You be very aware of who and what your conversations are about, from here on in," he warned.

"I will. But it sure will look like I'm awful stupid when I hesitate before I start to say anything."

Doty shook his head. "I mean it, kid. You can't be too careful. This is a damn sticky mess, and we're smack in the middle of it. We both want to be around when they all go to jail...It's too bad we don't have the vigilante committee any more. They all could do with a shave, and some tar and feathers. That was usually enough to wise them up, and make them leave town, rubbing their skin off in disgrace."

Jimmy moved off the desk and said, "I'm inclined to agree with you...I'll be careful, but I have to get home. Tell Alicia I was in, and that I'll call her." He pointed to the bills that lay on Doty's desk. "Take good care of those. I'm sure there'll be more coming."

Doty watched as Dale walked back across the room and out the door. He felt a lump of pride come up in his throat at thinking of what the kid was doing. If something should happen to him, no one would even know about it either. Only he and Corcoran. The whole damn mess was so far-fetched and ridiculous that if it were printed, the public would never believe it. They would think it a joke. "Damn it, I'm going to see that it isn't going to be dismissed as a joke," Doty told himself. He then turned to his typewriter, placed a sheet of paper in the roll, and started to type.

The majority of Billy's crowd had made themselves scarce in the past few weeks for one reason or another. Greg and Donnie had gone to the other coast for awhile, after their buddy Hollywood, the disc jockey, was arrested on a standing bench warrant from another county for not attending to a speeding ticket. The girls had gone on to other partners. Billy was the main person from his gang who remained in Fort Manson.

The colonel's gang quickly covered up any criminal involvement that he was ever drawn into. He was protected, because he knew too much to allow his getting caught up in the cogs of justice. As he was their only contact to the supply source, he felt secure.

Prior to Greg's pulling out, Billy had told him he felt he was being stalked. Greg only laughed. He wasn't leaving the house too much, only for work. His home had become a safe harbor from the storm.

Billy wasn't able to ask the department for protection, for if the colonel got the slightest hint he was squeamish, he would allow his eradication. For the first time, Billy could taste fear. He was scared. His house was a hell of a lot quieter now that the gang had pulled out. He hated it like this. He'd never realized till now the reason he'd always maintained a full house. He disliked being alone. Tonight was especially bad. He'd quit his job and come into business for himself, painting. He could always be home before dark. He had thought maybe if he changed routines it would make the feelings go away, but it hadn't. It had only gotten worse. He flopped down in the chair, reached for a cigarette, and found an empty pack. "Damn," he exclaimed, as he crushed the empty pack in his right hand, annoyed at himself for running out. He sat there watching television. The longer he sat, the more he hungered for a smoke. He could have used one of his joints, but he felt he needed all his senses keen and his faculties alert. He decided he'd chance going to the corner store for a pack. He left the TV running, as he'd soon return.

He paused before going out the door into the dark night. He'd gotten terribly hesitant lately venturing out without a chaperone. "Hell," he said, after the urge for a smoke overcame his intuition. He ran down the front steps to the security of his car. He shut the door, locked it, and then turned the key in the ignition. It started with a roar. He put the car into gear, backing out of the driveway while using his rear view mirror. He felt the road come up under the rear tires, then the front. He put it into drive. The car started forward. He then glanced into the mirror and his heart sank. His tongue became so thick with fear he couldn't speak. He had difficulty driving, keeping his eyes to the front. It was hard to keep the car on the road.

The reflection in the mirror showed a black man sitting in the rear seat.

Finally, trying hard to cover the fear fast overcoming him, Billy spoke. "Just what the hell you doing in my car?"

"Jus' yo' keep your han' on the wheel, man. Yo' do as ah tells ya to do," the black man said, in a forceful but demanding tone.

"What do you want? Money? I don't have much, but I'll give it to you," Billy stated.

"No," he said. "Yo keep on drivin' and turns where as tells ya." Coming to the front of the back seat with his body, he leaned his right hand over the front seat.

Billy saw the bowie knife. It glistened in the streetlight as they passed underneath. "Where do you want me to drive?" asked Billy. If he could only find out what the man wanted with him. "Do you need a fix? Man, I could help you there. Is that what you need? Huh?"

The black man only said, "When you get to Cleveland Ave, turn right and head south."

Billy was bewildered. He had to buy some time to think. He had to slow his racing mind down. "I need some cigarettes. Can I stop here and get a pack?" he asked, as he slowed down and pointed to the convenience store.

"No, you don't need any. I have some." The black man reached in his pocket, drew out one cigarette and lit it. He handed it to Billy.

Under any other circumstances he wouldn't have taken a smoke from a black man, let alone smoked it after it had been in his mouth.

Now he was desperate. He took it and dragged on it, never noticing it was a neatly-rolled reefer. The first drag relieved him. "All right," he said. "That's more like it." *No one that means you harm could be giving you a weed,* he thought. He drove more relaxed, while he continued to draw deep. Before realizing it, he'd driven all the way through town.

As he pulled up to the red light on the airport road, the black man spoke. "Turn left here. Go until I tell you to stop." He moved the knife at a threatening angle.

Billy could feel himself losing touch with reality. Now was when he needed to keep hold of it. *Damn weed,* he thought. He turned left, as he was told.

They drove until all signs of inhabitants were gone.

"Now, pull over to that dirt road," the man said, as he pointed. "Go down it as far as you can drive, " he instructed Billy.

"Where the hell are you making me go?" Billy asked in a slurred voice. Getting no answer, he drove to the end of the dirt road and stopped. Then he started to turn around.

"Now whaa...a...a"

The black man hit him over the head with the end of his bowie knife. Billy slumped in the front seat.

The black man moved quickly. He accomplished with Billy what he had to before he came conscious again. He made sure his blow wasn't too hard. He didn't want him unconscious long. Just sufficient to be less resistant.

Billy opened his eyes and looked around. The first thing he noticed was a giant headache. He tried to bring his hand to his head, but couldn't move it. Quickly, he moved his head to one side, then the other. Both his hands were bound and tied to a stake pounded in the ground. He couldn't move his legs either. They were spread eagle and tightly secured to stakes also. He rolled his head from side to side, lifting it off the ground to view as much as possible. He was naked! His eyes located the black man about seven feet away, sitting against a tree smoking. "Hey! What the hell are you doing to me? What you done?" Billy yelled, struggling to get free.

"Ain't no usen try'n to get yo self free. I got you tied, better' in a heifer fo slautin'." He laughed, then rose from his perch against the tree. He walked over to Billy and stood looking into the frightened face looking up at him.

"Why you doing this to me?" Did I ever refuse you dope or pot? What? Why?" Billy begged.

Instead of answering, he reached in his shirt pocket and retrieved another reefer, lit it, then leaned down and put it to the white man's lips.

Billy nuzzled it between his lips and took a deep drag.

The black man left it there. Billy kept sucking feverishly, as if subconsciously knowing he'd need the high, carefree feeling it produced. The lit end glowed as the smoke was drawn out the other.

His narrow eyes followed the black man around. "What are you doing with that?" he asked, then spit the joint out of his mouth. "You're just trying to get me high. Why?" he yelled in a fever-pitched squeal.

The black man calmly walked over to Billy and glared into his eyes. Slowly, he said, "That's more than you'd do for my Delilah. She was suppressed and had to take her torture without a high."

Billy's eyes opened wide. The picture flashed in his brain who this man was, and why he had him trussed up for slaughter. *Oh, my God!* he thought. He opened his mouth and tried to talk convincingly. "Hey man, you don't want to do this to me! I'm a brother, and you know we don't hurt our own. Come on, undo me! I'll make it right with you about Delilah. I did know her, but I didn't have anything to do with the way she died," he lied.

"How in the hell could you be a brother of mine?" asked the black man, speaking with better pronunciation.

Frantically Billy said, "No really, I'm part nigger. Leastwise, my old lady said my old man was. Damn! Just look at my hair. It's kinky, like a nigger's. My lips are big and thick. I hated her for it all my life. She thought no matter who your old man was, you're supposed to love him. She said, she found no fault in falling in love with a black man. He was from Barbados. His skin wasn't very dark. They passed him off as an Indian. Indian, hell! He was a nigger!" screamed Billy. "Now, come on, brother, untie me and I'll get you another girl. I could get you a little rabbit. Huh? How'd you like that? A little white meat, huh?"

The black man didn't answer.

Billy was desperate. He was starting to panic. He talked as fast as his mouth could run. His head moved several times to each one of the black man's movements. The black man moved very slowly but deliberately. Haste was not of the essence. He was enjoying watching Billy squirm.

Billy fell silent. His wide eyes watched the back man prepare for the ceremony. First, he took out what looked to Billy like a fine piano wire, about fourteen inches long. He laid it on the large table napkin, next to the knife he'd placed there moments earlier. To Billy it seemed like an eternity. He was panicking and his face showed it. The beads of perspiration stood out all over his body. His mouth was dry, and he couldn't gather enough spit to wet his tongue. The next thing out of the bag was a box of salt. This made Billy scowl. The final thing was a broom handle about twelve inches long. Seeing this, Billy opened his mouth to scream.

With a swiftness in contrast to all his prior movements, the black man filled Billy's mouth with a gag, muffling the scream, that now lay gurgling in Billy's throat. "Those are a pair of Delilah's pants. I thought it only fit'n that you be shown the same courtesy." That was the first time the black man had spoke through all the dialogue Billy had delivered. It would only be his voice from now on that would be heard. Billy's had been silenced with a pair of panties. "You should've taken more advantage of the weed while you had the chance, weirdo. My goodness," he mocked, "Aren't you a likely specimen laying there all staked out, and naked as a jaybird. Now ..." he said, as he picked up the broomstick, "I'd like to know if you did the broom handle to her first, or last."

Billy shook his head violently from side to side.

The black man continued, untouched by Billy's actions." Knowing what she told me about you, I'd suspect you'd do it first, to prove to her she could take it. At least 'show' her she could take it." He smiled at Billy, who lay motionless in fright. "I think I'll do it first. Think you can take it?"

Billy shook his head rapidly from side to side. A scream stuck in his throat.

Then the black man took his bowel knife from the napkin and flashed it in front of Billy's eyes. "Then I could always use this, to make it fit easier."

Billy shook his head wildly from side to side. Cries in his throat strained to get out.

"Then you'll chance the stick, without the knife's help?" asked the black man, waiting for Billy's answer.

Billy figured he stood a better chance of a little hurt from the broom handle than from having the knife used to enlarge the hole. Maybe that's all this mad man had in mind. He was sure he could endure, it for he'd been in this position before. It wasn't too uncomfortable. Of course, the broom handle was rigid. Billy had no choice. He had to lie there and let the black man subject him to whatever he deemed.

The black man spit on his hands and ran the broom handle through them, wetting it. Then he rolled it in the salt he'd poured on the napkin. Much stuck.

Billy didn't submit without a struggle, or an attempt to scream. When the black man, without mercy, shoved the wooden broom handle up his anus, it stung like hell. He could barely endure the pain. Finally, however, the force of the stick stopped. Billy stopped struggling and lay there with fists clinched. Tears rolled down his cheeks.

"Did Delilah cry, Billy?" the black man asked, noticing the wet face.

Billy was in excruciating pain. He couldn't hear or concentrate on what the man was saying. He just hoped he'd go away and leave him alone. When the pain had gone its limit, numbness set in.

Then Billy caught a glimpse of the black man picking up the piece of wire. His eyes glared in horror as the black man stood over him, very slowly winding, then unwinding the wire around his hand. First one hand, then the other. He kept this up, until the look on Billy's face told him that he knew what the wire was intended for. He smiled, then knelt down over Billy's nude body.

"Too bad I'm not kinky like you are, weirdo, or I'd take advantage of this position," he said, as he straddled Billy's nude body a little below his groins.

By this time, Billy was frantic. He was pleading with his eyes and making all kinds of noises in his throat. All to no avail.

The black man took the thin wire and looped it under the two sacks of flesh hanging between Billy's legs. He rubbed it back and forth to tantalize Billy. It succeeded, for Billy was in a hysterical frenzy with fright. Then the black man crossed his hand over and took the opposite end of wire with the other hand. "Have the name of Delilah on your mind, weirdo, when you meet your maker. May God have mercy on your soul." With a quick jerk, he gave a pull to the wire. The fleshy sacks that once were Billy's severed from his body and fell to the ground.

Blood immediately started to spurt and the black man sprung up with the same swiftness he'd used castrating Billy. As he did, he gave the broomstick that still protruded out of his rectum one final kick home with his boot. The force of this entering Billy's insides could be heard as it tore through flesh and bones. Billy's body gave one final twitch, then lay motionless.

The black man walked back to Billy's car and retrieved the plastic bag off the rear floor. As he approached Billy's bloody body, he opened it. He tipped it up and out fell garbage. He distributed it all around Billy's lifeless form, threw the bag down and walked away. He never looked back. His mission was completed.

He drove Billy's car to within walking distance of the highway and parked it. Then he took a rag out of his pocket and wiped the car clean of his prints. He threw the keys in the tall grass and walked down the road toward the lights on the highway.

Chapter 30

The pain was unbearable, and Yarbrough knew what he was in for. He'd experienced this pain the last time, only it wasn't so severe. He clutched his chest and gasped for breath, as he fell to the floor.

Colonel Watson heard the thud outside his office door, and came running out. He saw Yarbrough lying on the floor. "Smith! Call the rescue squad! *HURRY!*" he yelled. He loosened Yarbrough's clothing and tried to make him as comfortable as possible.

Smith came running. "What in the hell happened, anyhow?" he asked.

"I don't know, but I think he's having another heart attack. He'd just left my office, when I heard the thud. I found him like this. That's all I know."

By this time the hallway had started to fill up by others who had heard the commotion.

Colonel Watson yelled, "Get the hell out of here. Give him some air."

The rescue squad come running in, carrying a stretcher. They placed it on the floor beside Yarbrough. One medic gave him oxygen with a portable mouthpiece attached to a tank. Then he strapped it to his face.

The other medic looked for vital signs. He looked at the colonel and shook his head. "Let's get him loaded and make a quick trip, or he won't make it."

Within seconds they had him on the stretcher and in the waiting ambulance.

"Call the nearest area unit, and tell them to open the way. They're coming through," Watson bellowed. "Smith, I'm going to the hospital. You hold down the fort till I get back." Watson ran out the rear exit. His car could be heard squealing out of the parking lot, sirens wailing.

"Everybody get back to work," Smith yelled to all that stood around.

Things had happened so fast it took time for his words to register.

"He sure did look white," Eva said, as she and Ruth walked back to the front desk.

"Yes, he did."

Watson arrived at the hospital. Shortly afterwards Sheriff Myers joined him.

"Sheriff," the colonel said and solemnly nodded.

"How is he, Don?"

"They're still working on him, Hank, but it sure doesn't look too good."

"What happened, Don?" Sheriff Myers asked.

"I think he's had a heart attack. The Doc's in with him now."

"Has anyone called his wife yet?"

The colonel motioned toward the nurses' station. "I asked the nurse to call her at the shop where she works."

"Good."

A noise drew their attention. They both looked up, as the doctor approached them, after emerging through the double doors. All men exchanged handshakes.

The doctor was somber as he spoke, "Gentlemen."

"How is he, Doc?" the colonel asked.

"He's in guarded condition. All I can tell you is that he's resting now. We have him monitored and he'd holding his own. The first twenty-four hours are the most crucial. We have to give it that much time, then I can tell you more. My educated opinion is that he'll never regain full control of his bodily functions. That part of his brain appears to have been damaged. I won't be able to tell for sure until I get the results back from tests. I don't dare try them until he becomes more stable....I have to get back in there with him."

"Sure, thanks, Doc." the sheriff softly said.

"Oh yes, there's no need in telling his wife until we are definite. So until we get the results, it's just between us."

They both agreed with the doctor.

"Men, I have to get back in there, if you'll excuse me." The doctor turned and exited through the heavy double doors.

The lawmen both looked at each other.

The sheriff was the first to talk. "We can't do anything here. Come on, we'll see if we can head his wife off before she gets up here. She can't be of any use here. It would only tear her up."

Both men walked down the corridor in silence.

With Yarbrough not being able to come back to work, Sheriff Myers set out looking for new recruits. He called the academy in Miami. The next graduating class would be out in the spring. They'd just have to make do until some prospects came on the scene. They were having no luck in the city with recruits. He blamed it on the grand jury convening for investigation of his department. He was personally overseeing the books being placed on order, for viewing by an independent firm. He thought of all the troubles he'd had since taking over the department. He'd never imagined he'd have all these problems. *No wonder Yarbrough had a heart attack,* he thought. He was a young man, but he couldn't hold up under the pressure. If the colonel hadn't lightened his own load he imagined he'd have difficulty doing his job also. He felt he was lucky to have such a loyal and trusted friend. Hank was sure the investigation would turn out all right. The colonel had reassured him that they'd find nothing. He could trust the colonel. That man knew what he was talking about.

Woody made another trip to the colonel's office.

Watson was surprised to see him. "Hey, what are you doing back again, so soon? They couldn't be talking that much, are they?"

Woody laughed. "No. There hasn't been any change in their talking. I've been transferred, and I thought I'd better get these to you while I had the chance."

The colonel looked disappointed. "I sure do hate to have you transfer. You've really been a big help to me."

"Well, Colonel, I have a chance to take a better job at another substation. It pays more money and that's the name of the game."

Watson looked at him and said, "I wish I'd been able to pay you more to make up the difference in what you'll make."

Woody had heard about the investigation and he wanted out, as fast as a rat deserted a sinking ship. He wasn't going to be making any more money, but he would have the advantage of bowing out from under the colonel while he had the chance.

They shook hands and bid each other farewell.

The colonel was alone in his office. As he was without anything pressing, he picked up a tape at random, put it in the recorder, and turned it on. Then he leaned back in his chair and listened. It was a telephone conversation between Jimmy and Alicia. The usual lovers' telephone conversation. He listened a few minutes, then a puzzled look appeared in his eyes and on his face. *I wonder if that was before they had their fight?* he thought. He turned off the tape player and took the tape out, reading the date Woody had printed on it. "Hell, that's recent," he said. He placed it back in and listened more intently. *Maybe they'd be in a fight on the phone,* he thought. He listened all the way through. Nothing about a fight was mentioned. There should've been. The colonel unlocked the drawer of his desk and fumbled about looking for tapes on Jimmy. He hurriedly placed a recent one in the player and turned it on. It was a telephone conversation between Doty and Jimmy, the night Share was murdered. The colonel's face suddenly turned beet red. He pounded his desk with his fist. "Sonofabitch!" He'd been had.

He listened as he heard them discuss what Doty would do to help Jimmy cover it up. The evidence that he, Watson, was going to use for Jimmy's indebtedness to him. Watson was livid. Then came a feeling deep inside of him he wasn't familiar with, as, until now, he'd always had the upper hand. Now he was being patronized, and he didn't like it. He felt like he could murder Jimmy right then and there, but he had to control himself. "Damnit!" he said under his breath. "He wasn't capable of doing it! I didn't think he was." Watson found consolation in crediting himself for being right about Jimmy's capabilities. It wasn't much, but his ego was at a low ebb and needed a boost. He'd been set up, put on the hot seat. He still held the upper hand, though. Jimmy didn't know he'd been bugged, so the colonel could act with the element of surprise. Being his defense, Doty wouldn't be able to disclose anything about Jimmy. *He shouldn't have a damn thing!* The colonel again felt in command. He knew he had tied up all the loose ends now.

After the sinking of the aircraft in the Corkscrew Swamp, he felt with the evidence submersed it was a done deal and no one the wiser. The drugs were well on the way to being dispersed throughout the country. Those that actually did the digging of the hole and submersion of the aircraft were either dead, missing or dying. He had gained control again. It was his world and no one was going to tell him what to do anymore.

He took the tape out of the player and put it in the drawer with the rest, then he locked it. He took a small black book out of his shirt pocket and printed Jimmy's name in big bold letters on the very top of the page. He closed it with a movement of determination and put it back in his pocket. Just as a smile spread across his face, cold and calculating, the phone rang. He picked it up and grunted a sound. Someone at the other end did all the talking. Watson placed the phone back on the hook and rose from his chair.

Watson wasn't prepared for the scene in the front office when he left. Two young people sat huddled together in a chair, each embracing the other. They looked as if they'd met a ghost, and it'd left its mark on them. After they told the shocking story of going out in the woods to park, and of what they'd found there, they agreed to go back out and show the deputies where "It" was. But they absolutely refused to view it again. They both sat there and cried like babies.

It was ironic how they'd been prepared to experience the adult pleasure of life then, yet now sat scared like the two kids they were.

Watson and his gang loaded into cars and drove to the spot the kids told them to. Leaving the young ones in the car, the sheriffs' men trucked in. They gasped in horror when they laid eyes on the body.

Lemmon was the first to see the man's face.

The rest couldn't take their eyes off what remained of the lower half of his torso. "That's Billy Carter, Colonel! My God, that's Billy! What in the hell's going on?!"

Colonel Watson walked over to have a closer look, then asked the coroner to come closer for a look. He wanted to remove the article from Billy's mouth. Everything rung a bell, and clicked into place in his mind. The proof he needed would be the knowledge of what was in his mouth.

"Sure, go ahead and remove them if you want to," said the coroner. He couldn't imagine one of "them" wanting to touch such a mess.

Watson looked around and found a stick, then used it to tug and pull the gag out of Billy's mouth. He'd bit into it with such force that nothing remained of the panties but an embroidered "D". "D for Delilah," was the only the comment the colonel made.

Lemmon and Deets looked at each other. "I never did trust that little bastard," said Lemmon.

"It's not nice to speak ill of the dead," said Deets.

The colonel spoke. "Hey man, you're overlooking one important thing. This solves two of the murders that have been giving us a fit. Can't you see that Delilah's friend avenged her death? He must have made sure of having the right man too, for him to go through all these preparations." He pointed, "Look, even the garbage to complete the scene. I think he even met a worse death than the one he doled out. Man, that sure must've hurt." With no show of emotion, the colonel turned to the coroner. "You might as well take him to the morgue. We've seen all we want to."

"You mean you don't even want to have the crime lab boys to go over things out here?" asked the coroner.

"Nope. In fact, you can even pull the ramrod out of his rectum."

Deets laughed. "Rectum. Hell, it killed him!"

They all laughed.

"We'll do a routine investigation, but as far as we're concerned, it's wrapped up. So is the Lesso girl's and the black woman's deaths." He turned to leave.

Deets started to follow the colonel out. "Now all we have left is the man from the newspaper."

"Yep," was the only comment the colonel made.

All but the coroner and his crew loaded in their cars. The rosy glow from the lights on the ambulance reminded Deets of another night, ages ago it seemed, when the Manning kid's death took place.

They drove in silence, each man silently feeling the anguish Billy must have gone through before his death.

"It was terrible, but you know, he deserved it." Lemmon said. "I suppose you live like a sadist, you have to take the chance of dying like one."

The colonel said, "How true." He had another type of revenge and punishment in mind.

Colonel Watson made sure the release was ready for the paper when Jimmy came into work. He told him to run it over to Doty, so it could make the morning paper. It would make one more point for the sheriff's department before the grand jury met.

Jimmy took the paper and left. It sounded logical to him. They did actually find out who had killed two women by discovering the death of one man. All the gory details were in the report. Doty would have to tone that down some, he thought. Doty had always had to interject his own commentary into prior reports, giving them the color the department had left out. Well, in this one, nothing was left out.

Doty cringed when he read it. "Holy Mary of Mercy. That poor sonofabitch sure did meet his maker in a hell of a mess, didn't he?"

Jimmy didn't have time to stay and talk. He had to go on duty. "I'll talk with you later about it. Will you get it out in the morning's paper?" he asked.

Doty looked at him in amazement. "What! Are you kidding, and miss the chance of a Pulitzer Prize? You bet it will make the paper," Doty said with excitement in his voice.

Jimmy hadn't seen him this elated over a story, and Jimmy was happy for him.

Meanwhile, the colonel drove in haste toward the *News Leader*. He talked to himself the short trip down Anders Avenue. He would wipe that two-faced sonofabitch out! He was sure he could do it, and make it away unseen. He had to eliminate Dale. Not just because of the fact that the bastard had pulled the wool over his eyes - no one had ever done that and gotten away with it - but he was dangerous to Watson's long-run organization. He'd make it look like a sniper hit-and-run. Cops were always expected to be on someone's grudge list.

He spotted Dale's car parked by the paper's door. Pulling in the shadow of a large tree would keep him from being seen. He'd be able to observe those going in and out of the door. Mainly, he'd be able to hit Dale and leave fast, for he would aim well, as he'd done with the Manning kid. He'd shut him up, too! This time he'd see that the job was done more smoothly. No notes to mess up his plans this time. Damn, that kid would have to have threatened him with exposure to Hank. He'd showed him, though! Just like he would Dale.

He sat so involved with the thoughts of past deeds and the upcoming planned one that he didn't hear or see the man who quickly approached his car in the darkness.

"Hello, Colonel," the man said hoarsely.

It startled the colonel. He jumped up and glanced toward the voice, but he couldn't see who was talking to him. "Who is it?" he asked. Fright, for some reason, was creeping up on him fast. There was something about the voice. "Come on out of the shadows, where I can see you."

What do you want?" he asked, trying to control the fear from showing in his voice.

"It's too bad, Colonel, that you had to take the whole pie and reduce our ranks locally. What did you do with Ruocco, Colonel?" The man's voice hardened.

"What are you talking about? Who's Ruocco?" the colonel asked, innocently.

"Knock it off, Colonel. You're the one! We used the process of elimination and we got to *YOU!*"

The colonel started to open his car door. His thoughts of Dale were replaced now by the confrontation with this man accusing him of something he knew nothing about. He'd get out and face the man who was mistaken about something. He'd straighten him out!

Then a glistening of metal caught his eye ..."No. Don't!"

Jimmy turned to leave when it suddenly sounded like all hell was breaking loose. Nam all over again.

At first everyone just stood or sat, frozen to their spot. Then, in a split second reflex, everyone hit the floor at the same time.

Jimmy had already crouched to the floor, heading toward the sound of the shots with his gun in hand. He shouted back over his shoulder for every one to stay down. By the time Jimmy got to the door, the shots had stopped as abruptly as they had started. He opened the door and stood back. No response from outside. So he darted out through the door and took cover behind one of the cars parked close by. He cautiously moved, an inch at a time, getting the advantage of viewing something... anything, but not yet knowing what he was looking for.

He peered out around the end of the car, hesitating a moment at what he saw. He then walked carefully toward the bullet-riddled car.

The door was open on the driver's side and the lifeless body was hanging out. Colonel Watson's head reached the ground, while the feet were still in the car.

After Jimmy looked around again, he holstered his gun and walked toward the car.

Doty joined his side from out of nowhere. "You all right, kid?" he said. "I sure was worried when you disappeared. I didn't know what you were walking into."

Under the streetlight, they both viewed the lifeless, bullet-riddled body hanging out of the car. Doty reached down and picked up the black book that had slid to the ground out of the colonel Watson's pocket. He leafed through it and handed it to Jimmy.

There, first on the list, was Jimmy's name in big, bold print.

"Looks like he had you dead to rights, my boy. Someone beat him at his own game, before he got his chance at you."

Jimmy was shaking, and yet he felt relieved. He knew the kingpin of the whole crooked operation lay dead at his feet.

From out of the crowd that had gathered, Alicia came running and threw herself in Jimmy's arms.

He hugged her to him and kissed her wet cheek. They then turned and walked away from the scene that by now was bustling with lawmen flashing lights and sirens.

Doty sat at his typewriter a long time. The words just wouldn't come. He'd waited for so long; now it all seemed so senseless to have wasted his time. He wanted so very much to write the expose', but he couldn't find the proper words. He repeatedly tore out papers from his typewriter and threw them in the paper basket. He paused and propped his elbows on his desk, arms bent upward. On his cupped hands, he rested his head and closed his eyes. Suddenly he moved, as if spurred on with a sudden impulse. Taking a fresh piece of paper and putting it in the typewriter, he began to type. He was on his way to a feature article on the recent happenings in the county.

An hour or so later, as he reread the newly composed article in his hands, he smiled. It wasn't exactly what he had wanted to do all these years, but he felt it would serve a better purpose than for him to settle a vendetta he had sworn to settle.

EDITORIAL
BY
STEVE DOTY

I recently had the pleasure of reporting openly the disclosure of wrong doings of the sheriff's department in this county, and the sadness to admit that I was part of the public that condoned their actions. Had I, or you, my dear reader, lifted a finger to seek federal help, there would be life right now in the young lives that were so coldly and callously snuffed out. I don't mourn those getting killed who were involved in the dirty racket; they got what was due them.

Yet, it is not for me, or any mortal, to judge or punish

them. But to survive as a democratic republic society, we have to fight to keep our freedom, as our forefathers fought to start out great nation. Their struggle must not have been in vain. We must preserve it, no matter the cost, or be forever doomed to domination by tyrants like the colonel. His rule is not where it would end, dear reader. His was only the beginning. The bitter end would be complete rule by communism. The part between the beginning and the end is where we are right now.

In order to change the end, that looks inevitable right now, we have to keep their plan from being carried out. As the man who pounded his shoe on his desk, so many years ago at the U.N. saying they would take us over without a shot being fired. In order to do this they have to split us from within, using people like the colonel and his henchmen. Their greedy tactics will make it materialize, unless the free in spirit and body exert themselves to hold onto our precious freedom, which was given to us 200 short years ago through a long and fierce struggle. The colonel and the greedy groups have to be held in check, drummed out of the county, state and federal governments.

I still have to believe that the majority of the people in our county are good, law-abiding citizens. We far out-number the corrupt political machines in the minority.

GOD HELP US IF THEY AREN'T.

We have to ban together and keep freedom ours. If need be fight for it, as they did 200 years ago. We may have to do it again, but maintain our freedom we must, no matter the cost. It's precious. Ask any immigrant to our land. They'll tell you how sacred it is going to bed, and waking up free, no longer dominated by a police state.

We must make it known to all communist and fascist organizations and the syndicates that our county is a "hands-off" domain. We must set an example for our communities; show them that there is something that can be done to weed out the wrong doers. Place them behind the bars.

We must not sit idly by and allow this to happen again

right before our eyes. We must get involved; see that justice be done swiftly to those guilty of atrocities that have been allowed to run rampant in our county.

GET INVOLVED, MY FRIEND. IT'S THE NAME OF THE GAME!

Jimmy put his fish pole down on the ground.

His movement drew Doty's attention. "What's the matter, kid?"

Doty reeled in his line, and placed his pole on the ground also. "Want to talk about it?"

Jimmy picked up a handful of pebbles in his left hand. Taking one in his right hand, he tossed it in the water. Then a second, then a third one. Slowly, the rings stretched out and dissipated. The only sounds were the plop, plop, plop, of the stones hitting the water. An occasional animal could be heard scurrying about.

Doty didn't press. He'd known for some time that Jimmy's pent up emotions from the past few months were about to come to a head. So much had happened. Doty picked up a pebble and tossed it in the water. He was trying to get Jimmy to identify with him. If he'd just open up, he'd feel better; Doty knew he would.

"Come on Doty, let's take a walk, ok?"

"Sure."

Several minutes passed in silence. Each pulled at a sprout of grass now and then.

"You know, Doty, I feel sort of let down."

"Yeah, I know."

"You know, I thought when this mess all cleared up, it would give me peace of mind. It didn't come. In a way I feel cheated. Somehow I feel with having to give up so much, I should feel grateful it's all over. I don't. I feel cheated. Is that wrong, Doty?"

"Naw. I think it's only normal. I understand how you feel."

"Well, even with the knowledge of Watson's no longer having a grip on the county, Costello and his group's political future crushed after a term in prison, and Sheriff Myers run out of town, I feel we are no further ahead. I feel cheated. I can't help it. I don't know how to handle this feeling, cause I don't know what is causing it. I should be happy. I have a good job. Alicia and I are happily married. We are expecting a baby. Why Doty?"

"Well, Jim, I'm no physiologist, but I'd say you psyched yourself up as the pressure increased. Then when the whole mess blew up, it was a sudden let down. You've given of yourself, beyond what could be expected."

Doty's words were hollow, like Jimmy's feelings. "Doty, I don't expect sympathy; I only did what I felt was right. The feeling I can't understand is the lack of self-gratification. I at least thought I'd achieve that, once this mess was exposed."

For the first time, Doty knew what Jimmy was trying to express. "Kid, I think I know what you mean. It was like me. All I could think of was writing that expose'. But when the time came, I felt, well, guilty somehow. I couldn't single myself out and stand alone, pointing a finger at everyone else. I looked, and I had three fingers coming back at me."

"Yeah, Doty, guilty. That's the way I feel. Remorseful. Even though I helped tear down Costello's and Stewart's political career. I feel pity for them now. Not hate. That's weird, too, because I know they'd not hesitate to rub me out."

"I think Costello has to fear for his own air now. It will be especially rough on him in prison serving time with men he helped to put there. For once an indictment in Leeward County stuck, and manifested into jail terms instead of a plea bargain. I don't imagine the syndicate holds him in too high esteem either. Surely Sheriff Myers won't show his head for some time to come, being run out of town in shame, as he was. I hear his wife finally made her break with him and went north."

"Gee, I hope she can eventually start a new life and find happiness. She deserves it. This all had to be rough on her. Thank God the kids were young enough; it all didn't leave an impression on them. That's what I mean, Doty. So many innocent people got hurt, or lost lives. They got caught in the middle."

"Well, kid, look at is this way. Be satisfied with the fact you tried. As a result of your efforts, we have a new sheriff."

"Yes, but the Governor only appointed Williams acting sheriff as a token, because he was black. Not because he's qualified, with over twenty-five years in law enforcement. He's a just and compassionate man, though. Oh, it's the same old crap all over again Doty. Just a big hassle. Things are sad."

"Look, Jim, when the grand jury received the testimony from people who had been afraid to talk prior to the colonel's getting killed, they started the new beginning. There is a whole new regime in there now. They're going to make their mistakes, but I do believe Williams will try to succeed. He's a good man. Yarbrough will pose no threat to anyone anymore. He is no more than a vegetable. So, kid, look at it this way. You've done what you could; now it's up to the taxpaying public to see that it doesn't happen again."

Jimmy stopped, stooped down, and picked up another handful of shore gravel. He stood sifting it back and forth in his hands. Suddenly, he threw the whole handful in the water, in one final protest. It hit the water with such a splash, it startled the birds from their perch.

"Damn, Doty, you're right. Let's get back to our fish poles. We got some fish to catch for supper."

As they walked off, jabbering away to each other, the birds' last rustling of their wings could be heard, as they settled back on their lofty perch high in the Florida pines.

THE END

Contact Irene Crout
tchnglo@verizon.net

or order more copies of this book at

TATE PUBLISHING, LLC

127 East Trade Center Terrace
Mustang, OK 73064

888.361.9473

www.tatepublishing.com